I0789024

CAN YOU HEAR ME

Geonn Cannon

Supposed Crimes LLC • Matthews, North Carolina

Dedicated to the two women without whom this book would have ended up being much different, and come out much later.

For Sarah
Once an inspiration for my characters, and now an inspiration in everything else. I've called you Jodie, Nicole, Dash, Chelsea, and now Noa, but the most important thing I've called you is friend.

For Kate
Who became a fan of someone who was a fan of hers, which turned us into friends. The other half of the Mutual Admiration Society, it's an honor to write for you.

PART

I

// MISSION DAY -193, SIX MONTHS PRE-LAUNCH //

THEY TOLD her to sit in an office chair in front of the camera. There were monitors to her left and right but the screens were turned away from her. The rest of the studio was dark, but light was coming out of a door on the far wall. People with headsets and clipboards spoke to their opposite number on the other side of the country, two people with the same job working to make what happened next look effortless. Behind her was a backdrop of the Boston skyline. Lights shone down on her but they weren't powerful enough to blind her or hot enough to make her sweat.

Colonel Noa Laurie was in her dress blues. She sat with her shoulders squared, one leg crossed over the other with her fingers laced together on the knee. They'd offered to do her hair when she showed up but she refused. Her dark hair was pinned up into a perfectly coiffed helmet, per regulations. She did let them put some makeup on her, but she asked for there to be as little as possible. It still felt caked on.

"Colonel? Are you there?"

The question came from her earpiece. She smiled at the empty space just above the camera. "Yes. Can you hear me?" A microphone was pinned to the lapel of her jacket.

"Loud and clear," the other woman said. "I just wanted to touch base and say hello before we went on the air. I'm Sofia."

"Hi, Sofia."

"It's a huge honor to speak with you this morning. I covered the incident when it happened, and I just couldn't believe you made it through."

Noa lowered her gaze, centering her emotions. She focused on the cuffs of her uniform jacket, the way the wool rested on her wrist. She remembered the day, that endless day, she had watched her entire crew die. She saw her wrist speckled with blood and a horseshoe-shaped bruise which was later diagnosed as a broken radius. Though she was still sitting completely still, she could feel the seat vibrating underneath her as thrusters pushed her against the stubborn barrier of the atmosphere.

"Colonel?" Sofia asked again. "I think we lost her..."

"No, I'm here," Noa said. "Sorry. My mind was wandering."

Sofia said, "Okay. It's going to be about forty-five seconds."

"I'm ready."

A producer had appeared behind the camera. Noa kept looking down at her hands. She took a deep breath and let it out slowly. She could hear faint music through her earpiece as the other studio came back to a live broadcast.

"Welcome back," Sofia Kennedy said to her audience. "Eight years ago, we were all witness to a horrific tragedy unfolding in the skies as the International Space Station suffered a catastrophic failure that cost the lives of four of the five crew members. And of course we all remember the moment from that day which gave us all hope: a small capsule raining down with so much debris, carrying the sole survivor of the disaster. Joining us this morning from Boston is that survivor, Colonel Noa Laurie."

Noa smiled a moment before she raised her eyes to the camera, looking through her lashes before lifting her chin to face the lens fully. The producer gestured to let her know they were live to the studio in Seattle.

"Thank you for being here, Colonel," Sofia said.

"Thank you for having me." Noa remembered the endless interviews after the disaster. Everyone looking at her with complicated and unqualifiable emotions. Awe, shock, pity. Some didn't bother to hide their judgment, asking themselves the same thing Noa asked herself in the aftermath. Why her? Why was she the sole survivor? Had it been a courageous act, or was she a coward only spared because she was running away? Today's interview was bound to be different, but she couldn't shake the anxiety of waiting for a bombshell question that tried to blame her for what happened.

"—have obviously been over this time and time again. We're not here to rehash what happened to you eight years ago. I just wanted to put you at ease about that."

Noa's smile was genuine. "I appreciate that."

"You're here not as a representative of NASA or the Air Force, but for the private aeronautic company Astraea, which is based here in

Seattle."

"That's right," Noa said. "I was approached by Enver Crane, the brain behind Astraea, and asked to participate in a new project they're putting together. As everyone knows, the... incident... that thrust me into the public eye caused all kinds of problems for future space travel. The debris of the station is up there floating around with all the rest of the space junk, like a minefield of shrapnel for anyone who goes up next."

Sofia said, "What exactly do you mean by space junk?"

"Humanity has always had a problem with littering wherever we go, and space is no different. Defunct satellites, derelict experimental craft, booster rockets, tools. Before the disaster on the station, the United States Strategic Command had tracked nearly eighteen thousand specific artificial objects in orbit around our planet. There are over one hundred and seventy *million* pieces of debris smaller than a centimeter that we can't hope to track but could also cause devastating damage to a spacecraft. And of course, what happened to the station has only increased that number. Imagine driving down the highway and the car ahead of you sends a pebble flying into your windshield. Now imagine that pebble was traveling at over seventeen thousand miles per hour and there was no oxygen on the other side of the glass."

"Chilling," Sofia said. "You're here today because Astraea has a plan to reduce this problem."

"That's right. Obviously the debris needs to be dealt with before anyone can even begin repairs on the station, and the problem has gotten so bad that missions to the moon or Mars are out of the question simply because we can't get out of our own backyard. That's what Enver is hoping to change with this new project.

"It's called the Orbital Debris Independent Eradication engine. Or the ODIE engine, for short. The ODIE is a one-person spacecraft which will launch later this year from the Mojave Airport. Its skin will be triply reinforced to ensure no mishaps occur."

Sofia said, "If the technology exists to protect the ships, why don't they just make the shuttles out of that?"

"It simply isn't feasible financially to do it with every ship, even for someone of Mr. Crane's resources. And ships aren't the only thing at risk. That pebble I mentioned earlier could just as easily tear a hole in a spacesuit. We can't wrap all of our astronauts in the material. The ODIE will be one-of-a-kind, specifically made for this clean-up mission."

"How will the ODIE work?" Sofia asked.

"The ship will have multiple methods of clean-up. The first is a tow system, in which tethers latch onto larger pieces of debris and tows them out of orbit. They can either be dragged away from Earth's gravity or pushed down to be dealt with by reentry. There will also be a magnetic system which gathers medium-sized objects and carries them along to a centralized hub where they can be dealt with. Lastly, and my personal favorite, is a laser guidance system."

"Lasers?" Sofia asked.

Noa grinned. "I can visually target the smaller pieces of debris and destroy them by ablation. Eradicating them down to nothing so they no longer pose a threat."

"Sort of like *Space Invaders?*"

Noa laughed and nodded. "Yes, actually, very much like the video game. Astraea wants to reassure everybody that this isn't a dire situation for us on the ground. The debris is only hazardous for future space travel."

Sofia said, "It's not just a video game, it's a bit like the early explorers, bushwhacking through the forest to clear the way for expansion."

"That's exactly what it is. When this mission is complete, the space around our planet will be eighty-five to ninety percent cleared of dangerous debris. The door will be open for future missions to Mars and beyond."

"I think we're going to leave you with that exciting prediction. Thank you again for taking the time to talk with us this morning."

"It was my pleasure, Sofia."

"Colonel Noa Laurie," Sofia said to her own camera, near the other ocean.

The camera light went dark. The producer smiled at her. "You did a great job."

Noa smiled nervously. The producer walked away, and someone came to unhook her microphone. They moved quickly and efficiently, probably setting up for another interview or the next broadcast. Noa slid off the seat and stood up as the crew vanished through the open door at the back of the studio. The lights were still on but the room had emptied out so quickly that she felt as if the lights had been shut off as well. She looked at the backdrop of Boston.

"Okay," she said into the silence.

There was a weight beside Jamie Faris in the bed when she woke up. She spent a few confused minutes with her eyes closed as she tried to make sense of it. It didn't take long for her mind to clear and realize it was just her wild man, her stalwart companion, her dedicated guardian. Almost as if he realized she was thinking about him, Cisco threw his full weight against her back and began snuffling at her ear and neck. Jamie brought up one arm in defense, burrowing as deep into the pillow as she could to escape the assault.

"Leave me alone, you beast," she muttered through laughter.

"Okay. Okay, you win!"

The dog leapt off the bed and disappeared out into the hall. Jamie found her phone on the nightstand, rolling over to further tangle her legs in the blankets as she checked her email. It was as much of the internet as she allowed herself, and that was only because it was a necessary evil. Clients had to find her somehow, and everyone expected email availability. This morning there were two more requests for custom items, income she might never have gotten without the internet. Her original intention was to never set foot in the information age, but one day it was easier to get a cell phone than a landline, and it seemed like all cell phones came with the internet whether she wanted it or not. It was easier to compromise than fight.

Cisco barked downstairs. Jamie kicked her legs free of the blankets and sat up. Stretched, twisted left then right, and lifted both arms over her head before she stood. She took off her pajamas and put on a pair of shorts and a baggy plaid shirt, buttoning it as she headed downstairs. She let Cisco outside on her way to the kitchen to put on coffee. The dog barked outside. She looked out the window as a wave of big black birds took off with her companion in hot pursuit.

Jamie's brown hair fell over her right eye and she absently pushed it back up, tucking it behind her ear. She'd forgotten her glasses and didn't feel like going upstairs to get them. She stared at the coffee maker as it ticked and began radiating heat. She closed her eyes and breathed deeply, hands flat on the counter. Long slow breaths.

"Fuck you, Louis," she whispered.

In the beginning she let herself say it as loud as she wanted. Her neighbors were just far enough away that it didn't matter. She let herself say it as often as possible, with as much rage as she could muster, until her throat was raw and she curled up in a ball on the floor. Cisco had found her in that position far too many times, whimpering with worry and licking her hands and face until she got to her feet. So now she only said it once per day. She tried to wait as long as possible but lately she hadn't been able to make it past breakfast.

It had been something like thirteen months and four days since the perfect life she thought she had blew up in her face. It was strange how a year could feel short and endless at the same time. She still thought about that day, as vivid as it had just happened. Did Louis wake up knowing it was the last time they'd be in bed together? The last time they made love, did something in his brain say, "Well, that's that, no more with her"? She hadn't even known to be looking for signs.

He chose to do it over dinner. He kept his hands on the table near the silverware. "James," he said. She'd looked up, mouth full and surely looking like some kind of dumb animal as she chewed. "I think we can both admit this isn't working."

He then explained to her how they both felt - which was really how *he* felt and how he thought she should feel - and told her it was probably best if he finished dinner and then went to pack. She'd saved him the trouble. Why wait until they were done eating if she'd suddenly lost her appetite? So she went upstairs, packed a bag for him, and left it by the front door. He slumped toward her, head bowed, hands in his pockets.

"Go," she said. "And I'll spend the time you're away trying to decide if I let you back in when you come back."

He kissed her forehead. "I'm not coming back, James."

It figured that would be the one promise he managed to keep. She waited for the other shoe to drop: the revelation that he'd been seeing another woman on the side. But he still lived in town and, as far as she could tell from her trivial stalking, he was still single. So it wasn't that he wanted something different. He just wanted out. Away from her. Away from the life she thought they'd been building together.

"Fuck you, Louis," she said again, grimacing halfway through as she realized she'd gone over her quota. She pushed away from the counter and went outside. Her driveway was eighty yards long, stretching across her rolling front lawn and ending at a tree-lined street. She crossed the driveway and went up the gentle slope to the barn. She propped the door open with a piece of cinder block so Cisco could get in when he was done hunting.

Her main work area took up much of the space in the barn. There was the work table with the various tools of her trade, all carefully put away. Her lathe and saws stood against the far wall. The air was thick with wood dust, polish, varnish. It was her sanctuary, her true home. The house was just where she slept and ate her meals, a box where she could keep her stuff. This was where she felt most comfortable, especially now.

There was another table in the barn, against the far wall. The corner of the table was occupied by a small black box about the size of a toaster oven. It was a Galaxy amateur radio, gifted to her by a client who no longer wanted it cluttering up her garage but also didn't have the heart to just throw it away. "It's an expensive little thingie," she said. "Maybe you could get more use out of it than I did."

Jamie took it and let her niece set it up. She spent a few minutes fiddling with the dials that night, but she never picked up any signals. Her interest quickly waned, and now it stood mostly forgotten and half shrouded in wood shavings.

Jamie took a seat, switched the radio on, and winced at the squelch of static produced. She scrolled through the frequencies, pausing when there was silence. The microphone was a palm-sized black stone attached to the machine with a thick, curled wire. She picked it up and squeezed the button as she brought it to her lips.

"Breaker, one-nine, breaker one-nine. Come on back now, ten-four."

She chuckled and dropped the microphone on top of the machine. Sometimes she picked up faint transmissions from Indianapolis, and more frequently she could hear truckers talking to each other out on the highway. She assumed that was what the internet would be like if she ever ventured onto it: a lot of noise with whispers of something far away that might be interesting. It was a fun toy but not anything she would want to waste time with.

Jamie put the microphone back on top of the machine and went to her worktable. The emails she'd gotten that morning were for a lamp and chair. The lamp would be easy. She had a few ideas already, so she would do a couple of sketches for the client to approve before she actually wasted any wood. She pulled her stool over and got to work, the radio already forgotten on the table behind her.

// Mission Day 1, Launch //

THERE WAS a Motel 6 not far from the Mojave Airport, its parking lot full to bursting with the vehicles of journalists and space junkies. Train tracks ran parallel to the road, the bare-metal cars rattling through a desolate landscape reminiscent of a version of the 1950s Noa had never experienced except through movies. To the north, not that far away, the Piute Mountains stood between the desert and the verdant Sequoia National Forest.

Noa woke up well before dawn though she hadn't fallen asleep until past midnight. She moved to the foot of the bed and sat with her elbows on her knees, eyes closed, focusing on little things she took for granted: the way her feet rested heavily on the carpet, the effortless weight of her ass on the mattress, the way the air felt against her skin. She was wearing boxer briefs and a tank top, loose clothes because soon she wouldn't have the luxury of feeling naked without inviting danger.

A foot extended from under the blanket and touched her hip, sliding along her hip to lift her shirt, then moving down so the toes could curl around the waistband of her underwear. Noa smiled without looking back.

"Go back to sleep," Noa whispered.

"I should. I have a really big day today."

Noa looked over her shoulder. Kelly was lying at an angle, her hair a mess, pillow folded in the middle under her shoulder.

"Oh yeah?" Noa said. "What have you got going on?"

"I'm going to hang out here in town for a few hours. Maybe see a movie."

"I'm going to outer space."

Kelly snorted. "You always have to one-up me, don't you."

Noa laughed quietly. She twisted and crawled catlike up the bed, noticing how her hands sank into the blankets and mattress. She perched over Kelly and bent down to kiss her arm where it lay across her chest. She tasted like sweat and sun-baked sand. Kelly moved her arm and settled onto her back. Noa pressed her face into the valley between Kelly's breasts and breathed deeply. They met in flight school, when the adrenaline of flying helped disguise the fact they weren't very compatible as a couple. The sex was amazing, but they just didn't work.

Kelly was now married to a very open-minded woman. She knew about Noa, knew they occasionally got together and had sex, and she encouraged it. She had lovers of her own. Noa was, depending on her mood, jealous and suspicious of the arrangement. But she'd spoken to Kelly's wife and was reassured that everything was on the up-and-up. Plus it meant that she got to have great sex with a woman she respected without the tangle of commitment.

"Are you nervous?" Kelly asked.

"It's an experimental craft, so there's always a possibility something could go wrong." She brushed her bottom lip over Kelly's nipple. "But Enver is a genius. All the test flights went perfectly. The bugs got worked out a long time ago. I learned that thing inside and out. So if someone else tried to fly it, there's a bigger chance of a mistake. But not with me."

Kelly put her hands in Noa's hair and lifted her head up, bending down to kiss her. "Self-confidence is so sexy in a woman."

Noa nipped Kelly's bottom lip and slid her hands down the other woman's side. She rolled and smiled when Kelly yelped in surprise. Her legs automatically tightened around Noa's hips. She flattened her hands on Noa's chest, and Noa spread her fingers wide on Kelly's back. Kelly laughed and hunched her shoulders as she lined up their faces. She brought up one hand to brush it across Noa's face.

"What are you doing?"

"Using your weight on top of me," Noa said, kissing Kelly's fingertips, "to say goodbye to gravity."

Kelly made an adorable noise and bent down to kiss her. She stretched out, covering as much of Noa's body as she could.

"Mind if I do something while I'm up here...?"

"Go crazy," Noa said.

Kelly began moving against her. Noa closed her eyes, holding tight to the woman pressing down on top of her. She moaned when Kelly kissed her neck, gasped when one of Kelly's hands reached between their bodies and ventured into her underwear. After this morning, it would be two full years before she saw another human being in the flesh. She intended to make the best of her final morning on Earth.

The sun was just beginning to color the sky when Jamie carried the lamp out to her truck. She secured it in the passenger seat, strapped it in with the belt, and headed toward town. The lamp was a rectangular tower with round holes of various size cut out near the top. She'd made it out of cherry and used a varnish so it was darker at the top than the bottom. The client had requested it to look like a melting candle, and she felt she'd gotten as close to that as possible.

Her house was a ten minute drive from Corwin, a town so small and quiet that people passing through it might think it was a ghost town. Two roads formed a cross with a flag in the intersection. To the north, the post office and grocery store. South, police station and laundromat. East, mostly empty storefronts with two small restaurants and a VFW hall that doubled as a senior center. West, a video store that still offered VHS along with their DVDs, a bookstore, and a home furnishing store called, creatively enough, Corwin Home Furnishings.

The front window displayed some of Jamie's work: a chair, a wardrobe, a long flat table. She took a moment to admire how it looked before she went inside. None of the lights were on, so it took her eyes a few seconds to adjust to the dim room. It always smelled like dry flowers and candles which had just been snuffed out.

She blinked until the familiar layout faded into view. Handmade pieces crowded around furniture donated from estate sales, traded, or rescued from the dump. The stuff she brought in was always the biggest draw, something she took a lot of pride in, but it was easy to see why based on the competition.

Alf Dooling, the owner, hustled out of the back room, pumping his arms like he was trying to get through a crosswalk before the light turned green. Behind him, she could see the TV sitting on top of his desk showing what appeared to be a live shot of clear blue skies. He was just a shade over five feet tall, slope shouldered with powder-white hair, but she'd seen him haul a recliner into the back of someone's truck without even breathing hard. He waved one gnarled hand at her as he went climbed onto the raised platform behind the counter.

"Sorry, dear. I got all caught up watching this thing on the news. You haven't been waiting long."

"I just got here," she confirmed, even though it hadn't been a question. "I'm on my way to drop off my last commission, so I wanted to see if there was anything you needed."

Alf tapped his fingers on the counter as he thought. From the back room, she heard a snippet of a reporter's voice. "...Enver Crane, CEO of Astraea Aviation, is here with us today at the Mojave Air and Space Port where..."

"You know," Alf said, "there was a fella in here the other day asking about a rocking chair for his wife. She's pregnant, you know, and he thought it would be good for when the baby came and for the, uh, for the..." He gestured vaguely near his chest.

Jamie said, "Breastfeeding?"

He made an uncomfortable face as he searched the countertop. "I made a note of his phone number here somewhere."

Jamie was willing to wait. She looked toward the back room. She vaguely recognized the man on the screen as Enver Crane. He'd invented a website or built a piece of the internet, and now he had all the money in the world. The newspapers seemed to treat him as a benevolent force of science instead of a Bond villain. The wind was whipping at his hair and suit jacket, and he was squinting against the desert sun. He smiled at the reporter as he listened to her question.

"What's going on?" she asked.

Alf followed her gaze. "Hm? Oh. Some kind of new plane."

"Oh." Jamie never went anywhere, so she couldn't have cared less about the elites of the world getting from New York to Paris at a slightly faster clip.

Alf held up a slip of paper. "Found it! I told him you'd give him a call next time you had a sec."

"Thanks, Alf." She glanced at the address, folded the paper, and put it in her back pocket.

He rested both hands on the counter. "You doing okay out there?"

She nodded. "I'm keeping busy. Lots of orders coming in on email. I had a client last month who said I'd get a lot more traffic with a website, but I don't know. It would be like standing in the middle of the street with a sign, right?"

He shrugged. "I meant with, you know... Louis has been in here a couple of times."

Jamie grimaced and shook her head. "I'll talk to you later, Alf. Thanks for the recommendation."

"Jamie..."

She was already at the door. She turned around to push it open with her shoulder and gestured at the back room. "You better hurry or you'll miss the new plane taking off."

When Alf looked back toward the office, she stepped back out into the sunlight. Her mind was occupied by the commission, already planning out each piece of the rocking chair, and pushing down her irritation at Alf for bringing up her ex-husband. Months later, even after the events taking place in the Mojave actually impacted her life, she wouldn't remember seeing the news report.

Noa took a luxuriously long shower, standing under the spray even after the water went cold. Her next shower would be in two years, the one thing that was almost enough to make her call off the whole mission. She angled her face to the faucet and let the water flow over her face. It flattened her hair and coursed down her neck, over her shoulders to follow her spine. She felt it pooling at the bridge of her nose near the corner of her eyes. She had always loved showers and baths. They felt cathartic, meditative, and there was literally no way to have one in space. It wasn't fair.

She stopped dwelling on the bad things and focused on the good. She had someone looking after her house. Her car and bike were in storage. All the loose ends of her life were neatly tied or packed away until she was back on solid ground. It felt good to have everything settled and no outstanding stress, but there was also something strange about putting her affairs in order. It felt unnervingly like planning her own funeral.

When she finally left the bathroom, Kelly was dressed and packed. "I think you just drained the Mojave of all its water."

Noa grinned. "Worth it." She kissed Kelly goodbye. "Say hello to Lisa for me."

"I will. Good luck." She tugged on the towel tucked under Noa's arms. "Maybe you can come see me when you land."

"It's a date." She kissed Kelly once more, stroked her hair, and let her go.

Kelly left, and Noa dressed for her departure. Enver Crane had requested a specific uniform for the cameras: navy blue slacks, polo shirt with the Astraea logo on the left breast, and a leather jacket. He wanted to evoke the golden age of aviation and dashing test pilots like Chuck Yeager. "Only this time, with women. Yeah? Women power!"

She put on the outfit and examined herself in the mirror. Not bad at all. She would probably grace a couple of magazine covers, show up across the internet in memes and on Twitter. Enver had asked for the outfit because it made her look cool and beautiful. People would respond to that, would share pictures of a woman who looked beautiful and badass, and that would draw attention to the very important work they were doing. Plus there was nothing wrong with looking good.

They sent a driver for her, a young black man buzzing with nervous energy whose shirt collar was already darkened by sweat. She put on her flight cap on the way to the car and introduced herself. He grinned, showing most of his teeth.

"Of course you are," he said, extending his hand. "I'm Stephen. I worked at Astraea on the ODIE design team. I can't tell you how thrilled I am to be your chauffer today. The last piece of our design." His eyes bugged out slightly. "Uh, not that you're a component or a tool or anything like that..."

Noa put a hand on his shoulder. "It's okay. I've been to space before, so I know that I'm a cog in a much bigger machine. Just get me there in one piece, okay?"

He nodded. When they got in the car, he told her the radio was busted so she could put in her earbuds. She was grateful for the offer so she wouldn't seem rude, but she did like to block out the world during the last leg of her journey. She put on some fast music, a ritual before all of her test flights. She always chose a female vocalist and she always played it as loud as she could. It wasn't a long drive to the airport but there was enough time for at least one full song. She chose Serena Ryder's "Got Your Number" and turned it up as Stephen pulled out of the parking lot. She tapped her fingers on her knee as she watched the town roll past.

It was hard to believe anyone chose to live here. Judging from the empty storefronts, not many people did. There were fast-food restaurants with signs which hadn't been able to stand up to the constant assault of the desert sun, leaving them faded and abandoned-looking even if the stores were still technically open. All the buildings were pale stucco or brick. They reminded her of old westerns and ghost towns. As goodbyes to Earth went, she would have hoped for something a bit more vibrant.

The Mojave Air and Space Port looked like a military base, the entry road flanked by the only greenery she'd seen since arriving. The place was packed with vehicles, cars and trucks, vans, and people unloading camera equipment. Most of them were crews from Los Angeles and the surrounding area, and she saw someone she recognized from CNN jogging alongside the road with a cameraman in tow. Stephen showed his ID to a guard without rolling down his window and was waved into the private staging area.

Noa pulled the wire of her earbuds and let them fall as the ODIE came into view. Her home for the next twenty-six months was waiting on the runway as if impatient for her to show up. She got chills just looking at it. On the surface, the ship wasn't exactly elegant. It looked like a flattened beetle painted white and black, covered with solar shields and energy panels. The back flared out to house the thrusters and flattened out to either side to form long elegant wings.

Stephen said, "I fought hard to call it the ORCA, but I was outvoted."

"I can see the resemblance," she said. "What would ORCA have stood for?"

He shrugged. "I would've figured that out once the name got confirmed."

Noa laughed. "Oh, is that how naming stuff works?"

"Don't tell anyone."

Enver Crane had seen them arrive and jogged over to greet her.

"Colonel Laurie!" He held his arms out to either side. He was a lanky man, but she'd seen enough photos of him with his shirt off to know his wiry frame was threaded with muscle. He was a surfer, a biker, a thrillseeker who also happened to have one of the most brilliant minds in the northern hemisphere. He was also movie-star handsome, with a stunning smile and blue eyes that sparkled. His hair was a sandy blonde which was just long enough to be pushed around by the desert winds. He had been blessed in so many ways it would've been easy to hate him if he wasn't also charming as hell.

Today he was wearing a white V-neck under a tan blazer. He shook Noa's hand, then did the same to Stephen.

"Thank you for picking her up, Stephen. She's going to be doing plenty of driving in the next few months, so I thought we'd give her a little break, huh?" He grinned and slapped Stephen on the shoulder. He had an accent Noa had eventually decided was a mixture of Turkish and Toronto, a combination she couldn't describe but nonetheless found accurate. He focused on her. "Are you all set? Do you need anything?"

"No, I think I'm good," she said.

"Fantastic." He reached into the breast pocket of his jacket and withdrew a small paper bag. He tossed it to Noa. "Here, for you."

She caught it easily. "What's this?"

"Peanut butter rice krispie balls."

Noa stared at him. "What?"

"You said you liked them."

"I love them." She opened the bag and looked inside as if she expected a trick. She gasped when she saw them, four perfectly misshapen globes. "Where in the world did you get these?"

"I made them."

"You..."

He was already walking away from her. She pulled out one of the treats and bit it in half as she hurried to catch up with him.

"You're about to take command of the vessel I saw in a dream when I was a teenager. It's taken billions of dollars - no exaggeration - to get to this point, and it would be nothing but a hunk of metal on a runway without your talents. I can spend an hour at a stove."

"Thank you so much." She held the bag out to Stephen. He reached in and took one of the treats. "This is a perfect snack. How did you even know?"

He said, "At our first meeting about the project, I asked you what the perfect snack food was."

She vaguely remembered, but she'd thought he'd been breaking the ice with a softball question. She finished the first ball and went for a second.

Stephen broke away and headed for a group of other Astraea

employees. They were standing in front of a stage which faced a wall of bleachers full of the journalists whose cars she'd seen outside. There were also angel investors and others who had provided the income to make this day possible. Many of them ended their conversations when they saw Enver approaching, and Noa felt their eyes on her as she followed him onto the stage. Video cameras were hoisted onto shoulders while photographers began snapping still shots.

Enver was the type of man who could request an introduction but chose not to. He clapped his hands as he approached the microphone and the crowd fell silent. Noa stayed a few steps behind him, feet shoulder-width apart and hands clasped behind her back.

"Welcome! Welcome, everyone, thank you for being here on this very special day. Behind me, you see the ODIE, a revolutionary ship which will make amends for years and years of neglect and laziness." He raised one arm and gestured at the sky as if he was palming the top of a snow globe from the inside. "Our planet is currently wrapped in a tangled ball of barbed wire. Tiny pieces of metal swirling, swirling around, impacting each other, causing a cascade of projectiles, any one of which could prove deadly. The government created this minefield, and now they are doubly terrified of it. They are terrified of what it can do, and of how much it would cost to fix."

He dropped his arm and smiled.

"I am not terrified. Neither is my pilot, Colonel Noa Laurie, whom I'm sure you all remember from the ISS incident which pushed the space junk situation into a critical area. She faced a hellish situation that none of us can even begin to comprehend. She was alone in space, the very systems that were keeping her alive were failing, and she came through the other side stronger. A phoenix from the ashes. There could be no one else better suited for this mission.

"In a few moments, Colonel Laurie is going to board this vessel and take off into the sky. Imagine the next time you got into a car, the door would seal, and you wouldn't be able to leave for two years. Just imagine that! She'll have a bit more room, of course, but I don't think any of us would be quite as willing as Colonel Laurie is." He looked back at her. "Right?"

Noa gave him a thumbs-up. "Ready to go."

"Glad to hear it!" He faced the crowd again. "Now, I would go through all the bells and whistles for you, but there will be time enough for that later. We have a very small window in which to launch, so we're going to get Noa safely up into the air before we take care of the dull stuff. Let's go!"

He turned and began jogging to the edge of the stage. Noa was startled but, with no other option, jogged after him. She heard laughter from the crowd and she couldn't help smiling as well. Enver jumped off the stage but she took the stairs. There was no need for showboating at this point, when any misstep could lead to a sprained ankle and a scrubbed mission.

Enver looked over his shoulder at her. "You ready to go back to space, Colonel?"

"Hell yes," she said without hesitation.

She tilted her head back as she ran, casting one last look at the clear blue sky. There were clouds on the horizon, miles long but wispy enough that she knew they'd be gone in an hour or so. Between the ground and her destination was the firmament, the place where all of human life and history unfolded since the dawn of time. She was about to break through it for the second time and she wanted to make sure she appreciated its beauty before she said goodbye.

The picture that would be on the front page of most websites later that day, and on magazines and newspapers for the rest of the month, was Noa standing on the wing of ODIE, feet planted apart, twisting at the waist to look back toward the gathered ground with one arm in the air. The sun was shining to one side of her, providing an aura without casting a shadow on her face. It would run under the banner of THE NEW FRONTIERSWOMAN, focusing on her mission to make future exploration possible.

When she saw it later, even though she hated when people focused more on her looks than her accomplishments, she had to admit the picture was damn good. It was iconic, the kind of picture she could imagine ending up in history books. For most of the past decade she'd feared she would always be remembered as the sole survivor, a memento of an unspeakable tragedy, but now Astraea was offering her the chance to be something else: the woman who cleared the way to Mars.

It was time to get to work.

// **MISSION DAY 23** //

NOA WAS sick of space.

She was sick of her little bunk. It was a nook above the main command center and, a bed inside of a smooth-walled alcove which was just barely wide and long enough for her. She was sick of the lack of gravity, which sent her stomach into spirals whenever she turned too fast. She knew it was just a matter of acclimation. The irritation would fade once she got used to her surroundings. It happened the last time she was in space. She went from awed, to frustrated, to practically begging for her mission to end early, to wishing she would never have to leave.

Between the command center and the thrusters was what Enver had called her "life space." It was where she had her meals, exercised, and did interviews. All of her personal time, which amounted to about two or three hours every day, was spent there. The rest of the day was spent either in the command chair or asleep.

She was currently in the chair, eradicating a small cluster of debris using the lasers. It had been fun for the first few days, like the video game she'd compared it to in so many interviews, but even that quickly lost its appeal. She was feeling bored and stuck in a monotonous routine that wouldn't end for another seven hundred and some odd days.

The cockpit reminded her of being at the dentist. It was a cramped space, specifically designed with her proportions in mind. Control panels lined the walls to either side of her, just inside of arms' reach. It was all very exact. If anything had happened to her, Astraea would have needed to find someone who was her exact height to take over. The chair was nylon and cotton canvas, not comfortable but once again built to her specifications. It allowed her to sit at an incline, facing forward where four screens showed her what was ahead and to either side of ODIE's nose. She could also recline the chair completely when she wanted to nap.

She reached out now and flicked the radio switch. "Astraea Command, anyone down there?"

There was a low hum of the open line for a few seconds. "Good morning, Colonel," a male voice said. "How's everything going up there?"

"Five by five," she said. "Just checking in."

"All systems are normal." She could tell from his voice that he had leaned away to check the multiple screens showing ODIE's current position and operations. She knew that everything was normal. She would have felt if anything was amiss. "How are you feeling?"

Noa rolled her eyes. She didn't know what requirements Astraea had for people manning the communication desk, but a degree in psychology seemed to be a common thread among them all. Everyone wanted to know how she felt or where her head was at or if she was having any curious dreams.

"Nothing to report," she said. "Are we on track for the clearance rate?"

"Looks like it." He paused. "Is anything wrong with your instruments? You could have checked that yourself."

She bit back a sigh. "I know. Sometimes it's better to hear it from someone else."

"Okay. Enver is going to be in the office in about... uh, I guess maybe an hour from now if there's anything you want to discuss with him."

"That won't be necessary," she said. "I'll go ahead and clear the line now."

"We'll continue monitoring down here," he said.

She turned the radio off. She unfastened her harness and pushed herself up and back, floating weightlessly over the top of the chair and into her life space. She did still appreciate the ease of zero-g living. Once she was out of the command area, she twisted so that she was face down. She tapped the wall with her foot and gently propelled herself forward to the cabinet which contained her snacks. She hummed as she searched for something to eat, singing under her breath.

"I need your help tonight, alone I can't win this fight, I tri-i-i-ied to call..." She looked toward a spot on the ceiling and addressed the ship's automated systems. "Vera, play Radiation Canary."

An automated voice responded. "Album?"

"Shuffle all."

There was a pause before music began filtering through all the nearby speakers. Enver had told her she could upload any music she wanted. "You can upload every song you've ever loved and you'd still have room. Even though you'll probably be filling more memory space than they used for the first Moon landing. But times change!"

She retrieved a baggie of dried fruits and floated to the dinner table to eat them. She'd expected pushback when she asked about a vegan diet for the mission, but Enver was ecstatic. A vegan menu was much simpler to maintain in a limited space. Couldn't exactly send a bunch of cattle up in ODIE with her. So she got her way, and now the lower compartment of ODIE was full of freeze-dried meals to last her for the duration of her trip.

"Sinfully Citrus," she read off the package, quirking her lips to the side. "I don't know what's so sinful about lemon, lime, and orange, but Enver does like to give quirky names to things."

She carefully opened the package and removed a dried piece of food. She had to reseal the package so the rest of it wouldn't scatter, and she held the bag against her stomach as she chewed the first piece. Eating was so methodical in the ODIE that she worried she would skip meals just because it was so much of a hassle. Her foot kicked one wall and she began to drift in the opposite direction.

The ugly truth was that she was bored. The work was important and it required her full attention, but it was monotonous. She destroyed everything that was small enough for a laser and she hooked anything bigger. She worked in quadrants, moving over large swatches of the planet in a single bound. If she kept to a straight line, she could complete an orbit in under two hours. Enver's plan caused her to travel so erratically that it took just under thirty hours to circle the planet. She was moving at incredible speeds - almost five miles a second - but it still felt like she was crawling along.

"Vera," she said.

"I'm here, Colonel."

Everything Vera said was prerecorded, but sometimes it was easy to pretend she was actually having a conversation with someone. Vera had access to the internet and could answer pretty much any question.

"Tell me what you know about... ah... ramen shops."

A pause. "A ramen shop is a common and very popular type of restaurant which specializes in ramen dishes. They originated in Japan. Shall I keep going?"

"Yes, please."

"Okay." Another pause as the voice loaded an article for the systems to recite. "While some ramen shops prepare orders on-site, others rely on pre-packaged meals..."

Noa tuned her out. What she was saying didn't matter as much as having someone else's voice in her ear, someone who wasn't a technician or an engineer or, god, a reporter. She closed her eyes and ate another piece of dried fruit, drifting, kicking her feet slightly as if she was floating in a pool. She had over seven hundred days left. Eighteen thousand hours. She was a genius and a problem-solver. She was confident she could figure out some way to fill them all without going absolutely bonkers.

But at the moment, she would learn all about the fascinating world of ramen shops.

// MISSION DAY 97 //

JAMIE LIVED far enough out of town that the sound of a vehicle was usually enough to get her attention. The mail truck's engine was a familiar grumble, as recognizable as any of the creaks or groans in her house. Occasionally a tractor-trailer would take a detour on its way out of state, or hunters in their obnoxious 4X4 trucks would shake the windows. She tried to ignore them as much as she could, and it helped to have the machinery and her earplugs to help push back the intrusions.

She was working on the table saw, ears plugged against its piercing whine. Cisco was sprawled in the doorway with his head in the sun. She saw him sit up in response to something outside but ignored it until he got to his feet. She shut off the machine, took out the plugs, and listened as she heard what had gotten the dog's attention: a familiar but unwelcome sound, an engine that had slowed down to pull off the main road onto her driveway.

"Damn it."

She took off her safety glasses and examined herself. The front of her apron was covered in sawdust. Underneath she was wearing an old flannel and jeans that were ripped at the knee. She waved a hand though her hair to get rid of the dust she knew was there and walked to the door of the barn. Cisco looked up at her with a confused expression. In the past he would have run out to greet the car, but now things had changed in a way he didn't understand. Jamie patted him on the head as the car parked next to her truck and her ex-husband climbed out.

Louis had let his hair grow out a little, shaggy on top and shorter on the sides. She could see a little gray at the temple and it suited him well. He was a big man, a college hockey player who never let himself lose the muscle, and he always flashed his wide, crooked smile as if he anticipated someone taking his picture. Today he was in a burgundy shirt, unbuttoned at the collar, and a charcoal suit jacket. Jamie crossed her arms over her chest as he approached.

"What are you doing here, Louis?"

He stopped. "I'm visiting my wife."

"Ex-wife."

"No one is ex-anything yet."

She turned her back and went into the barn. "Then bring the papers."

"James, I never said I wanted that."

"Then I must have picked up something in your body language. The way it picked up and walked out the door, and then moved into a little apartment in town. The way your mouth said you weren't coming back. The clues were subtle, but I'm pretty good at interpreting that sort of thing." She busied herself cleaning up her work, even though she didn't plan on stopping for the day. It gave her something to do with her hands and a reason not to look at him. Louis had followed her into the barn but remained just inside the threshold. She could see his shadow on the floor.

"I just want to talk, James. Can we... talk?"

"You had a chance to talk. You could have looped me in on whatever conversation you were having with yourself, but I guess you didn't need my input. You decided the best choice was to leave. You made that decision. Don't force me to do the dirty work. Don't make me the one to file the papers when this was one-hundred percent your decision."

Louis sighed heavily. "James–"

"Jam-ie, Jamie, my goddamn name is Jamie." She picked up the piece she'd been cutting when he arrived and lifted it as if to bang it against the saw. Her mind caught up with her in time, warning of the potential damage to the machine or herself if a piece snapped off and went flying. She placed it gently on the table. "You've called me James since we started dated."

He said, "You should have said something."

"After the first dozen times of you ignoring me, I thought it was easier to just let it go." She turned to face him. "Why did you come here, Louis? Did you get lonely? Are you sick of frozen dinners and fast food? If you're not here to deliver divorce papers, then what? Did you miss the dog?"

"I did, actually." He looked down at Cisco and smiled. "Hey, boy."

Jamie muttered, "God," and turned away from him. "I'm pretty sure everything you left in the house has been moved into the sewing room." It was a small room off the kitchen, narrow and not much use for anything but storage. "If you want it, get it and get out."

"I was hoping we could have lunch. I could take you to Jack's~"

"Where we had our first date? What the hell are you doing, Louis? Are you trying to ask me out?"

He sighed yet again. Jamie was starting to hate the sound. "There's no reason this has to be the end."

"Yes, it does. After what you did~"

He rocked his head to the side. "Well, hold on, it's not like I cheated on you or left you for another woman."

"No, you just cut me out of the entire process. You made the choice, you elected to put our marriage on hold or whatever it is. You weren't happy so you walked away. I don't plan on changing to accommodate your hissy fit, so you'll just be coming back to the same old boring wife I've always been."

Louis looked tired. "I just wanted some space to think."

"I would've given it to you. I don't care if you had doubts, you asshole, I cared because you left. You just left. I care because you're still holding on because it's a safety net for you. You don't want to completely cut ties in case you want to come running back. And look here, look what we have. You're asking me out to lunch? At *our* place? Fuck you, Louis. File the fucking papers and end this."

He ran a hand through his hair. "I caught you on a bad day. Why don't I call~"

"I really don't want to damage any of my tools by throwing one at you, so leave. Just *leave*."

"I care about you, Jamie. I want you to know that."

She walked toward the pegboard. "Oh, hell, I need a new hand planer anyway."

Louis ducked his head and ran for the car before she could unleash the tool. She watched him back across the yard and down the driveway. She didn't relax until his car was actually out of sight, breathing hard and feeling the urge to smash every surface in the barn until her anger was completely spent. Cisco sidled up next to her and lifted his head to lick her hand. She looked down at him, tears in her eyes, and crouched down to give him a hug.

"Thanks, pal," she whispered into his fur.

When she felt capable of standing without her knees giving way, she let him go. She wanted to yell, scream, curse, but she didn't want Cisco to bear the brunt of that anger. She looked around the barn and her gaze landed on the radio sitting in the corner. She stormed over, pulled the chair close, and sat down. She switched it on, jabbed at the frequency until the static cleared, and she brought the microphone up to her mouth.

"You son of a bitch, you fucking asshole... how dare you walk in here, act like nothing happened. Like you didn't blow this up. Like it was no one's fault. It was *your* fault, and if you think I'm giving you another chance, you can just go fuck yourself, do you understand? Go fuck yourself!"

She exhaled sharply and put her head down in the crook of her elbow. Her face was hot and her eyes stung. She took a deep breath, smelled her own sweat and the sawdust on the table, and let the breath out so sharply that her whole body shook with it. And then...

"Hello? Who is this?"

Jamie sat straight up and stared at the radio.

Noa had decided there was peace in monotony. She could be alone with her thoughts. She could center herself and meditate when she wasn't shooting down debris. The monitors showed a clear swath of space behind her, though other junk was going to drift into the void within a few hours. It was like mowing a lawn where the grass actively tried to keep itself at a uniform height. She wasn't a pioneer, she was a gardener of the cosmos.

And, by her reasoning, she had earned a break. She called Astraea with a progress report and then reclined her chair. There was a spacesuit in the back compartment just in case she was required to leave the vehicle for exterior repairs or if there was a breach. She had taken the Snoopy cap from the suit, the Communications Carrier Array colored black with a white stripe over the top of the head, and was using it to keep her hair under control. It also kept her connected to the radio without moving her arms. Plus, in her own opinion, it made her look cool.

She was half-asleep with her fingers laced over her stomach, feet crossed at the ankles. There was a fizzling of static in her ear and a voice warbled through the ether. She opened her eyes as the signal became stronger in the middle of what seemed to be a very vitriolic rant.

"–think I'm giving you another chance, you can just go fuck yourself, do you understand? Go fuck yourself!"

Noa had both eyes open now. She waited for a response to the woman's rage, assuming it was some kind of radio broadcast or television show that somehow got picked up. She looked at the radio readout and only heard silence. No, not silence. What was that, shaky breathing? Crying? Was somebody... crying?

"Hello?" she said into the Snoopy cap's microphone. "Who is this?"

Silence for close to a minute. Then: "Hello?"

Noa raised an eyebrow. "Is everything okay down there?"

More silence. She checked the readout and didn't see anything amiss. There was a screen where she could receive text messages from the ground, but it was blank.

"Who is this?" the other woman asked.

Noa laughed. "Who do you *think* it is?"

"I don't know. I don't usually, uh, I don't use this very often."

"Yeah, I can tell," Noa said. "I don't recognize your voice. But it's not exactly crowded up here. Where is the usual guy?"

Silence. She didn't know if there was a delay or if the other woman was just taking her time.

"I'm not sure."

"Well, who else is there?"

"Nobody."

That was enough to make Noa stop smiling. "What do you mean 'nobody'? You're alone?"

"Well, my dog is here..."

"Your dog?"

"Cisco."

Noa blinked and looked at the monitors. "Why do you have a dog?"

"Okay, who is this?" the other woman said.

"That's a really strange thing to ask. You understand that, right?" She chuckled softly. "What's your name?"

"Jamie Faris."

"Well, Jamie Faris, I'm Noa."

"Noah? Like with the Ark?"

"No H. Just N-O-A." It was becoming clear that whoever this Jamie was, she wasn't ignorant and she wasn't playing dumb. "Jamie, you're not at Astraea, are you?"

"I don't even know what that means. Like I said, I'm not really a radio, uh, user. Sometimes I hear truckers on I-74, but I never really talk to them. Do you need a license to use these things? God, I'm not breaking the law, am I?"

It was Noa's turn to be silent. She rested her head on the cushion behind her, staring at the ceiling above her. Was it possible a civilian had somehow hacked into Astraea's signal? But no, if she'd done that she would know who she was talking to. Jamie seemed legitimately perplexed by the situation. I-74... where was that? Ohio? Somewhere in the East, she thought.

"Hello? Noa?"

"I'm here," she said softly. "Jamie, can you tell me exactly where you are right now?"

Jamie said, "Why?"

"Humor me."

"I'm in my barn. My house is on the other side of the driveway.

About twenty miles outside of Indianapolis, Indiana, United States... Earth."

Noa couldn't help but laugh at the last bit. "Can you do me a favor? Google the name Noa Laurie." She spelled it again. "Tell me what you see."

"I can't."

"Why not?"

"I don't have a computer."

Noa was stunned. "You don't have any internet access at all? What about your phone?"

"It doesn't get very good reception. Look, um... I'm... I'm sorry. I'm having a really bad day, and I wanted to scream about it for a little bit. I didn't think I would actually find someone who was listening to this particular frequency."

Noa looked at her monitor. She made a quick note of what frequency the communications were currently on. There should have been safeguards to prevent a civilian from getting anywhere near the ship's communications. She knew that Enver had jury-rigged a state-of-the-art radio system so they could be in contact no matter where she was above the planet, but there were also firewalls. There were dedicated frequency bands. What was happening should not have been possible.

"I'm going to turn the radio off now."

"Don't!"

Noa wasn't entirely sure why she reacted that way, and she had to think before she continued. It was simple enough: she enjoyed hearing someone else's voice. She was speaking to a real person who didn't care about her progress, who wasn't doing a job, who wasn't adhering to strict guidelines about what could be talked about over the radio. It was the closest she'd come to a real, authentic conversation in over three months, and she was practically giddy about it.

"Just... don't go. Please? I'd like to talk longer. I don't know how long we'll be in range of each other, but I'd like to just keep talking."

Jamie said, "Okay. But... what do you mean in range? Are you moving?"

Noa smiled. "Wow, you really have no idea who I am, do you?"

"Should I? Noa is a pretty name. I feel like I would remember it."

"Thank you. And... I guess there's no real reason for you to know me if you don't watch TV or go online."

Jamie said, "So you're famous in certain circles?"

"Yeah. It depends on who you ask."

"You said 'down there' a minute ago. Are you in Canada?"

Noa laughed again. She hadn't laughed so much in a very long time. "No. I'm afraid if I tell you where I am, you'll think I'm a liar."

"Okay, you've piqued my curiosity."

"I'm in outer space."

Jamie leaned back from the radio, staring at the dial. It was a crazy person or a prankster. Some bored trucker playing a trick on the newbie. She scooted her chair closer and brought the microphone back up.

"People aren't going to space anymore," she said. "Not since the ISS disaster."

"Oh, I'm well aware." There was still humor in Noa's voice, but Jamie didn't feel it was directed at her. It was just general amusement at the conversation. "I know this is probably very hard to believe, but I'm over two hundred miles straight up in a prototype spacecraft designed to clear up all the space junk that's preventing other missions from getting out of our atmosphere. My name is Colonel Noa Laurie. I'm currently working with Astraea Aviation. This would all be so much easier if you could check the internet."

Jamie pulled out her phone but, as expected, there was no real signal. If she tried to get online it would take forever to load a single page.

"I swear to you, I'm telling the truth. And I can't begin to tell you how great it is to hear someone else's voice. I didn't know how badly I needed a conversation until you started talking."

"These Astraea people don't talk to you?"

"Sure they do. But that's all mission spec and progress reports. How am I feeling? How is the ship operating? It's all mechanical. Sometimes I do video or radio interviews, but that's all prearranged. Most of the time it's answering questions from grade schoolers about how I go to the bathroom. Kids are great, but they aren't the best conversationalists. Do you ever just... get lonely?"

Jamie felt a twist inside her chest at the question. She rubbed her right hand over her left shoulder in a sort of self-hug. "Yeah. Of course I do."

"So you understand. I don't know how long this is going to last, but I don't want to cut it short."

"How is it even happening?"

Noa said, "I haven't the faintest idea. Enver, the brainchild of this whole thing, gave me a radio that can pick up the Astraea signal no matter where I am in the world. I could be over Australia and they'll come in loud and clear. But it's supposed to be impenetrable to private radio signals. Even if you have the right frequency, all you should be hearing is static."

Jamie examined the radio closely. "I don't know what's different about this set. I rarely even pay attention to it."

"Maybe it got hit by lightning like Johnny 5."

Jamie beamed. "*Short Circuit*. I love that movie."

"It's a good one," Noa said. "Whatever is causing this, I think it depends on your end. So whenever I get out of range of your signal, we'll be cut off."

"Do you have any idea when you'll be in range again?"

"There's a lot of math involved. Hold, please."

Jamie put down her microphone and leaned against the back of her chair. She covered her face with both hands. It was insane. There was no way she was actually talking to an astronaut who was orbiting the planet. It had been almost a decade since anyone went up. She barely remembered hearing about the space station disaster and she didn't even know any details, but she knew it killed everyone aboard except for one person. She also knew it resulted in such a mess that no one could launch without having their ship torn to shreds.

Then again, everyone knew that space was off-limits, so why would anyone stick to such a blatant lie? Why would they go to the trouble of making up Astraea and the mission? It would be so much easier to just claim she was in Canada or, hell, Chicago. There was no need for a lie, let alone one that was so immense. She didn't know if she believed in things that were too bizarre to be made up, but... and if... then that meant...

"Are you still there?" Noa asked. "Jamie?"

She brought up the microphone. "I'm here."

"I'm going to be back in this general area in just under twenty-five hours. Since you faded in, I have a general idea of when I entered your range."

Jamie wore a big clunky watch which she'd inherited from her father. She pushed up her sleeve to make a note of the time: thirteen minutes past one o'clock.

"So we just need to make a note of how long it takes to start fading. How do I sound?"

"Sounds perfect on my end," Jamie said. "A little static, but not bad considering it's coming from outer space."

Noa sighed, not without humor. "You still don't believe me, do you?"

"Would you believe you? I mean, a hundred percent without a doubt?"

"Absolutely not. You're entirely right to doubt me. I just wish there was a way I could prove it. Wait, let me check the schedule. Is there any chance you could get to Miss Shepherd's second grade class at Lafayette Elementary School in Utica, New York by nine tomorrow morning?"

Jamie twisted her lips. "It's doubtful."

Noa laughed. "Well, I had to ask. I don't see any television interviews in the next little bit."

"How about this? I humor you for the rest of this conversation. Then tomorrow morning, I head to the library and look you up online. If everything checks out, I'll be back here in the afternoon."

"Perfect solution!"

Jamie said, "I find it hard to believe you're bored, anyway. If you really are in space, I mean."

"Are you kidding? It's been three months. I'm by myself. I have my routine, and that's it. There's music and movies, and I have some books, but the work gets as monotonous as anything else."

Jamie laid her arm across the edge of the table, holding up the microphone with her other hand. "I guess I understand that."

"So tell me some more about yourself, while we're still connected. What's your job?"

"Woodworking. I make furniture."

"Get out of here. You make furniture? I thought it was all mass-produced crap."

Jamie grinned. "Yeah, between the two of us, *I* have the unbelievable job."

"Well, it sounds pretty cool to me. Are you working on anything right now?"

She looked over at the work she'd been doing when Louis showed up. "Right now I'm working on a night table. I sell my stuff to a shop in town, and I occasionally do custom orders from the owner's customers. I also have email."

"Oh, you have email. So you're not a complete dinosaur."

"Against my wishes. I needed a phone, and it was easier to get one of these *Star Trek* doohickeys than a landline."

Noa said, "It's the future."

"Said the spacewoman."

"Touché."

"So tell me something. You expected me to know who you are based off just your name. Are you famous or egotistical?"

Noa laughed for a while at that. "Well, maybe both. I've been on magazine covers and I've been on television multiple times. A lot of people tried to make me an icon for one thing or another. A female astronaut, an allegedly good-looking female astronaut, an allegedly good-looking openly gay astronaut."

Jamie raised an eyebrow.

"Oh. Indiana is sort of Bible Belt, isn't it? Did I just make you recoil in horror?"

"No, no. I'm... I'm actually bisexual, so I don't have a problem with that." She hadn't admitted that out loud to many people, and it felt oddly freeing to make the confession to a stranger. "I was just trying to deal with the fact I'm talking to a celebrity. I don't think I've ever talked

with someone who has been on TV before. I'm a little starstruck."

"*Starstruck*," Noa said.

"No pun intended. And what do you mean 'allegedly good-looking'?"

Noa grunted. "It means people like to take my picture for some reason. My flight school asked if they could put my picture on the cover of their brochure. Forget the fact I'm a Colonel in the Air Force, forget the fact I flew forty-seven combat missions or that I have a brain for math and science that most people would kill for, they just want to know if I'm comfortable posing on the wing in a bikini."

Jamie said, "Wow."

"Sorry. I didn't mean to go off on you like that."

"It's obviously a sore spot."

"I always think I'm used to it, but sometimes it makes me upset." She sighed heavily. "Sorry. We were having a nice conversation and I went and ruined it with my rant."

Jamie was using one leg to swing her chair back and forth. "I don't think you've ruined it. We're just getting to know each other. And since you went there, how about I balance the scales and tell you why I was screaming into the radio?"

Noa said, "I admit, I'm curious. You don't seem like the type of person to shout obscenities for no reason."

"I'm not, usually. My husband, my ex-husband, my... whatever he is. The guy I was married to who decided to walk out but refuses to actually divorce me came by. He seems to think there's still something to talk about. As far as I'm concerned, the marriage is dead. The second he walked away without even a conversation... I can forgive a lot of stuff, but I'm not going to forgive the fact he made a marriage decision entirely on his own. Does that make me a bitch?"

"Personally, I think you're in the right. He left. Now he regrets it and he wants to undo the mistake without consequences. Do you want him back?"

Jamie shook her head. "Not really. He decided the marriage was over once, so what's to stop him from doing it again? I have better things to do than sit around waiting for a ticking time bomb to go off in the bed next to me."

Noa said, "He might also use it to manipulate you. You take him back, but the threat of walking out the door is always there. You'd be walking on eggshells the rest of your life."

"Exactly! Thank you."

"Devil's advocate, I don't know him, you, or the relationship. Maybe things were fine before..."

"No," Jamie said. "No, there were problems, I'm not saying he just made them up. We fought. He was jealous of my bisexuality, always afraid I was going to leave him for a woman even though I never gave him a reason to think that. He could be close-minded and set in his ways. I don't know if I would have left him or stuck it out for the long haul, but he removed himself from the equation. He gave me room to think. And I decided he was right."

"Wow," Noa said. "Good for you."

Jamie shrugged and rolled her eyes. "I keep making gestures I know you can't see. But I don't know. I think part of it is just being stubborn. I don't want to be like a... a..."

"A toy he got bored with."

"Right. Exactly. Hm." She tapped the microphone against her lips. "I turned this on because I wanted to feel better. I wanted to scream without scaring the dog. I never expected to find someone who actually made me feel better. Thank you, Noa."

"You're very welcome, Jamie. And I was tapped into the radio because I was bored and too lazy to shut it off. I'm extremely grateful I left the line open. And I really hope this is something that can be recreated tomorrow. I feel rejuvenated. You'd be surprised how much it helps to just talk to somebody. Just a normal person."

Jamie said, "Anything I can do to help an astronaut. I feel like a superhero's sidekick right now." She looked at her watch. "We've been talking for a while now. Is the signal still coming in clearly on your end? There's a little static here, but not much."

"Same. If you have somewhere you need to be..."

"No," Jamie said. "But if you need to get back to your work, I can sign off."

"I have a little time. I'm curious to see how long this little anomaly lasts, and the easiest way to do that is to keep talking. Right?"

Jamie nodded. "Right. So come on, Major Tom, sell your story. Tell me how you ended up floating up in space."

Noa said, "Ninety-seven days ago, I was in the Mojave Desert..."

Jamie leaned back and put her feet up on the table. She let her eyes drift along the wall behind the radio set, past the shovel and rake and pitchfork hanging by the door, to the swath of blue sky she could see beyond the house. It was ludicrous to think she was using this crappy little radio to talk to someone in outer space. There was no chance it was real no matter how convincing Noa might be.

Then again...

What if it was?

// MISSION DAY 98 //

THE SKY was still all pinks and purples when Jamie woke the next morning. She took Cisco out for his jog and continuously found her eyes drifting upward past the horizon. She'd been on the radio for close to an hour before the signal became too weak for them to continue their conversation. They hadn't even had a chance to say goodbye. When she finally accepted Noa had traveled out of range, she turned off the radio and stretched her tired legs. She felt elated, even better than she'd felt before Louis showed his insufferable face. She'd spent the rest of the afternoon on work, at several points discovering that she had started to whistle as she worked the saw.

Now that she'd had time to sleep on it, the entire conversation with Noa seemed like a hallucination. She didn't know what she wanted to believe. She wanted to think there was an astronaut up in space waiting to hear from her, but how absurd did that sound? If she mentioned it to anyone they would think she'd lost her mind.

Maybe she had lost her mind. Or maybe she'd passed out from rage and dreamed the whole thing. She'd written down the astronaut's name so she would be certain she remembered, and she could feel the slip of paper in the back pocket of her jeans. If it was a hallucination, it was the strongest she'd ever experienced. She had a muffin for breakfast when they got back to the house and left Cisco to watch over the homestead while she made the drive into town.

The library was a former church on the edge of town. Very little had been done to change the exterior after the building changed hands; there was still a steeple, and the stained-glass windows still reflected down onto the long shelves of books instead of pews. The head librarian always said the building had been built as a quiet space where people could be enlightened, "and that's exactly what it is now!"

Jamie arrived at nine, a half hour before the doors opened. She sat in her truck, elbow against the window and finger curled across her lips, watching the clouds. Her mind drifted from Noa to Louis, to figuring out what his motive was. Did he really want her back? Did he regret throwing her away so cavalierly? Maybe she was being too stubborn or overly sensitive. She could swallow her pride and let him back in. Let him learn from his mistake. And she could learn, too. She could watch him for signs he was getting ready to flee again.

Someone knocked on her passenger window, startling her. She turned and saw the head librarian, Myra, smiled apologetically at her through the glass.

"Sorry, Jamie! I didn't mean to startle you. Are you waiting for the library?"

"I am, yes."

Myra waved for her to come with her. "Come on in, then. We're not technically open for another ten minutes, but I saw you sitting out here and felt bad."

Jamie got out of the truck. "Sorry. I was just kind of inside my head."

Myra grinned. "That's my favorite place to be." They walked up to the building together. "I haven't had a chance to put out the new releases yet. I think they're supposed to have arrived last night."

"I'm not here for books this time. I have plenty of reading at home. I actually need to use the internet."

Myra stopped with her hand on the door, twisting to look at Jamie over her shoulder. "Really?"

"Is that okay? Do I need to sign up for it or anything?"

"No, no, your library card gives you access to all of the library's facilities. I'm just a little surprised is all. Everyone knows you don't like the internet. Louis once told Gina that y'all don't even have a television."

"I held out for as long as I could."

Jamie followed her into the library. The lights were out over the stacks, but she could see the computers against the far wall were already booted up. Their screens glowed in a way she found ominous in the dark architecture of the church. Her mind filled with half-remembered scriptures about false idols, with images of dead-eyed teenagers staring at their phones, and she wondered if satisfying her curiosity was worth becoming one of those minions.

Myra had gone around the circulation desk and pulled out a binder. "You just have to sign in here, and you log into the computer with your library card number. Password is your last name."

Jamie signed the sheet for Computer 1. She walked through the shelves - pausing only once or twice to examine a book that caught her eye - and pulled out the chair for the appropriate computer. She examined the screen for a moment. She could do this. She knew the basics of computer usage. The internet was easy. Children used the internet. She reached up and tapped the screen. Nothing happened. She held her finger against the icon for Google Chrome, but nothing happened.

"Dear?" Myra said.

"Mm-hmm?"

"It's not a touchscreen."

Jamie blushed. "Right." She found the mouse and guided it to the icon, clicked. A window popped up with the familiar logo. The keyboard was on a little drawer which slid out from under the table. She pulled it forward and carefully typed Noa's name into the box. This was it. The moment of truth. Her fingers hovered over the 'enter' key, then dropped like a bird dropping to capture a worm. The screen shifted to the results, the top of which was an image of Colonel Noa Laurie.

"Fu-uck me," Jamie said, then clapped a hand over her mouth. She looked over her shoulder but Myra had fortunately gone into the back and hadn't overheard.

Ears burning, Jamie faced the screen again. She clicked on the NASA profile picture so that it filled the screen.

Noa was gorgeous, nothing "allegedly" about it. It looked like a school picture, with her posed in front of a gray backdrop. An American flag was on one side, what she assumed to be a NASA flag on the other. She was wearing a blue jumpsuit with the flag patch on her visible shoulder. Her hair was down, long and thick and black, draping over her shoulders. She was smiling wide but not showing her teeth. One eyebrow was arched as if she'd just heard an unexpected question, her chin down, her eyes sparkling.

And her eyes. Her *eyes*. She had gorgeous blue eyes.

Jamie clicked back to the main page to avoid the risk of being caught gawking. She found an official biography on Wikipedia and clicked, skimming through the dry bits - Bachelor of Science in Mechanical Engineering, Air Force pilot, over fifteen-hundred flight hours - and saw a section title "ISS Disaster." She scrolled down. Before she could read anything, she saw another image of Noa which was just as shocking as the first, but for different reasons.

In the new picture, Noa was lying in a hospital bed. One side of her face was peppered with small red marks. One arm was in a cast and the edge of a bandage poked out from the collar of her gown. She was looking at the camera but not smiling, and the white of her left eye was dark red. The caption read "Colonel Noa Laurie after recovery of her capsule."

Jamie read the article and remembered hearing about the disaster when it happened. Noa was aboard the station with two other NASA astronauts and two Russian cosmonauts. On the morning of February 19, a design flaw in one of the modules failed in spectacular fashion. A slow leak was noted, and Noa joined the other astronauts in an attempt to locate its source. They were spread throughout the length of the station when the faulty module explosively depressurized.

"I don't remember much of what happened next," Noa was quoted as saying. "The only reason I got out was because I was closest to the Soyuz. I waited as long as I could but no one else showed up."

The majority of her injuries were caused by delaying so long to separate the capsule from the rapidly self-destructing station. She waited so long for people who were most likely already dead that she risked her own life, almost lost her own chance for escape.

The article continued, revealing that a movie about the incident had been released about three years earlier. Noa was played by Charlize Theron. Jamie clicked over to the movie's page and made a note of its title so she could look for it at the video store. Then she went back and printed out the biography. After a moment's hesitation, she also printed out the portrait. She went back to the front desk where Myra had reappeared.

"I printed a couple of pages," Jamie said.

"Okay! They're a quarter each. Looks like you have five pages here."

Jamie paid two dollars and waved off her change.

"Astronauts, huh?"

"Yeah," Jamie said, a bit embarrassed and more than a little worried Myra would ask why she was printing out a picture of such a beautiful woman. "I'm... there's just, uh... someone asked me for a NASA-inspired... headboard."

"That's so interesting!"

"Yeah. Yeah, so. It's inspiration, hopefully."

Myra said, "Well, good luck! If you need to print anything else out, you have a little bit of credit."

Jamie thanked her and took the pages back to her computer. She didn't really know why she had lied. She could have taken a minute to explain what happened the day before, tell the story in a way that made it believable. Telling another person might even help her come to terms with the fact it was real. But telling another person might make it too real, and therefore less special. It had only been a day. It was much too early to share something this magical with the world at large. Or even just one librarian. She sat down and shuffled the pages so Noa's picture was on the top. It wasn't as sharp as the computer image, but that was to be expected.

She checked the counter at the bottom of the screen. She still had a half hour of internet use left, although she knew that would be reset if the library wasn't busy. She went to YouTube to see if she could find any of the interviews Noa said she had done. A set of headphones hung from the side of the desk and she put them on. She wanted to learn as much as she could about Noa before she left the library.

Noa was supposed to be back in range around one-fifty. She had plenty of time, but she wanted to get lunch while she was in town, and she also had to stop by the video store to see if they had a copy of Noa's movie.

The cap of Noa's marker hung in mid-air a few inches away from her face, just where she left it. She had a large whiteboard against the wall, and she was using it to calculate range. She first picked up Jamie's signal at approximately 1303 local time. They were able to talk for fifty-eight minutes before the signal started breaking up, and by sixty-three minutes it was completely gone. Factoring in her speed and the constant of Earth's rotation, she would be back in range in twenty-four hours and forty-nine minutes. So at approximately 1350, she would be able to turn on the radio and hopefully speak to Jamie again.

Or maybe the radio would refuse to connect. Maybe whatever had caused Jamie's radio to find the ODIE frequency would fail. Hell, maybe Jamie would forget all about it. There was no reason for her to be excited when any number of things might go wrong. But she would be sure to wear her Snoopy cap and keep the frequencies open just in case.

The first thing she'd done upon waking, in her morning conference with Astraea, was requesting a private conversation with Enver. He had been summoned and she heard his voice within fifteen minutes.

"Theoretically," she asked, "is there a way for the communication systems to pick up signals from private radios on Earth?"

"N-o-o..." He somehow spread the two-letter word into three syllables with three different tones. Certainty to confusion to curiosity. "You shouldn't," he amended, "but I won't go so far as to say it's impossible. Did something happen? I can schedule a diagnostic to see if we need to shore up the security..."

"No, that's not necessary." She didn't know if she was more concerned about having contact cut off or Jamie getting in trouble, but she wanted to avoid either situation. "It was just a little music. I enjoyed it. I'm thinking of it as a perk."

Enver agreed to leave the communications as-is, but he wanted her to let him know if the situation changed. She promised she would keep an eye on it.

Now the clock was the only thing she was actually keeping an eye on. She went about her work, following her pre-planned route to collect a huge wave of debris. One of the rear-facing screens revealed the open path behind her. The items she'd just grabbed were too big to be ablated and couldn't easily be knocked out of orbit. So she tethered them, magnetized them, and let each piece attract others. It was like the most dangerous version of Wooly Willy anyone had ever played. She would haul the pieces with her until she was close enough to detour up to the collection hub, where they were compressed. Astraea had sent it up a year before her launch. She liked the hub. She called it Hubert, but only when no one was around.

It was almost time. She slipped the cap over her hair and waited. She felt like she should do something, but she hadn't done anything the day before. The ship's systems had just picked up Jamie's signal and latched onto it. She drummed her fingers on her thighs. She scanned the monitors. Every wave of static made her breath catch in her throat, and she examined every hum of white noise for evidence of a voice hidden under the distortion.

Noa had just looked at the clock again when Jamie's voice came through.

"~ting, one two three. Testing, testing..."

"Jamie?"

"Noa?"

Noa smiled so wide it hurt her cheeks, the bubble of laughter caught in her throat as she realized the first contact wasn't a fluke. "Hi!"

"Hello! Hello, to the spacewoman."

The laugh broke free at that. "I guess you checked up on me and determined I was telling the truth."

"I did. According to Google, Colonel Noa Laurie did launch three months ago. So that checks out. And I watched a couple of interviews you did on YouTube. You definitely sound like yourself. But there's one thing you lied about."

"There is?"

"Allegedly good-looking? Colonel, I'm a bit concerned about your eyesight."

Noa laughed and felt her cheeks warming. "Well, thank you. But now you have me at a disadvantage. You know so much about me while I barely know anything about you."

"What do you want to know? There's not much to tell."

"Family?"

"One older brother who passed away when I was a teenager. Younger sister who I don't get to see very much because she moved to Cincinnati a few years ago. I miss my niece and nephew, but we talk on the phone. I live in a little town called Corwin. There's not a lot to do here, but I live a little ways outside of town in a neighborhood of about... oh... thirty people or so. I can go an entire day without seeing anybody but the mailman if I choose."

As she was talking, Noa had an idea. She unstrapped from the command chair and floated backward, propelling herself to the back of the ship by gently running her hand along the wall. The cap brought Jamie's voice with her as she drifted toward one of only two windows on the ship. She placed her hands on either side of the circular seal and looked outside toward the planet. Indiana was sort of pinched between two Great Lakes, their long thin bodies pointing in Jamie's general direction. Heavy clouds obscured the area but she didn't trust herself to pinpoint Indianapolis even on a clear day.

"There's something else you didn't tell me," Jamie said.

"Oh?"

"I... I didn't realize you were... I mean, I knew about the space station, of course..."

Noa's smile faded. "Oh."

Jamie was silent for another minute. "I can't imagine what that would have been like. I know it's probably a sore spot for you, I just wanted you to know that I'm aware of who I'm speaking with. The fact you're a hero."

"I'm not a hero," Noa said. "I was just the one who happened to get out. I got lucky. I... I had to leave everybody behind." She drifted away from the window. "That Soyuz capsule was the only way off the station and I disconnected it. I took it away from anyone who might have been crawling there." She realized she was cascading fast, but she couldn't stop herself. "I'm glad I lived, don't misunderstand me. But I spend so many nights wondering if I should have stayed even one second longer if it would've made a difference."

"I'm so sorry," Jamie said. "There's nothing I can say to something like that. But I think... well... all I know is what I read on the website. But if you had been the next closest person, wouldn't you have known that seconds mattered? And wouldn't you have wanted whoever got to the capsule first to get themselves to safety? I might not know you very well, but I have an idea of the kind of person it takes to be an astronaut. Selflessness, courage, heroism."

Noa said, "I literally ran away."

"You saved the only member of the crew you had the ability to save. Just like anyone else on the station would have done. You had to make an impossible choice in a matter of seconds. Hell, less than a matter of seconds, probably. The entire world was literally blowing up around you. No one has a right to judge the decisions you make in that situation. The only thing that matters is the results, and the results are that you survived and came home. Do you think anyone on that space station would be disappointed with that?"

"Probably not," Noa said quietly. Her eyes were watering. Tears worked differently in space. They accumulated in the corner of her eye, slowly growing until there was a blob of moisture big enough to obscure her vision. She pushed away from the wall to retrieve a towel.

"Me neither. The plane was going down and you put your oxygen mask on first. The house was on fire and you crawled out the window. It's self-preservation. It's what we're supposed to do as human beings. Have you been beating yourself up about this for eight years?"

Noa blotted the tears away from her face. "Well... off and on, maybe. Maybe a little therapy. Although I think you helped me more than the doctor did."

"Do I send the bill to Astraea or to you directly?"

Noa laughed. "Knowing Enver, he would probably pay without even looking at it. Him or one of the people he pays to take care of that stuff for him." She sniffled and straightened her legs. She twisted and faced the window again. "Before we started talking about the incident, I was going to tell you I'm looking down at Indiana right now."

Jamie said, "Really? Hold on... ahh, the microphone cord doesn't reach that far. I was going to wave to you."

"I can't exactly see you."

"It's the principle of the thing."

"Sure." Noa rested her cheek against the wall. The planet really was absolutely gorgeous. Greens and whites and blues. There was a haze around its perimeter that indicated how life could exist on its surface. The atmosphere, so vital but so insubstantial that there was no solid edge to where it ended. "I appreciate the thought that there's someone down there who knows I'm here."

Jamie said, "Lots of people know you're there."

"Right, they know I'm here the way they know someone is in the White House, or someone is probably in an airplane flying from New York to Los Angeles. I'm a face on TV to them. And the people at Astraea, they just think of me as a component of their ship. I'm not even the only part that can report to them about what's happening. You know *I'm* up here. You know I'm a person, a human being. I like that. I appreciate that. I woke up thinking about you."

"Really? I'm touched. I mean, I woke up thinking about you, too, but that's mainly because I thought you might be a dream."

"That's fair."

Jamie said, "So... what's the plan going to be here? Are we going to talk every day now that we know it works?"

"I wouldn't mind that," Noa said, "but keep in mind my options for socializing are extremely limited. You probably have a life, friends, work, things that are more important than staying tethered to a radio for an hour every single day."

"You're overestimating my social calendar. I would be happy to take a break now and then to talk to an astronaut. There's a very good chance I'll run out of conversation in about a week, though. You should be prepared for that."

Noa said, "I consider myself warned. Do you have a pen and something to write with?"

She imagined Jamie looking around the space in the silence that followed. Finally: "Yes, I do now."

Noa floated over to the chart she had made earlier. "I can give you the times I'll be within range over the next couple of days. If you want to talk, that's when I'll be available. If you want to skip the day, that's fine, too. I won't expect you to call me every single time I happen to be over Indiana. Although I promise you I wouldn't mind."

"We'll see how it goes, I guess."

"Okay, get ready." She gave Jamie a second to get her pen ready. "Tomorrow, I'll be in range from approximately 1440 until 1540. The next day, 1530 until 1630..."

Jamie had put down the microphone, using a stub of a pencil to quickly scribble down the numbers on a piece of scrap wood. They marched in uneven columns down the side of the plank. Noa was speaking slowly, but it was still an awful lot of numbers. She also wasn't entirely confident about military time, but she could work that out later. Her finger and thumb ached where she was holding the pencil, but she managed to mark all the times Noa would be in range over the next two weeks.

When she finished, Jamie retrieved the microphone. "Got them. A lot of these are in the middle of the night for me, you know."

"For me, too. Our schedules overlap... a bit. I think my morning begins earlier than yours, but it's close enough that we might be asleep at the same time."

Jamie looked at the times between 0100 and 0700. A whole week where they would sleep through their opportunity to talk. It was ridiculous, and those days were relatively far away, but she still felt cheated by losing them. She doubted they would even talk every day, but the fact there were days when they wouldn't be able to seemed unfair. Jamie propped the plank up against the wall.

"We can play it by ear," Jamie said. "If you're busy or I'm away from the radio, we won't beat ourselves up about missing a day."

"Sounds good to me. So... we're still uneven."

Jamie returned to her seat. "What do you mean?"

"You know what I look like. How about you?"

"Oh." Jamie looked at the print-out of Noa's portrait which was now hanging on the table above the radio. She thought of what she'd seen in the mirror that morning and reached up to push a wave of hair out of her face. "Well... when people want to get on my good side, they claim I look like a young Jodie Foster."

"*Taxi Driver* young or *Little Man Tate* young?"

"Closer to *Little Man Tate*. I'm not saying I agree with them, but it has been said more than once. Also, I have glasses. You know what they say... boys don't make passes at girls who wear glasses."

Noa said, "That just leaves them for other girls to pick up."

Jamie laughed nervously and teased the hair above her ear.

"I used to use glasses as, uh, as a way to mark my prey. Girls in glasses usually read a lot. They look at computers a lot. Those were the kind of girls I was interested in."

"Oh, so you're a predator?"

"I never hunted anyone who wasn't willing."

Jamie looked at the picture again. She could certainly believe that. "So you've been with a lot of women?"

"Uh..." Noa chuckled nervously. "I suppose. Sexual partners are different from actual relationships. Especially when you're an astronaut, especially when you have a certain amount of fame."

"Especially when you're scorching hot."

Noa laughed loudly. "Stop. What about you, Jamie? Not a predator?"

Jamie shook her head. "Uh, no. No, not a predator. Not a lot of chances to be a predator in Corwin, Indiana. Even if I had the guts to come out as bisexual, there aren't a whole lot of options in a town this small. People get assigned identities in towns like this. The Librarian, the Mailman, the Grocer, the Bisexual."

Noa said, "Maybe they're just being private like you are. Maybe they're waiting for someone else to take the first step."

"Doubtful."

"Have you lived there all your life?"

"Yeah. Well, since I was eight."

Noa said, "So have you ever actually... I'm sorry, that's too personal."

Jamie said, "Have I ever actually been with a woman? Is that what you were going to ask?"

"You don't have to answer. It's incredibly inappropriate for me to ask."

"It's fine. I've been with one woman. She was older than me. She was the one who got me into woodworking." She closed her eyes and remembered being in the woodshop. She was twenty, and Sharon was almost forty. Jamie remembered being transfixed by her hands. They were large, strong, rough. There were scars and callouses from years of working with wood. Jamie would go over when she got off work and Sharon would teach her the craft.

"Did you seduce her? Did she seduce you? Was it a tawdry teacher-student thing?"

Jamie said, "I could tell you, but I don't want to ruin the fantasy you've got going."

"No, please. The truth is always better. Well... not always..."

"She worked out of her garage. I would hang out there in my little Wade's uniform... oh, Wade's is a local burger place. We had to wear these godawful orange and yellow polo shirts. We were talking, and she smashed her thumb between two pieces of wood. I thought she'd cut off her thumb or something so I ran over. I took her hand and started to examine it, and that turned into just stroking her fingers and palm. It was hypnotic. I knew what I was doing, but I couldn't stop. And she didn't try to stop me. So I just kept stroking, wrist to fingers."

Maybe you should go, Jamie.

But maybe not...?

Jamie...

"We kissed," she said softly, chewing her thumbnail and looking out the window. "She pressed me against the cabinet she was building. And after that, uh... um..." She smiled and raked her fingers through her hair. "Uh, there was also a door she was working on that we ended up using as a nice, flat surface. I'm sorry. You probably don't want all the graphic details."

Miles above, Noa had unfastened the top button of her own polo shirt, one finger hooked in the collar. Her other hand was resting against her stomach, fingers gently curled. She blinked her eyes back into focus and forced a chuckle.

"Yeah, no, that was... that's fine."

Jamie had slumped slightly in her seat and pushed herself up. She was slightly breathless at the memory she'd just relived. "After that," she said, "we met up a couple of times before she decided it was too risky. The age gap, the appearance that she might be taking advantage of me, the whole nine yards. After that, I decided it was easier to pursue men. I kept my feelers out for women who might be interested but I never found anyone. Sharon eventually got married and moved away, so I lost the idea of someday going back to her for old times' sake."

"That's too bad."

"Yeah, I was pretty bummed about it. But then I met Louis. Things were fine for a while, so." She tapped her foot against the floor and looked at the clock. "I think we should spend the rest of today working out the ground rules. Or... not rules, but just... we've established this link works. Whatever it is and however it happened, it was recreated.

But I know you can't exactly drop everything to talk for an hour whenever you're over Indiana."

"And you should be able to leave the house," Noa said. "I don't mind missing a couple of days."

Noa looked at the board. "In five days, you'll be overhead at six o'clock. That's dinner time. So I can have a meal with you. Plus it will give me time to think up things to tell you."

"Sounds good. And you have the schedule now, so if anything amazing happens, you can always drop me a line."

Jamie said, "You really wouldn't mind that? I can't help but think you're doing this amazing work and I'm just this... little fly that pesters you."

"I'm working pretty much twenty-four hours a day, seven days a week. Even when I'm asleep, there are screens in my little nook which will wake me up if anything goes wrong. I have to constantly be on duty just in case there's an issue that needs to be resolved. The only people I'm allowed to speak with are Astraea personnel who have been cleared. People I've never met and who are only there because it's their job. Talking to you is the only relief I get. I understand if it gets boring for you~"

"Wait, wait, wait." Jamie closed her eyes and pressed the tips of both middle fingers against her temples. They were just going in circles. "Let's just get over ourselves and admit we both enjoy this. So I'll get on the radio every couple of days to shoot the breeze and keep you sane. You'll tell me about your adventures in space. It'll work out for both of us."

Noa sounded relieved. "That sounds great."

Jamie began swinging her chair back and forth as she tried to think of something else to say. She didn't know how she would fill an hour of conversation with this woman, but she was determined to fulfill her part of the bargain. She wanted their exchanges to be a two-way street, and she had all kinds of questions she wanted to ask. She would have to dig deep in order to find stories juicy enough to earn similar revelations from Noa.

// Mission Day 99 //

JAMIE WORKED the entire day, focusing on her current project and not the clock. Okay, she occasionally looked at the clock. And from time to time she would look at the radio. When 1440 rolled around, her hands itched a little. There was a lonely woman in space who would probably drop everything to talk with her. But no. No, she didn't want to get into the habit of talking to Noa every day. Their conversation the day before had used up all of her interesting information. If she did go over and turn on the radio, she would just sit there in awkward silence waiting for Noa to say something. That was hardly fair.

So she worked through their window of opportunity. She did take a moment to wave at the sky when she thought Noa might pass over, but otherwise she focused on the arm of her chair. Cisco chased birds and squirrels in the yard, occasionally coming inside to keep her company. Her work was hypnotic and calming. She thought of it like therapy, a time when she could allow her mind to wander and go over everything in her life.

When she finished work, she went inside to make dinner. A plastic rental box was sitting on the edge of the kitchen counter, right where she'd left it when she'd gotten home the day before. *Fall of Icarus*, the movie about Noa's experience on the space station. She felt strangely guilty about having it, like she was cheating somehow. She knew that if she asked, Noa would tell her anything she wanted to know about the incident. But watching the movie seemed like a shortcut. It felt like she was invading Noa's privacy, even though it had been seen by millions of people all over the world.

But when she finished cooking, she carried the DVD into the living room with her food. She put the disc in the machine and sat in the middle of the couch. She folded her legs in front of her to make a place to set her bowl, and Cisco jumped up to settle against her right side. She idly realized that if Louis had been there, he would have wanted to sit against the arm of the couch and force her to lean against him. No, not force. That was much too strong a word. She would have felt obligated to use him as a pillow. She settled in and hit play.

The movie began with Noa as a child, the daughter of a Florida science teacher who raised her alone after her father died in combat. He was an Air Force pilot - surprise, surprise - and Noa promised to follow in his footsteps. She also fulfilled her mother's dreams of being a scientist, going to college and earning her degree. The movie skipped ahead to Noa on the space station. Charlize Theron had grown her hair out and colored it black for the role.

"What do you think?" she asked Cisco. "She seems pretty cool, right?"

Cisco hurrumphed, more irritated at having his nap interrupted than anything else.

When the disaster happened, it seemed to come out of nowhere. Noa was thrown against the walls of the station like a pebble in a tin can. She got herself to the capsule and latched herself in. Then she waited. The camera lingered in a close-up. A red alarm light strobed across her face. Her forehead and right cheek were bleeding. There was a thick cut across her right eyebrow. Her blood was black and the beads of her sweat were red when the klaxon flashed again. There was no music so her ragged breathing filled the air. In the distance, a low and steady rumble.

"C'mon," she muttered. "Please, please, please, come on. Come on, guys."

Jamie found herself clutching her pillow. Her food had been set aside, forgotten and ignored even as Cisco ate the last of it. Jamie couldn't take her eyes off the screen. She held her breath as Noa finally reached up and sealed the capsule. She began crying immediately, wiping away the tears and smearing her blood as she began the separation procedure.

"What am I doing, I know she survives." She looked at Cisco and her empty plate. "Hey! Oh, who cares."

The music swelled as the capsule plummeted through the atmosphere, tumbling end over end. The cut over Noa's eye began bleeding down the side of her face. She was sobbing now, the sweat thick on her face. Jamie teared up, too. It was extremely clear how much Noa sacrificed to wait for her crew, how close she had come to dying as well. The scene faded out to after the crash landing, to an unconscious

Noa's recovery by EMTs, cutting to a montage of her surgeries and eventual recovery.

The next scene: Noa sitting on the edge of her hospital bed in a gown. She was battered and bruised, facing the window with a thousand-yard stare. The door opened and Clea Duvall - playing Noa's girlfriend at the time - rushed in. She crouched in front of Noa and looked up at her, holding her hands gently. She massaged the knuckles. Noa looked down at her without emotion.

"Are you okay?"

Noa blinked. "I should've... I was supposed to have died, Robin."

Robin shook her head. "No, baby. No. No one was supposed to die. It's a miracle you survived." She stretched up and cupped Noa's face with both hands. "You came back to me."

They kissed. Or rather, Robin kissed Noa, who didn't respond. Robin put her arms around Noa's shoulders and hugged her as tightly as she dared.

"You came back to me."

The camera held on Noa's face. She was still staring at the window as if she was still alone in the room. Jamie wiped her cheeks. She pulled up her sleeve and pushed up her glasses so she could dab at her eyes. When she looked at the screen again, she was looking at Noa's naked body. She yelped and jabbed the remote at the screen in an attempt to turn it off.

Technically it was Charlize Theron's nakedness, but Jamie had long ago stopped thinking of her as the actress. It felt like Noa and it felt like a horrible violation. She was blushing but she forced herself to look. It was just a movie and she was an adult. Noa was sitting on the edge of a bathtub with the lights off. She had her eyes closed as she gently examined the bruises and stitched wounds that covered her body. The internet had a list of how many bones she'd broken and how many surgeries were required to put her back together, but Jamie hadn't bothered to memorize those facts.

Robin turned on the light, leaning against the doorway in a T-shirt. "Noa?"

"I'm never going to live again," Noa said. "I'm never going to be myself ever again. I have to be this new person. This new, broken stranger. I might as well have died. It would have been better."

"Noa..." Robin looked down at her feet. "When you say things like that, it makes me wonder if you... if to you, I'm just part of some other world. A world you're not part of anymore."

"Maybe you are."

Robin stared, tears in her eyes. "Wow. Okay." She stood up straighter, sad and angry. "I'm going to sleep on the couch tonight."

"Robin."

Not looking back at her. "What?"

Noa, touching one of the bruises on her leg. After a long moment: "I love you. I'm sorry."

"I'm sorry, too."

Jamie shook her head and paused the movie. "You stupid woman." But then again, she understood how Noa felt. If someone was watching a movie of her life, maybe they would say the same thing about her rejecting Louis' overtures. He didn't cheat on her or abuse her. As far as she knew, he hadn't seen anyone romantically since walking out on her. And in a town as small as Corwin, the talk would have gotten back to her quickly.

But then again, was that enough? Didn't abuse her, so she has to forgive him? What about happiness? What about the dread she felt when she considered letting him back into the house? She liked her new routine. She liked sitting wherever she wanted on the couch and not turning the act of cooking dinner into a debate. She could soak in the tub for up to an hour without someone coming in to try to "fix" whatever was wrong.

She decided against starting the movie again. The rental lasted for seven days so she could take some time to process what she'd already seen. She bent down to kiss the top of Cisco's head and took the bowl he'd so helpfully cleaned into the kitchen. Her hands were sore from the full day of work, the fingertips dry and cracked. She submerged them in the sink and rubbed in moisturizer to prevent the cracks from getting deeper and becoming a problem. She would also apply Skin Shield when she got upstairs, even though it stung like hell. A little pain now to avoid constant pain later.

When she was done in the kitchen, Jamie turned out the downstairs lights and made sure everything was locked up. Cisco followed her and she allowed him to stake a claim on the bed while she went through her nightly routine. She would take a bath, give her hands some TLC, and read a little before bed. Hopefully it would take her mind off the movie and the fact it would be another couple of days before she talked to Noa again.

// Mission Day 100 //

THE SPECIAL widescreen monitor on one wall of Noa's living space showed a live feed of Jill Hood-Colby's fifth grade classroom in December Harbor, Washington. Noa had spent the past forty-five minutes answering the questions of kids from the entire elementary school. They were clever, engaged kids and she enjoyed talking with them. She didn't even mind performing a few "Wonder Woman" moves: backflips, dives, and "flying" toward the camera.

The interview ended when the bell rang for recess, and the kids filed past the camera to say goodbye. Noa waved to all of them and thanked them for their interview. The teacher appeared at last. She was a pretty brunette in a green sweater over a white blouse.

"Thank you again for taking the time, Colonel. I wanted you to see this..." She held up a drawing of cartoon astronaut standing on the moon. "I found this on Shannon's desk. She's the one who asked if you had to be good at math to be an astronaut."

"That's amazing! Is she good at math?"

"I have a feeling she's about to get a lot better," Jill said. "I'm sure you received more requests than you could possibly honor. It really means a lot that you agreed for such a small audience."

Noa said, "I grew up in a small town myself. I know how easy it is for them to get overlooked just because they might not have the best internet coverage. How are the laptops, by the way?"

Jill whistled and shook her head. "Extravagant. Mr. Crane really didn't have to go to so much trouble."

"I'm sure he was giddy about it. The only thing he likes more than playing with computer is spending his money on other people. The benefits it brings to your school are just collateral damage."

Jill laughed. "We certainly appreciate it. My daughter appreciates it, too. She's been bouncing off the walls about this all week."

"Your daughter was in the class?"

"Isabel," Jill said. "I doubt she'll end up going into the sciences, but I know you've inspired her to go after her dreams."

Noa remembered Isabel, the excited girl who got extremely shy when she actually got a chance to pose her question.

"Tell her good luck!"

"I will." She looked above the monitor at the clock. "Anyway... as much as I'd love to sit here talking to you all day, I'm sure you have a thousand things that need your attention."

No, god, please, stay, talk my ear off, I'm so fucking lonely, Noa thought, but outwardly she smiled and nodded. "Yeah, kind of a one-woman show up here. I should probably make sure I'm not drifting toward the Moon."

Jill laughed. "Good luck, Colonel."

Noa thanked her again and disconnected the chat. The screen went black with a NO SIGNAL message emblazoned across its center. Noa sighed heavily and pushed off the stool with her fingertips. She drifted backward and stretched so she was facing the ceiling. "Vera," she said, "play... play, uh... instrumentals."

The air filled with soft music.

"Volume, ambient level."

"Of course, Colonel."

She bent at the waist and pulled off her shoes and socks. She stowed them in the proper shelving and wiggled her toes as she brushed her hand over the wall. It was enough momentum to gently float her back toward the command center. All she had was time. Time to fill, endless hours. She'd been in space for one hundred days, two thousand four hundred hours, and she was still at the beginning of her tenure. One small sliver of the full length of her trip. Talking to students did help the time pass, but those brief spots of joy were few and far between. Soon the novelty would wear off, the requests would taper off, and she wouldn't even be able to count on those distractions.

Noa settled in the chair and strapped herself in. She had passed the window for talking to Jamie before she logged in with the class. It had been two days since she talked to her new friend and, even though the silence had been planned, she couldn't help worrying the connection was lost. There was no way to check it, no way for her to call Jamie if the radio was off. It was ridiculous to feel withdrawal. They'd only had two conversations. She'd only known Jamie for a grand total of four days.

She checked the monitors. The ship had been on autopilot while she talked to the kids. Everything was in the green, which was both good news and bad news. Good, because it meant she wouldn't have to go back over the same area. Bad, because it supported her theory that she wasn't entirely necessary for the mission's success. She knew she was vital, knew that there were minute calculations that required her presence, but every time the automated system succeeded without her intervention, she suspected Enver could have tweaked the whole thing to make a human component unnecessary.

Noa bumped the back of her head against the chair. "Vera. Random trivia."

"Okay." A pause. "Did you know Karen Everett of Radiation Canary is married to Laura Cowan of the Femme Reapers?"

"I did know that, Vera. That is very old news."

"Okay!" The voice was obnoxiously chipper. "I'll update my information!"

Noa rolled her eyes. "Yes, please do that."

"You sound exasperated, Colonel. Is there anything I can do?"

"No. Just..." She made a looping motion with her finger. "Keep up the small talk program."

"Okay!" A pause as it accessed a subroutine or a file. "ODIE is currently traveling over the Pacific Northwest region of North America. Median current temperature is 64 degrees..."

Noa stared at the ceiling. It would be another three days before Jamie made contact again. Maybe by then she would have found a new rhythm. Maybe by then, the idea of spending an hour talking to some woman from Indiana she didn't even know would be a hassle instead of a reward.

"Yeah," she said under her breath. "Maybe."

But it didn't seem very likely.

Myra shook her head as she pushed the book cart past Jamie. "Pretty soon you're going to be addicted to that stupid thing. You'll get a computer at home and then I'll never see you."

"It's not as bad as all that," Jamie said. "It's just this... this project I'm working on."

"I don't know," Myra sighed as she continued on. "Two visits in one week. It's a worrisome trend."

Jamie grinned and faced the computer again. She was back so she could read about the movie, figure out how much of it was fiction. She finished the movie that morning, unable to wait any longer to see how things worked out. In the final scene, Noa said goodbye to Robin. Their relationship was completely broken beyond repair. They were sitting cross-legged, facing each other on a cracked runway at an abandoned airport. It was just before dawn and the sky was still pale purple-blue.

Robin put her hands on top of Noa's.

"There's something beautiful about a woman in pain."

Noa had scoffed.

"I don't mean like in a sociopath way. I don't want to *cause* her pain. But seeing a woman in pain shows you the primal part of her. It shows you who she might have been before the world decided being a woman makes you inherently weaker. A woman in pain is... raw and powerful and brutish. And when she gets through the pain, that beast is always a part of her. It makes her stronger."

Robin had leaned forward and kissed Noa then. It was a goodbye kiss, but it was passionate and lingering. Jamie found herself ridiculously jealous of it, but she'd pushed down the feelings to focus on the end of the film. The last shot was Noa alone on the runway, arms resting on her knees. The rising sun hits her face and she smiles. The screen faded to black on that shot and a Radiation Canary song played over the credits. She was reaching for the remote control when one of the roles caught her eye.

NOA LAURIE as NASA SCIENTIST

Jamie went back and carefully skipped through the scenes, watching the background. There was so many extras, so many out-of-focus people milling about in the background, but few of them were women.

Finally, Noa appeared. Jamie jabbed the pause button so hard she hurt her finger. Beau Bridges was the mission director. During the press conference, Noa was sitting behind him in costume. She wore a white blouse and black slacks, her hair pinned back in a ponytail. She wore almost comically large eyeglasses but it was obviously her. Jamie had smiled and waved at the screen like a doofus.

Now she was back at the library looking for everything she could find on the movie. The first stop Jamie made on the internet was Amazon. She had an account because it was the easiest way to get some of her oils and tools, plus she could also get lotions and creams to keep her hands from being destroyed, so she was able to purchase her own copy of *Fall of Icarus*. Google revealed photos of Noa and Charlize Theron at the premiere. The actress was glamorous as always, but Noa looked nervous and uncomfortable in every shot.

The movie seemed to have done okay, critically. It made money. There were critics who claimed it was wrong to portray Noa as a hero. There were others who thought that the director went out of her way to make Noa seem tragic. Some thought the nude scene was cheap. Charlize defended it.

"It was important to see her in that moment, stripped bare, no bandages or barriers. She had all this armor on her... the space suit, the bandages, everything - and it hid who she was. That scene where she's sitting there naked, you can see the damage that was done. You can see very clearly what she had gone through to survive. It wasn't about being naked, it was about not hiding anymore."

"You tell 'em," Jamie muttered under her breath.

She managed to leave the library without printing anything, although the white gown Noa wore to the movie premiere had tempted her something awful. She was on her way to the truck when she spotted a small pond had formed in a ditch that ran alongside the building. Two ducks were sitting in the tall grass between the water and the building. Jamie made her way over and one duck waddled in the opposite direction. She crouched so she wouldn't frighten them, but both watched her warily.

Noa wasn't going to see any random animals for two years. She would never have the simple pleasure of looking up and seeing a flock of birds take off out of a tree. Escaped dogs wouldn't come running up to her on the street. No stiff breezes in her hair. No feeling the dew under her wet feet when she went out just after dawn.

She took out her phone and opened the voice recorder. There was something she could do for Noa that would also help fill their time, but she didn't think she could do it off the cuff. She needed to prepare, and these ducks were the perfect place to start.

"There's a library in Corwin that used to be a church," she said. "It's a long rectangular building, white with chipping paint, and a tall steeple on the front. It's both magnificent and, uh, frail-looking. The stained-glass windows are still there. Outside, in a strip of grass that needs to be mowed, there's a small puddle left from the last time it rained. A couple of ducks are sitting by it. The one with a green head is trying not to act scared but I don't think he wants me hanging around..."

She didn't know if she would actually have the guts to share the observation, but even if it turned out to be corny, it would be better than an awkward silence. She smiled at the duck and continued describing it into her phone.

// MISSION DAY 103 //

JAMIE DIDN'T celebrate birthdays or Christmas, but she still recognized the feeling people talked about. That pit of stomach, tingling hands feeling that the day was indescribably different than other days. She woke up excited and full of energy. She went for a jog with Cisco and tired the poor pup out. She sang under her breath while she cooked breakfast. It wasn't even noon and she was already looking at the clock in anticipation.

Noa would be in range at six o'clock. She finished her chair and emailed the client that it would be available for pick-up the following day. She made an early dinner to distract herself and skimmed the notebook page where she'd made a list of conversation topics. She finished a few minutes before six and carried her food out to the barn. The sun was just touching the treetops, and the light was fading. When she was a kid, she would have considered this prime playtime. There were trees to climb, hills to roll down, bikes to ride. Cisco seemed to have the same idea: as soon as he realized she was just going to sit in her chair for a while, he ran out of the barn in search of something more exciting.

She turned on the radio and started eating. Her watch beeped at six o'clock. She traded her fork for the microphone.

"Calling occupant of interplanetary craft. Anyone listening?"

Static. Silence. Suddenly she was worried that something may have gone wrong. Or worse, maybe Noa decided she didn't want to be bugged and changed the frequency. That was probably it. At some point over the past few days, Noa realized having a civilian take up her valuable time was foolish at best and hazardous at worst. She didn't need some nobody woodworker tying up—

"Is it really you?" Noa said.

Jamie grinned so wide that the muscles seemed to stretch. "Who else would it be? Do you get a lot of unauthorized communications up there?"

"Mostly telemarketers," Noa said.

"Well, have I got a deal for you."

Noa laughed. "It's great hearing from you again. I've missed you."

"Really?"

"Of course. It's been nothing but work and interviews up here since the last time we spoke. You might be surprised to learn this, but space is pretty dull."

Jamie stirred her food. "I guess people can get used to anything, huh?"

Noa said, "That's the truth. I've been looking at the clock all day waiting for you to show up. Sorry if that sounds clingy."

"Not at all. In fact, I've been doing the same thing." She looked down at the table. "I have, um... I guess confession is kind of a strong word, but I don't know what you'll think about it. I watched your movie."

"Oh." Her voice was flat, impossible to read. "What did you think?"

Jamie said, "We don't have to talk about this if it's an awkward subject."

"It's fine. I want to know what you thought of it."

"I thought it was amazing. And sad, and tragic." She chewed her bottom lip. "It showed me how strong you were. Even after I discovered you were on the ISS, it still didn't really register that you went through hell to get away."

Noa said, "Okay, that's fine. Now forget about it."

"What? Is it not accurate? The internet—"

"It's accurate," Noa said. "I was a consultant on the movie, they listened to me about everything, I'm fine with it as far as that goes. But I can already hear it in your voice, Jamie. The pedestal. Turning me into a superhero or something. A celebrity. Please, please don't. Don't build me up in your mind to be this miracle. I'm just a person. I'm a person who happened to almost die in a very dangerous job but I was lucky enough to escape. Don't make me into something to be impressed by. I'm a human being. I loved the fact you'd never even heard of me when we first started talking. I don't want to lose that."

Jamie said, "Okay. I'm sorry. I shouldn't have watched it."

"You didn't do anything wrong. Hell, if there was a movie about you, I'd probably try to get Enver to stream it to me up here."

Jamie laughed. "That would be a very boring movie. More like one of those old PBS shows about guys in plaid doing projects in their garage."

"Bob Vila!" Noa said. "I remember that show."

"I'm more furniture-focused than home renovations. But who knows, maybe there's an audience for it."

"You never know," Noa said. "What else have you been up to the past few days? Any change to the situation with your husband?"

"Ex-husband." Jamie tilted her head to the side. "Is that accurate? At what point can I refer to him as an 'ex'? Do I have to wait until the papers are signed, or is the title official as soon as I know I'll never let him back into the house?"

Noa said, "I think you can call him an ex as soon as he walks away. The paperwork is just a formality at that point."

"I agree. And no, he hasn't been by or tried to call. I think he's giving me time to miss him."

"Did you? Maybe just a little?"

Jamie shook her head. "I was too busy missing you to give him any thought."

"Aw. That's so sweet. Thank you."

Jamie blushed and took a bite of her food. "I'm eating my dinner right now. Mushroom risotto."

Noa groaned. "I'm jealous."

"You shouldn't be. It's all just frozen from the supermarket."

"Don't take it for granted. I'm having pad thai and apple wedges."

Jamie said, "That doesn't sound so bad."

"It's fine. It's relatively delicious compared to some of the stuff we have up here. Can you imagine planning your meals two years in advance?"

"God, no. Even shopping for a week can be a pain."

Jamie said, "Yeah. But it's fine. It's all good food that Enver let me choose myself. But what I wouldn't give for some piping hot soup in a bread bowl."

"I love bread bowls."

"They're the perfect dish."

Jamie scooped up some rice. "If we talk tomorrow, I'll make something really delicious and you can live vicariously through me."

"You don't mind eating that late?"

"Not if it can help you out. Any requests?"

Noa sighed. "Brown rice. Anything with brown rice. For some reason, I'm really craving it."

Jamie made a note. "Sounds good to me. I'll see what I can whip up. This actually goes along with some other notes I had about possible conversation topics. You're homesick. You're stuck up there and you don't get to enjoy the little things. So I've started noticing the little things so I can share them with you."

"I'm intrigued. Give me an example."

Jamie said, "I went for a walk yesterday afternoon. I knew I had to get it in before the rain started, but I kept putting it off until there were big heavy rainstorms to the west and bright skies to the east. I could see streaks of rain up in the sky, against the clouds, and it moved in like a curtain. I got a burst of ozone smell, like the rain was inside of a flower that had just bloomed, and then I heard the first drops hit my neighbor's mailbox. So I started running so I wouldn't get caught. I got back to the driveway just as it started to pour. Cisco ran up ahead of me to hide in the barn, the coward, but I just let it hit my face. I stood on the porch, sweaty from the walk but cooled by the breeze brought in by the storm, and I just watched it rain for a while."

Noa was silent for a long moment. "Wow. That was beautiful."

Jamie said, "I know talking about the weather is cliché..."

"No, that wasn't just talking about the weather. You... wow." Noa sighed into the microphone as she searched for words. "You made me feel like I was there. I'm positive I've gone three months without seeing rain before. Or seeing it and just not taking the time to appreciate its beauty. I miss it. I miss the rain, I miss *wind*. This was such a gift. Thank you, Jamie. Please, please, keep it up."

Jamie moved her notebook closer. "I have more."

"Give me whatever you have."

"Don't get greedy, Stargirl. I want tit for tat. I know you're bored with space, but I think you're just taking it for granted."

Noa said, "Fair enough. Hold." Jamie could hear rustling. "I've been strapped in the command chair. Floating backward now into the living area... spinning around to float up to the porthole. Looking outside..."

"At Earth?" Jamie spoke in a whisper. She tried to keep the awe out of her voice, but it was hard. She was talking to someone who was looking down at the entire planet. "Tell me what you see. Please?"

Noa said, "I see... I see North America. The eastern seaboard is off to the right, and the sun has already set there. All the cities are lit up. Big blobs of gold with streams coming off of it in all directions. And the line between night and day is right over Indiana."

Jamie twisted to look outside. She put down the microphone and walked to the barn door. She hugged herself as she looked at the sky. It was deep purple to the east and slightly brighter to the west. It was undeniably night; she could see a sprinkling of stars over the house.

"It looks like there's a storm above Texas," Noa continued. "Jesus. The lightning... how far is Texas from Indiana?"

Jamie hurried back to the table and picked up the microphone. "I don't know. Uh, something like a thousand miles."

"I'm covering them both with my hand right now."

"Wow," Jamie whispered. Even though it was just a matter of perspective, she couldn't help but think of Noa looming above her like a giantess whose hand could span the continent.

Noa said, "There's an aurora over the edge of the globe. Jamie, this is fucking beautiful. I can't believe I've been looking at this every day without seeing it."

"Like me with the rain and food, I guess," Jamie said.

"Yeah. Yeah, I guess so." Noa said, "Jamie, I hope you don't take this as desperation, and you can say no if you want, but I don't want to skip any more days. We have the overnight flybys coming up where we won't be able to talk, but the days coming up... the seven, eight, nine o'clock windows..."

Jamie said, "I'm with you. I didn't want to skip them, either. I like talking to you too much. The days when I knew you were available but we'd agree not to talk were like torture. Even when I didn't have anything to say."

Noa said, "Good. Okay. So tomorrow..."

"1850. With a big dish of something made with brown rice."

Noa laughed. "Right. And I'll try to find something to share, even if it's just commentary on the movie. I like talking to you. I like hearing you laugh."

Jamie smiled but almost immediately let it fall. Were they flirting? It felt like flirting, but she was so out of practice. And she didn't routinely flirt with women. Maybe Noa was just being kind. She was being overly friendly because they'd gone so long without speaking. And honestly, there was a great chance it was just wishful thinking on her part. Noa was gorgeous and gay. Jamie had just watched a full movie where she was played by one of the most beautiful women in the world.

"Are you there?"

"I'm here," Jamie said. "Sorry. I just..." She lowered the microphone and closed her eyes. If she couldn't be honest here, safely behind a microphone with someone who wasn't even sharing her atmosphere, then what hope did she have of being honest with anyone else? "I was just trying to figure out if you were flirting with me."

It was Noa's turn to be quiet for a long moment. Jamie closed her eyes and berated herself for asking. After the whole speech about being treated like a person, not being put on a pedestal, and~

"I was," Noa said. "It wasn't intentional, but I admit that I am. Is that okay?"

Jamie tucked her hair behind her ear. "Yeah. It's fine with me. If we were having these conversations on a date, I would consider it a roaring success."

"Would you walk me to my door? Kiss me goodnight?"

Jamie chuckled nervously. *I would invite you in for coffee,* she thought. "Depends on if you play your cards right, Colonel. You know, treat me nice and tip the waitress well."

Noa said, "I'll keep that in mind. Those are very good standards."

"Thank you."

"So... you said you wrote down a couple of things to describe to me. What else do you have?"

Jamie picked up her notebook and flipped to a back page. She had written it down on a lark, more for herself than for Noa. She felt guilty about telling Noa she looked like Jodie Foster, an extremely misleading (in her opinion) version of the truth. So she had stood in front of the bathroom mirror with the bath towel tucked under her arms and forced herself to be honest about her looks.

"I have me," she said. "I have pictures of you, and interviews, and all you have is what I give you. So I have a description of myself."

Noa said, "I'm intrigued."

Jamie's ears burned. "Okay... total honesty. I'm average. Height, weight, looks. Maybe I'm a little taller than some women, but not by a lot. Dirty blonde hair, at the moment closer to brown than anything else. Shaggy in the front but short at the back, just because it's so much less hassle. I'm thinking of going full blonde the next time I get it cut, but I haven't made the decision yet. Big granny glasses. Blue eyes. Big smile."

Noa laughed. "You sound adorable."

Jamie ducked her chin and shrugged. "You might not be the first one to use that word." She hooked her feet on the base of the chair.

"Have you been working on anything interesting?"

"Yeah," Jamie said, looking over at her workspace. "I just finished designing a changing table for the couple I made the rocking chair for. They liked what they saw, I guess."

Noa said, "Aw, babies. They're not for me, but I'm glad there are people out there willing to be parents."

Jamie said, "Yeah, and maybe they'll let me hold the baby when it comes. I don't need one of my own, but I don't mind holding one for a few minutes."

"Sure, as long as you can give it back when you're done."

"You'll have to be sure to take notes when you hold it. I want all the details."

Jamie said, "It's not due for at least two months."

"You think you'll get bored of me in two months?"

"No, I didn't mean that. I just... well, I guess I hadn't thought about the long-term of this arrangement. You have two years left up there, right?"

Noa said, "Twenty-three months, give or take."

Jamie chewed on her thumbnail. "Well, I can't just abandon you. What kind of friend would I be if I did that?"

High above, floating in front of the porthole, Noa wiped a hand over her face. She felt like a high schooler who'd just found a Valentine in her locker. "Well, good. That's good to hear."

"Except for the weeks when we'll be sleeping together." Noa arched an eyebrow. "Oh god. I meant... I meant when the schedule... we'll both be asleep~"

Noa laughed and pushed away from the wall, letting herself drift wide into the center of the room. "I know what you meant, but it's fun to hear you scrambling."

"You're cruel, Stargirl."

"Is that going to be a permanent nickname?"

Jamie said, "It doesn't have to be."

"I'll give it some time. I don't mind it right now." She could see the command chair now. "I should come up with something for you. Plains Jane?"

"Pass."

"Sexy Voice?"

Jamie laughed nervously.

"I'll figure something out eventually."

"We should have plenty of time."

Noa turned to look at the numbers she'd written on the board, showing her when she would be in range of Jamie's radio signal. Over seven hundred more days, give or take the sleeping weeks.

"Yeah," Noa said with a smile. "We have plenty of time."

// **MISSION DAY 104** //

"YOU'RE LYING."

"Why would I lie?"

Jamie was pacing in front of the radio. It was just past seven-thirty. They'd been talking for over half an hour, mining the past for embarrassing stories to tell. It was dark outside and Jamie had turned on all her work lights so she could see, even though they were positioned in a way that meant she was still mostly in the dark. She was in jeans and a baggy shirt that kept falling open to reveal the T-shirt underneath.

Noa was in shorts and a tank top, sitting with her back against the curved wall of her living space with her bare feet floating out in front of her. She was eating ice cream, one of the very limited pints available on the ship and which she'd been saving for a special occasion.

"It just seems so precious."

Jamie rolled her eyes. "I was a child! I'd never had sex before. I kept hearing sixty-nine, sixty-nine. So I guess I just figured out that grown-ups could have sex sixty-nine times. And once they hit the number, that was when they graduated to... I don't know."

Noa laughed and shook her head. "I can't decide if I want to ask how old you were when you found out the truth, or if you've hit the magic number yet."

Jamie narrowed her eyes. "I'm not sure I want to answer either of those questions."

"Aw, come on."

"Fine. I was eighteen and the guy I was fooling around with asked if I wanted to sixty-nine. I told him we'd already done it once and I was too tired to do it sixty-eight more times in a single night."

Noa cackled and fell, drifting toward the floor.

"It's not funny!" Jamie said, but she was laughing as well. "Besides, he was terrible at it."

Noa allowed herself to roll onto her stomach and pushed forward to float across her table. "Well, most guys are, from what I can tell. It's amazing the species has survived so long."

"They have their charm."

"Says the bisexual," Noa said.

Jamie sat down. "Don't get snippy just because you restrict yourself to a single sex."

"I don't think I'm missing out too much."

"Have you ever tried?"

"Never been tempted." She crossed her legs at the ankles and stretched her arms above her head. "My mother was very supportive and liberal. When I wore neckties and blazers to school in tenth grade, she asked if I felt like I was supposed to be a boy. I told her I just liked how comfortable the clothes were."

"And pockets."

"And pockets. And when you're a girl wearing a necktie and blazer, the other lesbians in your class tend to flock to you."

Jamie said, "I'll bet. You probably look great in a suit."

"I look okay."

Jamie arched an eyebrow and pictured it in her mind.

It was more than okay.

// MISSION DAY 106 //

JAMIE, LYING on the floor with her feet in the desk chair, staring at the ceiling. "...a long road with a ditch on the left, and a row of trees. On the right, there are houses every fifty or a hundred yards. We're not out in the middle of nowhere, but we have room to sprawl. If you go walking close to dusk, you can hear all the birds up in the trees. Sometimes you see big swarms of them take off to find somewhere else to roost. Tonight, I just stood under one of the trees for about half an hour. There must have been a thousand birds up there just screeching at each other. Cisco was going nuts."

"I'll bet." Noa's back was touching the 'ceiling' of her living space, her knees bent so she could keep her bare feet flat against the cool surface. "What color was the sky?"

"The same color it always is," Jamie said.

Noa smiled. "Tell me anyway."

"Pink and yellow where the sun was setting," Jamie said, "and a deep blue straight up. And in the east, it was the deepest velvet purple. Like you could just reach up and run your fingers across it. My grandmother used to have a chair with a material that you could draw on. You push your finger through it and change the direction of the nap so it looks lighter. My brother and I used to squeeze behind the chair so we could draw secret pictures on it. We'd play tic-tac-toe a lot, too. It was easy to erase the board if one of us started to lose."

"So you're a sore loser?"

"I'm a terrible sport," Jamie said.

"Hm," Noa replied. It wasn't necessarily a laugh, but there was a touch of amusement in it. She had been listening with her eyes closed, partially to envision what Jamie was telling her but also to rest. She was tired from a long, long day, but she wasn't going to cut their day short. It was 2103, and she had another hour before she could go to bed. Jamie sounded sleepy as well. Her voice was a little rough but Noa liked it.

Jamie said, "Sorry, I got off track."

"That's okay," Noa said quietly. "I like your tangents."

"I bet you compliment all the girls' tangents."

Noa chuckled.

"Where was I in the story?"

"The color of the sky."

"Right. By the time I started walking home, it was full dark. I had a flashlight. There were little frogs on the corner, and I convinced Cisco not to terrorize them. I can sort of hear them croaking right now. Can you hear them in the background?"

Noa strained hard. "I don't think so."

"Too bad. Maybe I can record sounds for you. Frogs. Traffic."

"I don't miss traffic. Besides, I'd rather hear your voice than frogs or revving engines."

Jamie said, "You get really flirtatious when you're sleepy."

"Yeah. Izzat okay?"

"Mm-hmm."

Noa smiled. "Tell me more about the frogs."

// MISSION DAY 107 //

NOA PERCHED on the lip of the command area, her toes balanced in a way that would've been precarious in a gravity environment. She had one hand out to the side against the edge of the opening to keep herself from swaying. She examined the bells and whistles around her station, the things she took for granted because she knew them all backwards and forwards. "We have a towing system for the bigger pieces," she said, "which I activate from a panel above and to the right of my head. It took me six full months of training for nothing else, but I finally got it down. I can lasso better than Annie Oakley."

"Yee-haw," Jamie said. "What do you do with them once they're lassoed?"

"I carry them along behind me until I meet up with the hub again. Then it's a complicated system of magnets and getting the right angle so I can disconnect and the debris will get pulled into the hub. That's where it gets compacted and sorted."

Jamie said, "Wow. And you do all of that every day?"

"Yeah. But it sounds more impressive than it is. Same as driving your truck. You get in, turn the key, angle it down the driveway, apply the right amount of gas, turn the wheel just right. It's all a matter of training and learning how the system works. There is a little talent involved, but anyone with the proper education could do it."

"Not me."

"Of course you."

"Mm-mm. I'm scared of heights."

Noa laughed.

"Besides, I was never very good at science or math." She put her free hand behind her head. "Can I ask you a sincere question? I mean, I know you've been honest with me so far. But you also have a tendency to deflect with humor."

"Me? Never. But I promise to answer you as sincerely as I can."

Jamie said, "How the hell are you not terrified right now? Given everything you went through on the space station, losing everyone like that, barely surviving. How could you possibly get back into another spaceship and go up there? It wasn't a mistake you made, it wasn't a mistake anybody made, it was just a bad piece of machinery that failed. Aren't you terrified it will happen again?"

She rested the microphone on her chest as she waited for an answer. After almost a minute, she checked her watch to make sure they were still in the window.

"Noa? You don't have to answer that if you don't want to."

"It's fine," Noa said quietly. "I'm just thinking. No one had the guts to ask me that question on the tour, and even if they had, I don't think I could have given the truest answer. Honestly, I *am* terrified. When Enver approached me with the opportunity, I was physically sick to my stomach at the idea. He gave me a week to consider it, and I spent the entire time thinking of reasons to refuse. But I realized I couldn't let it beat me. This was my only chance to face it and come back on my terms. I was kept in the loop on the progress of the ship. I saw it being put together. I listened to Enver and met the team who created it, and I have faith. But I know it's space. I know anything could go wrong at any moment. Coming up here and doing my job is how I move past it."

"You have my respect for that."

"Thank you. I don't think I realized how difficult it would be, two years by myself. If I didn't have these conversations with you to look forward to, I think I would've gone insane a long time ago."

Jamie hissed through her teeth. "Bad timing for that confession, considering we're about to sign off for six or seven days."

Noa looked at her clock and saw Jamie was right. "Oh. Well... we could make contact tomorrow. It wouldn't be a full hour, but we could at least say goodnight to each other."

"That sounds perfect. I haven't been able to say goodnight to anyone in a long time."

"Neither have I. I look forward to it." She looked at the time again. "We should go ahead and say our goodnights now, before the signal starts to fade."

Jamie smiled. "You just want to go to sleep."

"I'm so tired."

Jamie laughed. "Me too. Sweet dreams, Noa. I'll see you tomorrow."

"Can't wait. Sleep well."

Jamie got off the floor and stretched, turned off the radio, and rested her hand on top of its casing. She patted her thigh and Cisco, realizing they were finally going inside, hauled himself to his feet and followed her outside. She turned off the light and paused on the grass just outside the barn, taking a moment to enjoy a darkness as complete as she was likely to get. The neighbors had their porchlight on, but they were far enough away not to pollute the sky too much. There were patchy clouds to the north but a clear spray of stars spread out directly above her.

She doubted she would be able to see the ship. It was at the far edge of their communication window, which was probably somewhere over Wyoming or something. Jamie took a deep breath of night air and looked toward the road. Cisco nudged her hand, eager to go into the house and get his bedtime treat before settling down for the night.

"What does it smell like out here, buddy?" she asked.

Cisco huffed.

"Come on. Noa's counting on us." Cisco remained silent. "Fine. I'll give you some time to think about it."

As she started across the lawn, Noa was shutting down her instruments for the night. She sent a Sleep message to Mission Control and they sent back a "Sweet Dreams" message. She propelled herself forward and turned the lights down to the night setting. She stripped out of her clothes, stuffing them into the small shelf that would wash and dry them overnight.

On the ISS, she'd worn a dark blue NASA onesie, but there was no reason she couldn't sleep in the nude on ODIE. She crawled into her nook and slipped her feet into the large sleeping bag attached to the wall. It was a cocoon that kept her from floating around the cabin while asleep. She zipped herself in and let her body go limp. Without gravity, there was no need for a pillow or a soft mattress. Once or twice she still woke up with a terrifying sensation that she was falling, but it was worth it for the most comfortable and solid sleep she'd ever had.

"Goodnight, Jamie," she whispered.

She folded her hands on her stomach and, quite literally, drifted off to sleep.

// MISSION DAY 108 //

A COT had been moved from the storage room of the house and set up next to the radio. It was a skeleton of hollow pipes with a rigid green fabric stretched across it. Jamie struggled for much longer than she wanted to admit to get it open. It was less complex than a tent, but she couldn't quite figure out how the legs should go. She finally succeeded and draped her blanket across it. Her two pillows were fluffed and placed at the top near the wall.

It was after ten o'clock - 2211 - when Jamie heard the crinkle of static she now associated with an open line to ODIE. She was bringing to the microphone to her mouth when Noa broke the silence first.

"You there, Lighthouse?"

Jamie blinked. "Lighthouse? Are you talking to me?"

Noa chuckled. "I was trying it out. I'm starting to keep track of my days by when you'll be available. Is it okay?"

"I kind of like it." Jamie sat down on the side of the cot. "So I'm used to settling in for a long conversation with you. It's kind of weird that we're just checking in."

"Yeah," Noa agreed. "I'm sorry, but I'm too bushed to actually have a conversation..."

Jamie said, "I'm right there with you, trust me. I was just pointing it out. I'm probably not exhausted as you are, but... yeah, it's late. I... I did something you might find silly. But don't laugh."

"Oh?"

Jamie lay down and pulled the blanket up over her legs. "I have this old army cot, and I moved it out to the barn so when we said goodnight,

I could just go to sleep."

Noa smiled. She pushed away from the wall and moved into the command section. "That's not silly at all. That's possibly the sweetest thing I've ever heard." She began turning off the lights.

"Oh, stop."

"It is. So you're just camping out?"

Jamie looked up at the crossbeams of the barn, which were mostly lost in shadow. "Yeah. It's a little spooky out here. But I can handle it. I'm tough."

The ODIE was dark, save for the few lights that had to remain on. The pale green-yellow glow fell across Noa's face as she climbed into her nook. She stretched out and pulled the halves of her sleeping bag around her.

"Are you lying down?" she asked.

Jamie said, "Yeah." She rolled over. "I'm on my left shoulder."

Noa shifted. "I'm lying on my right shoulder. Facing you."

"Oh hey, there you are." She closed her eyes and imagined they really were lying in bed, face to face. "Are you in your space jammies?"

"I'm in a pair of shorts and a T-shirt." She wet her lips and considered how to phrase her next question. "And you?"

Jamie chuckled. "Oh, come on, Colonel. I know you're dying to say it."

Noa blushed. "What are you wearing?"

"A baseball shirt and underwear."

"What's a baseball shirt?"

"You know, uh... gray on the chest and dark blue sleeves."

Noa said, "Oh. Okay."

They lapsed into silence. Noa's eyes were closed, and she envisioned the scene below her in the barn. She imagined Jamie curled on her side, legs tucked up, one hand under the pillow. She imagined herself on the cot beside her. She could hear Jamie's breathing over the microphone and, after a moment, noticed how slow and steady it had become. She brought her hand up and lightly stroked her own cheek. When she spoke, her voice was just barely above a whisper.

"Jamie?"

"Mm?" Her eyelids fluttered open, and it took her a moment to remember where she was.

"I think you were falling asleep."

"Shit. Sorry."

Noa said, "Don't apologize. I was just worried about the radio."

Jamie rubbed a hand over her face. "I'm worried about keeping you up. The radio will be fine."

Noa opened her eyes. "I don't want to say goodbye to you knowing it'll be a week before I hear your voice again. I'm going to miss you."

"I'll miss you, too."

"Jamie..."

"Mm-hmm?"

"Jamie."

Jamie smiled. "Noa."

They fell into silence again. They were both in their beds, snug and tucked in, eyes closed, minds shutting down just enough to believe they were together. Jamie could almost feel the weight of Noa beside her even though the cot wasn't wide enough for two people. Noa could feel Jamie's legs pressing against hers under the thick material of the cocoon. She brushed her cheek again and imagined it was Jamie reaching for her in the dark.

"What happens if we fall asleep with the line open?" Jamie asked.

"Probably nothing."

Jamie's voice was fading. "I can leave the radio on for a while."

"Mm-hmm," Noa confirmed. "You better not snore."

Jamie chuckled. "I bet you're sick of sleeping by yourself."

Noa's smile faded. "Yeah..."

"Goodnight, Noa."

"Goodnight, Jamie."

Jamie didn't plan to sleep. She was just going to close her eyes and imagine herself lying in bed next to Noa. She thought she could hear Noa's breathing over the microphone, but it might have just been the wind against the side of the barn. Logically she knew that any sounds Noa made would come from the speaker part of the radio up on the table, but she could've sworn the whispers were coming from right next to her on the pillow. She moved her hand closer. Her lips brushed the lines of the microphone and she felt like it was Noa's mouth.

It had been so long since she'd been kissed passionately. Even before everything went wrong with Louis, kisses were relegated to quick pecks on their way out the door. Sometimes they would kiss during sex but there was something mechanical about it. Her dream kiss with Noa was something else entirely. It was about standing together and experiencing each other without words. It was lips and tongues using a completely different language.

Noa didn't dream. She didn't fall that deep into a sleep. But she could hear Jamie on the other end of the connection as she gave up consciousness. Long deep breaths turned into sighs. Quiet smacking noises when her lips parted and then closed again. She made the softest noises that barely made it across the line, but Noa was listening hard enough to hear them. She struggled to keep her breathing steady. She hugged herself inside the cocoon, dragging her fingers up the outside of her arms just lightly enough to cause goosebumps.

Jamie could feel Noa's weight against her, could almost taste her breath. Jamie moaned quietly and shifted under the blanket, the movement just enough to shake her out of her dream. She blinked her eyes open and looked around the barn. Sections of the wall were lit up in red-orange halos, the misshapen shadows cast by her tools making it look like stage setting.

She was aroused by her dream and awake enough to be embarrassed by that. She didn't know how long she'd been asleep. More concerning, she didn't know if she'd said anything in her sleep while Noa was still listening. She brought the microphone up but stopped herself from speaking. If they were still connected, she didn't want to wake Noa. She listened carefully before she thought to look at her watch. They'd left the window fifteen minutes ago.

Jamie got up on her knees. She put the microphone down, turned off the radio, and rested her hand against its face. It was still warm.

"Goodnight, Noa," she said again. "I'll see you when you come back around. Your lighthouse will be here waiting."

She lay back down and pulled the covers up. She was too tired to bother turning off the lights, let alone going all the way back inside. She could rough it for one night.

// MISSION DAY 111 //

LILY FARIS was three years younger than Jamie, but she was taller and more voluptuous, so Jamie always ended up feeling like an awkward teenager next to her "womanly" little sister. Jamie arrived to find Lily speaking to the restaurant hostess and hugged her from behind, squeezing tightly until Lily began pounding on her fists and demanding freedom. When Jamie let her go, Lily turned around and threw her arms around Jamie's neck. The hostess watched the whole ritual with a pair of menus in her hand, weight shifted to one foot in anticipation of leading them to a table.

They were seated under a huge window with random orange panes alongside the clear glass. It cast a beautiful golden hue over the table as they settled themselves and gave their drink orders. Jamie decided that since she didn't have to wait by the radio for Noa's call, she could take the day off work and drive the hundred miles to Cincinnati for some family time. She left Cisco with the neighbors so he could continue his courtship of their beagle, called to let Lily know she was coming, and hit the road.

When the waitress left, Lily folded her arms in front of her on the table. She arched an eyebrow and smiled. "So," she said, "glad to hear everything worked out."

Jamie was confused. "Worked out?"

"With Louis."

"Nothing is worked out," Jamie said.

Lily's face fell and she examined Jamie's face again. Realization dawned on her and she sat up straighter. "Oh. *Oh.* Okay. Well, congratulations are still in order."

Jamie said, "What the hell are you talking about?"

"You! I could hear it on the phone, and then that hug when you came in, and now you're sitting here looking like a confused puppy but your eyes are still shining. I thought it was because you worked things out with Louis. But you *met* someone, didn't you?"

Jamie blushed and occupied herself with unfolding the napkin on her lap. "I don't... it-it isn't..."

Lily leaned across the table and lowered her voice. "Boy or girl?"

Jamie took a deep breath and let it out slowly. "Girl."

"Whoa, sis!" Lily fell back into her seat. "Good for you! Is that why you wanted to see me? What's her name? How did you meet her? Oh, wait, is she *here?*" She sat up straighter and scanned the room as every other patron had just become a suspect.

"She's not here! Everything else is... complicated. I wanted to see you because I wanted to see you. It's been forever."

Lily gave up her search. "It has. Did you get my email about Beth?"

"First place in the Chen-Graham Math Competition. Very, very cool."

"She's already talking about all these colleges she wants to apply to. She's fourteen and she's already planning everything."

Jamie said, "Maybe she's just trying to give you time to save up."

Lily cringed. "Oh, god, don't talk about that. I shudder just thinking about what it's going to cost to send her somewhere that really challenges her mind. Serves me right for having a genius. How *did* I have a genius?"

"Our mama," Jamie said. "It skips a generation."

"Oh-h-h, that makes sense." She sighed and skimmed the menu. "Everything looks so good. Oh!" She looked up as if she'd just had an inspiration and slapped the table twice. She aimed a finger at Jamie. "Hey, what's your girlfriend's name?"

Jamie said, "That trick hasn't worked since high school."

"It worked once!"

"I don't want to talk about her. It's... I don't know what it is. It's very complicated."

Lily hummed and looked back at the menu. "If it was anyone but you, I'd guess that it was an internet dating thing. You probably didn't even know you could date people online."

"Is that where people get those computer viruses?"

"HTTP STD," Lily said.

Jamie laughed. She pretended to read her menu, but really she was trying to push down the urge to spill her guts. Noa had become so special to her in a relatively short amount of time, but nobody knew about her. It didn't seem right.

"She's beautiful," Jamie said. "Absolutely gorgeous. And she's funny. And a genius. I know Beth is the next Einstein, but Noa..."

"Noa?" Lily said. "What an unusual name."

Jamie kicked herself. "Yeah. Noa. N-O-A. She's the smartest woman I've ever met."

"Beth should meet her."

"She... yeah, she absolutely should. I bet they'd hit it off."

Lily said, "But...? Come on. You're holding something back. What's the catch? Is she married?"

"No. No, nothing like that." She chewed her bottom lip. "There's a reason she can't be here. And it's very complicated, and I don't want to tell you because it would take too long to explain."

Lily's face was screwed up in her attempt to understand. "Well... okay, what does she do?"

"I can't tell you that, either."

"Well, crap, Jamie."

Jamie said, "This is why I didn't want to tell you any of it! There's too much I can't talk about, or I could talk about but you would never believe me."

"So why did you give in after, like, thirty seconds of interrogation?"

"Because I want to talk about her." Jamie was surprised by her eyes watering up. "She means so much to me, Lily, and no one even knows about her. I don't talk to her with anyone. And I feel like I just met her, but I already care so much about her." She put her elbows on the table and put both hands over her face. A moment later, Lily was on her side of the table and pulling her into a hug. She kissed Jamie's hair and squeezed.

"She sounds pretty special."

"You have no idea." She sniffled and wiped a hand across her cheek. "I feel bad for her, getting stuck with someone like me."

Lily thumped her ear. "You shut up about stuff like that. Are you forcing her to spend time with you?"

Well, she doesn't exactly have a choice... "No."

"Does she run away as quickly as possible when she leaves?"

Technically she's always running from me at something like eight miles a second. "No."

"Is she spending time with Jamie Rose Faris, the coolest and funniest and dorkiest creator of the finest furniture I've ever seen?"

Jamie laughed. "Yeah."

"Then she's not getting ripped off."

Jamie kissed Lily's cheek. "Thanks."

Lily went back to her side of the table. "Is she still in the closet? That's why you can't talk to anyone about her or go out with her."

"Right," Jamie said.

Lily nodded sagely. "Her secret is safe with me. Can you tell me anything about her? I want to know who can make my big sister go from laughing to crying in the space of a minute."

Jamie tried to think of something that wouldn't give away Noa's identity. "She's the bravest person I know. And strong... she's so strong. She went through something so harrowing, I can't believe she isn't a basket case who refuses to leave her house."

Lily looked star struck. "God, she sounds amazing. I want to meet her so bad. Maybe just bring her as a friend? Or I can be at your house when she drops by?"

"It's not that simple."

"Okay, okay." Lily gave a resigned sigh.

Jamie plucked at the napkin on her lap. "She calls me her lighthouse."

Lily made a pained noise and clutched her chest, sagging forward over the table. "You didn't have to tell me *that*. Why, why is she so adorable?" She made a sound that was almost a growl. "Okay, go ahead. Tell me. What do you call her?"

Jamie almost didn't answer. "Stargirl."

"Oh, I hate you. I hate you and your stupid relationship."

"Sorry."

"God, you're awful. You're a tease. I hate you so much."

Jamie put a hand over her mouth to stifle her laughter as the waitress approached to take their order. She sighed as Lily went over the contents of something on the menu. She hadn't really said much about Noa, given next to no real information, but it still felt as if she'd been in a stuffy room and someone finally cracked a window. She could breathe. Not only that, but Noa finally felt like a real person who actually existed in her life, not just a voice on the radio and a picture on the wall.

When the waitress left, Lily crossed her arms over her chest and glared at Jamie. "I can tell you're not going to give any ground on this secrecy thing, so I have some requests."

"Shoot."

"One, the next time you see your lady, warn her about me. Tell her that if she ruins this~" She gestured to indicate Jamie's whole demeanor. "~that I will track her down and make her regret it."

Jamie nodded. "Okay."

"Two, don't screw this up on your end. You have someone that makes you look like your sixteen again. But you sometimes get in your own way. Especially when it comes to dating a woman. So don't find reasons to screw this up. Identify problems and work through them, if you can. If this woman is as special as you say she is, she deserves that from you."

"Yes, ma'am."

Lily said, "Three, I want some of the fries that come with your meal."

"No deal."

"You're a bad human being."

"Is there a four?"

Lily said, "Yes. If there's anything about this woman's identity that requires you keeping it a secret, then keep it as long as you can. Protect it if you have to. If you open an oyster too soon, all you have is sand."

Jamie said, "You know, I may have been wrong about genius skipping a generation."

Lily winked. "Don't be too impressed. I heard it on TV or somewhere."

"Well, your sage advice is still very much appreciated."

"Does that mean I can have your fries?"

Jamie yanked her hands away. "Forget it."

"I hope you choke on them," Lily said.

They stuck their tongues out at each other, briefly reverting to their preteen selves before they laughed and found another topic of conversation until the waitress returned to take their order.

// MISSION DAY 112 //

"ASTRAEA COMMAND to ODIE." The man's voice came out of a speaker near her workout area. "Are you receiving, Colonel?"

Noa was finishing up her morning exercises on the treadmill. She knelt to disconnect her harness and catch her breath before answering. "Loud and clear," she said as she propelled herself back toward her chair. "Everything's five by five. Just finished my morning routine and my oh, so tasty breakfast paste. How are things going on the ground?"

"We're in perfect shape down here, Colonel."

She strapped herself into the seat. "What's your name?"

"I'm Doctor~"

"Name," she interrupted. "First name. You can call me Noa, and I can call you... what?"

"Uh, Max."

Noa relaxed. The straps tightened slightly around her shoulders and waist. "How was your drive this morning, Max?"

"My..."

"Your commute." She scanned the screens as she talked. She had two quadrants to clean out in the next two hours. "The drive from wherever you live to where you are right now. What did you see?"

Max didn't answer for a long time. Finally he said, "There's... a Starbucks not far from my building. I was going to stop there, but the line was too long. It wasn't even a busy time. And where are all these people coming from? All I wanted was a cup of coffee and suddenly ever person in this neighborhood decides~"

Noa tuned him out. She didn't want to hear his bitching, she wanted to be reminded of the planet she was so homesick for. In the four days since she'd heard from Jamie, space had seemed so much darker and bleaker than she remembered. She wanted Indiana mornings. She wanted dogs digging holes and chasing birds across a field. She wanted to envision things, wanted word pictures, and she would have said so but Max was suddenly off to the races.

She continued to ignore his rant about Starbucks customer service and focused on her checklists. Systems were running in the green. ODIE was currently above the southern tip of Africa. According to her chart, she would be within range of Jamie's radio at 0140. She wished there was a way to take a nap in the middle of the afternoon and wake up for their conversation, but she knew that wouldn't work. Jamie would have to know about it, and turn the radio on, and there was no way for them to set that up.

"Max," she said, interrupting what was obviously going to be a very long rant. "I want to double-check to confirm tomorrow's schedule. I have it up here, but I just want to make sure we're on the same page."

"No problem, Noa."

She regretted telling him to call her that. She realized she'd been trying to duplicate her rapport with Jamie, but she wasn't going to get it from some grumpy scientist named Max.

"Is Enver around today? I'd love to talk with him."

"I think he's coming in soon. Okay, the schedule... You're talking to a Cape Town elementary school today..."

Noa kept her irritation silent, but she made a face. She could speak three languages, but Afrikaans wasn't one of them. That meant she would have to use a translator, which meant every question would take twice as long and all her answers would get relayed by someone who wasn't a scientist but meant well... She loved the kids no matter where they were from, but translators could be a pain in the ass.

"Colonel?"

"What?" she snapped.

"I just wanted to be sure we were still connected."

She said, "We're always connected, twenty-four seven. I'm listening."

Max hesitated. "Is everything okay up there, Colonel?"

She was lonely and grumpy and she missed her friend. She wanted to abort the mission. Forget about Mars. Two nights ago she had a dream in which she literally landed in an Indiana field right next to a barn. She remembered crawling out of the ship, its hull still smoking from reentry, and walking toward the barn as Jamie came out to see what all the commotion was. But Jamie's face had been blank, just a blur that sort of resembled a young Jodie Foster.

"Max?"

"Ma'am?"

"Can you access the internet from your terminal?"

He paused again. "Yes, ma'am. I don't think I'm supposed to…"

"Then use your phone." Enver had the ODIE on a firewalled computer. He was anxious about the potential for terrorism if someone hacked into the ship's systems, so there was no way for her to get online. "I need you to look someone up for me."

She could almost hear Max's chair squeak as he looked around to see if he was being watched.

"Come on, Max. I'm the tool, right? You've got to keep the tool happy."

Max said, "I don't think anyone calls you the 'tool'…"

"Please," she said.

"Okay, okay. What do you need?"

"Jamie Faris." She started to spell it, then realized she wasn't sure about the spelling. "Try all versions. J-A-M-I-E, J-A-I-M-E. Faris with one R, two, with an A or an E… She's in Indiana."

Max said, "Okay… Not finding much. Uh. Dentist?"

"No."

"Uh… male or female?"

"Female."

"Okay, uh… I'll check… uh… social media."

Noa said, "Furniture. She makes furniture."

"Colonel, I don't think I'm supposed to be using this time to look up old college friends of yours…"

"It's important, Max. Enver wants you to keep me happy, right?"

"Right…"

"Please."

He sighed. "I'll keep looking."

Noa pulled the controls closer. She targeted a few nearby and eradicated them as she discarded more of the people Max found. A lawyer, another dentist, a man, an elementary school teacher. There seemed to be an infinite amount of Jamie Farises in Indiana. The more Max offered, the more impossible it seemed to find the one she was looking for. She was even suddenly afraid that by looking, she had somehow broken whatever spell allowed them to talk.

"Colonel? Mr. Crane just arrived."

"Excellent. Let me talk to him."

"Just a second."

She waited as the swap was made. Seconds later, she heard Enver over the speakers. "My favorite flyer! Max tells me you wish to speak to me. Is everything okay? You're on a private line, no one is listening in. Complete honesty, my dear."

Noa didn't want to admit to her loneliness because she didn't want

Enver to try and fix it. She could have admitted it to Jamie in a heartbeat. She could have poured out her heart about every fear she was feeling, gotten it off her chest, and moved on.

"There's nothing," she finally said.

"Are you certain? Noa, there's a human component to this. I understand that. Confessing fear or pain is to be expected in your circumstances. They won't be held against you. If there is anything you require, even if it's just a therapist brought in to~"

"God, no," she said. "No therapist. I'm just feeling logy."

Enver said, "I don't know that word."

Noa sighed. "It means I'm tired, Enver. And there's nothing you can do to fix that from down there, so I shouldn't have brought it up."

"Of course there is something we can do! We can increase your restful periods by... let's see... we'll have to work out a time that would actually do you good without unduly increasing the time you'll spend in orbit."

Noa snapped to attention. "Increase time?"

"Well, yes. I could add one hour to your sleep period, but then we would have to off-set that by adding time to the end of your mission. One hour per day for the remaining seven hundred days is, ah, seven hundred hours, obviously... which would add a month to your job..."

"Forget it," Noa said. "I don't need more sleep. I'm not spending another month up here."

Enver said, "You would be perfectly fine. There are fail-safes involved which means you would have enough food..."

"It doesn't matter. The mission will end when it's supposed to, if not before. Forget I said anything about being tired."

"Colonel..."

"Enver, I'm fine. Trust me. I'm just having a couple of bad days in a row."

He sounded skeptical. "If you are certain that's all it is."

She looked over her shoulder at the chart. In seven days, her window to Indiana would open at 0730. She would be awake, and it seemed reasonable to assume Jamie would be, too.

"I'm certain," she told him. "Everything will be much better in a week. Trust me."

// MISSION DAY 115 //

JAMIE ROLLED onto her side, punching and folding her pillow before dropping her head back down. Her sleep was sporadic. Some nights, even the act of slipping into REM sleep was enough to startle her awake. It was the second night in a row where she couldn't get comfortable. The night before she had tried taking a long bath and masturbating before sleep, and tonight she'd tried warm milk. Warm milk was disgusting and so far didn't seem to have done anything but irritate her stomach.

She looked at the clock and saw it was seven minutes past four. She squeezed her eyes shut and pressed the pillow against her face. She needed her sleep. She needed to be alert so she could work in the morning. If she was groggy, there were so many things that could go wrong in a workshop. She tried not to think of the cabinetmaker she sometimes did business with who only had three fingers on his left hand. She was just one bad day from ending up like him. She would be mortified to explain that to Noa on their next–

Jamie lifted her head off the pillow and looked at the clock. 4:09. She tried to remember what day it was, what the chart said. Was the window open? Was it about to open or was it about to close?

Cisco's legs twitched when she threw back the blanket. He lifted his head to watch as she grabbed her robe off the hook and ran from the bedroom. By the time she reached the stairs, he was running beside her with a frenzy that matched her own. She loved dogs. He had no idea where she was going or why, but he wasn't going to let her go alone.

She sat at the kitchen table to put on her shoes. A heavy-duty flashlight the size and weight of a hammer was on the counter, and she grabbed it up as she went outside. The beam was a blinding yellow which turned the grass a strange shade, but her head was tilted up toward the sky. She stopped halfway to the barn and moved the flashlight so it was smothered against her hip. The night stretched out in every direction. There wasn't even a hint of daybreak on the horizon, no man-made lights to mess up the view.

"Look at that, Cisco," she said softly.

It was like the cover had been taken off the planet, opening up space and bringing her closer to Noa than she'd ever been.

That thought reminded Jamie of her goal. She continued into the barn and turned on one overhead light, just enough to see by, and went to the chart. She'd been dutifully marking off the days, worried she would forget where they were on the schedule, and today was one-hundred-fifteen, and Noa would be in range starting at 4:10. She checked her watch. Three minutes ago. Her heart pounded and her hands shook as she picked up the microphone and turned on the receiver.

"Noa?"

The frequency was silent. She imagined Noa in the spaceship, tucked away in her little sleeping bag, fast asleep. She needed her sleep as much as Jamie did, and they agreed there wouldn't be any late night conversations. Jamie reluctantly turned off the radio, slipped the microphone onto its hook, and pushed the chair back under the table. She walked back outside and looked up at the stars.

She knew that being in range didn't necessarily mean ODIE would pass directly overhead her house. It might not even mean she was passing over Indiana. Even knowing that, she still had to look.

Smoothing the bottom of her robe against her thighs with one hand, Jamie sat down on the dewy grass and lay back. She turned off the flashlight but held it against her chest so she wouldn't lose it. Once she was settled, she stared straight up. It gave her the illusion of proximity, like she could just reach out and touch it. Space was just right there... right above her. She could reach up and cover the stars with her hand, fingers spread wide. She could pinch the moon between her thumb and forefinger.

A light glinted against the atmosphere, something small and fast which left a streak of white in its wake. While she was watching, it became bigger, and soon she realized it was coming closer. She sat up in the grass and watched as the shuttle - a large white ball - landed in the field where her neighbor's house was supposed to be. Jamie got to her feet and approached the vessel. It was huge. Smoke curled up off its curved, and it seemed lit from behind. A hatch opened on its side and a short flight of stairs descended onto the grass.

Noa stepped into the doorway. Her spacesuit was silver and form-fitting, just like those cheesy scifi movies from the fifties, and her head was enclosed in a glass bubble. Jamie approached as Noa descended the stairs on ridiculous high-heeled boots. They stood in front of each other on the grass, and Noa bowed to take the helmet off. When she straightened, Jamie reached out and touched her cheek, letting her fingers spread wide to cover as much as possible.

"Stargirl."

"Lighthouse. Here I am. What do you want?"

"I..." Jamie wanted to talk to her. Wanted to spend an hour talking to her, wanted to hear what was happening in space and stories from Noa's life. She wanted to let Noa live vicariously through her and experience the world she so obviously missed. She wanted a friend, companionship, a sounding board, a therapist...

Noa said, "What do you *want*, Lighthouse?"

Jamie said, "I want you to fuck me."

Her eyes opened. She realized she'd said the words out loud and covered her face with one hand. She was still lying in the grass, and Cisco had settled in beside her. The poor pup was probably confused about what was happening but he was still right there by her side. She sat up and brushed at her robe to rid herself of any bugs that might have been clinging to her. She got up and looked at the sky one last time before she led Cisco back inside. The clock above the sink revealed she'd only been asleep for about ten minutes. There was still at least half an hour left in their window, and she had an idea of how to use it.

Jamie went upstairs and shut the bedroom door behind her. She crouched beside the bed, opened her bottom drawer, and took out a small purple toy. She didn't like the technical word for it. The world had made that word dirty and embarrassing, so she just called it her device. She took off her robe and climbed back into bed. She stayed above the covers and pushed her pajamas down just past her knees.

There was a horizontal grip on the device she could hold onto, with an extension she could guide with her middle two fingers. Squeezing with her thumb and forefinger activated the vibrating egg inside the extension. Squeezing the other side with her pinkie and ring finger released a small amount of lube. She liked the device because it involved more skill than a standard, blunt toy. Plus it was a great hand exercise, strengthening her fingers and dexterity.

Jamie put one hand behind her head and settled the other between her thighs. She pictured Noa's face, her eyes and her smile, listened for her voice. She thought of the night they'd fallen asleep together and smiled, wetting her lips as she applied pressure with her thumb. The device began buzzing in a slow, steady rhythm. Her breath hitched in her throat and she repositioned her shoulders on the pillow. Her bare feet slipped across her sheets. Her toes curled as she lifted her hips to meet her hand. The device numbed her fingers as she applied a little more lube and increased the vibration.

She imagined Noa's dark hair let loose, falling across her face. Noa's hand, slender fingers pushing it out of the way to unveil her eyes. Jamie grunted at that image. Noa's eyes, her smile, her laugh. Noa's voice. The line of Noa's throat, the curve of her shoulder revealed before it disappeared under a bra strap. And then, Noa's fingers closing around that strap to draw it down, her other arm coyly lifted to cover her breasts.

"Noa," she said aloud. When she realized there was no one to overhear her, she spoke louder. "Noa... come fuck me, Noa. I want you so bad." She groaned and closed the fingers of her hand around her hair, pulling it just enough to feel it but not enough to hurt. She smiled when she realized Noa had the perfect name to moan, to cry out, to punctuate her orgasm.

She used her middle fingers to push the extension into herself. Steady pressure from her thumb and index finger kept the vibrations building. The base of the toy bumped against her clitoris and she moved her wrist to stimulate it further. She imagined it was Noa's tongue, heart pounding as she writhed under her own touch. She saw Noa's face shining with sweat, hair wild, lips wet with~

"Noa!" She bucked against her hand, gasped, trembled. She folded her knees together and slid her free hand down her throat. She cupped her breast through her pajama top and squeezed as she came. She flexed and stretched her toes as her body relaxed. She stretched out on top of the mattress. She moved her hand so the toy rested against her mound, still vibrating in tune with her orgasm, sending lovely little jolts through her whole crotch.

"Noa," she said again, eyes open and focused on the window. The curtains were open just enough for her to see the glass shining with moonglow, as if providing a spotlight for her. She chuckled at the thought. She turned off the device and set it aside, kicked off her pajama pants, and pulled her shirt over her head. She wasn't ordinarily the type to sleep naked, but something seemed right about it. She kicked the clothes onto the floor and settled on top of the blankets again. This time when she tried to fall asleep, her brain shut off without a fight.

At that moment, high above in the ODIE, Noa shifted in her sleep. She turned her head as if in response to hearing her name. "Jamie?" she murmured. She knew it must have been a dream even if she couldn't remember the details. Just a few more days until she saw Jamie again. She smiled as she fell back to sleep, hoping she could slip back into whatever dream had woken her.

// MISSION DAY 118 //

JAMIE, IN plaid boxer shorts and a tank top, took her coffee out to the barn within minutes of sunrise. She still hadn't showered, her short hair sticking up in crazy spikes. She had slipped her feet into boots without tying them and they flopped loosely around her bare feet as she marched across the lawn. Even Cisco wasn't willing to accompany her on this excursion. She sat down at the radio, switched it on, and held the mug under her nose as she waited.

Noa tucked away her sleeping bag, shut the nook, and used her bare toes to propel her across the living space to her coffee. She was still in her underwear, her hair pinned back and rising above her head like a thorny black cactus. The pouch with her coffee was automatically heated and it burned her fingers slightly as she removed it from the slot. She took a drink and sighed blissfully. Worth the burns. She took another sip and turned to look at the chronometer as it clicked over to 0640.

She didn't know how early Jamie woke up. There was a chance they wouldn't reconnect until tomorrow, but she was excited at the possibility they might be awake at the same time. She closed her lips around the spout of her coffee pouch and took another sip.

"~od morning, good morning, sunshine..."

Noa's smile was immense and authentic. "Are you singing to me, Lighthouse?"

Jamie almost spilled her coffee in her haste to put it down without looking. "Hey! Hi. Hello. Oh my god, you're still there."

"I'm still here for a good long while, Jamie." Noa settled against one curved wall, her feet flat against the bulkhead beneath her. She liked the position because it made her feel like Spider-Man. She flexed her toes against the cool metal. "It's really great hearing your voice again."

Jamie raked her fingers through her hair as if Noa could see her. "I wasn't sure you would be awake this early. I wasn't sure I'd be up this early. I just couldn't wait a whole 'nother day to see you again."

Noa was touched. "You missed me?"

"Well. That, of course. Yes, I missed you. But I also have a confession to make. It's kind of an awkward confession. As embarrassed as I am to tell you, I feel like I owe it to you. Or maybe you'd prefer not to know. Fuck..."

"You've got me curious now."

Jamie cleared her throat. "The other night, uh... I, uh... I was having trouble sleeping. And I had this dream. You were in the dream. And when I woke up..." She swallowed the lump in her throat. "I sort of, um. I... masturbated... thinking about you."

Noa blushed and arched an eyebrow. "Is that so."

"I feel terrible about it. I feel like it's an invasion or a breach of friendship or... or... something. I don't know. But the more I thought about it, the more I thought it would be worse not to tell you. I want you to know I respect our friendship and I'm not... I want to be frie~ I'm more than happy just being friends with you. I'm not trying to make this anything that it's not."

"Jamie."

"Hm?"

"I've had dreams about you, too."

Jamie cheered up. "Oh! Oh... *Oh.*"

Noa laughed and pushed an errant hair away from her face. "I didn't bring it up because... well, I didn't feel guilty about it. I thought we had a nice flirtation going. But I'm glad you confessed. At least it's out in the open now. So I feel much more comfortable saying I'm attracted to you."

Jamie looked at the photo of Noa still hung above the radio. "You are?"

"Mm-hmm." Noa looked toward the window. "To be completely honest, since we're in a confessional mood this morning, I'm a bit frustrated that I don't know what you look like. The young Jodie Foster thing is fine, but I don't want to picture Jodie Foster when we talk. I want to picture you."

"That's fair," Jamie said. "I'm... not exactly comfortable with myself. It's not a huge issue, but the general thing where I hate to have my picture taken. I wish I could just take a picture of myself and send it to you."

Noa almost asked *how much would you be wearing in the picture,* but she didn't want to tease Jamie's obviously real guilt about her fantasy. "That would be ideal. Unfortunately my circumstances don't really allow that as an option. You paint such beautiful pictures of the world around you. Do that for yourself. Let me see you."

Jamie worried her lip and looked away from Noa's image. "But I'm not—"

"Lighthouse," Noa said, "I don't care what you're not. All I care about is what makes you the person you are, whatever that might be."

Jamie took out her phone. She opened the camera and flipped the lens so she could see herself on the screen. She grimaced at the dark smudges under her eyes, the crazy brown weeds of her hair, and balanced the phone against the radio.

"Okay," she said. "Close your eyes."

Noa obliged.

"The features I like best came from my mother. They're the parts of her I see when I look in the mirror. My blue eyes, my smile, the bump in my nose. I have her long neck and broad shoulders, her long arms. She was a tall woman, taller than I am, but I still got some of her lankiness. I tend to slump over my work so I overcompensate when I'm out in the world by standing up very straight. It makes me look taller than I am. I wear plaid shirts unbuttoned over T-shirt, tank tops, whatever, and usually jeans or khakis. Comfortable stuff. Casual.

"And my face..." She pressed her lips together and squinted at her phone's camera. She pretended she was describing someone else, a complete stranger, and tried to be objective. "My eyes are striking. Not like yours, and a different shade, but still nice enough to compliment. When I smile, I think my cheeks look chubby, but it's not a bad look. My eyebrows are thin, but not because I pluck them. I wish they were thicker, to be honest, but it wasn't in the cards. My glasses are bigger than they need to be, but I like the big frames."

Noa smiled at the vision she was putting together.

"But my hands are my best feature. I love my hands. They're rough, with chipped nails and callouses and cuts. The fingers are strong. I have little white nicks on my knuckles where a tool slipped or I dropped a piece of wood, and there are shallow ditches where the damage was worse. When I met my husband, he called them 'man hands.' I told him they were a woman's hands, he just didn't spend enough time with the right women."

Noa laughed. "I like a woman with strong hands."

"Yeah, I'll just bet you do."

Noa's eyebrow twitched at that, but she decided not to press. "That was perfect. Plus it gave me a chance to hear you talk a lot. I've missed your voice."

Jamie said, "Yeah? How was the description? Will it work when you're trying to picture me?"

"I think it'll do." She looked toward the porthole. "I don't settle well."

Jamie frowned. "What do you mean?"

"With people. Relationships. I don't settle with other people very well, so I tend to jump from one to the next when things get too serious. I don't cheat. I was cheated on once and I'll never do that to anyone else. I don't know exactly how I'd run away in this situation, but I thought you deserved full disclosure if we're going to keep doing... this."

"Okay." Jamie pulled her legs up into the chair, crossing them in front of her. "So are we, like, dating now? Is that what this is?"

Noa shrugged. "I don't know. I know I look forward to your calls. I know how much I missed you this past week. And now I know that you dream about me, which makes me happier than I expected. I like you, Jamie. It seems like you like me."

"I do. Very much so." Jamie was surprised to hear herself say that. She hadn't expressed an interest in anyone since Louis asked her out. She grinned. "So I guess we're sort of a couple now. Of course, I still can't tell anyone about it because no one would believe I'm really talking to a celebrity astronaut."

Noa said, "And I can't tell anyone just in case they consider it a security breach and maybe cut us off. I really don't want that to happen."

"Me neither." Jamie looked at the clock. They had time left, but an hour never seemed as short as when she was on the line with Noa. "You know, yesterday was actually the three-week anniversary of when we first made contact."

Noa said, "Wow. I didn't realize."

"Well, we spent one week without contact," Jamie said. "It might not officially count."

"I think it counts." She had to move in order to see her chart of days and times. "Our next blackout period is going to start on Day 137."

Jamie said, "I'm already dreading it. We better get in as much conversation as possible before that happens." She repositioned herself again, feet on her seat and knees where she could rest her arm across them. "So what's for breakfast this morning, Stargirl?"

PART
II

JAMIE WATCHED with dread as Louis' truck rolled down the driveway at a quarter to eleven. She had finished breakfast and gotten an early start on that day's project knowing she would stop early for lunch. Noa would be in range at eleven and they were going to have lunch together. They'd just gotten past their second week-long break and, if anything, it had been harder than the first. Jamie threw herself into her work and spent time on home improvements like pulling weeds and fixing the gutters. She found herself looking toward the radio multiple times a day like it was a phone she was waiting to ring.

Louis parked next to her truck. She crossed her arms over her chest and stood in the barn door. He hadn't called to let her know he was coming, of course, so she didn't know how long to expect the visit to last. She flexed her fingers as he crossed the grass toward her. He moved slowly, scanning the surrounding yard for Cisco. It took all of Jamie's willpower not to scream at him to hurry up.

When he was close enough for normal conversation, she said, "What do you want? I have a busy day."

"I didn't come here to fight, Jamie." He stopped a few feet away and put his hands in his pockets. "I think it's time we talked."

She shrugged. "You had your chance to talk."

Louis said, "I couldn't talk then. I didn't know what I needed to say, what I wanted to be said. But I think we've been apart long enough."

Jamie shook her head. "No."

"James—"

"What, you get to decide when we take a break and you also get to decide when that break ends? Do you think I was just sitting here waiting for you to come back and rejoin the marriage?"

He took a slow breath. "No, you made it abundantly clear that you didn't appreciate what happened. Trust me, I've taken that into account. I know I screwed up." He came closer. "But think about everything we've been through, James."

She bit back an angry sigh. She closed her eyes and worked her neck from side to side. Was it so hard to use her actual name and not the pet name he'd chosen for her?

"I came here to take you to lunch," he said. "We can sit down, have a nice conversation about everything that's happened."

Jamie forced herself to maintain eye contact with him, refusing to look at her watch or in the direction of the radio.

"I don't have time to go all the way to town for lunch."

He smiled and gestured at the truck. "I figured you would say that. I have a bucket of fried chicken from Crisp's in the truck. Mashed potatoes and corn on the cob. I thought maybe we could spread a blanket out on the back yard and have a little picnic. Remember when we used to do that?"

Jamie said, "Of course I do."

There were bright spots in their relationship. She'd agreed to marry him, after all, and she'd thought they were happy right up until he walked out the door. She remembered when he got down on one knee to propose. It was so traditional, cliché, and corny, but she still found herself sobbing so hard that she could only nod her assent when he showed her the ring. It was a simple gold ring, no diamond since they both believed that whole market was a scam and a waste of money. She remembered falling asleep with her head on his chest and listening to his heartbeat. She remembered lying awake at night thinking about the future.

But he'd also left her. He abandoned her, and she would never forget that.

"We were just on hiatus," Louis said. "We can get through this even stronger than we were before. And I know I can't just walk in here like nothing happened. I know I have to win you over again. I'm willing to do whatever it takes to get *us* back."

Jamie twisted her wrist to look at her watch. Noa was five minutes away. "You walk away... you stay gone for a year. And you expect me to have been waiting for you that whole time? Do you think my life has been on pause this whole time? I've been thinking, too. And I know I've told you this in no uncertain terms, but maybe you need it spelled out for you. Our marriage is over. I'm ready to file the papers."

Louis was blinking at her, his face a mixture of shock and confusion. "But... no, you said you wouldn't..."

"It's been long enough, Louis. I realized waiting for you to make the next move was just being cowardly. Just being passive. I'm done letting you make decisions for this relationship, Louis. If you won't file, then I will. This marriage is over. We're done. That's it." Another furtive glance at her watch. "Now please go."

He stepped closer. "James..."

"Jamie, fucking *Jamie*, you asshole." She couldn't contain her irritation anymore. She had an irrational fear that if Noa entered the window and didn't hear her voice, if she wasn't there waiting when the conversation began, she would never be waiting again. And now Louis was standing here talking about saving the corpse of their marriage and calling her the wrong damn name. "Get out of here, Louis. Take your damn chicken and *go*. We're not going to talk this out. You're not going to convince me to change my fucking mind and let you back in, not as badly as you hurt me. I don't care if you're scared or lonely or whatever the hell prompted you to come here after all this time. I'm doing just fine without you." She aimed a finger at the road. "Go. Now."

He turned and walked away at what seemed like a glacial pace. Jamie looked at her watch again. It was eleven o'clock, and Noa was probably already on the radio trying to reach other. She drummed her fingers against her bicep and almost cried out when Louis walked around to the passenger side of his truck. He took out the fried chicken, placed it on the ground, then walked around the bed of the truck. She seethed with anger as he started the engine. He shifted gears. He backed up. Every single step of reversing away from the house took ages, and she was furious by the time he finally pulled back out onto the main road.

As soon as he was gone, she turned and ran to the radio. She switched it on, grabbed the microphone, and crouched in front of the table as if using the chair would take any longer.

"Noa! Noa, are you there?"

There was no delay. "I'm here, Lighthouse. Good to hear your voice. I thought maybe I'd gotten the schedule wrong."

Jamie took off her glasses, releasing a shaky breath of relief. She covered her eyes with her free hand. "I was so worried I'd missed you."

Noa furrowed her brow, one hand resting on the wall. She could hear the tremor in Jamie's voice and, after a moment, realized she was crying. "Jamie? Is everything okay?"

"It is now," Jamie said.

"Talk to me." Noa let herself drift freely across her living space. "It's what I'm here for, after all. Tell me what's wrong."

Jamie pulled the chair over and climbed into it. "Louis was just here. He showed up right before eleven, and he said it was time to start putting our marriage back together. After all this time, I'm supposed to jump up and down and welcome him back. He wanted to date me again. He had chicken and he wanted to have a picnic on the lawn. All I could think about was missing you. I was afraid if you came into range and didn't hear me, you'd leave and I wouldn't get to talk to you until tomorrow."

Noa said, "I would have waited."

"You would've?"

"For you?" Noa said. "I'd wait as long as it took."

Jamie brought the microphone up to her lips. She lowered it, closed her eyes, considered what she wanted to say. She ran her thumb over the now-warm plastic. She brought the microphone back up.

"I think I'm falling in love with you."

Noa blinked. The brief history of women - and one poor misguided man - telling Noa Laurie they loved her was not a happy one. There were stalkers after she became a public figure, there were two girlfriends who were far more invested in the relationship than she was. Those declarations were always codewords for her to back away and start looking for new living arrangements. It usually marked the beginning of the end. Now, however. Now, from Jamie, it made her feel breathless. She rested one hand against the wall and touched the collar of her polo shirt with the other.

"Are you still there?" Noa asked.

"I am. I was just giving you time to process. It wasn't a small thing, what I just said."

"No. It definitely wasn't. I don't want to treat it like it was something trivial." Her feet were a few inches above the curve of the wall, her shoulders also not quite touching anything solid. "I really like you. I like spending time with you. I work my tail off the rest of the day so I can justify spending an hour talking to you. It's the best part of my day. It's a part I never anticipated. And if I was the kind of person who could say those words this early, or at all, I'd be saying them back to you. The only reason I'm not is because of who I am. It has nothing to do with how I actually feel. Does that make sense?"

Jamie said, "Kind of. I know what you mean, at least."

"Good. Because at the very least, I have a very intense crush on you. And it's been a while since I considered this mere friendship. I don't know what label I'd put on you, on us, but I know friend is too small of a word. Is that enough?"

"It's more than enough, Noa." She wiped at the corner of her eye. "Even if nothing comes of it, that's enough for me."

Noa said, "Okay." She rolled her head back until it touched the wall. "Do you want to talk about your husband?"

"My ex-husband. And no. Time with you is too precious to waste on that asshole." She took off her glasses. "I want to talk to you about beautiful things. It's extremely hot today. Ninety degrees, fifty-four percent humidity, and not even a breath of wind. When I took Cisco out for his run, we left just after dawn but it was still sweltering."

ODIE was kept at a steady 73 degrees, but Noa felt the heat as if the environmental controls had been broken. She could see Jamie, beads of sweat on her upper lip and the curve of her throat. Probably dressed in shorts and a lightweight top. She had stopped under a tree, she said, and opened the bottle of water she was carrying. Noa could see it, Jamie's lips parted as the water spilled across them. Jamie's tongue flicking out to gather the drops on the corners of her mouth, tasting sweat.

Noa touched her own throat, licked her own lips, and could almost feel the heat bearing down on her as Jamie described it. Her fingers popped the top button on her polo shirt and slid inside. She stroked her collarbone. Jamie was telling her that when she got home, she had to change out of her sweaty shirt.

"Did you take a shower?" Noa asked.

"A bath," Jamie said.

"Describe it."

Jamie looked at the radio. "Describe... my bath? Or the bathroom?"

"Both."

Jamie bit her bottom lip before she complied. "It's a little square room with an angled ceiling, because it's right under the roof. The bath is in the corner under the window. That's fogged glass. I have all my soaps and shampoos and stuff on the sill. The bath is big because my ex is tall and he wanted plenty of room. I'm smaller than he is, so I tend to float a little bit." She grinned. "Well, not as much as you float, but still."

Noa smiled. She was imagining Jamie naked, settled in the tub full of cold water. Washing away her sweat, cooling her skin. Dragging the washcloth up her shoulder and down between her breasts.

"Jamie."

"Mm-hmm."

"The next time I'm over Indiana at night, I want you to take a bath with that window open. Can you see the sky from it?"

Jamie was blushing furiously. "Yes."

"Good. I want you to run a nice bubble bath. I want you to settle in. And I want you to open the window so I can look down and see you. I mean, I won't~"

"I know," Jamie said softly. "I'll do it."

"Yeah?"

"Mm-hmm."

Noa smiled. "Will you think of me?"

Jamie felt a prickle at the back of her neck. "Are you... I mean, are you asking...?"

"You know what I'm asking, Jamie."

"I will," Jamie said.

"Good," Noa said so softly it was almost a sigh.

Jamie shifted on her seat, crossing one leg over the other. She nervously tucked her hair behind her ear. She looked up at the chart to see how long she had to wait to follow through on her promise.

// MISSION DAY 164 - SUMMER, CONTINUED //

AFTER DINNER, Jamie went upstairs and ran a bath. Her plan was to take a long soak and then go directly out into the barn for her conversation with Noa. Tonight she was purposefully going to be a little late. She retrieved the book she was currently reading off her night stand as the tub was filling. The book's cover showed a drawing of an astronaut reaching out for something, and Jamie ran her finger along the upper curve of the helmet. She'd been reading a lot of science-fiction lately, even though she knew it was really nothing like what Noa was experiencing. Reading the books felt like getting a glimpse of her world.

She turned off the tap and settled in the water. She read for a while, trying to focus on the story, but her mind was too easily distracted. In the end she put the book on the edge of the bathtub. Water from her hand beaded on the cover, already sinking into the paper and causing irreparable but cosmetic damage. That was fine with her. She didn't trust a book without a little bit of damage to it. Bends in the spine, creased pages, rips and tears and ghosts of coffee spilled across the back cover. A damaged book was one that had been carried around and read time and time again. A damaged book was someone's friend and not just set dressing on a shelf.

She closed her eyes and sank lower in the water, lifting her legs to rest her feet on either side of the faucet. She moved her hands to create a current. The water lapped against her shoulders, up the nape of her neck to wet her hair before sliding back down over her chest. Her breathing grew shallower. Her body became limp. Her entire body was weightless. It was easy to ignore the bits where she was touching the sides of the tub and just imagine she really was floating.

She thought about Noa, about their plan. Her eyes were on the window, slowly blinking until the one time they stayed closed. The bathroom was the second floor, and the only way anyone could see in was if they were in the sky. Not that she actually expected Noa to literally see her. But she smiled at the thought.

When she began to dream, she was so relaxed that it built itself as a subtle layer over reality. She knew she was still in the bath but, in the dream, she was holding the mic. She could hear the static and whistles across the frequency band. Then she heard Noa's voice as clearly as if she was actually speaking.

"*What was that? Is it raining there?*"

"No…" Her lips barely moved, the word coming out on a breath. "*I'm in the bath, like we talked about,*" she said in the dream. "*Is that okay?*"

"*Of course it's okay. It was my idea. Why wouldn't it be okay?*"

Jamie's lips curled into a smile. "*Because I'm naked. It might be awkward.*"

"*I don't mind. Would it make you feel more comfortable if I was naked, too?*"

Jamie let her neck roll along the cool edge of the tub, sinking lower. She flexed her toes as the dream gained more substance and pushed the real world into the background. It didn't matter that the radio was in the barn. Her right hand curled into a fist, gripping only water, but she could have sworn she felt the textured plastic against her palm. Her left hand glided across her hip. She turned her knees inward as if she planned to stop its advance. Her lips parted.

"*Maybe,*" she said in the dream.

She saw herself in space, floating outside of a round porthole. She pressed her hands against the glass - plastic…? What did they use to make windows in spaceships…? - and watched as Noa unfastened her harness and floated up. Noa swam forward and put her palm against the window. Jamie did the same, fingers splayed, and whatever the material was dissolved from the heat of their skin. Noa smiled, her hair waving out behind her like a cape.

Jamie pressed her palm against Noa's. Noa threaded their fingers together and squeezed.

Jamie sat up so fast that a wing of water shot out and splattered against the floor. "Shit!" she said, then, "Sorry, I--" She didn't know who she was apologizing to. The dream conversation felt so real that it took her a moment to realize she was alone. She sank back down and looked up at the window, open at Noa's request. She filled her hands with water and brought it up to her head, letting it pour down her face as she pushed her fingers through her hair.

She squeezed her neck where it met her shoulders, then kept one hand there while the other continued lower. She circled a nipple with her thumb and made a quiet noise of arousal. The hand on her neck began a slow, rhythmic massage while the other stroked her skin under the water. She imagined herself floating above the ground as she skimmed her hip, went up the outside of her thigh to her knee. Her hand submerged again, moving along her inner thigh.

"Noa," she whispered. "Watch me, Noa."

Her legs eased apart as her hand sank. She bit her bottom lip in anticipation of the touch. She wondered if Noa would ask her to describe what she was doing, if she did, how detailed she would be. She was normally very shy about this sort of thing. The idea of someone watching her masturbate was completely out of her comfort zone. Or it should have been. Maybe it would have been with anyone other than Noa. Her only reservation now was that Noa couldn't actually see what was happening.

Jamie crossed her middle two fingers and pressed them against herself. She grunted softly and used the angle of her hand like a bellows to push water against her sex. She shivered and arched her back, lifting her breasts out of the water before sinking back down into it. She pictured Noa floating above her near the ceiling, her hands pushing against the wall to descend so that she was over Jamie's position.

"Please," Jamie whispered as she pushed her fingers into herself. She gasped quietly and saw Noa in a tight T-shirt, her legs exposed by her shorts. She said Noa's name like a mantra, the syllables blurring together until she grunted it once through clenched teeth. Her toes curled and her hand curled into a fist against her throat.

"Hah. Hm." She moved her hand up to her mouth, fingers resting against her lips as she slowly opened her eyes. She looked at the clock without moving her head and saw that Noa had been in range for three minutes. It was ridiculous to think she had somehow heard or sensed what had just happened, but still Jamie smiled at the thought.

She remained in the water until her skin stopped tingling and then stood up. She wrapped a robe around herself, not bothering to towel off, and left the bathroom without draining the tub. Cisco looked up as she passed through the kitchen but it was too close to bedtime for him to accompany her. She put on her sneakers and took a second to look out for neighbors before setting out. The barn light was already on so she could just walk straight to the radio and sit down.

There was a burst of static when she turned on the radio. She was used to it by now, but her heart still did a little jig every time it happened. Noa heard the same interference as a quick hiss over the line. She was sitting cross-legged in her bunk. Her hair was down and spread out behind her like a wing. She'd been sitting still long enough that every strand was motionless. When she heard the hiss, she sat up straighter and turned her head toward the living area.

"You there, Stargirl?"

Noa's face lit up with a smile. "There you are. I was afraid I'd have to go to bed without seeing you tonight."

"Sorry. I lost track of time in the bath."

"Oh…"

Jamie could feel the heat of her blush in her cheeks. "I was thinking about you."

Noa processed that. "Oh."

"I just hopped out of the bath and came here to talk to you. My skin is still wet. All I'm wearing is my robe and a pair of sneakers."

Noa kept her breathing steady. "Oh."

Jamie laughed. "I think you're stuck on a loop, Colonel. Say something else."

Noa slowly fell back against her sleeping bag. "I'm taking it all in, Lighthouse." Her hands were resting on her stomach. After a moment of consideration, she hooked her thumbs in the waistband of her pants and pushed them down her legs. She pushed the pants away with the heel of her foot and let her underwear follow.

Jamie heard the rustling of cloth. "What's going on?"

"I'm undressing." Jamie's breath caught in her throat. "For bed. Changing into my pajamas."

"Of course," Jamie said. She crossed one leg over the other, her hand pinned between them. "Do you always sleep in pajamas, Noa? I know I have my favorite comfy pair, but some nights when it's really warm out, I just skip them entirely and sleep naked on top of the sheets. The breeze from the fan feels amazing on my skin."

The last bit of Noa's outfit drifted away from her. She stretched out in her sleeping nook. "Is it hot there tonight, Jamie?"

"It's pretty warm. Humid." Jamie resisted the urge to laugh. She felt wanton, seductive. She felt like she was a siren or something, whispering these naughty things into the microphone. Her fingers curled under the edge of her robe. "I probably won't bother with pajamas tonight."

Noa hummed softly. She let her hands move across her thighs, easing higher toward her hips.

Jamie pulled gently at the robe, fanning herself slightly. "Noa…"

"Mm."

"I came for you. I want you to come for me."

Noa gasped and moved her hand between her thighs. "Jamie…"

Jamie squirmed on the seat. "Do they let you have toys up there?"

"Just… fingers. But that's okay. I'm… pretty good with my fingers."

"I'd like to be the judge of that."

Noa laughed, low and throaty. "You want to know what I'd do to you, Lighthouse?"

Jamie moved her hand, fingers spread on the seat of the chair. She hitched herself forward until she was straddling her forearm. She looked up through her eyelashes at the picture of Noa on the wall.

"You're so beautiful," Jamie whispered.

"Are you touching yourself again?" Noa asked.

Jamie swallowed. "Mm-hmm."

"Good," Noa sighed. Her eyes were still closed. She pictured Jamie in her robe, wet hair clinging to her forehead and cheeks. If she had been there, she would have picked Jamie up, put her on the cot, and let the robe go flying. The tip of her tongue played against the edge of her mouth. She had drifted and her head bumped the wall. Every thrust of her hips moved her entire body, and she knew she was no longer in her nook. She wasn't even sure which way was up, but it didn't matter at the moment. She hadn't been laid since the day of the launch. Five and a half months of nothing but her hand for company. And now there was someone to share the moment with. She wasn't going to squander that by worrying if she was 'upside down.'

"Spread your legs, Lighthouse."

Jamie uncrossed her legs and placed her pointed toes on the ground. Her robe had fallen open to reveal one breast, but she was too preoccupied to adjust it. She was still riding her forearm, imagining it was Noa's leg.

Noa quickly licked three fingertips and put that hand between her legs with the other one. She rubbed her clit with one, using the other for penetration. Her movements were quick and certain, just like she knew Jamie's tongue would be.

"My tongue is on you," Noa whispered.

"I feel it." Jamie moved her hand up to touch herself. She was wet, and so sensitive that her entire body jerked when she brushed her labia. She cried out softly. "I feel it, Noa. I feel you."

"I feel you, too."

"What am I doing?" Jamie asked.

"Licking me," Noa said. "You're gonna make me come."

Jamie rolled her head back on her shoulders. "Fuck."

They breathed heavily at each other. Jamie was squeezing the microphone so hard she was sure the button would be imprinted in her thumb well into the next day. Her tongue flicked out and licked the grill of the microphone. Jamie was usually quiet when she came, but she made a point to vocalize a little so Noa could hear her. She tried not to sound too "porn," but she wanted Noa to hear. When she finished, she moved closer to the table and put her head down.

Noa's breathing filled the room. She thought maybe her neighbors would overhear, but she knew the sound from the radio didn't travel very well. She didn't care either way. Let them listen. Jamie used one fingertip to lightly draw lines on the smooth wood of the table. She touched just enough to pretend it was Noa's skin.

"I want to taste you," Jamie whispered against the microphone. "I want to feel your skin against my lips and taste your sweat. I want to lick your thighs and taste how wet I made you."

"Keep talking," Noa gasped. "I'm so close, Jamie."

Jamie wet her lips. "I want to look up your body and see you watching me. I want to feel every tremor in your body when it's under mine. I want to lay next to you in bed and not know if it's your hair or mine tickling my cheek when my hand is between your legs."

Noa cried out. She groaned Jamie's name. Jamie felt an aftershock of her own orgasms and wondered how long it had been since she'd been this aroused in a single night. She was shaking and sweating. After a moment, the radio signal fell silent. She lifted her head and pushed her hair out of her face.

"Are you still there?" Jamie asked.

"Mm-hmm," Noa said. "That was amazing."

Noa said, "It was."

They lapsed into silence again. Jamie laughed. "I feel like I just actually got laid."

"Me too."

Jamie looked at her wrist and realized her watch was still upstairs. "I don't know what time it is. How much longer do we have?"

Noa spun to see the chronometer. "We have a little time."

"Would it be okay if we just lay here and listened to each other breathe again?"

"I was going to suggest the same thing. Is that cot still out there?"

Jamie looked down at it. "Yeah."

"I'm getting in my nook. Right side."

Jamie lay down on her left arm. "Left side."

Noa said, "Close your eyes, Lighthouse." Jamie did as she was told. "I'm there with you. We're lying in bed together. We just had the most amazing sex, and now we're exhausted. Sharing each other's air. Making each other warm on top of our tangled sheets. I'm stroking your hair. My thigh is between yours. I'm having trouble keeping my eyes open, but I don't want to stop looking at you."

"I kiss you," Jamie whispered.

"I move my hand to the back of your head."

"My tongue is in your mouth... fuck... do we have time~"

Noa chuckled. "Sorry, no."

Jamie said, "I can't believe we just did this."

"Do you wish we hadn't?"

"Absolutely fucking not."

Noa smiled and bit down on her thumbnail. "Good. When we say goodnight, I want you to turn off the radio, go into your house, and get in bed. Naked, on top of the sheets, just like you said. I'm going to give you... five minutes?"

Jamie said, "Okay."

"In five minutes, I'm going to say goodnight to you."

"Okay," Jamie said again. "I'll see you tomorrow? For our goodnight before the long... fuck! Fuck, tomorrow is our last night."

Noa shushed her. "It's okay. It's just a week. We can make it through."

Jamie kept her eyes closed. "Can we?"

"After what we just did, I'm going to need a week just to recover, sexy."

Jamie laughed. It was a strange, giddy sound, but she didn't hate it. "I'll go to bed every night at ten o'clock, local time. I'll be naked. And I'll think of you."

"I'll think of you, too." Noa swam back to her nook. "Okay, Lighthouse. I'm counting the clock. Five minutes from now, I'll say goodnight to you out loud. You better say it back."

"I will. Until tomorrow."

"Until then."

Jamie got up and reluctantly turned off the radio. She made sure she was decent, turned off the light, and hurried across the lawn. Her property was dark, and only one distant neighbor's porch light was on. There was no one outside that she could see. She was counting in her head as she locked the back door, patted her thigh to get Cisco to follow her, and went upstairs. She doffed the robe and climbed into bed. Cisco curled up at her feet as she watched the alarm clock.

Noa slipped into her sleeping bag still naked. She zipped herself up and settled in, her body still sensitive from her orgasm. When the chronometer ticked over the fifth minute since they parted ways, she craned her neck so she could see Earth through the porthole.

"Sweet dreams, my lighthouse. Goodnight."

"Be safe," Jamie whispered to the moon through her window. "Sleep well, my woman in the stars." She chuckled, put a hand over her face, and pressed her foot against the soft weight of Cisco's back. He shifted and rolled over to lay on top of them and she was grateful for the warmth even if it did mean she couldn't get up until he decided to move again. It was fine. She slipped her hands under the pillow and closed her eyes, basking in the afterglow.

Noa listened to the humming of the ship around her, its complex systems on autopilot for the next eight hours. ODIE was a technological marvel, one of the most advanced vessels ever created in human history.

There were scientists who would have given anything just to spend one hour inside of it. She realized she was falling asleep inside what was probably the most important invention of the century. And yet, at that moment, she would have traded it for the bedroom in a turn of the last century farmhouse somewhere in central Indiana.

Jamie and Noa fell asleep within minutes of each other, though there was no way for either of them to know that. There was also no way for either of them to know that, at several points in the evening, they both reached out into the empty space beside them in search of something that was infinitely farther away than either could reach.

// MISSION DAY 233 - AUTUMN //

NOA SLEPT with her earpiece in, the small wire of the microphone leading along her jaw toward her mouth. She woke at 0650 and blinked at the blinking lights above her head. Moments later she heard a burst of static. She smiled drowsily as she pictured Jamie on the little cot in her barn, hair mussed from sleep, reaching up to turn on the radio with her eyes closed. Her glasses were probably on the edge of the table with the book she read before going to sleep. The image formed in Noa's mind in the few seconds it took for Jamie to speak.

"Mm. Morning."

"Hi there." Noa's voice was rough. She hadn't taken a drink of water yet. She pushed her hands into her hair, careful not to disturb her radio. "How'd you sleep?"

Jamie shifted on the cot. Its metal skeleton groaned and protested and her pajamas rasped against the blanket. "Not very well. This cot isn't very comfortable."

"I'm sorry."

"S'okay," Jamie said. "It's worth it to wake up with you."

Noa brushed the back of her hand over her cheek. It had been ten days since they spoke, since the two month anniversary of 'sleeping together' for the first time. The absences were rougher now than they'd been at the beginning, when Jamie was just a friendly voice at the other end of the line. Now they were... what? Lovers? They'd certainly been intimate with each other enough times to qualify for that title, but they hadn't seen each other naked. They hadn't actually even touched.

It had been four and a half months since Noa first heard Jamie's voice over the radio. Now she felt as if they knew each other better than any of her past girlfriends. She could picture Jamie's house with crystal clarity. Jamie could tell when Noa was irritated or just tired based on the tone of her voice. And now, over the past ten weeks, they'd learned about each other in a whole new way.

"How long do you have before they start bugging you about work?" Jamie asked.

"Only about twenty minutes," Noa said. "Not enough time for anything fun."

Jamie murmured, "Too bad. I'm going to go into the house... draw a nice warm bath..."

"Stop!"

"Slide my foot into the bubbles..."

"Sto-op!" Noa laughed, covering her face. "You are such a bad person. I'm not going to the morning briefing wet and frustrated."

Jamie laughed. "I can't help it. I've missed you."

Noa said, "I missed you, too."

A few days ago, the calendar told her it was the beginning of autumn. It was her absolute favorite season and, since Jamie wasn't around, she asked Enver to describe his drive to work. She could tell he had been distracted by something on his tablet when he answered. "Hm? It was lovely. Very quick." When she pressed about the change of the seasons, he said, "This is California, Colonel! They don't even know what season it's supposed to be. It's sun season."

Noa said, "What does it look like there?"

"Oh, Noa," Jamie said, "it's gorgeous. I've been writing things down all week. Right now, one of my neighbors is out mowing the lawn. I can almost smell the cut grass and... can you hear the hum? That low drone? It's the last gasp of summer. Probably the last time they'll have to mow this year.

"The leaves have started changing color. It started at the end of the street and slowly came west, like there were little elves going to work every night and they slowly made their way from one tree to the next. Right now all the trees are big starbursts of red and orange and yellow. They haven't started falling yet... well, most of them. There are a few small piles. When Cisco chases after birds or rabbits, he hits them they turn into big fiery explosions. I love going for a walk at sunset when there are purples and golds in the sky and reds and yellows in the trees.

"The sunset is like the day is pulling a sheet across everything, and the leaves change color because they're dying, but it's just gorgeous. It's grace in destruction, I think. Accepting the end without sadness or grief. I think I'd like people at my funeral to wear bright colors. Pastels. Make it the brightest celebration going on that day so everyone stops and takes notice."

Noa had tears in her eyes which, of course, couldn't fall without gravity. She blotted them away. "That's a gorgeous thought, Lighthouse. That's what I want at my funeral, too."

Jamie stretched with a grunt. "I thought waking up together was going to be a sweet thing, not talk about death and funerals."

"It's sweet," Noa said. "Trust me. My heart is so full right now."

"I'm glad. Mine is, too."

They remained silent for a while after that. Noa closed her eyes and imagined herself on a cramped, uncomfortable cot in Jamie's barn. She could feel the breeze through the door even though she was certain Jamie would have shut it when she went to bed. She could see the morning sunlight creeping across the lawn. Jamie's weight was against her side, breast on her arm and foot teasing her calf under the blanket.

"Noa," Jamie whispered.

"Mm."

"You fell asleep, babe."

Noa opened her eyes. "Oh. Sorry."

"It's okay. I liked hearing you breathe."

"That sounds so much more romantic than claiming I snore."

"You don't snore. You breathe in very deeply and then let it out like a sigh."

Noa said, "You should hear me when I'm dreaming about you."

Jamie laughed. "I'd love to. But I think our time runs short. You probably have business to attend, and I don't have an outhouse here in the barn, so..."

"Okay. I'll be late tomorrow. Enver wants a progress report and it'll start at 0730 on the dot. I don't know how long it will take, but since our window opens at 0740..."

"So we miss a whole week, then we get twenty minutes, and we miss a whole other day?"

Noa winced. "I'm sorry."

"I'm not blaming... it's not your fault. Well... yes it is. Can't you just hover over Indiana for the rest of the mission and let the junk come to you? You've got magnets on that thing, right? Just kick them up super high so you're pulling all the junk from all over the globe to you."

Noa laughed. "I'll ask Enver about that when we have our meeting."

"You do that." Jamie sat up and kicked the blanket off her legs. She was only wearing a T-shirt since she'd gone to bed thinking of Noa, and she tugged the hem down out of instinctual modesty. "I have an outing planned for today. I'm only doing it so I can tell you about it, but I guess it can wait until the day after tomorrow."

"I'm excited!" Noa said. "Thank you for going to all this trouble for a homesick spacegirl."

"No, it's good for me. It's getting me out of the house, making me look up from the work table. It's a mutually beneficial arrangement, trust me."

Noa said, "Good. I can't wait. But for now, we better get dressed and start the day. It was so nice waking up with you, Jamie."

"I agree. Have a nice day, Noa."

"You too."

Noa disconnected. She left her sleeping nook and brushed her teeth, used the bathroom, and took what counted as a bath in zero-g. She was in the middle of rehydrating her oatmeal when the radio came back to life.

"Astraea to Colonel Laurie. Copy?"

It was so cold and professional compared to how she and Jamie greeted each other. "Loud and clear, Astraea. Who am I speaking to?"

"This is Aaron."

"Hi, Aaron. Tell me something about your day."

He didn't answer for a moment. "Um. It's five in the morning here, ma'am. The day hasn't really begun yet."

Noa shook her head. Why was this concept so difficult for so many supposed geniuses to understand? Why couldn't they conceive of the fact she needed a taste of home, no matter how small it might seem to them?

"Anything, Aaron. What did you do yesterday?"

"I was at work."

Noa strangled the air in front of her. It had been clear for a long time that she would've gone mad without Jamie's input, but never was it more clear than when she was forced to talk with Astraea's little robo-nerds.

"Never mind. Time to go over the schedule and review the past night's progress, yes?"

"That's right." Aaron sounded relieved to be back on-script.

Noa listened with half an ear, all that was required with these monotonous meetings. She thought about everything she'd shared with Jamie over the past couple of months. She wasn't a revelatory type of girlfriend. She was about the physical attraction and the sexual chemistry. There were a few relationships in her life that didn't reach the bedroom inside a week. Jamie was different. Jamie was a friend that she slowly became attracted to without having the benefit of seeing what she looked like or knowing how she was in bed. Not that she would be a disappointment sexually, if her radio prowess was any indication.

They'd spoken about the likelihood of meeting in person and whether or not their relationship would revert to friendship or if they would end up in bed together immediately. Jamie didn't see any reason to go through the motions of dating when, by that point, they would have spent over a year talking with each other.

"Besides," Jamie had said, "I don't know if I could restrain myself. Unless you have some kind of weird sexual things you need to ease me into."

"Weird sexual things?"

"Yeah, you know. Kinks, fetishes. The garnishes that make sex with a new person so exciting."

Noa had thought hard on that. "I can't think of... oh."

"Ooh, she's got one."

"No, I don't... not really... I... there's a thing I do when I get back from space, and I suppose it might be seen as kinky."

Jamie said, "Do tell."

"You don't realize how strange it is to go from gravity to weightlessness and then back to gravity. It screws you up inside, mentally. You forget how gravity works. It sounds bonkers, but it's true." Jamie had laughed at the word 'bonkers.' "It's especially bad when I sleep. I won't be used to a bed, or tossing and turning. There's a very real chance I'll just fling myself off onto the floor. When I got back last time, I was so terrified of smashing my head on the nightstand that I slept at the foot of the bed. So... when I get back to Earth, at least for the first few weeks, I... I want to..."

"You want me to tie you to the bed?" Jamie asked.

Noa blushed. "Maybe."

Jamie's breath was shaky. "That seems doable."

"Last time, eventually I got down to a surfboard strap attached to the bedframe. It had a leather cuff that I could put around my ankle. It was enough for me to feel grounded."

"Leather ankle cuff," Jamie repeated.

Noa had coyly asked, "Jamie, are you touching yourself?"

"Yes, Colonel."

"Colonel?" Aaron said.

Noa snapped out of her memory and backed up over the past few minutes to remember what Aaron had just asked her. The screen she was facing had a checklist, and she skimmed the last entry. "That looks good to me. What does it look like on satellite?"

// MISSION DAY 235 - AUTUMN, CONTINUED //

"THE RANCH is this big sprawling place next to a lake. It looks like something out of a picture book. Huge red building with iron fencing all around it."

Noa was wearing an Astraea T-shirt and shorts. She was sitting cross-legged above her dinner table with her eyes closed to better picture what Jamie was describing to her.

"I went really early. They told me to get there about half an hour early so I could get to know the horse first. He was huge... black, with white coloring on his face and chest. They said his name was Peter Pan, but I could call him Pete. So I fed him a carrot and let him get used to me for a little while before they took me out to this big field where we could follow a big track. I got up on the first try, thank you very much, and after that I was trying very hard not to fall off. Riding a horse is a lot more work than people think. You have to hold tight with your legs, keep your back straight and your shoulders square. You're not just latching on and letting it carry you somewhere, you're guiding it. You're working together.

"I thought it must be like you and the ODIE. You're not just sitting up there in a seat, the ship is part of you. And vice versa. It keeps you alive and you guide it on its journey. But I'm getting off track. Uh... I was on the horse. I think they gave me the gentlest horse they had, because he was extremely good-natured and very chill. When we got comfortable with each other, he picked up the pace a little bit so I could feel the wind on my face."

Noa imagined the wind, the movement of her body as the horse built up to a slow trot. She could almost feel the pull of gravity on her shoulders.

"Afterward," Jamie continued, "my back hurt like hell. My body wasn't used to such rigid posture and the jostling that came with it."

"Did you soak in a long bath?"

Jamie hesitated. "Yes... but I thought this wasn't supposed to be a dirty conversation."

Noa grinned. "I never agreed to that."

"You're such a bad influence. I'm the one who can just shut the door until I'm ready to face society. What if there's an emergency and you have your hand down your panties?"

Noa laughed and rolled backward. "I can multitask."

Jamie sighed wearily. "Yes, I took a bath. Pervert. I got myself all nice and soapy. And I lifted my leg up out of the water and watched the bubbles trail all the way down~"

"Wait, wait, wait," Noa said, "stop, you called my bluff. I have to talk with Enver in forty-five minutes and I don't want him noticing if I'm out of breath."

"You sure? I don't want to leave you hanging."

Noa said, "I'm sure. So what do you have on tap today?"

Jamie put her feet up on the table. "Work. I have a hope chest I'm making for a woman in town. She's going to give it to her daughter."

"What's a hope chest?"

"It's like a big cabinet where unmarried women keep things while they wait to find a husband. It's pretty archaic, but this is Indiana. Some people still need to be reminded women have the right to own property and own a business."

Noa said, "Or date another woman."

"Even if that woman is in outer space."

"Conservatives would probably be fine with our relationship, actually," Noa said. "No actual touching, no lustful gazes."

Jamie said, "I gaze lustfully at you."

"Oh?"

"I have your picture hanging on the wall."

Noa grinned. "Really?"

"Mm-hmm."

"Is it a sexy one?"

Jamie grinned. "I think it's extremely sexy. It's your official NASA profile shot. I would look for something sexier, but I have to print them off the library computer and I don't want to give the poor librarian a heart attack."

Noa said, "That's too bad. I have some pretty naughty shots out there. I don't think you'd find them online, though. I hope not, anyway. The only people who have them are..." Her voice trailed off as a thought occurred to her. "Hey, do you have your phone?"

"Yeah."

"Dial this number."

"Wait, now?"

"Yes now." She gave Jamie the number. "When she answers, put it on speaker so I can hear her."

Jamie listened to the buzz of the other phone ringing. There was a chance whoever she was calling would be at work or still asleep, depending on the time zone. She was about to say as much when the buzz stopped and she heard someone fumbling. She held the phone up in front of herself with the microphone in her other hand. She aimed the faces at each other.

"This is Kelly Bennett."

"Uh," Jamie said. "Uh, hi. You don't know me..."

Noa said, "Kelly? Can you hear me?"

"Noa?! I thought you were up in space."

"I am. It's a long story. The woman on the phone is Jamie Faris. Say hello, Jamie."

Jamie said, "Uh. Hi."

Noa said, "Jamie and I have become really close lately. Extremely close.."

Kelly's voice changed, more teasing. "Oh, I see. Goddamn, woman. They lock you in a tin can, shoot you into outer space, and you *still* manage to get lucky."

Noa laughed. Jamie blushed and felt the urge to put down the phone and run.

"Unfortunately," Noa continued, "I'm all the way up here, so I can't tease her the way I normally would when I flirt with someone. Do you know what I mean?"

Kelly's throaty laugh terrified Jamie. "I most certainly do. What can I do to help?"

"Do you still have the files I sent you?"

"Oh, boy, do I."

Jamie said, "Files...?"

Noa ignored her. "Put them on a DVD and mail them to Jamie."

"Are you sure?"

"A hundred percent. Jamie, do you have a DVD player?"

Jamie said, "Yes."

"Fantastic."

"I'll send everything I have. I can email them~"

Noa said, "She doesn't have a computer," at the same time Jamie started saying her email address. Jamie said, "Well, I have email."

"Oh. Right. Email, then."

Jamie recited her email address, then told this absolute stranger her mailing address so the mysterious DVD could be put in the mail.

"I got it," Kelly said. "I'll send them when I get home. Piece of advice, Miss Jamie. Wait until you're alone to open them. I've got to go. Noa, I want coffee when you get home."

Noa said, "We'll find a time. I've got to make a stop in Indiana first."

Jamie's ears burned. Noa and Kelly said goodbye, and Jamie hung up. "What did you just get me into?"

"Nothing, Lighthouse. We'll talk about it when you get the files." Jamie held back a sigh, chewing on her lower lip. Noa was able to read something in the silence. "Is everything okay? Should I not have told her about us?"

"No, that's fine. I'm actually thrilled someone knows how much you mean to me. But whatever these files are, it just imbalances us more. I can see you any time I want. I can go to the library and watch a video of you. But you don't even know what I look like. It's not fair to you."

"I guess not." Noa looked out the window. "I'd love to have a picture of you up here. I'd kiss it every night before I went to bed. But it's too late."

Jamie frowned. "What do you mean? Too late for what?"

"I'll never know if you're beautiful, objectively speaking. All I'll know when I see you is that you're the woman who has spent the last few months sharing the world with me. You'll be the woman who reminds me that I'm a human being when I start to feel like I'm just one more piece of machinery or a face on someone's screen. Are you worried I won't think you're pretty? Jamie, whatever you look like, you're the most beautiful woman I've ever known."

Jamie had tears in her eyes when Noa stopped speaking.

"Jamie? Honey, we're about to leave the window."

"Don't say it back."

"Don't say~"

"I love you," Jamie said. "Say it whenever you're ready, I just... I had to say it now. After that, what else could I say?"

Noa had one hand fisted against her chest. "I usually try to run when someone says that to me."

"Well, you kind of are running away. In the next couple of seconds, anyway."

"But I'll be back. Tomorrow. And the next day, and the next day, and..."

"I'll be here waiting," Jamie said. "Have a good day, Noa."

Jamie waited for a response, but the only thing that came over the radio was static. There was always something tragic about that sound. She hated it. The silent hiss of an open line that indicated ODIE had moved out of range. Soon it would be replaced with a rush of white noise that reminded of her a faucet left running in another room. She kissed her fingers and pressed them against the face of the radio. "See you tomorrow, Colonel."

// MISSION DAY 242 - AUTUMN, CONCLUDED //

THE MAIL came just after eleven. There was a padded envelope on the bottom of the stack with a return address in Seattle. KELLY BENNETT. Jamie was breathless as she walked back up the long driveway back to the house. Noa would be in range at 1430 - Jamie was getting very good at military time - which gave her plenty of time to investigate whatever she'd been sent. The envelope was bigger than she expected, and seemed to have a lot more than just a DVD inside. She refilled Cisco's food and water to ensure she would be left alone and then went upstairs. She closed the bedroom door and sat on the edge of her bed. Her breathing was shallow and her hands were shaking at what she was about to see.

First, a piece of notebook paper. She unfolded it and read the short note Kelly had included. "Hello, Jamie! Noa and I are very close friends-with-benefits. If she believes you can be trusted with this stuff, then I'm willing to send it. I thought you might appreciate printouts instead of jpgs on the computer screen. Enjoy."

Jamie put aside the DVD case and withdrew the 8x10 photographs. There were seven of them and Jamie took her time examining each one before moving on to the next.

One: Noa sitting in a wingback chair which makes her look tiny. She's in shorts and a tank top, long legs stretched out and balanced on top of an ottoman. She's wearing socks but no shoes. Her hair is a tangled mess. She's squeezing her eyes shut and pursing her lips in fake irritation at whoever is snapping the picture. She has a cup of coffee in one hand, the middle finger of her other hand extended.

Two: Noa in bed, lying on her stomach and hugging a pillow. She's very obviously naked, but nothing is showing. There are bags under her eyes. She's smiling in an unfocused way that indicates she was asleep seconds before the picture was snapped. Her right arm is bent over the top of her head.

Three: Noa naked. Undressed. Standing starkers in the doorway of a bathroom. Her hair is hidden by a towel, a toothbrush sticking out of her mouth, lips pinched shut around it but still curled in a smile. She is holding open her towel with her hip cocked to the side, flashing the camera with her right leg extended out to one side. The bathroom backlit her slightly, putting some of the detail in shadow, but it was still lit well enough to see details. Not that Jamie looked for details. She ignored the lean stomach, the subtle curve of her hips, the shape of her breasts with their small pink nipples. Or maybe they weren't pink. It was hard to tell in the lighting. Not that Jamie looked very hard.

Except she did look at that picture longer than the first two combined. Finally she shuffled it out of sight and moved on.

Four: Noa naked again, this time lying on her side. She is looking into the lens. The angle of her arm implies she took the picture herself, arching her back so her breasts are in the shot. She's smiling, biting her lip, eyebrow arched mischievously. The nipples were definitely pink.

Jamie wondered who the origin recipients of these pictures might be. Were they sent directly to Kelly? Had Noa taken them for herself and then just decided to share them with women she slept with? And who was behind the camera? Where were those people, who had been fortunate enough to share a room with a naked and playful Noa Laurie? Jamie found herself irrationally jealous of these anonymous photographers.

Five: Another selfie, an overhead shot that shows the whole length of her body. Her hips are twisted, one knee bent, to coyly cover her crotch. Her breasts are on display again. Her eyebrow is arched and her head tilted to the side as if waiting for judgment on the picture.

Jamie licked her lips. "I approve, Stargirl," she whispered as she shuffled to...

Six: Noa on a bed in a T-shirt, bare legs stretched out. Her hair is shockingly short, a mannish cut, which exposes her long neck. The collar of the shirt is wide enough that it has fallen to expose her shoulder. Her mouth is open and her tongue is touching the corner of her mouth. She looks young enough to be in college or maybe the Air Force Academy. There's a faded number 7 on the shirt.

Seven: Obviously drunk, leaning against a wall, smiling defiantly at the camera through her combed-forward hair. She's wearing a black T-shirt over ripped jeans. She's holding up both hands at chest height. The first two fingers of her right hand are curled around her thumb.

Her left thumb and forefinger are making an L shape.

Jamie went through the photos again, looking at each one longer every time. It took her until the second look before she realized the gestures in the final picture was Sign for N-L: Noa's initials. She laughed softly and shook her head.

"Colonel, you are adorable."

She finally put aside the pictures and picked up the DVD. The pictures were one thing, but the disc implied video. Jamie didn't know if she was prepared for that. Still, she went to the TV and put it in the machine. She turned on the screen and went back to the bed with the remote. She sat perched on the edge of the mattress. She stared at the blue screen for a full thirty seconds before she hit play.

A shaky image of a wide hallway with red and gold carpeting, camera aimed down before being brought up. A woman (obvious Noa) walking ahead of the cameraperson. She was wearing her dress blues, her hair up, low-heeled pumps hanging from the first two fingers of her left hand. She was swaying slightly and veered off-course to bump against the wall when she arrived at the recessed nook of her hotel room door. She took out her key card and fumbled to get it turned correctly. She looked over her shoulder.

"I'm going to order~" She grinned and her posture changed. She held up her right hand to partially cover her face. "What the hell are you doing? Stop that."

"Filming you," an anonymous woman said. She sounded sort of like Kelly, but it was difficult for Jamie to be sure. She'd only spoken to the woman once a week ago and had forgotten what she sounded like. Whoever it was, Jamie felt an irrational hatred of her.

Noa turned her back and swiped the card. "I'm sure it's riveting footage. Am I even awake right now? I feel like I might be asleep."

"How do you know I don't film you when you're asleep?"

"Creepy, Kel."

She followed Noa into the room and shut the door behind them. Noa walked across the room to the large picture window. She drew the curtains while the other woman turned on the lights. A soft orange-yellow glow came from between the beds and lit up the room. Kelly went to one of the beds and threw herself down on it. Noa dropped her shoes by the bed and let down her hair.

"I'm going to take a shower."

"Wait," Kelly said, "do something."

Noa stood at the foot of the bed. Jamie could see Kelly's legs - bare feet in nude stockings and just a little flare of a dark-colored dress. "What?"

"Come on, Noa. Give me something."

Noa gripped the lapels of her jacket and rocked her hips forward.

"Want me to dance for you?"

Kelly laughed. "Hell yeah, that's what I'm talking about. Take it off, sexy."

Noa threw her head back. "You're crazy. I'm going to go take a shower."

"Well, if you're going to be taking your clothes off anyway..."

Noa pursed her lips. She kept her eyes on Kelly as her hands moved down to the buttons of her jacket. She undid them slowly.

"And you're going to film it, huh? How do I know you won't stick it on the internet?"

"Uh-uh, this is just for me."

Noa turned sideways and slipped the jacket off her shoulders. "What if I want you to show someone?" She folded it carefully and reached so she could drape it respectfully over the back of the chair. Jamie smiled at this bit of formality, an example of Noa following the rules even as she bent them.

"Kinky," Kelly said.

The jacket slipped down Noa's arms. Her uniform blouse was long-sleeved with a small ribbon crossed at the collar. She reached up and undid that, then began working the buttons. She rocked her hips from side to side. Her movements were slow and sleepy, but she was doing her best. Jamie's toes curled in the carpet. She had one hand under her chin, the fingers resting on her lips as she watched this long-ago Noa swaying to unheard music.

"You look hot in that uniform."

"Anyone looks hot in a uniform," Noa countered. She tugged at the material of her blouse, which fell open to reveal a plain white undershirt. "Tailored and well-tended clothes make anyone look good."

Kelly said, "Okay, fine, but you started out from a much higher point than most."

Noa smiled. The blouse was gone now and revealed a white sports bra. She reached behind herself and unzipped her skirt. She swayed and bent at the knee as she pushed it down her legs. When she stood up again, she laughed.

"Is this really doing anything for you?"

"Oh, yeah," Kelly said, "amazing things."

Noa rolled her eyes. Under her sheer stockings were what appeared to be granny panties. Not flattering in the slightest, and in no way sexy. And yet, Jamie found her mouth very dry at the sight of them. She licked her lips and tried to work up some moisture.

"How's this?" Noa did a slow turn. Jamie's finger twitched on the remote, eager to pause, but she wanted to play it straight through the first time. Noa pushed her hair up and held it on top of her head as she planted her feet apart and moved her hips. "Is this what you were hoping for?"

Kelly said, "Uh-huh... getting there..."

Noa crossed her arms and lifted the sports bra off.

"Oh, Jesus," Jamie gasped.

The pictures were one thing. This was something completely different. Jamie had developed such intense tunnel vision that she'd nearly forgotten she wasn't in the room with Noa. In the time it took her to process what she was seeing, Noa had pushed down her stockings and underwear as well. She put a hand on her hip and flipped her hair with the other. She raised her eyebrows and grinned wide.

"Well? Can I please go take my shower now?"

"Mm-hmm," Kelly said. "Then you can come out here and take *my* clothes off."

Noa said, "Now *that* sounds fun."

Jamie turned off the DVD. She put the remote down and picked up the pictures, sorting through them again. She focused on the details: the fray on the collar of the 7 T-shirt. The mess on the bathroom sink. The black smudges under her eyes that were so dark that someone might think she'd gotten punched in the nose the night before. She ran her finger along the curve of Noa's cheek and smiled.

An hour later when she was sitting in the barn, she told Noa that the pictures and video had arrived. Noa laughed an evil laugh, and asked if she enjoyed them.

"Oh, yeah. Hell yes." Jamie felt herself blushing again. "But can I give you a theory about why you wanted me to see them?"

Noa said, "Absolutely."

"I told you that I could see you whenever I wanted. I have your NASA picture hanging over the radio. I watch your TV interviews. But all of that is polished and packaged. You have hair and makeup people and great lighting to make you look like this goddess. You wanted me to see the real you. Messy hair, bleary eyes, and pillow creases on your cheek. You wanted to kick away the pedestal I was trying to put you on so I could see the human."

Noa was hugging herself, shoulder against the hull beside the porthole. She was looking down at Indiana; she could find it very quickly now. "And?"

"If anything, I think you're even more beautiful than before."

Noa smiled and ducked her chin. "That's why it doesn't matter if I have a picture of you. Sloppy or polished, you'll always be my Lighthouse underneath. I don't care about the details, Jamie. I just don't. Are you six feet tall? I'll wear high heels to kiss you. Do you have big ears? Good, because I like nibbling on earlobes when I make love to women."

Jamie shivered at that. She also wished her ears were bigger.

"All I care about is if you have a penis."

"The only one I have is in the nightstand," Jamie said, "and it doesn't have to make an appearance unless you request it."

Noa said, "That's good to know. So... now that we've got that out of the way, what do you want to talk about for the rest of the hour?"

Jamie snorted. "Babe, I just spent a good hour looking at you naked. I want to touch myself."

Noa slid her hand down the front of her shirt. She unfastened her shorts. "Yeah? Tell me what you're wearing."

Jamie looked over her shoulder to make sure the barn door was closed. She scooted closer to the table and moved the microphone closer to her mouth so she could whisper as her other hand pulled at her belt.

// **MISSION DAY 309 - WINTER** //

THE LIGHT seemed smothered, like all of its energy was used up just reaching the window. Jamie knew what she would find when she got up, but she had to look anyway. She tucked her pajama pants into her boots, wrapped a cardigan around her T-shirt and then put a heavy coat over that. She wrapped a scarf around her neck and pulled it up over her face. Cisco followed her to the door but retreated when she opened it to reveal the world outside had disappeared. She took a deep breath of lung-freezing air and stepped into the whiteness.

The snow forced her to march across the lawn. Everything was utterly and completely still. It was like a minimalist painting: the trees just scratches of charcoal amid a few brushstrokes of blue and grey to create the illusion of drifts. Her neighbors' houses looked like igloos. She could see smoke rising from a few chimneys, signs of life, but no one else was attempting to go anywhere today. Their vehicles were cartoonish lumps huddled up against the sides of buildings.

The barn door was iced shut. Jamie grunted and strained her shoulders until she felt it give. The interior was untouched by the snow but full of frigid air.

"Frigidaire," she muttered through chattering teeth. "That's clever."

She sat at the radio and switched it on. She wished she'd brought gloves, because the plastic was almost too cold to touch. She pulled her cardigan sleeve up and hugged herself tightly.

"Noa?" she said in a puff of freezing breath. "Are you there?"

Noa flew to the porthole and looked down at where the east coast of America should have been. A wide, thick blanket of weather hung over them. "Jamie?" she said into the silence. "We're in the window, but... looking down right now, I really doubt we're going to see each other today."

"I hate this weather," Jamie said, chin on her chest, hearing only a white buzz of static on the other end. "It was perfectly clear this whole last week when we slept through all our chances to talk, and now this damn blizzard blows in. It's not fair."

"I've missed you this week." Noa rested her hand against the porthole. "I miss you every week, but it feels like it's getting harder to be away from you. I even thought about talking to Enver about changing my schedule. He wouldn't ask why, he would just make it happen."

Jamie tightened her coat at her collar. "You're probably not even trying to talk to me. You have eyes. You can see that we're not going to get a signal through this mess." She shiver-sighed. "You'd probably laugh at me for being out here."

"And what," Noa said, "You're going to trek through dunes of snow and sit in a sub-zero barn on the off chance you might hear me through the static? So at least I don't have to worry about you accidentally hearing me make a fool of myself."

Jamie cleared her throat.

Noa's breath had condensed on the porthole. She wiped it away.

"Noa?"

"Jamie?"

Noa remained by the porthole. It didn't matter if she was talking to thin air if no one was around to hear her. So she was going to keep talking.

Jamie closed her eyes and shivered. The cold of the microphone was now seeping through the material of her cardigan. She could go back inside and warm up with coffee or cocoa, bury herself in blankets by the heater. But if the clouds cleared and gave them the smallest opening, she didn't want to miss it.

It was just an hour.

// MISSION DAY 323 - WINTER, CONTINUED //

THE PATH between the house and barn was a slog of muddy grass and half-melted drifts. Jamie didn't mind the cold too much anymore but she hated walking through the morass of her front yard. She solved the problem by lining up two parallel lines of 2x4s from her porch to the barn door and then covering those with flat 4x4s to create a walkway. Normally she wouldn't have bothered; mud on her shoes was far from the worst thing in the world. But today was special.

She lit the woodstove so the room could warm up, looked at the clock, and turned on the radio. The room temperature had already gone up at least ten degrees when the radio static faded. Jamie picked up the microphone as Noa's voice came over the line.

"Good evening, Indiana. Anyone down there listening?"

"Good evening to you," Jamie said. They'd long ago discussed the possibility that someone else might happen across the frequency at the right time. It became an even greater concern after their conversations took on a sexual bent. There was nothing either of them could do to prevent eavesdropping, so there was no need to waste time worrying.

"I just finished my dinner," Noa said. "Lentil soup with cornbread and potatoes au gratin."

"Damn, you ate better than I did," Jamie said. "But I'm glad you had a nice meal. It's a very special day."

Noa said, "It is?"

Jamie rested her elbows on the table. "Yeah. I wasn't going to say anything because I didn't want to make it a big deal, but I woke up this morning thinking that it should be a big deal. Or at least I wanted it to be important." She took a deep breath. "It's my birthday."

Noa sat up straighter. "It is?! Happy birthday, Jamie." She shoved off from the bulkhead and swam over to her chart. She picked up the marker and wrote the current date. "I can't believe you weren't going to say anything."

"I never make a big deal about my birthday. It's too close to Christmas. Plus when you tell people, it feels like you're forcing them to say something back or, you know, buy you a gift. I don't like putting the obligation on people."

Noa said, "Well, if you'd told me ahead of time, I definitely would've run out to Target and picked something up for you."

Jamie laughed. "I know, I know. But there is something I wanted to ask of you."

"Name it."

"I want to dance with you."

Noa rested her hand on the wall. "I would love that, Lighthouse, but..."

"I know." Jamie pulled out a square of wood she'd carved for just this occasion. "But I have a plan." A few days earlier she'd carved a space out of the piece that was just the right size to fit the microphone with the side button pressed in. She placed it on the table and fitted the microphone into its niche. "Test, test. Can you hear me?"

She pulled the microphone out and released the button. Noa said, "I can."

"You're not going to be able to say anything while I'm hogging the line on my end. Sorry about that. But if you really want to dance..."

"I do."

"Okay. Stand up. Straight up and down, however you want to do it. Float if you want. Okay. I'm holding down the button now." She put the microphone back in its slot, then put her iPod near it. The song was cued up, a nice romantic instrumental that would give them plenty of time. "I'm going to be standing right in front of the table where the radio is. I have a pillow that I'm going to dance with."

Noa twisted to look into her sleeping nook. She disconnected her sleeping bag and pulled it out, folding it in half so she could hold it tightly.

"Close your eyes," Jamie said. Noa complied.

"I'm in a champagne-colored blouse and a knee-length skirt. Black stockings. Flat heels. I look fucking fantastic because I went all out for you." Noa laughed. "You're in your dress blues. I know you might have preferred something else, something civilian and less flashy, but this is my fantasy and it's my goddamn birthday, and you look hot as hell in that uniform, so that's what you're wearing.

"I'm already at the table when you come in. The lights are low and the piano is playing. You stop short of the table and hold out your hand. Everyone is looking but I don't care. I want them to see I'm with someone like you. So I take your hand. You lead me out onto the dance floor. We're the only ones out here but I don't feel self-conscious. I'm glad because it means I don't have to share this moment with anyone else."

She began to sway. Noa spread her fingers over the soft material of her sleeping bag. With her eyes closed, she could easily imagine it was the silk of Jamie's blouse. She lifted her feet as if she was dancing on a brightly polished dance floor. The restaurant was dark around them, save for a spotlight which just happened to be shining directly down on her. Jamie pressed her cheek against the sorry substitute for Noa's shoulder. She could feel the thick material of the uniform jacket against her skin.

"And I would hold you tight." Jamie's voice was so soft that she wasn't sure the microphone would pick it up. But this wasn't the sort of thing she could say loudly. "I would let you lead me though the song, and I'd never want you to let me go. And I would feel so lucky that someone like you was holding me."

Noa heard all of it. She moved her hand up Jamie's back and tightened her grip, almost convincing herself she could feel the shape of a shoulder under the material. She ran from relationships. Her companions were only there for sexual gratification, easily forgotten or discarded. Her emotions didn't run deep. The movie had to combine four of her real lovers just to create one realistic romantic subplot. She hadn't been ashamed. Her solitude was by design.

Her feet were moving in time to the music. She could almost feel the gravity, her weight returning thanks to the woman in her arms. Her heart swelled and she squeezed her eyes shut tighter to prevent any hint of reality from breaking through and ruining the illusion.

Jamie turned her head and thought she could feel Noa's hair brushing her face. When she tightened her embrace, she felt something more than the shapeless form of the pillow pressing against her chest. She felt curves of Noa's body and the buttons of her uniform jacket. The song faded to a brief silence before the iPod restarted it.

"I hate people making a fuss on my birthday," Jamie said. "I hate when they get dressed up and pay a lot of money for a meal just to honor me. But that's not what this would be. If this was real~"

"It is real," Noa said, even though she knew Jamie couldn't hear her.

"~it would be a celebration of who I feel like when you're with me. It would be in honor of having you in my life, which... I'm sorry, Noa, I don't think you like this sort of sentiment, but I feel like meeting you is a significant life event."

Noa pressed her face into the bag, wiping away the globule of water that had formed over her eyes. She was still blotting it when Jamie's voice became clearer.

"Noa? Are you still there?"

"I'm here, Jamie." She sniffled. "You just made me cry, which is a pretty complicated process without gravity to pull the tears away from my eyes."

"Sorry."

"It's okay." Her face was finally as dry as it was going to get. "That was beautiful, Jamie."

Jamie blushed. "I've been thinking about it all day. And then I made the rig for the microphone this afternoon."

Noa moved to the window and looked out. "You did all that just to dance with me?"

"If I had the material, I would have built a rocket and shot myself up there to dance with you."

Noa rested her cheek against the bulkhead. Jamie put her head down on the cold surface of the table. They stayed like that, eyes closed, listening to the dead air between them.

"It's cold here," Jamie whispered. "Still some dirty snow on the ground. And the sky is grey. Every time I see a cloud on the horizon, I freak out because I'm afraid it will block our signal. You're giving me anxiety, Stargirl."

"Sorry, baby."

Jamie hunched her shoulders. "I like when you call it baby. I've always hated it. But you make it sound sweet."

"Should I swap out Lighthouse?"

"No. I like that, too."

Noa said, "I'll alternate."

"Okay."

"You gave yourself a pretty nice birthday, Lighthouse. Can I tell you what I would do?"

"Please."

Noa drew her knees closer to her chest and wrapped her arms around them. She closed her eyes. "After our lovely dinner and our even lovelier dance, I would have taken you outside under the stars. I would have named the constellations as you nuzzled closer to me because it was cold and you didn't bring a jacket. So I would take off my uniform jacket and drape it over your shoulders. And your lips would be cold, but I'd kiss them until they were warm."

Jamie took a deep breath and let it out slowly.

"Then I would take you home. I'd take you out of those fancy clothes, and I'd lay you on your bed, and I would make love to you for the rest of your birthday."

"That sounds amazing," Jamie said quietly.

"I wish I could be there for it, baby." She looked at the chart. Jamie's next birthday was 364 days away, obviously, and that landed on Mission Day 688. She would still be in space. Her eyes welled up again. "I'm going to miss the next one, too."

Jamie said, "No you won't. You didn't miss this one."

"Yes, I will," Noa said. "Mission Day 688 means I'll be in the window at... five in the morning. We'll both be asleep."

"Oh."

"Yeah," Noa said.

"Fuck." Jamie closed her eyes and pinched the bridge of her nose. "Well, you know, it's a year away. Maybe I'll piss you off by then and we'll stop talking to each other."

Noa laughed. "Maybe so." She looked out the window again. "Last time I was up here, I kept thinking how amazing the Earth is from this vantage point. It's absolutely gorgeous. You think movies and TV prepare you for it, but nothing can. You look down and you see rivers and mountains and weather systems, and you turn your head slightly and you can see the curve of the planet and the atmosphere above it, and you see just how fucking fragile it all is, and everything becomes so precious...

"But now I look down and all I can think is 'that's where Jamie is.'"

Jamie sighed. "I feel the same way about space. Infinite cosmos, but I'm looking for one little shooting star." She lifted her head just enough to balance her chin on one fist. "Day 688 is a year from now... your mission ends around day 700?"

"Seven twenty," Noa said.

"So in a year..."

"Mm-hmm," Noa said. "Am I invited out to Corwin?"

Jamie sat up straight in the chair. "I do have a spare room."

Noa said, "I don't want your spare room, Jamie."

"Oh?"

"Not really. Is that okay?"

"Hell yeah," Jamie said, palms suddenly clammy. She rubbed them on her skirt.

Noa said, "So what else did you get for your birthday?"

"My sister sent me a big box of my favorite candy."

"Your sister... uh..." She squeezed her eyes shut and tried to remember. "God, you told me her name, I know you did. She lives in Cincinnati. Her kid is the one who set up the radio for you..."

Jamie waited a second to see if it would come to her. Finally, she took mercy. "Lily."

"Lily! Right. Lily. That's a sweet gift. Nostalgic and shows that she really took the time to think about what to get you."

"Yeah. She's sweet like that. We've always been close."

Noa looked at the clock. "Tell me about her. We have time left before the window closes. I want to hear about the Faris sisters."

Jamie thought for a moment and then leaned back in her chair. "Okay. When I was fourteen and she was twelve, our classes both went on a field trip to a place called the WonderLab Museum. It was a place where you could learn about science with exhibits and games. Like an arcade that taught you about electrons or whatever..."

Noa smiled and stretched out, hands behind her head, and listened to Jamie's story.

// MISSION DAY 332 - WINTER, CONCLUDED //

JAMIE HAD no idea if she should dress up for the dinner. She started to choose an outfit, then decided to just wear whatever she had on, then finally decided the restaurant was nice enough to require a little effort. She didn't want to treat it like a date and giving Louis any ideas. She finally settled on an outfit that was just nice enough that she wouldn't get turned away at the door but also wouldn't turn any heads. It was a church outfit: a heavy wool skirt and thick stockings to combat the cold, with a silk blouse so that, above the table, she would look professional and fancy. She exchanged her normal glasses for a pair with thin gold frames.

She had to park two blocks away from the restaurant. The sheer number of people struggling to find space was one of the things she hated most about the city. Indianapolis was small compared to most US cities, but it was still too large for her tastes. The traffic, the crowds, the noise, the trash. She hated it. She would have preferred meeting somewhere in Corwin, but Louis had insisted. Considering what she was there to say, she felt she owed him a nice meal.

Winter had rolled back over the city, but Jamie wasn't worried about the clouds since she and Noa were in a "dark week." All of their windows were happening overnight, so a little interference didn't matter. Jamie shivered and ducked her chin into her scarf as she walked from the parking lot.

There were tiny ice crystals in her hair, something she otherwise wouldn't have noticed. Her talks with Noa had made her focus on things like that. Little things, easily overlooked things, things that might have been an irritation without the context of sharing it with her new friend. Now it was a part of life on Earth, a thread to a woman who was starved for reminders no matter how small.

Jamie's boots were set with slush that melted immediately upon entering the restaurant's waiting area. A young Korean couple waiting by the aquarium was unwrapping their child from a pile of winter clothing. The hostess kept checking her phone under the podium but, judging by her body language, she was studying for something instead of just surfing Twitter. Jamie noticed all of them, along with the color of the carpet (red with gold accents) and the light fixtures (faux flames that flickered behind glass sconces).

It was amazing that she and Noa had spent over two hundred hours talking to each other. They discussed life ("I've always dreamed of seeing San Francisco, but the timing was never right or the funds weren't there. So when I got a dog, naming him Cisco seemed like a good reminder.") or the dreams they'd had ("ODIE was slowly filling with money. Coins, quarters and dimes and about a billion pennies, and I was sinking into it. I woke up when it was at my chest."). She was amazed they hadn't run out of things to talk about yet.

The door opened and pushed a wave of cold air inside. Louis' hair and the shoulders of his coat sparkled with water from the misty drizzle that had started falling after Jamie arrived. She stood to greet him and he took it as an invitation to hug her. She tensed and turned her face when he tried to kiss her. His lips glanced off her cheek instead of her mouth. The Korean mother caught the move and cringed, meeting Jamie's eyes with a sympathetic tilt of her head.

"I hope you weren't waiting long," he said.

"It was fine," Jamie said.

The hostess escorted them to a table close enough to the window that they could enjoy the street view, but not so close that they were freezing. Louis pulled out Jamie's seat. She hated the gesture but she didn't want to begin the meal with an argument. If she remained civil, then he would do the same. At least she hoped to god that would be the case. She crossed her fingers as she sat down.

"I'm so glad you called," Louis said as he took his own seat. "I've been thinking about what we're going to do next week."

Jamie was thrown. "Next week?"

"Christmas. I know you like to spend it with your sister's family, so I thought we could bring her out."

"Christmas?" Jamie said.

"Next week."

"Louis, I'm not here to talk about Christmas."

He looked legitimately confused. "We should start planning soon if we're going to be ready. Lily might make other plans, or—"

"I'm..." She shook her head. She'd had a whole speech planned and he had just pulled the rug completely out from under her. "Lily invited me to a play on Christmas."

A wrinkle appeared between his eyebrows. "That's... I figured we would have a big get-together at the house. With the tree and everything. I could hang lights."

"You think I brought you here to get back together?"

"Of course," he said. "With Christmas coming up. It was your birthday recently. I thought you'd finally decided to forgive me."

Jamie put her elbows on the table and put her fingers against her forehead. "Oh, god, I knew this was a bad idea."

"Then why?"

"I'm filing for divorce."

Louis actually flinched. He moved his hands onto the table, started to link his fingers together, then reversed the movement until his hands were back in his lap. He leaned forward. He looked around the restaurant. He had the audacity to look shocked. She finally got tired of waiting for him to find his voice.

"I've moved on."

His gaze snapped back to her. "There's someone else?"

"Yes. She knows about you, about this whole thing, but the longer it drags on, the more dishonest I feel. And I apologize, but I didn't even think about Christmas. I was focusing on the end of the year. I wanted to have this done with by the end of the year."

Louis was looking down now. "'She'?"

"Oh, for god's sake." Jamie closed her eyes and took a measured breath to steady herself. When she felt capable of speaking at a reasonable volume, she looked at him again. "Yes. She."

He took a long, slow breath. "You said the end of the year. You're not going to find anyone to draw up the papers this close to~"

He stopped talking as she lifted her purse and took out the manila envelope that had been delivered a few days earlier. She put it down on the table between them.

"Bruce in town helped me prepare them. No-fault, uncontested petition for the dissolution of marriage. All you have to do is sign and send them back."

Louis stared at the envelope. "This is some low shit, James."

She slapped her hand flat against the table. "Jamie. Jam-*ie*. Do you have a goddamn speech impediment? My fucking name is Jamie, and I've told you every time you call me James lately that I don't like it. Every single time. I hate being called James and you fucking know it."

The restaurant had fallen silent. The waitress was one or two steps away from their table and stood frozen, hands extended with menus which she slowly brought back to her chest. As Jamie's rage deflated, her embarrassment rose up to take its place. She sank back in her seat and tried to dissolve into it. The waitress cautiously closed the distance and put the menus down on top of the divorce papers.

"I'll... just leave these here," she said quietly.

Jamie watched her go, then stood up. "I'm actually not very hungry. Sign the papers, Louis. Send them to Bruce. It's the only thing left to do in this marriage." She took out her wallet and dropped a twenty on her empty plate. She hadn't ordered anything, but Louis might stay to eat and he was a lousy tipper. She also felt as if she was making amends for the blow-up. "Goodbye, Louis."

She kept her eye on the exit, avoiding the inevitable stares she was getting from the other patrons. She escaped out into the night and took a deep breath of fresh air. She didn't stop moving until she was at the corner. The only thing worse than causing a scene was the thought of everyone in the restaurant looking out the window and gawking at her. When she was out of sight, she pressed her back against the brick wall and tilted her head back.

Light pollution turned the sky into a faded velvet color, with only a few scattered stars visible. Just one more reason to hate the city, she decided. She walked the rest of the way to the parking lot and retrieved her truck. She barely noticed the bright and garish trappings of civilization as she sped past. City blocks gave way to freeways and overpasses, then apartment buildings and suburbs. There was still too much light and noise from traffic and streetlights, so she drove on.

Finally she reached houses on property that was measured in acres, wide open spaces like Corwin. She slowed down until her road was surrounded by the huge expanse of a wheat field. She pulled off on the next dirt road she found and drove until she was well away from the pavement. She parked and turned off her headlights. Up ahead she could see the tree line marking the edge of the field.

Jamie got out of the truck and walked out behind it. Her breath appeared in front of her, but she didn't care. She climbed into the bed of the truck and laid flat, arms out to either side of her. Now all she could see was a sky which was no longer obscured by a dome of electric light. She could see stars. She could see the moon hanging low off to the east. The world seemed to be a single flat plate underneath a twinkling sheet. Logically she knew that Noa was nowhere near Indiana, but she was looking up into space and space was where Noa lived.

"I know I'm supposed to wish on a star," she whispered, "but if it's all right, I'm just going to wish on you. So I wish for Louis to not drag this out. I hope that when I see you in a few days, I can tell you that I'm officially divorced." She closed her eyes and whispered, "Star light, star bright, wish I may." She opened her eyes and listened to the wind. Traffic was still audible in the distance but it was easy to tune that out.

She almost felt like she was actually drifting out in space waiting for ODIE to zip past her. Maybe if she held out her hand at just the right moment, she could grab hold and slip inside.

"You've been up there almost a year, Stargirl," Jamie whispered. "How much space junk could be left? Come home, baby. I want you here with me."

Jamie put her hands on her chest, stared up into the sky, and floated there for a while.

// MISSION DAY 341 - CHRISTMAS DAY //

"YOU'RE SITTING on the floor in front of the couch. Still in your pajamas~"

"Just a T-shirt over boxer shorts," Noa said.

"Right. I come in from the kitchen with two cups of cocoa. I'm wearing a full pajama set, because I'm a dork like that. Green and red plaid."

Noa said, "And big fluffy rocket ship slippers."

Jamie laughed. "Do they make those?"

"Mm-hmm. I'm going to buy you a pair."

"Sounds good to me."

Noa was mimicking the posture Jamie had given her in the fantasy, sitting with her back against the wall with her legs floating out in front of her. "What next?"

"I bring you the cocoa and bend down to kiss you. You put your hand on my hip and pull me down. I'm forced to straddle you."

"Forced?" Noa said.

"Completely against my will."

"Sorry."

"I'll forgive you." She inhaled through her nose, eyes closed as she imagined the scene. She had one leg crossed over the other, her hand on the lower thigh. The woodstove had made the barn toasty warm. "I kiss you harder."

"My hand slides to your ass. I pull you closer to me."

"Mm," Jamie purred and rolled her neck. "I let my hand move up your leg under your shirt. Your skin is so warm."

Noa's fingers tensed. "Do we have time to fool around?"

Jamie's eyes were still closed. "Yeah."

Noa took a deep breath. Noa shifted on her seat. Both had their eyes closed, giving themselves over completely to the fantasy scenario, whispering details to each other over the radio waves. Anything they didn't explicitly say was easily inferred by the other. They had done this enough times they were able to fill in the blanks. So they could see...

Noa put down her cocoa so both hands would be free. Jamie leaned back, her lips parted and inviting Noa to close the distance between them. The next kiss was just a glance, followed by a touch of Noa's tongue. Jamie also put down her cup and reached up into Noa's hair. It was unwashed and uncombed, a wild tangle, and Jamie threaded her fingers through it. Jamie's pajama top had big buttons that Noa could easily twist and release without looking.

"Take it off of me," Jamie whispered.

Noa complied, moving her lips down to kiss Jamie's neck as the pajama was slipped off. Jamie tossed it aside. The living room was bright with morning sun glistening on the three-day old snow. The Christmas tree sparkled behind Jamie as Noa kissed a path down her chest, to her nipple. She took it into her mouth and sucked softly, making Jamie arch her back and cry out. She hitched her lower body forward, repositioning herself even as she tried to rub herself against Noa.

"Baby," Noa whispered.

"Stargirl..."

The hand that pushed into Jamie's pajama pants belonged to Noa. It was her fingers that found she wasn't wearing underwear, that cupped her and made her cry out in pleasure. Noa's lips returned to Jamie's neck and worked a spot that she knew was a trigger. Her tongue pressed and circled and Jamie began moving her hips faster. Noa's hand in the small of Jamie's back tightened, guiding her.

Noa rolled her head back against the couch, eyes open as much as she could manage. She looked at Jamie and smiled as her fingers rubbed her.

"Fuck, I can see you," Noa said.

Jamie opened her eyes and looked down with a smile. Her cheeks were flush. "I can see you, too." She moved her hand under Noa's shirt, down to her shorts, and began touching her through the thin material. "I see you moaning when I do that..."

Noa cupped Jamie's cheek –

("That's three hands, baby," gasped breathlessly

"Fuck... th-the hand from... from your back...")

Noa cupped Jamie's cheek. She extended her thumb to brush over Jamie's bottom lip. Jamie took it into her mouth and held it with her teeth. Jamie came first, then redoubled her vocal efforts telling Noa what she wanted to do. How she would do it, how it would feel and what she would taste, and Noa surrendered to the assault without much of a fight.

Noa slumped against the wall and opened her eyes. She was on the ship, still. She was breathing hard, her slacks bunched around her knees with her underwear. Jamie lifted her butt off the seat cushion and tugged her pajamas back up. Her mouth was dry so she reached for the glass of water next to the radio. She drank half of it in one swallow.

"Merry fucking Christmas," Noa said.

Jamie put her wrist against her mouth to keep from spitting. "Well, I couldn't run out to Target and get you something special, so I gave you what I could."

"You can throw out the receipt."

"I'm very glad you approve, Stargirl."

Noa grunted softly. "God, when you call me Stargirl while we're fucking... I get chills, Lighthouse."

"Well, same when you call me 'baby.'"

They were silent for a moment. Jamie knew Noa was suffering the same withdrawal she was. The fantasy faded and now they were reminded that they couldn't touch, wouldn't touch for at least another year. Her shoulders trembled with aftershocks from her orgasm. She reached up and raked her fingers down the side of her neck, which made the tremors worse, but it felt good. She sighed and put her head down on the table.

"I put my head down. Would you play with my hair?"

"Sure."

Jamie smiled. "I have to leave as soon as the window closes. I'm going to see a play with my sister and her family."

"That sounds fun."

"Yeah. I'm going to tell her about you."

Noa sat up straighter. "Really?"

"Is that okay?"

"I'm... yes. I'm a little worried she'll think you're crazy, though."

Jamie said, "If I have to drag her back here so you can say hello, then I will. I just want someone to know about you. Someone who will be happy for me."

Noa said, "You could always record me. Do you have your phone?"

"Yes." Jamie was already fumbling to get it out of her pocket. She scrolled through looking for the voice recorder app. "You really are a genius, aren't you? All this time I could have recorded you talking dirty to me for those long weeks when you're not in range."

"We can record some stuff later. For now, let me say hi to your sister. Lily, right?"

"Lily. Yeah." She aimed the microphone at her screen, then hit play. "Okay, go."

Noa said, "Hi, Lily. This is Colonel Noa Laurie, and I'm currently in orbit above Indiana in an experimental spacecraft called ODIE. I've been talking to your sister for about two hundred and fifty days, and we've... we're, uh... how much detail should I go into here?"

Jamie blushed. "We've gotten very close."

"Hell yes, we have," Noa said. "Your sister is extremely special to me, and she wants you to know that. I look forward to meeting you when the mission ends and I get to come home. Until then, merry Christmas and happy new year. Give your sister a big, big hug since I can't."

"Aw, you're so sweet." Jamie stopped the recording. "She's going to go crazy."

Noa smiled, but she felt bad about the message. It would've been the perfect time to tell Jamie she loved her. But a lifetime of avoiding that milestone made her antsy about throwing it out. If she was going to say it, she wanted to say it at the perfect time. Somehow she didn't think the time would ever be right over the radio. She wanted to say it to Jamie's face, whisper it in her ear, feel her shiver when she heard the words for the first time. But then she would have to wait a whole year to say it. She didn't know if she would be able to hold off that long. And she would hate for the first time to be an accident.

"Noa? Are you still there?"

"Mm-hmm. Just basking in the afterglow."

Jamie chuckled. "I look forward to being with you in a real bed so I can just sprawl. Maybe burrow into some blankets if it's a cold day."

Noa thought about that. Every conversation they had required Jamie to go out into the barn and sit at a table for an hour no matter what the weather was like. That kind of dedication was astounding and humbling to her.

"I want to be completely sincere for a second."

Jamie sat up. "Okay. No dumb jokes, I promise."

Noa looked down. "Having you here, talking with you, these long conversations about nothing... and the conversations about ourselves, they're keeping me sane. Being up here is like being locked in a cage. I thought I had trained and prepared for that. But I haven't seen a human face in a year. I haven't shaken a hand or gotten a hug. But every time this radio buzzes and I hear your voice on the other end, I feel like I'm a real person. I'm not just a brain or a set of hands that knows which buttons to press. Thank you for this year, Jamie. Thank you for getting me through it."

Jamie wiped her hands under her glasses. "Wow. Well. First of all, you're very welcome. It would've been a pretty rough and lonely year for me, too. Without you, I..." She wrinkled her brow. "Without you, I might have taken Louis back. It would've been the path of least resistance. It would've been the easy and safe route. God, I didn't even realize you were giving me that strength. I owe you even more than I realized."

"I'm happy to have helped."

An alarm chimed. Jamie's watch beeped.

"Two minute warning," Jamie said. "There's so much I want to say to you."

"There's always tomorrow."

Jamie said, "Yeah, and tomorrow will only be an hour. And the next hour and the next hour. I want a whole day with you. An afternoon. I want a silence with you that lasts a whole hour without thinking I wasted a day. I want to fall asleep looking at you and I want you to be there when I wake up again. I want... I want to spend a whole hour on foreplay before I even start to think about letting you come. I want days with you. Long lazy weekends." She put her hand in her hair.

"I'm really smart," Noa said. "I can figure out a way to screw up the ship in a way that doesn't kill me but forces the end of the mission."

Jamie laughed. "Don't make light of my heartfelt sappiness."

Noa said, "I'm being dead serious. I couldn't care less about Mars or the future of space travel right now."

"Well, if you wanted to come down out of the sky and give me a Christmas present, you should have done it last night. Can you imagine all the internet videos saying people had finally seen Santa Claus? You could have been even more famous than you already are." She inhaled slowly. "Don't blow up the ship. What you're doing is important. The problems of two people don't amount to a hill of beans, or whatever that line is."

"If you change your mind..."

"I'll let you know." She blinked wetness away from her eyes. "See you tomorrow, Noa."

"Tomorrow. Have a merry Chzzzzsss..."

Jamie flinched. It never got easier to say goodbye, or to hear that signal cut out. She felt it in her chest, like the muscles in the center of her chest flexed against her heart. She put her hand on top of the radio and let it rest there for a moment just to be sure the signal was really lost. When the barn had been silent for a full minute, she turned off the radio and slipped the microphone into its cradle. She wiped away the last of her tears and took a deep breath, preparing herself for the rest of the holiday. A play! With her sister's family, whom she adored! She really shouldn't have to psych herself up for something so great. But after the morning she just had with Noa, anything else just paled by comparison.

// MISSION DAY 341 - CHRISTMAS DAY, CONTINUED //

LILY HELD the phone to her ear with one hand, using her left hand to plug the other ear as she listened to the message. She looked up at Jamie with an incredulous smile as she listened. They were standing on the street outside the theater. Lily's husband was inside with their kids. A line of cars stood between them and the street, and crowds of people were being corralled toward the entrance. Jamie had asked to stay outside to talk with her sister but also so she could have a few minutes of fresh air and relative space before she went inside with hundreds of other people. She also wanted to take note of the city's details so she could tell Noa when they talked tomorrow.

Lily handed the phone back. "Okay."

"So?" Jamie prompted.

"I guess I'm confused. This is the woman you were seeing the last time we had lunch?"

Jamie nodded. "We talk every time she's in range. It's only an hour per day, but it's been so amazing. We share everything."

"But it's not real."

"That's what people used to say about internet friendships and online dating. Just because we don't talk face-to-face or we didn't meet in a bar, it's somehow less authentic?"

Lily said, "But you met by *magic*."

"I didn't say magic! I said it was some fluke of my radio and her technology that... look, her ship has communication technology that lets her talk to her bosses no matter where she is in orbit. And somehow when she's over Indiana and my radio is on the right frequency, we can talk to each other."

"For an hour every day."

"Yes."

Lily laughed and looked down the street. "I don't want to belittle this, Jamie, but come on. You're not actually dating her."

Jamie looked down at her phone. "Because we don't go out to dinner together? Because we don't hold hands? I feel closer to her than I've ever felt with Louis."

"Because you only talk to her an hour per day! You don't have a chance to get sick or bored with each other. When you're mad, you can just turn off the radio and walk away. You don't have to work out your issues, you don't have good times and bad, you just have one hour per day, perfectly regulated. I'm sure that's nice and everything, but it's not a real relationship. You said she doesn't even know what you look like."

"It doesn't matter."

"Of course it matters," Lily said. "It might sound shallow, but it matters. And the first kiss matters. And the first time you go to bed together. None of which you've done."

"We've..." Jamie looked at the crowd around her and lowered her voice. "We've done things. We did things this morning."

Lily said, "That's great, Jamie, it's fantastic. But it's not the real thing."

Jamie shoved her phone into her jacket pocket. She refused to look at Lily. "I came here tonight ready to tell you about the most important relationship in my life, because no one knows about her, and I couldn't bear you *not* knowing about her anymore, and you treat me like a teenager who doesn't know how she really feels. And you know, I know how I feel, and I don't feel like seeing a play with you tonight. Tell them I'm sorry."

She started to walk away. Lily pushed away from the wall and gave chase. "Jamie, wait. Just wait."

"Enjoy the show."

Lily grabbed Jamie's elbow and stopped her. "Will you just stop walking for a second? God. Look at me." Jamie glared down the street. "Damn it, look at me."

Jamie turned her head and locked her anger on Lily.

"What's her name?"

"Noa."

"What is it?"

"*Noa.*" The tension faded from Jamie's shoulders. "Noa Laurie. Colonel Noa Laurie. Stargirl." She ducked her chin.

"Wow. As pissed off as you are at me, you still smiled when you said her name." It was her turn to look sheepish. "You know, the entire time you were dating Louis, you never smiled when you said his name.

Or maybe you did, just... not like that. And maybe I'm wrong. Maybe I'm full of shit. When you think about it, the fact you've kept up this conversation for almost a year says a lot. And she sounds pretty enamored with you, too."

Jamie said, "The things she says to me. No one has ever made me feel as special as she does. She changed how I think about my life. I thought I was happy with Louis when we obviously weren't. I was just content. Being with him was easy. Being with Noa is weird and complicated and it's so frustrating that I can't just reach out and touch her, but she makes me happier than I ever thought I could be. Everything I do, it's colored a little bit by the knowledge that she isn't there to share it with me. So I remember as much as I can to share it with her later. And when she does get home, maybe we'll get on each other's nerves and maybe we'll never be able to live together..."

"But if it works," Lily said softly, "then you'll have what everybody wants."

"Yeah," Jamie said. "Everything I know about her makes me want to know more. The only question I have is why she would ever waste time with me."

Lily clucked her tongue. "Oh, there's absolutely no mystery there in my eyes. You're the best Faris sister, after all." She held out her arms and Jamie stepped into the embrace. "I'm sorry I doubted you. But you know, I have to make sure you're not setting yourself up for a heartache."

"I appreciate that. It's supposed to be the older sister who looks out for the baby, you know."

"What do you have to look out for?" Lily put an arm around Jamie's shoulders and walked her toward the theatre entrance. "I'm perfect and I make genius choices. Look at my husband. Look at my children. Look at my job."

"Look at your humbleness."

Lily grinned. "Exactly."

Jamie kissed the side of Lily's head. She was actually grateful her sister had required convincing. It gave her a chance to defend her admittedly strange relationship in a way she never had before. Being forced to explain why she thought the relationship was as strong as anybody else's helped her shore it up in her own mind. Now more than ever she was convinced her love was real. What she and Noa had was worth fighting for, and she was up for the battle.

Noa was about to prepare dinner when she was interrupted by an incoming message from Earth. It was just a notification, meaning she could have ignored it if she was busy, but she was feeling lonely after her talk with Jamie that morning. She opened the channel and said, "This is the ODIE."

"Merry Christmas, Colonel!" Enver said.

She couldn't help but smile. "You're very enthusiastic for someone working on Christmas day."

"You shouldn't be the only one punching a clock today," Enver said. "How is everything up there? Are you getting ready for dinner?"

"I was just about to begin making it when you called."

Enver said, "Excellent! Excellent timing! Go to the pantry, please, and enter the following code." Noa moved to the wall and punched in the numerical password. Her food for the week was usually delivered on Sunday, brought up to the pantry from the lower decks where it was all stored. The screen flashed red and green and, a moment later, a small package appeared. She recognized Enver's handwriting on the note which read MERRY CHRISTMAS COLONEL.

"What is this?"

"Open!"

She took it to the table and opened it. Several packages of dehydrated food were secured to the tray inside. Noa examined each one: Portobello pot roast, pretzel rolls with pats of vegan butter, sweet potato casserole, mashed cauliflower, and carrots. Compared to what she normally got to eat, it was a veritable feast.

"What did you do?"

Enver was clapping. "Christmas dinner, Colonel! I thought you might appreciate something a little more substantial than your usual. And I was hoping by this point we would be near fifty percent of our goal, but you're surpassing your daily limits on a regular basis so we're at fifty-point-two-one. So it's also a celebration of you being ahead of schedule."

Noa said, "So I might get to come home early?"

"Well," Enver said, his sails deflating a bit. "Perhaps one or two days. I don't want to get your hopes up too far."

"Even so, this is very much appreciated." She took the tray over to her rehydration station and began preparing the food.

"I know one meal isn't much of a Christmas gift," Enver said, "but hopefully it's enjoyable. Is there anything else we can do for you?"

Noa watched one of the pouches expand to become food. *Was there something they could do?* Enver was an amazing man. He was generous. He was kind. If she asked him for something as ludicrous as giving an Astraea-strength radio to some random citizen who lived in Indiana, he would do it. He wouldn't even ask her to explain why she wanted it. But then again, if Jamie had a radio that could reach ODIE at all hours, they might be talking when Enver or his team had an important message to pass along. Even worse, they might cross wires and she'd be broadcasting her masturbation to a room full of space geeks.

"This is plenty, Enver. It's so kind and thoughtful. Thank you."

"Hm. Noa, you are aware I'm stupidly wealthy, yes?"

Noa smiled. "The paycheck you offered me for this mission indicated that, yeah."

"Just keep that in mind. You have a genie here and you're being very... ah... what's the word that means being offered a lot but only taking a little?"

She tried to think of one, but she'd never been very good at crosswords. "I don't think there's a word for that."

"Maybe there's a reason no one ever came up with one. Just think about it. The offer stands."

"Thank you, Enver. And I'll enjoy the meal. It looks absolutely delicious."

"The chef who prepared it assured me it was one of the best recipes in his book."

Noa took a bite and closed her eyes. "Mm, he may be onto something. This is fantastic."

"I'll leave you to it. And being ahead might not get you home much earlier, but it does mean that if you want to take it easy today, it shouldn't affect things too much. Like I said, let me know if there's anything else I can get for you."

The ship filled with silence after he disconnected. Noa sat for a moment and listened to the hum of the mechanics currently keeping her alive.

"Jamie," she whispered. "You could get Jamie for me."

When Santa didn't appear, she sighed and looked at her meal. It really did look delicious, and the one bite she'd taken while on the line with Enver had reminded her how hungry she was. It wasn't a good substitute, but at least it was something.

// MISSION DAY 347 - 354 //

JAMIE AND Noa shared their own private New Years' countdown at four o'clock in the afternoon. Jamie had champagne and Noa had a pouch of water, but they made it work. On the first day of January, she continued a tradition of getting a haircut. It was one way to discard the old and move forward fresh. This time she also took the plunge and told her hairdresser to color it blonde. She described it to Noa and assured her there was still enough to get a nice grip on "if anyone wanted to grab a handful of it, or just run her fingers through it."

On Day 349, Jamie described how the winter sun hit the window just right to warm her bed in the morning. "The first day it happened," she said, "I woke up hugging the pillow. It was warm and soft and I think I thought it was you."

On Day 350, they had dinner together just before six o'clock.

On Day 351, they had sex in the dark. Jamie turned out the lights and whispered what she was doing into the microphone. Noa's eyes were closed even though she had her environmental sensors lowered to 'night' settings. She let Jamie guide her hands, touched only where Jamie said she was touching. She was so immersed in the fantasy that she was surprised when her head bumped off the ceiling of her living space.

"You made me float away," she said quietly after her orgasm.

"Wow. I've never made anyone float before."

"My toes are tingling..."

Jamie said, "Wait, is that a good thing? I mean, that might be an oxygen problem..."

Noa laughed and reassured her that everything was fine with the oxygen.

Another dinner on Day 352, and Jamie was getting used to the odd meal schedule. She ate a small snack in the afternoon when she knew she wouldn't get a chance to eat before the sun went down. She didn't go vegan, but she tried to eat vegetarian meals whenever possible in solidarity with Noa. She hated talking about her food if she happened to be eating something with meat in it.

On Day 353, Jamie was almost late for their window.

"Emergency room?!" Noa said, moving across her living space to look down at Earth as if she could diagnose the problem from there. "Are you okay?"

"I'm fine," Jamie said. "I was more worried about not being here for our talks. We only have two more days before we're dark for a week. Time is precious."

"So are you," Noa snapped, irrationally angry at Jamie for being so dismissive of something that sent her to the hospital. "What happened?"

"Do you know what a jointer is?"

"No." She was practically buzzing, too anxious to care about the details. "Just tell me what you did. You're okay, right?"

Jamie said, "I'm fine. It was a dumb mistake and I'm fine. I just needed some ice and aspirin. The hospital visit was just to be thorough. I needed to trim a piece I was going to use for the leg of a table I'm making. I was feeding it to the blade and the piece kicked. Fortunately it went forward instead of straight back into me. Unfortunately it ricocheted off the planer and cracked me across the thigh. My whole leg was numb for about two hours. Luckily my neighbor Bryan is retired and drove me in to get checked out. I'm going to have a hell of a bruise."

"But you have all your fingers?"

Jamie grinned. "All ten, present and accounted for."

Noa said, "Good. I have plans for those fingers."

"All of them?"

"They all have very specific jobs."

Jamie said, "In that case, I'll redouble my safety efforts."

"You'd better."

Day 354 was their last full conversation before the next blackout. Noa's entire day had been spent trying to navigate a particularly nasty piece of space junk. Two satellites had become tangled in a tether, and pulled each other into a death spiral. It created a wide quagmire in which pieces of varying size were bouncing and colliding with each other. Noa's job had been to cut the tether and lasso the larger pieces without letting any of the smaller ones impact ODIE. By the time their window rolled around, she was utterly exhausted but unwilling to skip the date. She changed into her pajamas and curled up in her bed waiting for the signal from Indiana, forcing her eyes to stay open by watching the lights flash on the wall across from her nook.

"~lling, do you read?"

"I'm here."

Jamie said, "Oh, wow, you sound dead to the world."

"No, no. I'm here." She pinched her arm just above her wrist. "I just had a very long day. I'm just resting my eyes a little. I'm here."

"Are you sure? We can miss today. We still have tomorrow."

"We have goodnights tomorrow," Noa said. "Then a week of nothing. I'm not sacrificing a whole hour with you. I don't get enough of you as it is."

Jamie said, "Baby. Come on, you're obviously exhausted."

Noa wanted to argue, but she had to fight a yawn.

"Let me put you to bed," Jamie said. "You fell asleep on the couch. You were so tired that you didn't even wake up when I picked you up and carried you to bed."

"You think you can carry me?"

"I carry wood all the time. I've got arms, Noa, I got arms."

Noa said, "Mm. Okay."

"I put you down on top of the covers. I take off your shoes and socks, and I undress you as much as I can without disturbing your sleep. I loosen your belt and unbutton your blouse so its looser."

"So you can look at my boobs," Noa said sleepily.

"I don't have to sneak a peek because you'd show me your boobs whenever I want to see them."

Noa giggled sleepily. "Yeah. Sing me a lullaby."

"Don't get ahead of me. I take off my shoes and undress. I get into bed with you. I spoon you from behind..."

"Mm, I love being the little spoon..."

Jamie smiled. "I hold you tight. I kiss your shoulder and your neck. One of my hands is on your stomach. The other is stroking your arm, up and down, a very light touch. I reach up to move your hair away from your ear and I start to sing very softly... Wynken and Blynken and *Noa* one night sailed off in a wooden shoe. Sailed on a river of crystal light into a sea of dew..."

Noa smiled when Jamie said her name in the lullaby. She wanted to comment on it, but she also didn't want to interrupt the song.

"Where are you going, the old moon asked the three. We have come to fish for the herring fish that live in this beautiful sea..."

Noa opened her eyes and looked toward the porthole. She was over Earth at night, but she could see the sun shining over the far horizon.

"Jamie..."

"Mm-hmm?"

"I can see your tomorrow."

Jamie smiled. "Is it bright?"

"Oh, yes it is." Her eyes drifted shut again. "I think I'm going to sleep, Lighthouse. I'm sorry."

"Don't be sorry. I love the idea of watching over you. Go to sleep, Stargirl. I'll be right here."

Noa smiled. She wanted to talk to Jamie, she had been dying to talk to Jamie, but her eyes were just so heavy. "Keep singing, baby."

Jamie continued the song. "The little stars were the herring fish that lived in the beautiful sea..."

// MISSION DAY 367 //

JAMIE MADE two stops in Corwin - the furniture shop and a diner for a cup of coffee - and both Alf and her waitress commented on how happy she looked. She shrugged off their attempts to figure out the cause and headed out. There was a lumber supplier in Fort Wayne which, according to one of her clients, was open to providing discounts to self-employed designers like her. It would take her two hours to get there and two hours back, but she and Noa already had their window at eight o'clock. She was free for the rest of the day, and she was going to spend it "adventuring," getting inspired for things to tell Noa when they spoke again.

Two days earlier, they had celebrated the one year anniversary of Noa's launch. It was the halfway point of the mission, the point where they could count the time left before her return in weeks or months but no longer years. It was still an agonizingly long time, of course, but Jamie felt like the timeline clock had officially begun.

She hummed along with the radio the whole way to Fort Wayne, listening to whatever local stations she was able to pick up. They faded in and out, bursts of Dash Warren and new pop singers she couldn't tell apart. Their voices rose out of the noise, became clear, and then faded as she continued her journey. She smiled at the thought that for once *she* was the one moving through radio signals. Their sound waves moved through the air, grabbed onto her receiver, and then slipped away into the ether.

When she arrived, she headed to her meeting. She arrived early so she went to the park and sat next to a misshapen man-made pond. She watched the ducks. She had lunch at the first place she saw and people-watched. Suddenly everything was research for Noa. Jamie was noticing the minutiae of daily life because Noa didn't have that luxury. She'd never really thought about how much she would miss something as simple as traffic or eavesdropping on other diners if it was taken away.

Her meeting with the supplier went well. They worked out a deal they could both live with and she went home with some beautiful pieces of walnut that she already had ideas about. The drive home was spent fantasizing about the wood and what projects she might make with it. She would run some of the designs by Noa the next time they spoke. She reached down and rubbed her thigh where the wood had whacked it a few weeks ago. The bruise was almost completely faded, but the spot was still tender. Noa had offered to kiss it and make it better, but that had evolved into... something else.

Jamie parked in front of the house exhausted and sick of sitting in the truck. She decided to unload the walnut immediately just to give her legs a little workout. She carried the first load into the barn and stacked it with the rest of her materials. She turned to get the second load but stopped in her tracks when her gaze passed across the far wall.

Sawdust was spread across the tabletop like a fine powder. It was clear where she sometimes put her head down and where she rested her elbows. The cot was next to the table with the pillow set on top of her folded blanket for those nights she slept in the barn so she could say goodnight to Noa. The portrait was still hanging on the wall like a one-picture shrine. Everything was in its place except for one horrifying, glaring omission.

The radio was gone.

PART
III

SCREAMING DIDN'T occur to her. Jamie could do nothing other than stare at the empty space where the radio was supposed to be. All of her tools were there, or seemed to be. If someone had robbed her then maybe they'd focused most of their attention on the house. Realizing strangers had been in her home was the thought which snapped her out of the fog. "Cisco," she gasped, already running for the barn door. "Cisco!"

It normally took her thirty seconds to pass from the barn to the house. Today she crossed the distance in ten. She flung the door open and ran into the kitchen. If they'd done anything to her dog, if he was hurt in any way...

Cisco came around the corner with his overgrown puppy face twisted with concern and confusion. She dropped to her knees and wrapped her arms around his neck. He made a quiet and worried sound before twisting his neck so he could lick the side of her face.

"Okay, buddy," she said. "It's okay. You're okay."

Jamie realized she was trembling. Being in the house gave her enough distance to process what had happened. She stood up and took her phone out of her pocket, planning to call the police, but something on the fridge caught her eye: a manila envelope was clipped on the little board where she usually kept her grocery lists. She walked closer and felt her horror dropping off the edge of a cliff into rage, well aware of what it was even before she opened the envelope to look inside.

The divorce papers, signed and notarized. She tossed them onto the counter and went into the living room. The television was gone. So was everything on Louis' part of the bookshelf. She went upstairs and confirmed his winter jacket had disappeared from the closet. She was trembling as she looked for anything else he'd ransacked. She'd moved the majority of his things into a linen closet, and that was empty as well.

She felt violated, which was puzzling since this had once been his house. Then again, some might argue he'd given up the right to show up uninvited when he walked out on her.

Jamie finished her exploration of the house and confirmed that only Louis' things had been taken. She ended up in the kitchen and rested her hands on the counter. She took long, slow breaths in an attempt to calm herself down, but all she could think about was the fact she had a date with Noa tomorrow morning at 0850 and her radio was gone. Cisco bumped her leg with his head and whimpered.

"It's okay, buddy. It's not your fault. I should have trained you to rip out his throat when I had the chance."

She went back outside to her truck. It was late afternoon which meant Louis would still be at work. Normally after driving all day, the thought of getting behind the wheel again would make her weary. Today she felt lit from within and knew she could drive for another five hours if necessary. She gripped the wheel with a white-knuckle grip and kicked up loose dirt as she reversed out of the driveway. One of her neighbors was getting his mail and stared at her as she sped past.

Louis worked at the Sprint store, rising through the ranks and evolving from the guy who installed landlines to the supervisor who told high schoolers how to push handheld supercomputers on people who didn't really need them. He was actually the one who convinced Jamie to get her first smartphone and, even though it ended up being a good purchase, she slapped her palm against the steering wheel at the memory.

"Goddamn asshole," she growled. She realized she hadn't uttered her mantra in months, so she began chanting, "Fuck you, Louis," under her breath. She didn't stop until she reached the city limits.

The shop was in the closest thing Corwin had to a strip mall, next to a pharmacy and a family-owned pizza restaurant. Jamie parked right in front, slammed her truck door, and stormed inside. A young woman with purple hair and too many piercings stopped short with her arm extended as if she was going to escort Jamie deeper into the store. One look at her expression had told the girl that this wasn't a normal customer. She backed away quickly.

Louis was at the back of the store in his stupid black uniform shirt tucked into his stupid khakis. He was talking to a customer so he didn't see Jamie until she was right up on him. He looked at her and had the audacity to look surprised. The customer might have caused her to be quiet and civil, but then Louis opened his mouth.

"James?" he said.

She closed her fists in his shirt and used her momentum to shove him backward. He hit a wall display of cell phones and other techie devices and sent them all crashing to the floor. Every eye in the store was on them now, and Louis actually looked terrified of her. He had both his hands up and out to the sides so there would be no confusion about whether he had laid a hand on his wife.

"Where the hell is my radio?"

Louis' confusion returned. "What... your radio...?"

"I understand why you took all your shit, and you're welcome to all of that. Keep your garbage. But that radio was *mine*. A client gave that to me. You had *no right* to take it." She had an epiphany. "You only took it to hurt me, but you didn't have the balls to take Cisco or any of my tools or anything you thought really mattered to me. You took it because you were being a petty, weak asshole. I want it back. *Now*."

"Jamie," he said calmly, and she noticed that he actually used her name, "why don't we go in the break room and talk about this like adults, okay?"

"No. I'm not going to be here that long. Tell me where the radio is and I'll be gone. For good."

Louis scanned the room behind her. Jamie could feel the eyes of the staff on her, and the customer had retreated out of her view. She kept her eyes locked on Louis so she could see the red creeping up his neck, coloring his ears now. He was embarrassed. Humiliated. She realized confronting him at his workplace in front of his employees had been a bad idea, but she couldn't back down now.

"You think I took it to hurt you?" he said. "You think I'm that much of a petty asshole?"

"I'm learning you're a lot of things."

He carefully removed her hands from his shirt and brushed away the wrinkles. "I took it so you would come find me, so we could sit down and have a talk."

"You're holding it hostage?"

"I didn't think you would come barging in here like Xena Warrior Princess. It was just a goddamn radio. Does it even work anymore? I thought you would notice it was gone and, since it was from a client, you would..." He dropped his head and trailed off. "Look, Jamie, I signed the papers. If that's what it takes to get a fresh start~"

"You think divorce papers are a fresh start?" She touched her fingers to her head. "You are delusional, Louis. We're done. We're over. If this town was big enough for it to be possible, I would wish I'd never see you again. But since that doesn't look likely, I'll settle for getting my radio back."

Louis brushed his hand over the front of his shirt again. "It's... it's not going to be that easy."

Jamie advanced on him again. "What did you do?"

The front window was so covered with garish paint advertising their wares - ELECTRONICS! CLOTHES! DVD/VHS! PHONES AND ACCESSORIES! - but even so, Jamie could see half of the main shop lights were off. She was out of breath when she pulled on the door but still managed a sigh of relief when it actually opened. A bald man was bending over behind the counter, just his head and the shoulders of his bright blue sweater visible as the bells jingled over her head.

"We're closed, ma'am. Everything will still be here tomorrow."

"I'm looking for something specific," she said. "Please, it's an emergency."

He straightened and rested his hands on top of each other next to the cash register. He smiled knowingly. "It's always an emergency, sweetheart, and it never is. Trust me, whatever you need can wait until tomorrow."

"It can't. Please. The radio. My ex-husband brought in a two-way radio. It wasn't his to give away. He just did it... you don't care about any of that." She pulled out her wallet. "He said you gave him fifty dollars for it. I'll give you two hundred. It's all I can afford but it's probably a lot more than you'll get selling the thing."

He looked tempted, but shook his head. "I'm sorry."

Jamie pulled out another bill, one side of her brain doing the math on how much sandwich supplies cost. "Two fifty."

He smiled and shook his head. "I'm not negotiating here. When it goes up on the shelf, you'll be more than welcome to buy it for sticker price. But I'm not going to put it on the shelf until the loan period ends."

"How long is that?"

"Thirty days."

Jamie felt her insides twist. She put her hand on the nearest shelf to steady herself. A whole month without speaking to Noa was one thing, but there was no way for her to tell Noa when she would be back or why she left. Would she think something terrible had happened? Or would she assume Jamie had just gotten bored with their relationship and wandered away? Which would be worse? Would Noa even be waiting for her when and if she got the radio back.

"Fuck you, Louis," she muttered under her breath.

"Ma'am?" the shop owner said. "Look, I'm sorry, but this is the way it's done. If you can get the man who brought it in to repay the loan... two hundred dollars is much more than he'd have to pay back to get the radio back. I feel for you, but I really--"

Jamie said, "You're closing. Right. I'm sorry. None of this is your fault."

She turned and stormed out of the shop. She drove back to the Sprint store and parked next to Louis' truck. Her mind was racing the entire drive, but it never settled on anything in particular. It was like staring at a TV screen while flipping through channels where everything was on fast-forward. She knew what time the store closed and knew she wouldn't have to wait for him long. The sky was blue-purple when the employees started to come out. One of them who saw Jamie waiting ducked his head and moved faster to avoid being there for round two.

Finally, when the parking lot was nearly empty, Louis came out. He locked the door, gave the handle a good tug to make sure it was secure, and strolled down the sidewalk. He was almost to the car when he spotted Jamie getting out of her truck. He continued on but his shoulders slumped.

"Get it back," she said.

"Why?"

"Because it's important to me. You had no right to take it. You stole it."

He unlocked his door. "Then go to the police. File a report."

She assumed if she did that, the radio would be taken as evidence and it would be much more than a month before she got it back. She put her hand on his door and pushed it shut before he could get inside. He finally looked at her.

"Go to the pawn shop, pay back whatever money he gave you, and get my radio back."

"Okay. If you have dinner with me."

Jamie's stomach was churning too much for her to even consider food, but if that was what it took... She gestured at the pizza place. "Fine. Let's go, right now. Large pepperoni, on me."

"A *real* dinner," he said. "One where we can sit down and talk about our relationship."

Her heart sank. She knew the way Louis operated, and she knew it was never going to be a simple dinner. It would going to be a dinner at his little apartment, which would include wine, and then she would be too drunk to drive home. So she would sleep on his couch, if she wasn't inebriated enough to accept his invitation into the bedroom. Being with Noa but unable to touch her had strangely made Jamie feel lonelier than she'd ever been. A warm body might be too tempting to pass up after a few glasses. And even if she stayed sober, dinner would become breakfast. He would spend the entire time arguing for himself, convincing her of how easily they could slip back into their real lives, and maybe it really would seem like the better path.

"I'm not going to do that, Louis."

"You'd rather blow up our entire lives?"

Jamie said, "I'm clearing out the shrubs and weeds to make

something new."

Louis narrowed his eyes. "What do you mean, something new?"

He didn't remember. She'd revealed she was falling for someone else, and the damned fool didn't even register the information. Jamie knew she was going to say something stupid even before the words formed on her tongue. "I'm in love with someone else."

"No, you're not. No, because you wouldn't say that unless you've been seeing him for a while, and I would have heard about it if you were dating anyone. What, are you going all the way to Indianapolis for dinner or something? No. You're not seeing anyone."

"I never said it was a man," she said.

Louis scoffed. He looked across the parking lot. When he looked back at her, he saw something in her face that convinced him she was telling the truth. His features fell.

"No. No, you wouldn't do that to me."

"It has nothing to do with you. She's the person I fell in love with."

"You're leaving me for a *woman?*"

Jamie said, "You left me. Don't act hurt because I finally told you to stay gone. And the fact I fell in love with a woman doesn't reflect on you at all. It only means I'm bisexual, which you've known for most of our relationship."

Louis turned away from her and put his hands on top of the truck. "After the stunt you just pulled in the store, I suppose I shouldn't be surprised you'd also go gay, too."

"*Wow,*" Jamie muttered.

"It's that woman whose picture is hanging in the barn, isn't it?"

Jamie ignored the question. "Give me the radio."

"Or what? You'll divorce me? Humiliate me at work? Face it, *James,* you've already done your worst to me. You can have your radio back in thirty days when Adnan puts it on the shelf."

He opened his door again and this time Jamie didn't stop him. "This is cruel. This is just pointless cruelty."

Louis rested his hands on the steering wheel, staring in defeat at the wall through his windshield.

"It doesn't have to be this way. Our relationship doesn't have to end with us hating each other for doing cruel, petty things to each other. This can be a peace offering. It won't fix what's wrong with us, but we could at least be friends. We could be friendly with each other."

He started the engine. "Thirty days, Jamie."

"Fuck you, Louis." It was the first time she'd said it to his face and it felt better than any of the other times she'd said it. "I can't believe how much I hate you right now."

"There were two people in this relationship, Jamie. Yes, I walked out. But maybe you should start thinking about why I left. I love you. I still love you. Think about what you're doing. Think about if throwing away this marriage is worth a fucking radio."

He revved the engine. Jamie stepped back and watched him reverse out of the spot. She was still watching when his truck disappeared around the corner. She stood with her hands by her sides, crying softly. Night had fallen during their argument, and she lifted her head to look up. Most of the stars were washed out by the security lights. Dusk was still clinging to the edge of the horizon, getting ready to drop off and leave them all in darkness.

Thirty days was long enough for Noa to forget her. It was enough for the schedule to be forgotten, for both of them to get out of the habit of taking an hour out of every day to talk. Their conversation that morning was now the last time they would speak for an entire month, and it already felt like another life. It had been their second conversation after they'd been in the dark, so technically it would be five weeks where she only got to talk to Noa twice.

She hugged herself and walked back to her truck. On the drive home, she thought about one of the last things Noa had said to her that morning.

"I don't think of myself as an astronaut."

"Do me a favor. Take a peek out the window."

Noa laughed. "No, I know, I just... if we met in a bar and you asked me what I do for a living, I would tell you I'm a pilot. Then I'd take you out to my car and molest you a little bit. Wait, that's a tangent. I'm just saying that I fly things for a living, and it doesn't matter to me if it's in space or fifteen feet above a field. Flying is a career that killed my father and did its damnedest to kill me. But I still do it. I crave being off the ground."

"It's in your blood," Jamie said.

"Yeah. But this is the first time I've wanted to jump ship and get back on the ground. If I thought I could survive it and aim just close enough to your house that I could walk there, I would do it right now."

"No," Jamie had said flatly. "Don't. That would be wrong. Do you need latitude and longitude?"

Noa laughed. "I'm thinking too clearly right now. Ask me again tomorrow."

It had been the last thing she said before signing off. "Ask me again tomorrow." Jamie sat in front of her house, forehead on the steering wheel, and cried thinking about Noa showing up at 0850 the next morning and hearing nothing but static. Eventually she got out of the truck and went inside. Cisco attacked her as soon as she was through the door, a canine EMT desperate to diagnose and treat whatever was wrong with his person. She buried her face in his fur and took him upstairs. She got into bed fully dressed and hugged him, using his shoulder to muffle her sobs as she tried not to think about how achingly long a month could be.

// MISSION DAY 368-373 //

THE CHRONOMETER ticked over to 0850. Noa had her breakfast tray in her lap, chewing slowly as she waited for a signal. 0851 passed. Then 0852. She looked at the wall, looked at the timepiece on her wrist, and floated into command so she could double-check her trajectory. Everything was in the green. All of her timepieces were properly calibrated. She realized Jamie must have overslept and smiled at the thought of her running into the barn with hair mussed, robe trailing out behind her even as it fell off her shoulders. She settled in with her breakfast. Their window closed at 0953.

A day later, at 0940, Noa was preparing a whole shtick about Jamie being a lazy bum and sleeping through one of their precious windows. At 1049, she was no longer amused. Twenty-five hours passed and Noa worried through them all. She held her breath at 1030. She checked her communication systems. She even floated to the window and looked out to make sure she was over Indiana. At 1139, she sent a message to Astraea that she needed a diagnostic on her shipboard comms.

Everything came back in the green.

1120 on the next day, lunchtime, and silence.

1210, the fifth day without contact. Noa looked at the chronometer. She hadn't slept the night before. Her mind was full of godawful scenarios. A mangled truck in a ditch. A fire in the barn. She remembered Jamie injuring herself with a piece of wood, so maybe there had been another accident. She was actually nauseated by how many things could have been wrong.

"Jamie, in the blind," Noa said, her voice weak. "I don't... I don't know if maybe you're hearing this and just can't respond. I don't know what happened. I don't know if you can't respond or if maybe you're choosing not to." Her eyes filled with tears, which became bubbles. "Shit." She dabbed them away with her towel. "If I said something to scare you or drive you away... or if I... if it's because I didn't say something... I know how long it's been since you said you love me. Maybe you got tired of waiting for me to say it back. I want to. God, I want to." She rested her head against the wall and floated. Her whole body was adrift, arms and legs slack. "Jamie..."

On the sixth day - 1300 - Noa didn't say anything. She hung suspended in the middle of her living area and listened to the silence of the ship that ordinarily would've been filled with the sound of Jamie's voice. She thought she heard a burst of static and her heart nearly leapt out of her chest, but it was just white noise from a solar flare.

There weren't any requests for interviews, no schools scheduling her to appear at their assemblies. The novelty had worn off. Her launch was a year in the past, and other things were taking up the public consciousness. A war, a new Presidential election circus, a movie star having an affair... no one cared about the woman who was still up in space, still doing the same job, still just circling the Earth once per day. Some days she worried that even Astraea had forgotten about her. They called every morning, right on schedule, but there was a routine to each conversation. Maybe they had moved on like everybody else.

An entire planet had just forgotten her.

The following day, one week since Jamie inexplicably went dark, Noa strapped herself into the command chair in anticipation of her morning briefing. Instead of the normal anonymous voice, she was surprised to hear Enver come over the line.

"Colonel Laurie, are you receiving?"

"Enver. This is a nice surprise." She tried to put some emotion into her voice, but it wasn't a very strong effort. "To what do I owe the pleasure?"

He hesitated. "I'm not sure it will be a pleasure, Noa. We're in my office right now, just the two of us."

Noa remembered it well. Two walls were painted green, while the other two were all glass looking out on his team of engineers. The wall behind his desk had a recessed shelf where his awards stood proudly next to photographs of him posing next to various inventions. He also had a dirty tennis ball which he claimed had been given to him by Chris Evert when he saw her at a gas station.

("What, she just carries them around with her...?" Noa had asked when he told her this story.

"I assume not," Enver said, "but she happened to have one that day.")

"Is everything okay?" she asked.

Enver said, "I hope so. I've received several reports from my technicians about your demeanor. They're concerned. They say you've been lethargic and distracted. You're extremely brusque with them. One..." His voice trailed off. "Well, one of them said it sounded as if you had been crying."

Noa set her jaw. "I'm fine."

"Don't do that," Enver said. "Don't, don't play the hero or the strong woman, okay? Man, woman, it doesn't matter genders, anyone would crack under this pressure. It has nothing to do with female. My people are concerned for you. *I* am concerned for you. We knew going into this that two years alone in orbit was going to be a trial. If there is anything we can do to lighten that load or assuage the pain, please, let me know. Even if you need to come home, it will not be considered a failure. You've achieved over fifty percent of your goal. That is tremendous. We could make that work, NASA could make that work."

"The money you put into this mission..."

"That money is gone," Enver said. "We've proven the concept is sound, all right? We can try again in a few years but we'll spend more time on the human component. If you can't do it alone then no one can. We'll rework it, we'll add a second astronaut, or two! We'll find out what works. This mission will not go down as a failure even if you came home today. The only way I'll consider it failed is if something happens to you, physically or mentally. Please, Noa. I'm a rich man. If I can do anything to improve your situation, you only have to ask. If it's within my power, I will do it."

Noa looked at the array of screens in front of her. "Well... there might be one thing."

// MISSION DAY 375 - EIGHT DAYS SILENT //

JAMIE NEEDED to remind herself to eat. She forced herself to make a sandwich whenever she fed Cisco, but often she would find the last two-thirds growing stale on her plate hours later. She would give it to Cisco who still hadn't stopped looking at her with concern. Every morning she drove to town and sat outside the pawn shop. She'd gotten to know Adnan very well. She would ask if Louis had come back to take the radio. He always said no. She would ask if she could buy it. He always said no, but this time she could see the regret in his eyes. She knew he was just being a good businessman. She knew it was probably against the law for him to sell something before the thirty days were up. But she couldn't stop herself from asking.

On the sixth day, he invited her to sit down on the curb with him. It was just before seven in the morning. A cluster of kids in brightly-colored winter coats were standing on the corner by a church waiting for their bus. Adnan clapped his hands together in the cold.

"I don't know what the story is with this radio. I don't need or want to know. But you're here every morning at the crack of dawn waiting for me. You don't look like you're sleeping. Are you eating?"

"Sometimes."

Adnan nodded as if he'd expected that answer. "My wife makes this... casserole thing. It has broccoli and pasta. Chicken, carrots, peas. She's making it tonight. Come over, we'll feed you. I can tell you if your hubby has come by to get the radio so we can skip the early morning tomorrow. So you can sleep in, plus you can have a full belly."

The school bus arrived. She watched the kids climb up into it. "He could come back any day he wants. He could pay you back, take it, and smash it on the sidewalk."

"Why would he do that?"

"To hurt me."

Adnan sighed heavily and twisted his thumbs around each other. "Do you still have that two hundred and fifty dollars?"

"Yeah." She'd been saving a lot of money on food.

"If your ex-husband comes back and repays the loan, I have to give the radio to him. That's just the rules. But there's no rule stopping me from buying it from him before he leaves the store. I'll offer him the two-fifty. Then you can pay me back."

She looked at him. "Why would you do that?"

"Because I'm a good guy. And you seem like a good person. And if recruiting myself to be your lookout means you start taking care of yourself, then I'm willing to lend a hand."

She twisted at the waist and hugged him. He awkwardly returned the hug, patting her back before he leaned away to indicate she should let go.

Jamie touched her sleeve to both eyes, blotting away her tears. "If I'm going to take you up on that dinner invitation, I'm going to need your address."

Adnan's wife ended up doing the impossible: she not only got Jamie to eat a full meal, she got a laugh out of her. They managed to take her mind off Noa and the radio for a few hours. The next morning she woke up feeling rested for the first time all week. She decided to build on those good feelings by visiting her sister, so she called Lily and arranged to meet her in a small town at the halfway point between Corwin and Cincinnati. They would have lunch and do a little shopping, taking their time since Jamie didn't have to worry about getting back home to meet her window.

Lily was already seated when Jamie arrived at the restaurant. Lily held up her phone in a triumphant gesture. "I clocked it. This is ten miles closer to Corwin than it is to my house. You made me travel farther."

Jamie rolled her eyes as she sat down. "I'll buy you lunch to make up for it."

"Deal." Lily put away her phone. "So-o-o? How are things going with you and the space alien?"

"She's not an alien," Jamie said.

Lily said, "Well, close enough. I saw her on YouTube, and I'd like to blame those eyes on space radiation or something."

Jamie smiled and hunched her shoulders, feeling oddly proud of herself for becoming entangled with someone like Noa. She let herself enjoy that glow for a few seconds before she deflated it by revealing the whole thing might have come to an abrupt and painful end. Lily stared at her, wide-eyed and slack-jawed through the entire saga. When she finished, she shrugged and used her straw to push around the ice in her water glass.

"What an asshole," Lily said. "What if you broke into his apartment while he was at work and got the ticket?"

"Like he's not keeping it in his wallet at all times," Jamie said. "I said I hate him."

"I don't blame you after this stunt."

"No, I'm not..." She looked out the window. "I said I hate him, and I meant it. And I don't want to see his stupid face again because I'm liable to just black out and start punching. The thought of him being in the house when I wasn't there creeps me out. Like suddenly we're enemies."

Lily said, "He deserves it. He walked out on you without warning, and now two years later, he expects you to just come back to him? Like you've been waiting this whole time while he sorted things out? And *then*, when he finds out you moved on, he pulls some petty little stunt?"

Jamie nodded. "All true. But before he left, I loved him. I swore to love him forever. I cried so hard when he proposed, I had the hiccups for the rest of the night."

"So?"

"That's how I feel about Noa. I feel like I know her better than I ever knew Louis, but do I? I don't even know how she kisses. I don't know if she snores or steals the covers. What if someday the sight of her makes me sick to my stomach? What if I shout at her to stay out of my life?"

Lily pressed her lips together and looked down at her napkin. "It's a risk. Everyone has had a relationship go from absolute adoration to indifference."

Jamie put her hands on the sides of her head, fingers in her hair. "I don't want my feelings for Noa to change."

"Ha!" Lily reached across the table for Jamie's hand. "I'm sorry to break this to you, babe, but they're going to change. You're completely smitten right now. You're falling in love with her so it's to be expected. But like you said, there are bound to be little things about her that will drive you crazy. What if she smacks her lips when she eats? What if she's a slob?"

"I kind of doubt an astronaut would be a slob. Neatness is probably in their DNA."

Lily sat up straighter. "Okay, but that's not my point. At this point in your relationship, you're as in love with her as you'll ever be. But eventually that's going to change. You'll become used to each other, you'll take each other for granted, you'll piss each other off. You don't love her less, you just love her differently. Love evolves. It changes. It makes room for the faults. Like us. You and me. You get on my nerves sometimes..."

"What? When?"

"Shut up, stupid. I'm talking." She smirked. "But it doesn't mean I wouldn't kill or die for you. It just means my love is deep enough to survive some minor irritation. It means that even on our worst days, we're going to come back to each other. I'll have your back no matter what, just like you'll have mine. It's like diving into a pool. When you first hit the water, you go as deep as possible. But if you stay down there too long, you drown. Or... I don't know, become a stalker. I'm making up this metaphor on the fly. So you go back up to the surface and tread water. You can dip back under the water sometimes, but mostly you're right there on the surface. Everything will be fine as long as you never want to get back in the boat. If you really care about this woman, then stop focusing on what might go wrong down the road. Focus on how you feel in the moment and take each speed bump nice and slow. You'll get where you're going."

Jamie smiled slowly. "Wow. I didn't know you had all that in you."

"I didn't either. But I thought a lot about it. My marriage hasn't been all prom night and wedding cake, you know."

"Well, I appreciate your wisdom. And was that your subtle way of hinting that we've talked too much about me?"

"Not at all. You're the one who asked to meet up. I assumed that was because you had something you needed to say. And I know you'll be right back here if I ever need a sounding board or a free therapist."

Jamie looked down at the menu. "Not exactly free..."

"Hey, I drove an hour to get here. I'm not going to settle for a burger at McDonalds."

Jamie laughed and patted her sister's hand.

They had their lunch, and they discussed things that weren't related to radios or astronauts or their love lives. The good mood she'd gotten from dinner with Adnan and his wife was boosted almost back to her normal levels. They hugged goodbye in the parking lot - "You talk to outer space for an hour every day," Lily said into Jamie's hair, "you can pick up a phone and talk to your sister now and again." - and went their separate ways.

Jamie drove home and allowed Cisco to greet her before she went into the barn. The chart of days and times still hung near the portrait, with the past days marked off. Over two hundred hours of conversation. They still had about three hundred left. They weren't even at the halfway point of Noa's mission yet. In the grand scheme of things, missing thirty days was just a tiny hiccup. She went to the chart and drew a box around the month she would be without the radio.

Day 398 at ten in the morning - she didn't know if that was ten hundred or one thousand in military time - they would be back in contact. If everything worked out well. If Louis was true to his word and didn't try to trip her up again. She kissed two fingers and pressed them against the date.

"See you then, Stargirl. Wait for me. Please wait for me."

She looked at her tools and unbuttoned the cuffs of her sleeves. She'd barely touched any of her projects since the radio disappeared; she didn't want to risk getting distracted and losing a thumb. But now she thought it was time to get back to work.

// Mission Day 378 - Eleven Days Silent //

Cisco was dozing in the door of the barn. Jamie was at the scroll saw with her back to the door but, when she went to move the piece she'd been working on to the sanding table, she saw that Cisco had gotten to his feet and was watching the driveway. She put down the wood and pushed her safety glasses up into her hair. The National was playing loud enough to be heard over the machinery but, when she turned it down, she heard the sound of an idling car engine.

She walked to the door and watched as a young black man moved across her porch. He was wearing a yellow shirt under a blazer. He backed up almost to the steps, then walked to the side and peered through a window with his hands cupping his face.

Cisco made a quiet rumbling noise in his throat.

"Well, if he's not smart enough to follow the sound of power tools, he can't be that much of a threat," she said as if in response to him. The dog grunted again. "Okay, partner. Watch my back."

Her guest walked back to the front door and knocked again.

Jamie stopped in the driveway. "Help you?" she called.

He turned around, startled. "Oh. Oh! I hope so. I really hope so. Is your name Jamie Faris?"

"Yes."

"You make furniture?"

She was currently wearing goggles and a leather apron covered in sawdust. "Yes."

"Do you have a dog named..." He saw Cisco. "Named Cisco?"

"How do you know my dog's name?"

The man was obviously getting excited. He came down the steps. Jamie had a chisel in her apron pocket and stopped herself from reaching for it.

"Do you know Colonel Noa Laurie?"

Jamie would have been less shocked if he'd slapped her face. She felt tears pricking her eyes. She had no idea who this man was or why he was on her property, but if it had something to do with Noa... She swallowed the lump in her throat and, not trusting herself to speak without crying, nodded.

He exhaled with relief. "You have no idea how many Jamie Farises live in Indiana. At least you're a woman." He pulled out his phone and began jabbing the screen. "My name is Philip, and I have a message for you. And I hope to god it makes sense to you, because the other Jamie Farises were completely clueless. Okay. The message... is my lighthouse okay?"

Jamie sobbed. She clapped a hand over her mouth and felt her knees go weak. She heard Cisco bark and reached out her hand to him, calling him over to her. The dog stopped, wavering between his owner and the man who had apparently hurt her, but he obeyed. He went to her and Jamie wrapped an arm around his neck as if she was drowning and he was a buoy. Philip had retreated to the steps when Cisco came out of the barn.

"Is that from her?"

"Yes, ma'am," Philip said, still eyeing Cisco. "I'm supposed to wait for a response."

Jamie had no idea what to say, how to explain what happened. Noa had the easy bit, just a vague question that wouldn't mean anything to anyone but the two of them. How could she explain Louis and the pawn shop and her hope that things would be back to normal in nineteen days? Finally she settled on the truth. She looked at Philip and shrugged.

"I don't... I don't know what to say."

"Well," Philip said as he poked at his phone again, "I happen to know a guy who is pretty good at coming up with brilliant ideas."

"Colonel Laurie, do you read?"

"I'm here." She was in the command chair. She was completing her mission, methodically destroying space junk and lassoing what pieces she could and et cetera and so on. She felt like a garbage collector making her rounds. It was all muscle memory, shit she could do in her sleep, shit a monkey could have been trained to do.

"Hold please," the voice said.

Noa twisted her lips, irritated. Why call if they were just going to put her on hold? Then again, it's not like her time was precious. She rested her head against the cushion and took the chance to close her eyes.

"Baby?"

Noa sat up so quickly she strained the straps holding her to the seat. She fumbled with the clasps and freed herself with trembling hands. "Jamie?"

"Stargirl." Jamie laughed, and Noa could hear a trace of tears in her voice. Noa was trembling, her mood immediately elevated. At the moment it didn't matter where Jamie had gone or why she was back, all that mattered was that she was there. But she still had to know how.

Noa swam into the back of the ship. "How is this possible? Are you at Astraea?"

"They sent someone out to my house." Jamie looked over her shoulder. Philip was sitting in the dirt with Cisco, now best friends. She had moved far enough away that he couldn't overhear her. "I'm using his phone. He called Mr. Crane, who patched their phone into the communications array, and now we're supposedly having a completely private conversation."

"If Enver says it's private, I believe him," Noa said. "I can't... your voice. I've missed your voice." She closed her eyes. "Say my name."

"Noa," Jamie said, "my Stargirl, Noa."

"Lighthouse," Noa sighed.

Jamie took a deep breath. She could feel the wind again, the sun on her face. Everything felt right again. She smiled and explained what happened. Her eyes stung with angry tears, and Noa clenched her teeth as she listened. She wanted to aim her ship at Louis and crash it into him. She'd be able to get to Jamie and he'd be out of her hair. Two birds with one stone.

"I've been so nauseated the past two weeks," Jamie said. "The way I just vanished. The thoughts that must have gone through your head. I'm so sorry, Noa."

"It wasn't your fault." She looked out the window and realized she wasn't over Indiana. Since they were using Astraea's comms, they could talk whenever they wanted. "How big is the guy they sent to your house? Can you beat him up and steal his phone?"

Jamie laughed. It was a gorgeous sound, and it gave Noa strength. "I don't think that would be a very nice way to repay him for reconnecting us."

"You're right," Noa said. "It was worth a shot."

"Yeah. I don't know how long we're going to get. I swear to you, in nineteen days..."

Noa could see the chart from where she was. "Mission day 398 at ten-hundred."

"Ah, so that's how you say it."

"Jamie?"

"Yes, Noa?"

"I love you."

Jamie felt like she was the one in a vacuum. She was caught breathless, with an unexpected pressure on her chest. She bowed her eyes and squeezed her eyes shut.

"I'm sorry it took me so long," Noa said, "but your disappearance made me realize just how true it is. And I thought, if the worst had happened, I might never get a chance to let you know, and that was just devastating, so I wasn't going to wait another three weeks."

Jamie said, "I love you, too. And even without saying the words... I knew."

"Good," Noa said softly.

Jamie pressed her fist to her chest, just below her neck. "I think we should leave it at that. If we keep talking, I'm going to eat up this poor guy's whole battery."

"Okay. Nineteen days."

"It'll fly by."

"It won't," Noa said, "but it'll be worth it. Goodbye, Lighthouse."

"Bye, Stargirl."

She hung up, even though the idea of cutting off conversation with Noa was painful. She turned and walked back to Philip. Cisco was sprawled upside down across the Astraea messenger's lap, allowing a furious belly rub to be inflicted upon him.

"Be careful," Jamie warned, "he'll adopt you if you do that too well."

"I think this is my punishment for making you cry earlier."

Jamie said, "He's tough but fair." She held out his phone. "Thank you for that. You have no idea how much it meant to me."

"Sure, no problem." He took his phone back and freed himself from beneath Cisco. He brushed off the seat of his pants. "Is there anything else you need?"

Jamie started to say no, then thought of something.

Noa was buzzing with joy. She did a somersault in the middle of the living space, a move that she had no plan on how to stop, and ended up gloriously dizzy. She giggled like she was drunk as she stumbled back into the command center, stretching her legs out along the seat and strapping herself back in. Jamie was alive, she was safe, and the radio would be back in nineteen days. It was such a very long time, but now that there was an end to the silence, she felt she could handle it. Everything was easier with a deadline.

"Colonel Laurie?" It was another engineer.

"Copy!" Noa said, chipper as a receptionist on her first day at work.

"We're preparing a new file for your personal folders. Confirm delivery?"

Her personal folders were items that only she could open from the ODIE. She brought it up onscreen and watched as a new folder appeared and was populated with files. The computer chime when the upload was complete.

"I've got it, Command," she said, clicking on one at random. "Confirming files are--"

It was a photograph of a woman. Noa was confused until she saw the barn behind her and realized that she was looking at Jamie Faris.

"*Oh*," Noa gasped. "Oh, my god."

She clicked through the other photos, nine in all. Jamie, Jamie, they were all Jamie, portraits and full-body shots and profiles.

"Average, my ass," Noa muttered.

"Colonel?"

"Everything is fine, thank you, Astraea. Signing off."

She had tears in her eyes, which was ridiculous. Then again it had been an emotional day. She hated crying in space. She unstrapped herself from the seat and floated closer to the screens, her fingertips resting on the glass. Jamie was wearing a plaid shirt with flakes of sawdust scattered across her shoulders like dandruff. She was squinting slightly due to the sun and had her head tilted to the left, a wide smile spread across her face. Noa examined every bit of the picture as if it would vanish.

"Hi, Jamie," Noa whispered.

She reached back and pulled the keyboard to her. She clicked through the pictures. There was a full-body shot of Jamie, hands crossed over her chest. A dog was visible just behind her, caught mid-run. Noa laughed and said hello to Cisco. For some reason she'd been picturing a smaller dog. The next photo was a portrait, extreme close-up, her shoulders just barely visible at the edge of the shot. Jamie's eyes were beautiful and blue. Noa brushed her finger down Jamie's cheek.

There were six photos in total, and in each one Jamie looked awkward but happy. They were all taken in front of the barn except for one that was taken inside. Noa eagerly examined the room where they had fallen in love. She smiled so big her eyes watered when she saw the cot and, sure enough, there was her portrait hanging above the table. And even though she'd never seen the room before, the radio was conspicuous in its absence.

"Fuck you, Louis," Noa growled.

She flipped back to her favorite picture. The cameraman had obviously taken it without telling Jamie, snapping the shot while they were walking into the barn. She had her back to him but was looking off to her right, her face caught in profile. The light caught the dried tears on her cheeks and Noa ran her finger over the trail left behind. The other pictures were Jamie, posed portraits designed to show Noa who she was talking to every day, but this was the person herself. Casual and unguarded, the person she was in the quiet moments.

"Vera," Noa said.

The automated system chimed. "Yes, Colonel."

She scrolled to Jamie's portrait. "Can you please make this the desktop image for every terminal on the ship?"

"Certainly."

The default background - Astraea's logo on a field of cyan - changed to Jamie. Suddenly nineteen days didn't seem so long. Suddenly a year seemed manageable. What was a year? Just twelve pages in a calendar. She drifted back to her chair and strapped in. Her excitement level was back to where it had been on launch day. She would use the next few days to get back ahead of schedule to justify her hour-long breaks with Jamie every day.

"All right, Vera," she said, "let's blow up some damn space junk."

// MISSION DAY 384 - SEVENTEEN DAYS SILENT //

NOA WAS looking into Jamie's eyes when she came. She was lying in her bunk, bare feet touching the curved wall but the rest of her body free-floating. The tablet was floating right above her face with Jamie's portrait filling the screen. Noa was naked from the waist down, her shirt pushed up so her hands could roam as necessary. She grunted quietly with one hand between her legs and kept her eyes open as long as she could. Finally she relaxed, one hand on her thigh and the other on her stomach.

Their window had technically opened twenty minutes ago. She had started using the time to examine all of Jamie's pictures in an attempt to memorize every inch of them. She could've picked Cisco out of a lineup using all the same breed. Most importantly, she could see Jamie even when her eyes were closed. Jamie had invaded her dreams and made going to sleep her favorite part of the day.

"Most people would kill to be where I am, Lighthouse," she said one evening as she dressed for bed, "and I'm trying to spend as much time unconscious as possible. I hope you're happy with yourself."

She finally finished undressing and slipped into her sleeping bag. She zipped herself up and let her hands fall to the sides. There was no fidgeting in space... no need to fluff a pillow because she didn't have one, no need to toss and turn until she found a comfortable position. She pulled the tablet closer and scrolled through the images Jamie had sent her until her eyes were too sore to keep open.

"Sweet dreams, Lighthouse," she whispered.

As Noa fell asleep, Jamie lifted her head from the telescope and looked overhead with her naked eye. She'd seen the telescope on her first visit to the pawn shop but hadn't realized its potential until a few days after her dinner with Adnan and his wife. She had gone back and decided the price was worth it. Now she had it set up on her front porch and aimed at the western sky. There was a whole website dedicated to when and where the ODIE was visible. She visited it from the library computer and learned that it would be overhead at for three minutes starting at 2246. Its maximum height above the horizon would be 39 degrees in a WSW direction.

Jamie held her arm out with her fist on the horizon. NASA's website said that her fist would be about ten degrees, so she ticked it up three times to figure out where to aim the telescope. Her phone - brand new and purchased from the AT&T store in Odell - beeped when the time was right. She hummed David Bowie's 'Space Oddity' under her breath as she bent forward again. She allowed herself a little doubt as to the accuracy of the website's estimate, but then she saw it: tiny and shining so much it was hard to get details, but definitely more than a star.

She stopped breathing. She'd seen images of ODIE online, but this was the actual vessel. Noa was inside it right at that very moment. If she came to the window they could wave at one another. It moved slowly enough that she could follow it with the telescope. A few tree branches got in her way, and at one point she almost lost it through a cloud, but she recovered. The glow around the ship began to flicker after two minutes and, by the time her three minutes were up, the ship seemed to have vanished into the night.

A few weeks ago she was complaining that an hour with Noa wasn't enough. Now she was happy to get three minutes where they couldn't even talk.

Only two weeks left before she could get the radio back. And most of that was time they wouldn't have been able to talk anyway. They were going into the dark, when they would both be asleep while Noa was overhead. It wouldn't make the time pass any quicker, but at least she wouldn't feel like they were losing days.

"Goodnight, Stargirl," she whispered. "I hope you're thinking about me."

Noa smiled in her sleep. The tablet drifted not far away, the brightest thing in the ship, Jamie's face smiling down at the slumbering scientist.

// *MISSION DAY 397 - RECONNECT* //

ADNAN WAS shaking his head as he got out of his car. Jamie had seen him pulling into the parking lot and was waiting by the door while he was still pulling the keys from his pocket. She'd called him the night before because she'd heard from Louis' mother - who called the landline instead of his cell - that he was leaving town for a week. He wouldn't be there to repay his loan or retrieve the radio. She called Adnan and told him these details, and after quite a bit of begging, he agreed that maybe fudging the timeline by a few hours wouldn't be noticed.

Now he arched an eyebrow as he joined her.

Jamie gave him a skeptical look. "What, you're surprised?"

He chuckled under his breath. "No, no. But I'm glad you look better than you did a month ago. Sleeping well?"

"Yep," she said, "six or seven hours a night, and I'm back to work. Eating regularly. But I wouldn't say no to another plate of Louisa's casserole."

Adnan said, "I'll let her know. You're more than welcome any time."

Jamie stopped in front of the cash register. Adnan went behind the counter and began the process of opening shop. She tried not to drum her fingers on the glass, tried to look anywhere but the back office where he had the safe. She'd actually only gotten about two solid hours of sleep the night before. She kept tossing and turning and looking at the clock.

"She needs some time to prepare. We'll find a day that works for us."

Adnan sighed and said, "Usually I don't do this until lunchtime, but I'm not going to torture you. Stay there."

Jamie was bouncing on the balls of her feet when he came back with the radio. She was close to tears when she saw it. Adnan put the radio on a mat next to the cash register and Jamie couldn't stop herself from reaching out and placing her hand on top of it.

"I still don't know what's so special about this thing."

"It's... it's a lifeline."

"If you say so." He took out a ledger from beneath the counter, flipped it open, and found a pen to make a mark. "One shortwave amateur radio, brought in by Louis Rhodes thirty days ago." He marked a box. "Now available to be resold." He looked at Jamie and gave her a salesman's smile. "Good morning, young lady. Can I help you find anything?"

"A radio," Jamie said quietly.

He said, "You're in luck. I just put this one out today. Will it fit your needs?"

Jamie nodded, eyes filling with tears. "Yup."

"Fantastic. Let me ring you up." He poked the cash register buttons. "That will be a dollar-ten."

Jamie snapped out of her fog. "What?"

"Dollar and a dime."

"That's... you can't do that."

Adnan frowned. "Don't tell me what I can do in my own store. This is a pawn shop! We don't haggle here. One-ten."

"Adnan... you had to have given Louis more than that for the radio..."

He closed the book. "Maybe. I don't remember." He pointed at the radio. "But I know what that thing is worth to you, and I know how much it's been hurting you to not have it. Plus you're saving me the trouble of adding it to inventory. All things considered, I'm coming out on top. As long as you cough up the dollar-ten, of course."

Jamie leaned across the counter and hugged him. "Thank you, Adnan."

"I still haven't seen any cash."

Jamie laughed. "You drive a hard bargain." She took a five dollar bill out of her wallet.

Adnan said, "Don't try to give me a tip, either."

"Well, I don't have anything smaller."

He sighed and made change for her.

"Thank you, Adnan."

"I'm just running a business. I'll tell Louisa you're coming over sometime. We'll let you know what day."

"I'm free any night this week." She picked up the radio. It was heavier than she remembered, and she imagined Louis hauling it out to his truck. If he had dropped it, if he... she quashed that train of thought. Nothing bad happened, she'd stuck out the long silence, and soon they would be back on track. If she was able to get home and set it up in the next forty minutes, she wouldn't have to wait a whole day.

She drove as fast as she dared, not wanting to be held up by cops or an accident. Technically, Noa wouldn't be expecting her until tomorrow, but she couldn't wait. She had gotten a tutorial from her niece in everything she had to do and she hoped she would be able to do it on her own. Everything about talking to Noa seemed so magical that she was afraid the simple act of moving it from the barn to the pawn shop might have severed its connection. But she believed. She wasn't going to be pessimistic.

Her hands were shaking as she set the radio up. She checked its battery, ran her thumb across the glass covering the frequency dial, and swallowed the lump in her throat. She looked at the clock: it was 0909, and their window opened in sixty seconds. If Noa was listening. And if Jamie had set it up right. She'd put everything back the way it had been before, but with one major difference.

She crossed her fingers and picked up the microphone. The plastic was cold, but her fingers wrapped around it with a familiar, tight grip. She closed her eyes and waited.

"Please," she mouthed, unwilling to cover the sound of static with her voice.

Seconds ticked by. Jamie pressed the microphone against her forehead. It had to be 0910 by then. It could mean nothing. Maybe Noa was talking to Astraea, or maybe she was in the middle of a briefing. Maybe Jamie had just screwed things up and she could fix it by~

"~morrow," Noa said through a burst of static.

Jamie screamed and dropped the microphone. Fortunately she hadn't been holding down the button, so her panic wasn't transmitted. The microphone swung on its cord and she grasped for it as Noa continued talking.

"...last day without you," Noa said. "It's hard to focus on anything else knowing how close it is to finally being over. I think about hearing your voice tomorrow and the idea of working just evaporates."

Jamie brought the microphone up. "In that case, I can come back tomorrow if that fits your narrative better."

There was silence from ODIE for almost a full minute. Jamie's heart pounded. Noa was sitting under the porthole, legs folded in front of her, wearing her shorts and a thin T-shirt. She was eating a rehydrated fruit for breakfast. She stopped with the pouch halfway to her lips and stared across the empty space. She half-believed she'd imagined the voice. It wouldn't have been the first time she hallucinated

Jamie's side of the conversation. But all those times, she'd known it was coming from inside her head. This time sounded real. It sounded just like her.

"Jamie...?"

"Hi, baby."

"Jamie," Noa said again. "I-I thought... I thought it was tomorrow."

"I pulled some strings," Jamie said. "I couldn't stand to go another day without talking to you. Besides, today it's been three hundred days since we first made contact. I thought it had a nice symmetry. How are you?"

Noa said, "I'm... I don't know. I'm so surprised. I didn't... I was just talking to myself. Can you talk for a minute? I just want to hear your voice. Please."

Jamie said, "I suppose that's only fair. I went to the library a few times to watch your videos. I got to hear your voice, but you couldn't hear mine. So I'll talk while you adjust to having me back, okay? I have a surprise for you."

"You've been killing it with the surprises, Lighthouse. I can't wait."

"I've had a lot of time to think about our situation and the things that would make it perfect. I couldn't exactly figure out how to get video to work, so that was out. So I thought about what was within my power. I decided if I had to set the radio up again anyway, I might as well see if it worked inside the house. So I brought everything inside to see if I could still get a signal."

Noa said, "I'm in your house?"

"You're inside," Jamie said.

"Which room?"

Jamie bit her bottom lip.

"You put me in your bedroom, didn't you?"

"Where else?"

Noa laughed. "Kind of presumptuous, aren't you?"

"I was getting a little sick of masturbating in the barn!" Jamie laughed. "I knew it would only be a matter of time before my neighbors overheard us and thought I was torturing animals in there or something."

Noa couldn't help but put some seduction into her voice. "Ooh, so now I get to be as loud as I want with you...?"

Jamie blushed. She wanted to say it was too early for that. She hadn't had her breakfast yet, hadn't even showered, but it had been so long that even a little flirt in Noa's voice was enough to make her tingle. She crossed her legs and squeezed her thighs together.

"And now I can be completely naked when we talk."

"Yeah? Are you?"

"I can be."

Noa wet her lips. "Take your clothes off for me, Jamie."

"Yes, Colonel."

Noa shuddered at that, even though she'd found it corny when other lovers said it. She pushed aside her fruit pouch and quickly stripped as well. Her feet became tangled in the material of her shorts and kicking them free sent her spinning. Jamie toed off her shoes and pushed her jeans down with her underwear. She was wearing a button-down shirt but she pulled it and her undershirt over her head in one swift motion. Jamie sat down again as Noa was pinning her hair back so it wouldn't get in her face.

"Are you naked?" Jamie asked.

"Yeah."

Jamie closed her eyes and let her hand roam. She brushed a thigh, pretended it wasn't her own. She kept the microphone close to her mouth, pressing down the button whenever she gasped or moaned. Noa stretched out with her feet crossed at the ankles, her knees slightly bent. She touched herself with feather-light brushes of her fingertips across her stomach, hips, and breasts.

"I can picture you so much better now, thanks to those pictures."

"Oh." Jamie had almost forgotten about those. "I thought I may never have the opportunity again. I was in the middle of working, I-I'd just been crying--"

"You're gorgeous," Noa said. "You're absolutely gorgeous, Jamie. I looked at those pictures so much, I have them memorized. The color of your eyes. The way you smile. The curve of your lips. Now when I hear your voice, I can picture you, and I can see you sitting there naked for me, and it makes me wet."

Jamie gasped softly as her hand continued to explore. "I wish I could have sent pictures like yours."

"Me too. But these worked fine. I used them."

"You..."

"It was like you were watching me."

Jamie's mouth was dry. "I watched your movies. The-the Hollywood one, and the dirty one."

"Which one was your favorite?"

"The dirty one," Jamie admitted.

Noa grinned. "That one is my favorite too." She wet her lips and craned her neck as she touched herself. "I've missed you, Lighthouse. I'm so glad you're back."

"Me too," Jamie said. "Your hand is on my left thigh."

"Not anymore," Noa said. "I moved it higher."

Jamie gasped and sat up straighter.

"I'm rubbing you with two fingers," Noa said.

Jamie forced herself to form words. "I'm kissing your neck."

Noa brought her free hand up and brushed it down her neck, starting just behind her ear. The touch was just light enough to make her shudder. "I feel it. Do you feel me?"

"I do," Jamie said. "Missed you..."

"I missed you, too."

Jamie listened to the sound of Noa breathing. In that moment, the radio didn't matter. It wasn't a matter of distance or separation, they were truly together no matter where they happened to be sitting. Jamie had never felt closer to anyone than she did right then. She slid lower in her seat and imagined Noa's weight on top of her. She'd never had much of an imagination before meeting Noa, but now she could conjure entire worlds and scenes that didn't exist. Jamie's hand tightened on her thigh when she heard Noa coming, and they breathed through it together.

"I love you, Noa," Jamie whispered.

"I love you, too."

"I guess we get to say that at the end of our messages now, huh?"

Noa was breathless and red in the face. "Yeah, now that I stopped dragging my feet. I have time to make up for. I love you, James."

Jamie cringed. "Don't call me that."

"Okay. I'm sorry."

"It's okay." Jamie blinked away tears at the simplicity of the apology. She knew that even if Noa slipped up in the future, she could gently correct her. But she also knew that Noa would never use it in anger or as a weapon to prove her superiority. "Say it again," she asked, "but with the right name."

"Jamie," Noa said, "I love you, Jamie."

She sighed happily. "Thank you."

Noa rolled across the center of the living space. She was amazed at how easily they slipped back into the old rhythm, even after a month apart. Being with Jamie took away all the irritations of being locked in a tiny shuttle high above the planet. Plus the sex was better than masturbating, which didn't make sense. It was still her own hands touching her, but having Jamie there turned it from self-pleasure to something shared between them. It was the closest to sex she was going to get. And if she was honest, it was more like making love than most of what she'd done in the months leading up to the launch.

"I, um, ahem, I have... I've been writing down things to tell you when we reconnected."

"Hold, please." Noa swam back to her sleeping nook and stretched out on top of the bag. "I'm lying down in bed. Post-coital and sleepy." She put her hand against her cheek even though there was no pillow underneath it. "Tell me a story."

Jamie laughed. "It's morning."

"We missed enough nights. We can pretend today."

"Okay." Jamie took out her phone and looked for a good memory to share.

// MISSION DAY 400 //

THE SCREEN faded in from black as the camera swept past the band, over the blue floor of the performance space, and settled on the lanky man behind the desk. His tie was loose and his hair had been mussed by repeated raking of his fingers. He drummed his hands on the desk and sat up straighter as if he had just noticed the camera. When he smiled, his whole face transformed, and he gestured welcomingly.

"Hey, you came back! Welcome back to *Settle In, Seattle!*" The audience applauded. Rather than an auditorium full of people, however, this taping was attended by only a few dozen people who worked on the show and a scattered group of interns. "Four hundred days ago, you watched out next guest do something incredibly cool. Take a look."

The image shifted to ODIE sitting on a runway that rippled in the desert heat. A wave of sand lifted up and blew across the gleaming curves of the vessel. Audio from the radio played over the image.

"Everything green?" a man asked.

"Green as grass. We have a go?"

"We have a go! Whenever you're ready, Colonel."

The countdown began. The engines came to life. ODIE sped down the runway almost too fast for the camera to keep up with it. It reached the end of the concrete and lifted up as if it had hit an invisible ramp. The ship twisted on its axis as it rose, and the sun reflected off its sides as drew a white line of smoke through the clear blue sky.

"We have liftoff, ladies and gentlemen!" Enver Crane's voice was ecstatic. "We have liftoff!"

The image faded back to Nick Young at his desk. He looked off-camera to his sidekick, Hank Kingsley.

"I could do that if I wanted to."

"You just don't feel like it?" Hank said.

Nick shrugged. "Not enough runway. You know Seattle, all our streets are so uppy-downy. You can't find anywhere to get a good running start like that."

Hank said, "You ever gone down Highland Drive in Queen Anne? Take that fast enough and you might end up in outer space."

"I'll have to remember that." He faced forward again and drummed his hands on the desk. "Our next guest, joining us via satellite, was piloting that ship, and she's still piloting it now all these months later. Please give a warm welcome to Colonel Noa Laurie!"

The tiny makeshift audience applauded as a screen revealed the live feed from ODIE. Noa was wearing an Astraea Aviation polo shirt and khakis, seated against the wall of her living area. She had one leg crossed over the other, her fingers laced together on her knee. She smiled and waved to the camera.

"Hello, Nick. Thank you for having me back."

"We had to make sure everything was going okay for you up there. Now, first things first, Colonel. Your hair is kind of doing that kooky anti-gravity thing, but we have a lot of skeptics in the audience. Can you prove to us that you're actually in outer space right now?"

"Sure." She reached out and turned the camera to show her living space, the table and chair giving away the fact she was actually sitting on the ceiling. "How's that? I was going to spill marbles, but I didn't really want to clean them up."

Nick put a hand over his stomach. "Oof, okay, Spider-Woman. Stop. I think I'm getting queasy here."

"Sorry." She aimed the camera back at herself. "After four hundred days, I forget how weird it is that I can essentially 'fly'."

"You're a real life superhero!"

"Well, I don't know about that. But I'm actually not sitting on anything right now. I'm just kind of hovering."

"I stand corrected. You're Superwoman."

Noa laughed. "It's all science, Nick."

"That's what superheroes always say. Now you visited with us once before, back when the mission first began. You were very optimistic about the potential of what you were doing. How have things been going?"

"Things are going great. I'm past the halfway point of my mission and just the other day we got word that we've hit sixty percent of our goal."

"That's fantastic!" Nick said.

"Can I show you the view?"

"Oh, absolutely you can."

Noa took the camera and pushed off the wall with her toes.

Nick said, "I want to nip any conspiracy theories in the bud right now: Colonel Laurie has a very strict schedule, and she was only available for this video interview at a certain time of day, so we're recording this a little earlier than usual."

"That's right, Nick. Thanks for waking up early for me."

"I wouldn't have missed this for the world!"

Noa stopped next to the window and aimed the camera outside. "There you are. You can see Seattle right down there. And to the west, you can see where night ends and the day begins. The sun is rising over the Pacific right here."

"That's amazing." There wasn't a trace of the showman in his voice; he was too transfixed by the image to play up his role as host. "Wow. Uh, so. Sorry, I got carried away looking at that view."

"Happens to the best of us, Nick." She moved the camera so it was facing her again. "My day is pretty routine. Morning meetings with Astraea, then the rest of the time I'm a trash collector. I destroy what I can, I gather up what's too big to blow up, and in the end we're left with a much cleaner sky."

Nick said, "I'm sure you're allowed to have some personal time."

Noa said, "Absolutely. I have movies and TV shows, books. I have lots of free time to think and relax."

"I imagine it might also get really boring, as well. I like solitude as much as the next guy. Well, maybe a little more than the next guy. Well, I have a moat and a ten-foot wall around my house. The point is, even I might find it a little claustrophobic to spend two full years by myself."

"I'm not going to lie, it gets a little rough sometimes. Everyone who works for Astraea is absolutely wonderful. Just top-notch. And Enver is a big joker. I love talking to him because he can make me laugh even after the roughest day. But the habitable part of ODIE is a little smaller than your stage. Can you imagine staying in that area and not leaving for two full years?"

Nick shrugged. "It would be easier for me, because the people come here to talk to me. Present company excluded, of course."

She laughed. "I appreciate you making the effort for me."

Noa paused and looked away from the camera for a moment. She was about to say something which wasn't cleared, hadn't been discussed in the pre-interview, and would be completely out of the blue for everyone involved. She weighed the pros and cons of saying what she wanted to say, and decided the pros won out.

"Actually there's one person who has been keeping me sane for most of this mission. We talk every day. Not about the mission, but about ordinary things. Her job. The weather. Her dog. She makes me feel normal. She reassured me that people down there haven't forgotten about me. Her voice is what's gotten me through the hardest days and made me believe that I can finish this mission without sacrificing my sanity."

"Does this special lady have a name?"

"I'm not sure she'd like me saying it on national television." Noa grinned. "I didn't exactly clear this revelation with anybody. But I call her my Lighthouse."

The audience said "aww." Nick said, "That's adorable. What does she call you?"

"I don't see how that's relevant."

"You're the one who opened up this line of questioning, Colonel."

She fidgeted and finally gave in. "Stargirl."

The audience reacted again. Nick joined them, and then said, "Uh-oh, I think we've made her blush. I'm sorry, Colonel. I'm very glad you have someone keeping you grounded, as it were. Right now I'm being told that we have to wrap this up soon. I guess you have to get back to your mission. But I want to thank you for taking the time to talk with us. We want to have you back on the show when you can actually be here in person! So as soon as you're back, give us a call."

"I'll do that."

"Say goodbye to the people of Earth!"

"Goodbye, people of Earth!" Noa said, waving and smiling into the camera.

The feed died as the audience applauded. "Stick with us," Nick said, "we'll be right back with the Femme Reapers!"

"Goodbye, people of Earth!"

Lily, who had been keeping her eyes on the screen since Noa's unscripted revelation, slowly turned to look at her sister. Jamie had come to visit specifically so she could see Noa on the show, since Jamie didn't have cable. It was based in Seattle but the host was popular enough for several syndicated networks to air it. She hadn't known that Noa would say anything about their relationship for such a wide audience. She looked at Lily, who raised an eyebrow.

"She's talking about you, right?"

"She better be," Jamie said. "Otherwise she's got Lighthouses all over the world and I'm going to be one pissed-off woodworker."

Lily scooted across the couch and hugged her. "She looked like you did."

"What?"

"Your face when you talk about her? She had the same look on her face when she was talking about you." She squeezed Jamie hard. "My little sister is in love. With a damned celebrity! I mean, she was just on television! She was a guest on a national talk show."

"The second guest," Jamie pointed out.

Lily scoffed. "Like that matters." She kissed Jamie's temple. "Are you okay? She just gave up a really big secret."

"I'm fine," Jamie said. "I think it affects her more than it does me. The only people I really cared about finding out were you and Louis. And he is now officially my ex-husband. So screw whatever he might think about it. I'm glad people know she's happy, even if they don't know it's me."

"Aw, honey." She kissed Jamie again. "People still wouldn't know it was you even if she'd said your name. You're a nobody."

Jamie rolled her eyes. "Gee, thanks."

"Could've put up a big picture of you and everyone would've been like... okay."

"I get the idea."

Lily brushed the hair out of Jamie's face. "Big ol' nobody."

Jamie finally grabbed a pillow and leapt to defend herself, using it as a shield to drive Lily into the couch. She climbed on top of her and tried to pin down her flailing arms and legs without letting go of the pillow. Lily shrieked with laughter as Jamie continued to smother her.

"What's going on out there?" Lily's husband called from the kitchen.

"Nothing!" both sisters responded.

"Colonel?"

"Yes, Enver?" Noa was strapped into her command chair. She knew what he was going to ask, but she wanted to make him say it.

"Um." He hesitated. "Um, I've asked the communications director and everyone who is cleared for talking with you on the radio, and none of them seem to have any idea who this 'Lighthouse' is. I checked the records and there's no evidence that any one person speaks with you every day. So I suppose I'm just a bit perplexed by your interview."

She considered her answer carefully. "I've given up two years of my life to this mission, Enver. It also cost me a huge percentage of my privacy. You monitor my vitals, you provided every meal I've had for the past year, you check in on me every morning. I understand all of that. I get the need for it, trust me. I don't think you're some creepy asshole keeping me prisoner. I'm just part of your mission that requires monitoring. Lighthouse has been part of this mission since Day 97. She never affected communications or operations, unless you want to give her credit for raising my morale. I certainly do. And you saw what happened when I lost contact with her for a while.

"What I'm asking is if I can just keep her a secret. This one thing, this person who keeps the mission on track and keeps me sane. Makes me happy. I don't want to jeopardize what we have by explaining how we're talking because it might be a flaw, it might be some weird mistake in the security or the technology that you would have to fix if you knew it existed. I want her to just be mine."

Enver considered her plea. Finally he said, "It's a very small thing to ask, considering what you have given up for us. You may keep your secret, Noa. But if I may know one thing... this is related to the woman in Indiana, yes? Jamie Faris?"

Noa said, "Yeah. She's my Lighthouse."

"I don't..." He made a noise like he was shutting a door. "No, I don't care. However you are in contact with her, I will do nothing to jeopardize it."

"Thank you."

"You have nothing to thank me for, Colonel. I'm only respecting your basic human privacy in a relationship. Tell her thank you from me, in fact."

Noa said, "I will."

He cleared his throat. "Now, I believe you have had enough of a vacation today. How about getting to work and continuing your streak, hmm?"

She laughed. "Sounds good to me, Enver. I'll talk to you tomorrow."

She disconnected the radio and closed her eyes. The constant hum of the ship was like listening to its beating heart. She'd grown so used to it that now she had to really listen for it even when there was nothing else drowning it out. She let her hands and feet lift off the chair. In less than a year, she would be back on Earth and she'd likely never again experience anything like this. She slowed her breathing and just floated against the straps, moving faster than most people ever would but also feeling perfectly still. She let the utter silence wash over her. She felt the peace few people ever could on the noisy hive of Earth. She gave herself a moment to appreciate just how lucky she really was.

Finally she opened her eyes and smiled. "Vera."

"Yes, Colonel."

"Play Tom Waits. *Mule Variations*."

The bluegrass guitar of the song 'Get Behind the Mule' filled the ship. Noa bobbed her head along to the beat and drummed the fingers of one hand against the armrest as she got to work.

// MISSION DAY 416 //

THE APARTMENT building could have been nicer, but it certainly wasn't a slum. Louis' new address was a brick tower that reminded her of college dorms she'd seen on television and in movies, but everyone she saw on her way upstairs had a middle-aged slump to their shoulders that said they wouldn't know a party if one broke out around them. This wasn't a home people chose for themselves, it was the place they went to when they had no other options.

Louis lived on the fourth floor. She found his number, knocked, and waited. A few minutes went by, long enough that she was afraid he might be out, and then the door opened. He glared out at her.

"What do you want?"

Jamie held out the box she'd brought. She'd made it specifically for this purpose, a nice little cedar box about the size of a humidor.

"You missed a few things when you went through the house. I thought you might want them."

He stepped into the hallway and took the box. She glanced over his shoulder into the apartment. It was nice if a little spartan. She could hear the sounds of some *Law & Order* or another playing on TV. Louis opened the box and sorted through the items inside, pausing when he found one in particular. He held it up.

"Is this your wedding ring?"

"And the engagement ring is in there somewhere. Some earrings you got me that I never wear."

He looked down into the box again, his eyes shaded. "What do you want me to do with this?"

"I don't know," she said. "I thought maybe you could sell it, get some cash. It's not going to do me any good gathering dust in a jewelry box. And if it helps you out..."

"I don't need your charity."

"It's not charity," she said. "They're yours, you should have them."

He held up one of the earrings. "These were a gift."

Jamie shrugged. "I didn't like them. I'm just being honest with you, Louis. I'm not trying to be hurtful. I'm trying to do the right thing."

He continued to slowly dig through the box. "I just needed time, Jamie."

"If you needed that long to decide you want to be with me, then you don't really want to be with me. And this is just stuff. Keeping it for no reason would be petty. Consider it a peace offering or a clean break or whatever you want to call it."

"You changed your phone," he said. "You're not with Sprint anymore."

"Yeah. I figured that was for the best."

He looked up. "No one has seen you with anybody. You said you were with someone, but I've asked around. You're not out on dates, you're not going to the movies, there aren't cars parked at your house overnight..."

Jamie pushed down her anger. "Stop checking up on me, Louis. That's as bad as if you were sitting outside the house all night watching with binoculars. I'm not your business anymore. My girlfriend isn't your business, just like whoever you date is none of my business. I'd like it if someday we could be civil to each other. I know you aren't there yet, and neither am I, but it's a small town. It'll be even smaller if we can't get along." She rubbed her hands together. "That's all I wanted to say. I'll go."

She was almost back to the elevator before Louis spoke. "She'll get tired of you eventually. You're throwing this all away for nothing, James."

She smiled and pressed the button to call the elevator. She looked back at him. "Thank you for leaving, Louis. I never would have cheated on you. I never even would have entertained the possibility of a relationship when this woman came into my life. But you made it all possible. Thank you for that."

"James..." he said again.

The elevator arrived and Jamie stepped into it. "Call me whatever you want, Louis. I don't care anymore. Goodbye."

The doors closed on his frustrated expression. Jamie smiled to herself and tilted her head back. There had been a very small twitch the first time he called her James, but the second time she hadn't felt anything at all. If she needed any further proof that she was beyond any of his tactics, that had done it. He could call her James every single time they met in the future and she would let it roll off her shoulder.

There was only one nickname she answered to, and only one person who used it.

// MISSION DAY 438 //

THE TABLE was set for their dinner. The overhead lights were off, and a pair of candles stood to one side of Jamie's plate to provide ambiance. Noa had asked Vera to lower her lighting as well. Her tray was in front of her with the meal laid out before her. Jamie was surprised when she learned about how varied Noa's food supply was. "It's not all goo in pouches," she said. "People have been working for years on how to feed astronauts who are going to Mars. And of course Enver made sure he had access to that research for this mission."

Jamie unfolded a napkin and draped it across her lap. "Enver sounds like a good guy to have around in a pinch."

"He's remarkable. He has more money than anyone else in America - combined, probably - and he's using it to advance science and education. Plus he has this uncanny ability to think about seven or eight unbelievable things at once. It's like playing chess with someone who is doing calculus with his other hand."

Jamie chuckled and looked down at her plate. They were eating curry cauliflower burritos from a recipe Noa had carefully described to her the day before.

"This looks delicious."

"It's one of my favorites," Noa said. "I'm in my navy blue Astraea polo and khaki slacks."

Jamie said, "I'm wearing a white blouse and a black skirt. I had my hair done."

"Oh, yes, you did. I was going to say something. You look lovely. The blonde is beautiful."

Jamie grinned and touched her hair. "Thank you. You look nice yourself."

Noa waved off the compliment. "You're kind to say that, but I'm a mess. I had to come directly from work."

"You look magnificent to me," Jamie said. "Just stunning."

"Thank you."

They began to eat. It was difficult for Jamie with one hand occupied by the microphone. She considered using her device again, but she didn't want to block Noa's communication.

"How was work today?"

Noa shrugged. "It was fine." She chewed slowly and looked at her food. "Actually it wasn't fine."

Jamie paused and looked across the table. "What happened?"

"I... I saw a piece of the ISS. It was a sizeable piece, so I had to do some maneuvering to lasso it. So it was on my screen for a good long time. It was part of the habitation module." She worked her jaw from side to side. "It reminded me of how close I came to... how..."

"Hey," Jamie said softly. "I come around to your side of the table. I kneel down and hug you."

Noa closed her eyes. "I squeeze you tightly. Thank you."

"Any time." She imagined her arms around Noa. She didn't have the words to fix Noa's pain, so she didn't try.

"I would have given my life to save any one of those guys."

Jamie felt a pang at the idea. Then she said, "Then maybe they would say the same thing. Maybe if they knew that you, at least, made it home safely, they would consider it a win."

"Maybe," Noa said. "No... I know they would. That's exactly what they would think."

"I brush the hair away from your face. I wipe away any tears that are on your cheeks. You should honor them somehow."

Noa sniffled. "The last of them I ever saw was Anton Dragomirov. Cosmonaut. He had a bald head and this magnificent orange and white beard. He was always telling us stories about Russia like a stereotypical movie character from the eighties. He was a riot." She smiled as she remembered some of his jokes, but she needed to move on to the next crew member. "The other Russian was Lev Igoshin. He called himself the Black Russian because... well, because he was black... He didn't have an accent unless he was making a joke. He had two... two daughters... and he would use his personal time filming things around the station for them so they would grow up to become scientists like him."

"Did they?" Jamie asked.

"One of them is at MIT right now. The other one is still in high school, but she's a science ace. She'll get there when she's old enough."

Jamie smiled. "It's sweet that you keep up with them."

"I have to," Noa said. "It's the least I can do. None of the survivors blame me for what happened. We trained together, we knew each other. We were a family. It would be like getting angry at your niece for surviving a car accident which killed everyone else."

"That does happen, you know."

Noa said, "Yeah. But not with us. Their wives wanted to make sure I was taken care of." She looked toward the window. "I don't know why I thought I could do this before I knew you'd be here. I thought it would be easier if it was just my life at risk. I wouldn't have to worry about losing anyone else or putting someone else in the same position I was in. I didn't think about how goddamn lonely it would be. Thank you for being here, Jamie."

"There's nowhere else I would rather be."

"Go back to your side of the table. Let's finish our date."

"Are you sure you're okay?"

"I'm fine. Thank you. I squeeze your hand as you go back to your seat."

Jamie said, "Okay, back in my seat. You haven't told me about the American astronauts yet."

"Colin Morris and Isaac Buchman. They were good guys. Colin was a bit too much of, uh... you know, the southern cowboy type. He insisted on calling me 'ma'am' the entire time we were up there. Not because of rank. He was a civilian. But it was just how he was brought up. He would always sing old country songs. I got used to it after a while. I even bought an album by one of the guys he would sing because I missed it. I think Colin's version was better."

"What about Isaac?"

"He was older than me. Protective. Like you said about the others giving their lives to save mine. If Isaac knew only one of us could escape, he would have hit the eject button himself and then jumped back into the station. That doesn't make it any easier to accept, but..."

Jamie said, "It's still good to acknowledge it."

"Yeah," Noa said softly. "Is it strange that I feel as if you're right here with me? I feel like we're in the same room, we're... we're together."

"It's not strange at all," Jamie said. Except for the rare burst of static and the fact she had to hold down a button so Noa could hear her when she talked, she truly felt as if there was no distance between them. "I feel the exact same way."

Noa looked at the time and her smile disappeared. "Damn it."

Jamie looked at her watch. "Oh."

"I guess we should pay the check and get out of here."

Jamie said, "I stand up and take your jacket off the back of the chair. I help you into it."

"Thank you. Such a kind lady."

"It's just an excuse to squeeze your shoulders."

Noa laughed. "Sneaky. I like it. Let me walk you to your car."

"I offer you my elbow."

"We step outside."

Jamie tilted her head back. "Wow, look at all the stars."

Noa looked out the window. "Have you ever seen so many at once?"

"No. Never. I pull you closer to me."

"I look into your eyes. Are you wearing your glasses?"

Jamie said, "Well, sure. I have to see you. I can... I'm wearing contacts..."

"Don't. I want you how you are. You look beautiful in glasses. I touch your cheek and, when you close your eyes, I lean in and lightly kiss your lips."

Jamie parted her lips slightly in anticipation. "I... I, um, press against you."

"My other arm is on your waist."

"I have my hands on the front of your, at your, um, on the collar of your shirt. I move them up. Into your hair. The back of your head."

Noa smiled. "Thank you for the best date I've had in a very long time, Lighthouse."

"You're welcome, Stargirl."

"Enjoy the rest of your evening. I'll see you tomorrow."

"Goodnight, Noa. I love you."

"I love you, Jamie. Goodnight."

Jamie waited until they were actually out of the window before she hung up the microphone again. She rested her elbows on the edge of the table and put her face in her hands. In a few days they would have another eight or nine days without communication, and the thought of it was making her sick. She took a deep breath, blew it out through her nose, and finished her meal.

// MISSION DAY 441 //

"IT'S GETTING harder," Jamie said. "Being apart from you."

"I know, Lighthouse."

They were in bed together, though apart. Noa had her tablet propped up with Jamie's picture on the screen. Jamie had Noa's portrait framed and smiling down at her from the nightstand. When they spoke, they looked into each other's eyes. Jamie's fingers moved along the wrinkles in the sheet like it was Noa's T-shirt. They had just finished making love, a quick exchange of dirty talk and quiet moans stifled by their pillows. Jamie's nerves were still singing from her orgasm and she felt vulnerable enough to tell the truth.

"I'm going to miss you over the next ten days," Jamie said. "But I know it's worse for you. I can go into town, I can talk to other people. I feel like I'm abandoning you."

"You're not."

"I know. But it's how it feels."

Noa closed her eyes. "You're always with me, Jamie. Even when we can't speak, you're with me. I've never really felt that kind of closeness with anyone. I'm a love-them-and-leave-them type, you know. I'm always looking for the next takeoff. But if being with you meant I could never fly again, I'd be okay with that."

"I'd never take the sky from you," Jamie said.

"I know. That was beautifully said."

"It's from a TV show."

Noa smiled. "That doesn't diminish its sentiment. I'm just saying that if there was a choice between seeing you every day and flying, I would sell my plane."

"You own a plane?"

"Of course I own a plane."

Jamie said, "You never told me you owned a plane. That's so cool."

Noa chuckled and pressed her face into the pillow. "I'll take you up sometime."

"Thank you."

"I can tell you're falling asleep, so I kiss your forehead. I take off your glasses and set them... where?"

"On the nightstand," Jamie said sleepily.

"I set them on the nightstand. I brush my hand down the side of your face and kiss your lips, and I whisper goodnight to you. Goodnight, Jamie."

"Night, love."

Noa heard the static of a broken connection and blinked back tears. She hated how dependent she was on the relationship, but she also wouldn't trade it for the world. She turned off her radio and slipped the earpiece off.

"Vera, sleep mode."

The assistant was programmed to say "Goodnight, Colonel," when sleep mode was activated, but Noa turned that off. She wanted Jamie's voice to be the last one she heard, and if she couldn't have Jamie, she didn't want a goodnight. The lights dimmed without comment from the artificial intelligence and the only illumination came from the tablet propped up in Noa's sleep nook. She fell asleep looking at Jamie's face, just as she could have if the world was perfect and they were actually together.

// MISSION DAY 452 //

NOA'S GRIN collapsed as soon as she heard Jamie's voice. "Lighthouse? What's wrong?"

"Nuffik."

"Baby, are... are you crying?"

"Mm-mm. Efra-think s'fyn."

It was their first window in ten days. It was extremely early in the morning, but Noa could still tell that Jamie's voice was off. It wasn't from sleepiness and if she wasn't crying...

"Are you sick?"

Jamie said, "Don'th be silly. It's da middle of-" There was a long pause. "-April," she finished with a rough exhale.

Noa said, "Was that a sneeze or did you blow your nose?"

Jamie didn't answer for a long few seconds. Finally she said, "Both, actually."

"Poor baby. Get back to bed."

"I am in bed." She sniffled. "I have the microphone stretched out like last time when we said goodnight to each other. It'll be fine."

"Jamie..."

"I just lost ten days with you. I'm not going to lose another one just because my stupid body isn't cooperating. I need my Noa time more than..." She sneezed again, this time accidentally keeping the microphone button depressed. Noa's heart twisted when she heard the agonized groan that followed the sneeze. "Besides, I can always go back to sleep when the window closes."

Noa said, "I pull the blankets up over your shoulders, tucking you in nice and tight. I brush your hair back and place my hand on your forehead. It's beaded with sweat and very warm. I check to make sure you have plenty of Kleenex and then I go downstairs to make you a big bowl of chicken noodle soup."

"Don't go," Jamie whispered.

"I'm already back," Noa said. "You must have fallen asleep while I was making it. So I wake you by kissing your temple, right by your eyebrow, and I ask if you're up to having a little broth."

Jamie said, "I'm too queasy."

"I'll just leave it here on the nightstand. It can cool there for a while until you're up for it."

"Okay. Thank you."

Noa said, "I'm still stroking your hair. Do you want me to tell you a story?"

"Only if it's a true one. Something about you."

"Oh. Okay..." She searched for something she hadn't told Jamie yet. "After the ISS disaster, when all the interview requests died down and I was out of the hospital, I retired from active duty. I left NASA. I tried to settle back into normal life. I suspected that people would only think about me on the anniversary of the disaster or in one of those 'where are they now' website things that pop up now and again. I wouldn't miss the celebrity and the people demanding to know my every step, but I had no idea what I was going to do with my days. I thought about getting a job as an airplane mechanic, something normal like that.

"Then one day, the richest man in the world showed up on my doorstep. Literally, he just showed up by himself in a rental car. Not even a fancy rental, just whatever they had available at the airport. He doesn't care about showing off like that. He asked me if I was working and if I would maybe consider a job with him. He was going to give me a chance to go back into space. He was offering me closure. But I think in a way, and in a way neither of us could even know, he was giving me a way to find you.

"He found me because of the ISS disaster. I was on the station because I was an accomplished pilot. I became a pilot because of my father, who was my hero from the time I could crawl. I don't believe in destiny or fate or our lives leading up to one specific point, but if everything I've done and everything that made me who I am turns out to just be stepping stones to meeting you, then I'll take it. Good and bad, I'll take it all."

She waited for Jamie to answer. She looked at the clock after the silence stretched on. They still had over forty minutes left in their window.

"Lighthouse? Jamie?" She smiled. "Did you fall asleep, baby?"

Noa considered her options. As long as the radio was still on, the radio would broadcast whatever she said. She imagined herself sitting next to the bed where Jamie was recuperating, the tip of her nose red from repeated swiping of her Kleenex, lips parted as she issued tiny, wheezing snores. She could almost feel Jamie's fevered forever under her palm as she began to sing under her breath.

"Someday I'm going to build a boat from plywood and glue. I'm going to steal my mother's sail, head off into the storms. I'll bear any rough seas I find and I'm going to break through. I swear I'm not going to stop until I'm back in your arms..."

"Noa?" Jamie's voice sounded so small, so puny.

"I'm here, baby."

"You sing beautifully."

Noa smiled. "Thank you."

"I think I should go to sleep."

"That sounds like a very good idea. I'm stroking your hair. I bend down and kiss your cheek, and I wish you sweet dreams."

"I'm going to leave the radio on. Don't stop singing."

"I won't." She wet her lips. "And I won't take my eyes off you. To the edge of the world I'd follow you. Where the lighthouse can't reach, on some dark and foreign beach, or an undiscovered place. I will run to you, I will fall to you. My reward will be one glimpse of your face..."

// MISSION DAY 470 //

NOA SAT near the window with her fruit pouch in one hand, looking out the window with her legs stretched out in front of her. She was barefoot, dressed for bed in shorts and a tank top. Jamie had reported she was in pajama bottoms and a T-shirt. They were having a late-night snack together which fell into a comfortable silence not long after their initial hellos. Noa reached out with her free hand to drag one fingertip along the edge of her window.

"America is beautiful from up here."

"Yeah?" Jamie sounded sleepy.

Noa said, "The whole world is gorgeous."

"What's your favorite?"

"The Pacific Northwest," Noa said without hesitation. "You get everything there. Oceans, mountains, cities, forests. No deserts, but I find deserts boring anyway. Just huge stretches of sand. There might be something remarkable to someone else, but I don't see the appeal."

Jamie shifted on her cushion and stirred her fruit. "Sometimes I forget you can look at the whole world. Every country, every continent. What's it like when you come back from up there?"

"Well, last time when I came home, I couldn't get over how small it really was. It seems huge when you're down there. Borders seem to mean something. But up here you can tell just how... how..." She made a gesture with her hands. "How everything is everyone else's backyard." She looked out the window. "I'm not used to describing this to someone else. Usually it's all internal and I only have to worry about making sense to myself."

Jamie said, "You don't talk about it with girlfriends or, you know, Kelly?"

"Not really. I'm not really... I don't... you know, relationships that involve sitting around and talking to each other... I don't really do that a lot."

"You don't seem like a hit-it-and-quit-it type."

Noa was quiet.

"I'm sorry if that came off judgmental. I didn't mean it like that."

"No, it's..." She uncrossed her feet and straightened out so that she was parallel to the wall, the low-gravity version of fidgeting. "It would be fair if you were. It's not exactly a point of pride to have gone this long without having a serious relationship. But I saw what happened to my mother when Dad died. It was like she had to become a different person just to exist in a world where he wasn't there. He died and her life ended at the same time. When I became a pilot, I decided I didn't want to put anyone in that position. I was fine with risking my own life. I didn't want to risk anyone else's. I didn't want to make anyone hurt that much."

"That's so sad. It sounds so lonely."

Noa said, "It can be. But I'm not lonely. I have Kelly. I've had other lovers. The physical act can be enough to distract me for a while."

Jamie shifted uncomfortably on her cushion. "Oh right. Kelly..."

"Lighthouse?"

"No," Jamie said, "nothing. It's nothing."

"It didn't sound like nothing. Talk to me."

Jamie grimaced and put down her snack. "I... I didn't think about Kelly. Or all the Kellys who are probably waiting for you to come home again."

Noa remembered the promise she made to Kelly before she left. "I don't want to," she whispered, as much to herself as to Jamie. "I hadn't thought about it, and last time after I recovered I was really looking forward to meeting up with women I have pasts with. But this time I haven't even thought about any of them. And now that I *am* thinking about it, I don't want to. I only want to see you."

Jamie pulled her knees up and wrapped her arms around them. "When you say things like that, it makes me think... it makes me feel like maybe you're as excited as I am. And that is so shocking to me. Because I'm just me. You're... you."

"You have a lot to offer, Lighthouse."

"What if we fight?"

Noa smiled. "Couples fight. Healthy ones, anyway. I can't wait to bicker with you about not picking up my shoes."

"Why would you not pick up your shoes? Were you raised in a barn?"

Noa rested her cheek against the hull. "I'm still worried about what might happen on the mission. If I never get back to Earth for one reason or another and we never get to meet face-to-face. But for the first time, I'm not willing to walk away to protect you. Pretty selfish, huh?"

Jamie pressed her fingers to her eyes before she picked the microphone back up. "Yeah, pretty self-centered. And... and if something did happen to you, god forbid, I want to know I had spent every possible moment with you. I already have to deal with you being out of contact for twenty-three hours of the day. When you're here and available, I want you here. With me."

"Now who's being selfish?" Noa said.

"I don't care."

Noa chuckled. "Me neither." She looked up at the chronometer. "Damn it. Why do we always get stuck with the fastest hour of the day?"

"Bad luck, I guess."

"That can't be it," Noa said. "Absolutely nothing about this is bad luck."

Jamie wrapped one arm around herself, the other holding the microphone close to her mouth. "An hour per day, for... how many days has it been since we started talking?"

"Three hundred and seventy-three. Hey... last week was our anniversary. One year since we started talking. Sorry I missed it, baby."

"I missed it, too," Jamie said. "What's three hundred and seventy-three divided by twenty-four?"

"Fifteen," Noa said. "Fifteen point... five."

Jamie said, "So technically, we've only known each other for fifteen days. Just over two weeks."

"It's been a hell of a two weeks," Noa said. "We used every minute wisely."

"Yeah," Jamie said. She'd noticed a bit of a sibilant hiss in Noa's voice. She blinked away her tears. After this conversation, they would be out of contact for another ten days. "You're moving too fast, baby. I'm about to lose you."

"I'll slow down soon, Jamie. I promise. I love you."

"I love you, too."

She listened until static took over the white noise, then pressed the microphone to her forehead and closed her eyes.

// MISSION DAY 540 //

NOA'S TRAINING prevented her from panicking when she was woken by an alarm. There were any number of things that could go wrong on the ship, especially when she was asleep, but this wasn't a simple proximity alert. She freed herself from bed and walk-crawled up the wall to the command center. She was still in her underwear and hoped whatever was wrong wouldn't require a video feed to Astraea. She had just fastened herself in when the communications screen lit up.

"Colonel, are you receiving?"

"I'm here. Who is this?"

"Marcus."

"Tell me what we're looking at, Marcus." She was already examining her monitors and could see for herself that this was a red situation. Red was bad.

Marcus said, "We're still trying to determine that. We're not into the black, so we know it's not an imminent threat. You're fine, at least for the moment."

"You can understand how that's not exactly a comfort."

"Of course, ma'am. Hold, please."

Noa ran a diagnostic of her systems. She saw the problem before they did. "Astraea Control, please confirm status of GCR shielding in sector A-3-1."

"Checking now, Colonel." A half-minute later, Marcus said, "Oh, shit."

"So that's a confirmed?"

"What? Oh. Yes. Confirmed failure, Colonel. Shit."

His reaction was unprofessional as hell, but she couldn't really fault him for that. The ship's hull was plated with armor to protect her from radiation. The shielding was the only reason she was able to remain in space for two years without risking her health. Now, according to the computer, part of that shielding had failed and galactic cosmic rays had a direct line to her living area. She was relatively safe. GCRs weren't constant and she could withstand a little exposure without very much ill effect. It was like she was floating on a beach and occasionally being hit by waves. Not fun, but also not necessarily deadly. The true threat was the potential of a solar particle event. Just one of those would be enough to kill her.

Noa undid her straps. "Marcus, contact Enver and let him know what's going on."

"On it, Colonel. I'm... I don't know what I can do from here."

"You can't do anything from there. I need to get outside and see why the panel failed."

Noa pushed off the floor and propelled herself to the back of the ship to the one piece of safety equipment she had hoped she'd never need. She opened the compartment and saw the shining dome of her spacesuit staring back at her. There was no hurry. She could spend half an hour to follow proper procedure, so she fixed an oxygen mask over her nose and mouth to rid her blood of nitrogen. Now that she was sitting still with nothing to do but think, her mind betrayed her. She remembered the last time she'd been in this type of situation and her composure faltered, just a light tremor on the surface of an otherwise calm lake.

There was an alarm, a search for the problem... she remembered Anton floating up from below her.

"*We had this problem in Russia,*" he'd said. "*Cold air coming from outside. We light candle, see which way the flame danced. That is how you find leak. You make what is invisible so it can be seen.*"

"*I'll tell NASA your plan. I'm sure they'll be happy to let us run around the station with a couple of lighters like we're at a Coldplay concert.*"

"*You should not mock conventional wisdom! Old wives tales come from old wives, and old wives become old wives because they survive! And that is what we will do! Survive! You go back that way, check Rassvet. I shall check Leonardo. See? Cooperation!*"

Because she was to his left and he was to her right, because it was easier for her to back up for them to switch positions, he had gone toward the leak while she went to salvation. This time she only had to worry about herself. By the time she was ready to suit up, Enver had arrived.

"Colonel? Noa. Are you all right?"

"Everything's fine up here, Enver. Plan for disaster so every minor inconvenience is just part of the schedule." She was in the airlock now. She pulled the suit to her so she could begin her work. It was a bit like constructing a robot, attaching arms and harnesses to the rigid torso and connecting communications to the helmet. She pulled her knees up to her chest, rolled forward, and stretched both legs out into the LTA - Lower Torso Assembly. She hitched that up to her waist and attached the cooling umbilical to it. Once that was done, she pulled the upper torso close and wriggled into it.

"Colonel?"

"Give me a second, Enver. You know how long it takes us ladies to get ready in the morning."

Enver said, "My apologies. No rush. I merely wished to inform you we're examining the issue down here."

Comforting to know, but she also knew that despite his genius and wealth, there was literally nothing he could do from the ground. She attached the life support to the suit, checked to make sure it was working properly, and then locked the top half of the suit to the lower. She secured her helmet, slipped on her gloves, and flexed her fingers to make sure she had full range of motion. After a quick check for leaks, she carried her toolkit to the airlock. As she waited for the pressure to drop enough for her to open the door, music began to play over her speakers. It took her a moment to recognize it as Tom Petty's "Free Fallin'".

"Cute, Enver," she said.

"I thought we could use something to lighten to mood."

She smiled behind the glass of her helmet. The airlock door opened and she gripped the edges of the door to pull herself outside.

And she was in space. She was floating outside the safety of her ship, hanging by a thread. She turned toward the planet and stared down. Clouds were between her and the ocean. It was immense and so small at the same time. The distance from her toe to the top of her helmet covered entire continents. And yet the whole planet stretched out to either side, so vast that she couldn't see the curve without turning her body to look.

"You should've played a little Bette instead of Tom," she suggested.

"What... oh, 'From a Distance'," Enver said. "Yes, very true, that would work as well."

She tore her gaze away from the tremendous view and turned back toward ODIE. It had been over a year since she'd actually seen it with her own eyes. She put her hand against the side of it and used her wrist-mounted PDA to confirm she was at the correct panel before she disconnected it. The panel remained connected by a tether much like hers, and she pushed it to one side so it wouldn't get in her way. Each panel had an independent operating system so that if one failed, it wouldn't take out the entire shield. It also made diagnosing the problem much easier.

"Enver, this panel is dead."

"I'm reading that, too," he confirmed. "We're going over our options."

Noa said, "Don't cut me out of the loop here."

"The failed panel is relatively inconsequential. One of our engineers has suggested increasing the output from the neighboring panels to 'fill the gap,' as it were. There would still be a small bleed-through but nothing to be concerned about. In the event of a solar particle flare, you would have to take cover within the ship until it was past. We would have ample time to warn you when that was going to happen." He paused. "But..."

"That sounds like a big but."

"It is. Quite sizeable. We're not entirely sure why the panel failed in the first place. If the others begin to fail in the same manner, your protection will decrease incrementally."

Noa calculated the time she had left on the mission. "People have survived that long in space without any shielding at all."

"Yes, in the dinosaur era where they didn't know any better. We have options. But this is bigger than radiation, Noa. These panels are also designed to protect you during reentry. If more of them fail, you won't be able to come home without burning to a crisp."

Noa felt a chill. "What... um..."

"There are no real options here, Noa, there is just what we must do. You will boost the output of the panels while they are still fully operational. Plug the hole. And then you get back inside and you abort the mission."

She closed her eyes. "Are you absolutely~"

Enver said, "No debating. No questioning. If those panels fail, you cannot come home. That is a level of mission failure even if you clear the entire minefield. As it stands you are... you are... I don't have the percentages right in front of me, but you passed the halfway point a very long time ago. You've set back the clock by decades. Space travel is possible again because of you. And you have proven that the ODIE's systems are capable of maintaining life long enough to get a crew to Mars. These are all successes, Colonel Laurie. Just because you didn't cross the finish line is no reason to call it a failure. I, for one, plan to pop a bottle of champagne when this is all said and done."

"Cutting the mission short is going to cost your company a lot of money."

"Money? Stock options? Yes, Noa, I am going to lose some money if the mission is cut short, but whatever amount it is, I consider it the cost of saving your life and I will call it a bargain. Now boost the output of those panels, get into the ship, and we'll begin the procedures to bring you home."

The situation suddenly moved out of the abstract and into the real, and Noa realized one of the benefits to cutting the mission short would be that she would get to go home.

"Colonel?"

"I'm here. I'm just processing the situation."

"Take your time," Enver said, "but keep working while you process. With any luck, you'll be back on solid ground by tonight."

Noa twisted to look behind her at the planet slowly turning. *Jamie...* She faced forward again, gripped her wrench, and began opening the next panel.

It was time to go home.

Jamie rarely kept her phone in her pocket when she worked. It was sitting on the table where the radio had once sat, and she was aware of it buzzing as she fed a piece of maple through the whirring bandsaw. When the machine's sound fell silent, she heard the ringtone. It was Lily's. If Lily was calling this much, then it was either something incredibly dire or maddeningly mundane. She pushed her safety googles into her hair, took out her ear protection, and answered the phone.

"What—"

"Turn on the TV."

Jamie's irritation vanished. Lily sounded frantic. "What's wrong?"

"Just turn on the TV."

Jamie tossed her goggles down and started for the barn door. "What channel?"

"Any channel."

That made Jamie run. By the time she got into the house, her fingers were shaking too much to work the remote control. She was still clutching the phone to her ear.

"What's happening? Is it Noa? Is she all right?"

"I don't know. They said it was planned and everything is under control, but... I-I don't... I don't know."

Jamie found a network with a BREAKING NEWS - LIVE banner across the bottom of the screen. An anchor was talking and Noa's NASA headshot, the same one that had hung over the radio since they started talking, filled the upper portion of the screen. Jamie's heart leapt into her throat and she almost dropped the phone. Instead she jabbed the volume button with her thumb.

"—no word on a projected landing site, but it's expected that her current trajectory is going to take her somewhere near the southwestern United States. It makes sense that they would attempt to get as close to California as possible since that's where the mission began. It's also where Astraea is located. We're getting some footage taken from Twitter and Instagram, people with their cell phones taking footage as the ship passes overhead. Let's see if we can pull some of that up."

The image shifted to a shaky video that was clearly shot on a phone. It was being aimed at a cloudy sky as a yellow flame streaked across the horizon. It flickered and flashed, light reflecting off ODIE and the exterior hull burning against the atmosphere.

"This was taken in Alabama about fifteen minutes ago. Once again, this is the Astraea Aviation craft ODIE piloted by Colonel Noa Laurie reentering the atmosphere well ahead of schedule. We're not certain why the mission has ended, but Enver Crane did issue a press release before any sightings had occurred, which leads us to believe this really was an intentional scrubbing of the mission and not an error or emergency situation."

Jamie said, "Have... did they say if Noa is okay?"

"When I first turned it on, they said there's no way the ship could be coming in like this without a pilot. Even if the automated systems kicked in, there would be a sign. They said there's definitely someone in control up there."

Jamie dropped onto the couch. "Thank god. Thank *you*. Thank you for letting me know."

"You're welcome. I'm going to let you hang up so you can focus on the news. I hope she's okay, Jamie."

"Me too."

She hung up and put the phone down on the couch beside her. She folded her hands in front of her face and, though she'd never been a praying woman, whispered to whoever might be listening that Noa wasn't hurt.

The ship rattled around her. The turbulence was unbelievable, like she'd been floating through clear skies and then dived directly into a thunderstorm. ODIE shouted all around her in the only voice it had: squeaks and rattles and alarms. Warnings flashed on every monitor but she ignored them. She didn't need a screen to tell her it was much too hot inside the ship. She was dripping sweat and her skin felt like it was roasting inside her spacesuit. She made a point of not looking at the actual temperature. If she didn't know how hot it actually was, she could pretend it was simply a warm day in July. In Arizona. Under a tin roof. Where someone was barbequing.

"Goddamn it's hot," she gasped.

"Colonel?" Enver asked.

"I'm here, Enver." She blinked away the sweat. Her eyes were stinging but she focused on her trajectory. "I don't think I'm going to make it all the way to Mojave."

Enver said, "We've already made that determination. We found an alternative. The coordinates should be coming up on your screens now."

Noa reached up and dismissed the warnings, then dropped her hand back to the yoke to keep the ship steady. She saw the latitude and longitude and punched it into the map. An image came up and she blinked to make sure her eyes weren't deceiving her.

"What is that?"

"That's your landing pad."

Noa said, "That's *desert*."

"That's the Snakeridge Reservoir."

She zoomed in on the screen and saw a narrow ribbon of blue. She laughed. "You have way too much faith in my skills, Enver!"

"You can do it, Noa. I've been reassured by my people that it's possible."

"Possible. That's not a word I want to hear right now, Enver."

He laughed softly. "I know, dear, I know. But the alternative is a hard landing, and I'm not certain you could survive that crash."

"You're just worried I might scratch your baby."

"No!" He sounded aghast. "I would... I can't... you must believe me, the ship actually *could* weather a landing on~"

"I'm teasing you, Enver."

"Oh. Right. I'm sorry. Things are very tense down here."

Noa said, "Really? Why? What's going on down there?"

He laughed again. "Nothing much. Typical office drama."

"Tedious," she said. "I'm glad I'm missing it."

Sunlight streamed in through the window, actual sunlight filtered through the atmosphere and creating a day on Earth. Her monitors were smoking and sparking, and one had gone dark completely. She watched her altitude and, when the time was right, deployed her chute. She felt the drag as it unfolded behind her and the heat had dropped noticeably. The ship was still rattling as if it were about to break apart, more than a year of relying on its durability and now it seemed like it had been cobbled together out of scrap.

"How do I look, Enver?"

"You're cutting it very close, Colonel."

"Everyone's a critic." She looked at the screens. One of them had frozen, no longer providing useful information, so she reached up and jabbed the buttons until the status screen closed and revealed Jamie's smiling face.

"Take me home, Lighthouse," she whispered.

She had vastly higher control than she did on her last return from space, but it still felt like she'd been shot from a gun and she had to guide the bullet to the right target. The monitor directly in front of her showed the ground speeding by at a remarkable rate. Roads crisscrossed the landscape beneath her and she was able to catch fleeting glimpses of cars parked along the shoulder to watch as she passed overhead. A countdown clock appeared at the top of the screen.

"Brace for landing!" Enver said.

Noa held her breath. She kept her eyes glued to the monitor as the reservoir loomed ever larger. The impact rattled her, thrust her forward against the straps and then gravity flung her back into the seat. And then, for the first time in over a year, the ODIE came to a stop. Flotation devices erupted on ODIE's underside to prevent it from sinking. Her stomach twisted and squeezed around itself. She tried to reach for the straps to undo them, but her arms wouldn't work. Her head lolled forward until she forced it back against the cushion.

After an interminable amount of time, she heard voices outside, Astraea employees who had been sent out ahead to recover her. One of them popped the hatch.

"Colonel?"

"A-heh," Noa said, her tongue refusing to work properly. Her tongue had weight. How could she have forgotten that? But now moving it required fighting gravity, however minorly, and her brain was having a hard time figuring it out. "Here," she slurred. "I'm he-ah."

The Astraea ground crew, medics from the look of them, crowded around her in a space that had once been hers alone. She felt an odd sense of violation when one of them pushed a monitor out of the way so he could kneel next to her seat. Another one unfastened the straps for her. She expected to drift up but her body remained alarmingly frozen. She felt like she suddenly weighed a thousand pounds.

"Can't move."

"That's to be expected given how long you were in space." He fitted an oxygen mask over her face. She breathed deeply as he rested a hand on her shoulder. He might as well have punched her given how heavy it felt. "We're going to very carefully take you out of here and get you to a hospital where you can begin your recuperation. Just relax and let us take care of everything."

She nodded. They checked her vitals and declared she was safe to move. One of them brought in a backboard, and the others carefully lifted her from the chair and stretched her out across it. Straps were pulled tight across her legs and torso to keep her from rolling. When they lifted her, a simple change of altitude measured in inches rather than feet, her stomach shot up into her throat as if she had just plunged on a roller coaster.

"Colonel?"

She was still wearing the oxygen mask so she nodded. They moved slowly and she looked past them, watching as she was taken out of the ship she'd come to know as home. Her eyes welled up and tears fell, following the contours of her cheeks. The tears on the right side pooled against the strap of her mask. As she was lifted to be taken out of the ship, she reached out and touched the edge of the hatch. The medics stopped.

"Colonel, is there something wrong?"

"No." Her voice echoed hollowly inside the mask. "I just need a second."

"Absolutely. Take all the time you need."

Noa looked down past her feet. The light coming in through the hatch made everything look strange. The shadows were falling all wrong, and the cabinets and shelves looked less substantial. It already looked so small. She let her eyes drift past the nook where she slept, the spot where she had done a majority of her interviews and school presentations. She flattened her hand against the hatch. The metal was still warm, but not as scalding as it would be on the exterior.

"Bye, ODIE," she said so quietly that she doubted it could be heard through the mask. "Thank you for keeping me safe for so long."

The medics waited until she dropped her hand - it hurt to keep it elevated for so long - before they took her outside. She cried out and turned her head away when the sunlight hit her face.

"Oh, god, I'm sorry." One of the medics slipped his sunglasses onto her. "Enver warned me about that but it slipped my mind."

"It's okay."

She saw that they'd accessed ODIE by using a small boat. Once they were aboard, she was placed in the center. The man who had been doing all the talking told someone else they were good to go, and the boat headed back for shore. One of the medics looked down at her and she made an "up" gesture. He understood what she needed and propped up the backboard so she could see over the side of the ship. There it was, ODIE, bobbing docilely on the surface. Its surface was pockmarked and scorched in places, but it had done its job admirably. It had been her home. She was going to miss it like crazy.

The tears came back to her eyes.

"Welcome home, Colonel Laurie," the medic said.

She smiled behind the mask. "Thank you," she said. "It's good to be back."

PART

IV

ENVER HAD, of course, arranged for a private room at the nearest hospital. Noa barely remembered the ambulance ride or the doctors fussing over her as she was transferred into the building. One, a disturbingly young man named Bryan, explained it would be some time before she could move normally.

"The exercises you did while up there kept your body physically strong," he said, "but you still need time to adjust. You can't spend that long in a zero-g environment and then just go skipping along."

She knew all of this, of course. Her injuries after the ISS disaster meant she was hospitalized while she reacclimated to the world. The knowledge didn't make it easier for her to lie immobilized on a bed in a room where even the air felt heavy.

Enver had arrived at the hospital by the time she was admitted and taken to her room. He waited patiently near the sink as the nurse transferred her from wheelchair to bed. Noa smiled at him and waited until the nurse left before she spoke.

"Private plane?"

"Helicopter," he said. "A little nicer on the environment. I figured something or another from ODIE got leaked into the reservoir when you landed, so I'm attempting to balance as well as I can."

She held out her hand to him. "It's good to see you again, Enver."

He came forward and took her hand between both of his. "So grateful to see you in one piece. They told me while I was en route that everything checked out. You're good, right, you're fine? Everything...?"

Noa nodded. "Just weak. You never notice how much gravity there is until you get used to not having it. I'm feeling kind of puny lying here." She was also nauseated and dizzy. The edges of the room were wobbly. She was used to up and down being relative, but now they were firmly established. It was hard to look at any one spot for very long.

"Take your time getting back on your feet. The room will be paid up for as long as you need it. And if you need anything, absolutely anything, you just let me know."

"I will. Thank you, Enver."

"Of course." He reached into his jacket pocket and handed her a cell phone with a slip of paper covering the screen. The paper had a ten-digit phone number written on it. "I also got that for you."

Noa looked at the number. "What is it?"

"Just a phone, if there's anyone you want to speak with. That phone number goes to, ah, some furniture maker outside Indianapolis. I've no idea who she is, but she must be quite important to you."

Noa blinked back tears. "Thank you, Enver. You don't know how much this means to me."

"No, I don't. But if you ever want to explain, I'll listen." He patted her arm as gently as he could. "I'll give you a little privacy. There will be Astraea personnel right outside the door for privacy or if you should need them. Get some rest, Noa. You are officially off the clock."

She grinned and watched him leave the room. Once the door was closed, she looked at the number in her hand. She was exhausted, and the thought of talking to anyone else made her feel even more tired.

Then again, Jamie Faris wasn't just anyone.

Jamie almost didn't answer since she didn't recognize the number. She was glued to the news, who had stopped their live coverage when the ship landed. A helicopter over the reservoir caught footage of a disturbingly motionless body being carried out of ODIE on a backboard, but the anchor reported Astraea's official spokesman said Noa was okay. Jamie had been trying to find more information online using her phone's browser when it began ringing. She brushed her thumb across the screen.

"Hello?"

"I'm okay, Lighthouse."

Jamie had been seated but she shot to her feet, her hand over her mouth. "Noa?"

"Hi, baby. I'm so, so tired but I couldn't sleep without letting you know I was safe. They took me to a hospital and they're going to check me out, let me get used to gravity again. Maybe give me a little rehab. I don't know how long we'll get to talk—"

"You need to sleep," Jamie said.

Noa said, "I'll sleep in a minute. But Enver gave me this phone. And if he wants it back, he's going to have to fight me for it. So as long as I'm here, I'm going to be calling you as much as I can."

Jamie laughed. "I'll keep the phone by my side at all times, I promise." She sat down again, full of energy she didn't know what to do with. "You're on Earth." She laughed and pressed her fingers to her forehead. "That sounds so strange. But it's true. You're... you're here, you're really on Earth."

"I really am."

"I'm glad you're safe. Do... do you know how long it'll take before you're, uh, better?"

Noa said, "I don't. No one has ever been in space this long, so they're not really sure how much time I'll need to get back to normal." She paused. "I'd like to come and see you when I'm ready."

Jamie said, "You just saved me the trouble of thinking up a way to invite you without sounding desperate. Yes. Yes, please, as soon as you can." She laughed at herself. "Well... so much for not sounding desperate."

"It's nice to be wanted," Noa said, resting her cheek against the pillow. She could see out the window, at the bare mountains in the distance. She was again stricken by the weird vertigo in which everything in the room seemed to shift a few degrees and then snapped back. She closed her eyes. "I think I need to get some sleep, Lighthouse."

"Right, of course. Call me whenever. Day or night."

Noa said, "Day or night. No windows. Just whenever I need to hear your voice, there you'll be."

"And for longer than an hour."

"That sounds perfect."

Jamie said, "Get some rest, Stargirl. Welcome home."

Though Jamie wasn't the first one to say it, she was the first one who almost made Noa cry. "I'll talk to you soon."

They hung up and Jamie immediately added the contact to her phone. "NOA." She smiled at it, the smile growing when she realized it meant that Noa could call her at any time. She fell back against the couch and laughed.

Her Stargirl was finally home.

Noa slept most of her first day back. Nurses and doctors came into her room but not nearly as many as she would have expected. She had a theory that Enver had somehow made sure they stayed away unless it was an absolute emergency. A physical therapist came in on the second day to gauge her "situation." He estimated it would be about "six to eight weeks" before she was fully functional.

"But again," he said with an affable smile, "no one really knows what to expect. Your situation is quite unique."

"So it could be faster."

"Well, yes. But we must be careful not to rush things. Your body has been through a tremendous strain. Forcing it back to normalcy could cause more problems in the long run."

She nodded but was already calculating how long it would take before she could visit Indiana.

The following day, she convinced the nurse to bring her a walker. She was only able to make it into the hallway before she turned back and collapsed onto the bed in a panting, sweaty heap. She was scolded by both her doctor and the physical therapist, but the next day she did it again. She focused on which parts hurt the most - ankle, hip, back - and spent her time in bed stretching them. Her stamina was the biggest problem. Just the idea of walking to the elevator was exhausting, and she remembered Jamie said her driveway was something like the length of a football field. So a hundred yards became her goal.

She called Jamie every day. Their first phone conversation had taken place while Noa was sitting outside in her wheelchair, having been pushed there by an orderly. Holding a phone up to her ear was too much for her arm, so the phone was in her lap and connected to a Bluetooth earpiece and speaker. Just like the old days, she thought.

"It's gorgeous out here," Noa said.

"Describe it to me," Jamie said. She was sitting on the floor with her back against her bed. Cisco was curled up beside her. "God knows I've described enough weather to you. It's your turn."

Noa looked around. "There's a brick walkway around a huge water feature. There are some, uh, there's wooden furniture all around the perimeter. And sun shades so people don't have to sit in the heat. The ground is mostly AstroTurf, because we're so close to the desert. Although you'd think the water feature would defeat that purpose." She looked to her right and stifled a laugh. "There's a woman in a wheelchair staring at me. Hello, ma'am. Oh, she rolled herself away."

"What's it like having people around you again?"

"It's very strange. I keep muttering to myself or singing to myself, and then someone answers. But it's still harder to get used to gravity and the fact I can't fly anymore."

Jamie said, "Yeah, that would be a hard one to give up."

Noa dropped her head back against the cushion of her chair. "I feel so weak. It's frustrating as hell."

"I know, baby. But you need time to get back on your feet."

"I hate thinking about the fact you're just a few miles away~"

Jamie laughed. "More like two thousand."

Noa continued. "~and I can't just run out the door and go see you."

"I feel the same way. I wish I could hop on a plane and be at your bedside while you're recuperating. But beyond the price of the ticket, you need to focus on your health. And the things I want to do when I finally see you aren't very conducive to the healing process."

"Oh, really." Noa raised an eyebrow and repositioned her legs. "I'll just consider that incentive to get better as soon as possible."

They fell into a comfortable silence. Jamie stroked the top of Cisco's head. Noa scanned the garden for some detail she missed while describing it. Jamie glanced toward the clock and laughed when she saw what time it was.

"It's three-fifteen."

Noa looked at her watch. It was a quarter past twelve for her. "Okay..."

"You called me at two-fifteen. We've been talking for an hour. That's why we fell quiet. We're waiting for the window to close on us."

Noa laughed. "I guess we developed a rhythm, huh? We don't have to worry about that now. We could talk all afternoon if we wanted. Except you probably have to get back to work at some point."

"Work can wait. I don't care if we just sit here silently."

"We'll keep talking until the nurse comes to take me back inside. Deal?"

"Sounds good to me."

When she wasn't talking to Jamie or recuperating, Noa filled her time doing interviews. Enver convinced her it was the best way to control the narrative of the aborted mission. If she didn't tell her first-hand account, people might try to say she was at fault. Enver willingly took the blame for what had gone wrong. His design had failed and Noa was forced to take drastic action to save her own life. No other pilot could have done a better job, he insisted, and he would sign Noa up for another mission in a heartbeat. He wanted to be sure the public knew that truth.

And then there were interviews from her hospital bed.

There were long walks that only got her ten feet away from her bed, then twenty.

She graduated from a wheelchair to a walker. The elevator was no longer her final frontier, and she insisted to her therapist that she could attempt the stairs. The first day she was proven wrong. The second day she was also not quite able to get down to the next landing. After a week, she could get to the lobby, even though it left her too exhausted to walk back to her bed. She gratefully accepted a wheelchair and still considered it a victory.

Each day she reported her progress to Jamie. They talked, sometimes for twenty minutes and other times for an hour. They texted each other goodnight. Noa tried to be reasonable about how she felt, tried to be intensely critical of herself, but even under the harshest judgment she found herself falling deeper into love with Jamie.

Five weeks into her recuperation, she stopped at the intersection of two hallways and looked down at her feet. She caught her breath and rolled her shoulders.

"How far is this from my bed?" she asked the orderly.

He looked back the way they had come. "Well, we did two circuits this time. I'd say about a hundred yards."

Noa smiled and tightened her grip on the walker. "Yeah. That's what I thought. Okay. Let's keep going."

"Are you su—" He caught himself before he finished the question. Everyone in the hospital had learned to stop asking her that question. So he just put a hand on her back to help her balance and let her lead the way. She told herself she would spend one more week building her strength and stamina, regaining her ability to walk as unsupported as possible, and then she would ask Enver to make arrangements for her trip.

Two weeks later, she boarded a private plane with an orderly at her side and a cane in her hand, smiling too much to notice the lingering pain in her back.

// POST-MISSION - CONTACT //

THE SEATBELT cut across Noa's neck, but there was no more comfortable position for her to place it. She felt painted against the corner of the backseat, her legs pulled up and folded in front of her so she would take up as little space as possible. She had agonized over what to wear and finally settled on jeans and a button-down green plaid shirt. She was also wearing a straw cowboy hat, which had been a gift from Enver for reasons she couldn't comprehend. Whatever his thought process, she liked it more than she expected to.

Trees and houses swept by outside the window next to her head. The driver had his phone mounted next to the steering wheel in a position which allowed her to see the screen. He took a turn and she could see that the blue line of their route ended less than a mile straight ahead of their current position.

"Can you stop the car?"

The Astraea representative who'd picked her up from the airport - either Ted or Ben, she couldn't remember which - glanced up at his phone to look at her, then told the driver, "You can stop here." He looked at Noa again as the car slowed. "Is everything okay?"

"Yeah. I'll walk the rest of the way."

TedBen looked at her cane. "Are you sure~"

She glared at him. "I just spent a year and a half in a tin can, and another six weeks in a hospital recuperating. I want to get some fresh air."

"Yes, of course." He reached for his seatbelt.

"Alone."

"Enver won't like that."

Noa smiled. "He's a big boy. He'll get over it." She opened the car door. "I have my phone if I need to call you for a ride home. Otherwise, consider yourselves free."

TedBen sputtered. "We're supposed to stay with you for your entire trip."

"I don't want you to do that. Enver might be annoyed, but I'll be pissed off. Would you rather deal with an annoyed Enver later or a pissed-off me right now?"

To his credit, TedBen didn't even consider the question. "Enjoy your walk, Colonel."

"You're good people, Ted."

"It's Michael."

She was thrown. "Okay. Right. Michael."

Noa got out of the car and stepped away from the road. She gripped the cane tightly with her right hand, fingers curled around the ornate grip. She could feel the pressure rising along its thin length, like a tremor between her arm and the ground. Her feet seemed to weigh a thousand pounds. The idea of walking even a handful of steps made sweat pop out on her brow. She watched as the rental car executed a three-point turn and went back the way it had come. She smiled and waved when it passed her. She saw TedB ~ Michael ~ looking at her with worry but she just nodded her head to let him know she was all right. Once she was alone on the road, she looked in the direction of Jamie's house. She took a deep breath of fresh, unfiltered air, and began walking.

It was a gorgeous day. The sun was bright and the breeze was just enough to keep her from feeling too hot. She pushed her hat higher on her forehead and found a good step-cane-step rhythm. She wasn't sure what to call the place where Jamie lived. It seemed like a lot of people lived nearby, but the houses were too spaced out for her to consider it a neighborhood. The south side of the street faced a wide field, making it feel like the country, but in her mind the country had to be more rural.

She heard a car approaching and slow down, so she moved further into the grass. The driver rolled down her window and smiled, shielding her eyes with a flat hand. "Do you need a lift?"

"No, thank you," Noa said.

"Are you sure?" The woman was wearing sunglasses, but it was obvious she was looking at the cane. "It's no trouble."

"I appreciate it, but I just sent my car away. I'm looking forward to the walk." She took out her cell phone and held it up. "I can call them back just as quickly."

The woman said, "Well. Okay. If you're sure."

"I am. It was very kind of you to stop."

The woman drove on. Noa looked down at her feet, the way they had pushed some of the gravel away from the pavement. The ground was heavy under the soles of her shoes, as if she could feel it pressing up against her. Another long, slow breath and then she started walking again. Months of weightlessness left her feeling like a lumbering oaf. Every step felt sloppy and monstrous without the fluidity that came with a lack of gravity. Her heels, ankles, and calves burned, but she could feel the other side. She knew that she was close to the wall. Soon she would climb over it and, on the other side, be an inhabitant of Earth once more.

She had the address memorized and looked at each mailbox she passed. Finally she saw the right one and stopped. It was a simple metal box on a cross-shaped post. The name FARIS was spelled out with reflective stickers above the number. Behind the mailbox was a long ribbon of driveway that unspooled up to the large blue house. Noa had a lump in her throat as she looked at it. Jamie's home. The place where they'd had so many conversations. The place where Jamie had been when they fell in love. She squared her shoulders and tapped her cane against the pavement once before she turned and stepped onto Jamie's property.

Noa was halfway to the barn when Jamie walked out, head down, looking at something in her hands. Jamie was wearing a blue flannel shirt unbuttoned over a scoop neck T-shirt and jeans with the cuffs rolled up to reveal her naked ankles. Her hair had fallen over her glasses and she absently swatted it back with her free hand. A dog - obviously Cisco - was by her side and slowed when he saw the intruder. He faced her and made a sound so quiet that Noa couldn't hear it, but Jamie could.

First Jamie said, "Shush."

Then she followed his gaze and saw what he saw.

Her fingers curled tighter around her phone. She stopped walking, one foot still bent mid-step. Noa smiled nervously. She suddenly felt ridiculous in the stupid cowboy hat, but she didn't want to take it off now that Jamie had seen her. She smiled and stood still, putting her weight on the cane. They were standing about twenty feet apart. Noa didn't want to break the silence, didn't want to ruin the moment. She would have stood and stared at Jamie for another hour if given the opportunity.

Jamie broke the silence. "Noa."

"Hi, Lighthouse."

Jamie ran to her. Noa opened her arms and accepted Jamie into them, crushed by the hug. She closed her eyes and pressed her face against the warm softness of Jamie's shirt. It smelled like laundry detergent, flowers and lavender, and she also felt the abrasive rasp of wood shavings against her cheek. Jamie stepped back but kept her hands on Noa's waist. Her eyes were wet and, when she smiled, a tear trickled out down the side of her nose.

"You're here," Jamie said.

"I'm here."

"You're so small."

Noa laughed. "Hey!"

"No, I just mean... you're... I imagined you six feet tall. You were a giant in my mind. I can't believe you're shorter than me."

"Not by much," Noa said.

Jamie said, "No, not by much."

"I was going to greet you properly, but I..." She glanced past Jamie at the other houses nearby. There weren't any fences, so anyone could be watching them. "I wasn't sure..."

"What?"

"If you were out. If your neighbors..." She looked at Jamie's mouth.

Jamie realized what she was saying. "What neighbors?"

She leaned in and Noa tilted her head accordingly, parting her lips just as Jamie touched them. Noa had never considered herself a romantic kisser. Kissing was something done during sex or to greet an intimate friend. Kissing was a gesture or a means to an end. But with Jamie, the kiss was a culmination of everything they'd shared. Every word, every night spent listening for a voice in the static, every quiet moment after orgasm listening to the breathing of someone she'd never met. It all led to this first kiss, the first physical intimacy, the moment they finally came together.

It was worth the wait.

Noa turned her head slightly and felt Jamie's tongue against her lower lip. She let her cane dangle between her thumb and forefinger as she flattened her hand between Jamie's shoulders. The other hand moved down and pressed into the small of her back, guiding her closer. Jamie arched her back and let her body mold against Noa's.

Neither of them knew how long the kiss lasted, or how long it would have lasted if Cisco hadn't interrupted by bumping the back of Jamie's knees. Jamie looked down, which caused Noa's lips to graze her cheek and eyelashes. She closed her eyes and breathed in Jamie's scent as she scolded the dog. Her skin was buzzing to have Jamie in her arms, to actually hold her and hear every noise she made - the quiet "Shoo, go on," and the laugh under her breath as the dog grunted possessively - instead of hearing whatever happened to come through the radio.

They looked at each other without moving apart. Jamie brought her hand up and brushed it over Noa's cheek, down to her mouth.

"You're really here," Jamie said. "And you're... you're really you."

"I am." She stared into Jamie's eyes, almost giddy at the chance to really look at her. The handful of pictures she'd received had been enough for her to create a mental picture and gave her a template for her best dreams, but it was nothing compared to actually seeing her in the flesh. This was Jamie Faris, the woman who had kept her sane, and now they were together. She'd never seen anyone so beautiful. She laughed and shook her head. "I can't believe you called yourself average."

"Stop," Jamie said. "Your voice. I can't believe I'm hearing your voice. Say something else."

Noa whispered, "I love you, Lighthouse."

Jamie's eyes welled up again. "I love you too, Stargirl."

They kissed again. Noa leaned into Jamie, rising on her toes to make up for their height distance. Jamie noticed the adjustment and held her tighter. Noa could only hold that position for a few seconds before her legs began to shake and she almost knocked them over. She got the cane down in time, planting it in the dirt and leaning hard to keep herself from falling. Jamie's hands moved to her flanks, just under her arm, and Noa's skin tingled at the touch even through her clothes.

"What's wrong? Are you okay?"

"I'm tired. I-I walked a really long way."

"God, I would have come picked you up..."

Noa shook her head. "I wanted to walk. I just didn't think about how much it would take out of me. I'll be fine, I just need to rest."

Jamie had already guided Noa's arm across her shoulders. "Let's get you inside. I have a big bathtub. You can take a soak."

"That sounds like heaven," Noa said. "Thank you."

"Sure. Can you walk?"

Noa nodded. "If you help me."

Jamie said, "We'll take it slow."

They walked together, taking it a step at a time, neither of them in much of a hurry to separate. Noa smiled and rested her head against Jamie's as she was taken into the house. Cisco went with them, sometimes trailing and sometimes moving ahead to watch them like a disapproving chaperone.

She tried not to gawk too much at Jamie's house as she was led upstairs, but she couldn't help it. For so long Jamie was a mystery to her. Now she was actually in the woman's house. She could stare at Jamie all she wanted and burn those features into her memory. Her hand was resting on Jamie's shoulder but she moved it up into the short hair at the back of her neck. She scratched it and Jamie hunched her shoulders.

"You... have to stop that."

"Oh. I'm sorry. I thought you might like that."

Jamie said, "I do. A lot. Too much."

Noa smiled. "Oh. Gotcha. Filed away for later."

There wasn't much light on the stairs, but Noa was fairly positive that Jamie blushed.

When they reached the second floor landing, Jamie navigated Noa past an open door to their right. Noa glanced inside and stopped walking.

"Wait. Wait, wait."

Jamie came back to her. "What?"

"Take me in here."

"In the... bedroom...?"

Noa said, "I want to see the radio."

"Oh! Right. Yeah. Of course." She took Noa into the bedroom.

There it was. She'd placed it on a small table next to the window, near the foot of the bed. She remembered all the conversations they'd had on this little box of wires and coils. She slipped away from Jamie's grip and limped over under her own power. It felt like she had twin rubber bands connecting her knees to her ankles, and both were on fire. She ignored the pain. The office chair was slightly pulled out and she used the cane to maneuver herself into the seat. She sighed as the spring took her weight and she stretched her legs out underneath the table.

It was just a simple radio. She'd seen hundreds like it, or variations of the same thing, since she was a little girl. *"I'm looking out the window here. There's a sliver of the moon behind some clouds... what does it look like to you, up there?"* She reached out and put her hand on top of the radio, sliding her fingers across the cool plastic. *"I'm still in my pajamas. I'm going to go take a bath after the window closes."* Her thumb swept across the glass covering the dial. *"Right now I'm lying across my bed, imagining you on top of me..."* Noa unhooked the microphone and brought it up to her lips.

"Hello, hello. Anyone still up there?" She raised an eyebrow and looked back at Jamie. "I guess the neighborhood kind of died after I left."

"Looks like it," Jamie said.

Noa examined the radio with a critical eye. "Do you have any idea how it was able to reach ODIE?"

"I was going to ask you," Jamie said. "I thought maybe Enver Crane and his geeks would have figured it out when you were recuperating."

"They didn't tell me if they did. I don't think they were even looking. There was security in place, Jamie. Firewalls. Even if you happened to find the right frequency, even if this little mundane radio had the power to reach all the way to space, there's no way we should've been able to talk. There's no way it should ever have worked even one time."

Jamie put a hand on Noa's shoulder and squeezed. Noa liked the weight of it. "Maybe someone or something just knew how much you needed to hear a friendly voice."

"Like God?" Noa said.

"Or *a* god or fate or some random force in the universe." She moved her hand to Noa's hair and teased the strands. Noa closed her eyes and enjoyed the sensation of having her hair played with. "The point is that it worked. It helped us find one another when we needed each other the most. Does it really matter why?"

Noa shook her head. "I guess not." She leaned forward and pressed her lips to the front of the radio. "Thank you," she whispered. She looked over her shoulder. "Don't laugh at me for doing that."

"I won't. I'll also pretend I didn't do that same thing after some of our conversations."

"Good to know." She moved her cane and used it to stand up. Jamie helped her. "Now, I think you said something about a bath..."

Jamie pointed out where the soap and towels were, inviting Noa to take as long as she needed. Then she went out into the main house and tried not to lose her mind. She wandered downstairs with no plan. She wound up standing in front of the living room window looking out at the lawn. She could hear water running through the pipes as Noa drew a bath and her mind flipped again.

After all these months, after spending so much time with just a voice on the radio, with just flat images and an unchanging video, Noa Laurie was actually in her house. They'd touched and held each other and kissed. And *kissed*. What a kiss. Louis had never kissed her like that. She raised her fingers to lightly brush them across her mouth and realized she was smiling.

Cisco came up beside her. She crouched down and scratched the sides of his head. "Hey, pal. Stranger danger, I know. There's somebody you don't know in the house, and that's never fun. But she's a good one. She's a really good one. I think you're going to have to get used to her. Okay, pup?"

He considered the offer and, while he had some misgivings, he was willing to give Jamie the benefit of the doubt in a situation she had given much more thought to than he had. At least that was how she interpreted the fact he began licking her face.

She shoved him away, patted his side, and went into the kitchen. She poured a glass of water from a pitcher she kept in the fridge and added a few cubes of ice. She took it back upstairs and knocked lightly on the bathroom door.

"Noa? I thought you might want a glass of ice water."

"You can come in."

Jamie still hesitated before twisting the knob and sticking her head inside. Noa was settled in the bath, thankfully only visible from the shoulders up due the bubbles she'd added. Her hair was pinned up with a few strands hanging free around her neck. She smiled when she saw Jamie noticing the field of white foam.

"I hope you don't mind," she said. "I haven't really had a chance to pamper myself with a real bath in... well, in years, actually."

"No, you deserve it after everything you've been through. I'm sure the water feels like being weightless again."

"You're not wrong." Noa lifted one foot out of the water. Jamie watched the bubbles trickle down her ankle and her calf. She flexed her toes. "It's absolutely amazing."

The foot disappeared again. A hole was open in the foam now, softly swaying with the motion of Noa's leg going back underwater. She imagined those legs, those gorgeous legs, currently naked and wet and in the same room she was in.

"Jamie."

"Mm?"

"The water?"

"Yeah," Jamie said, still staring at the bubbles.

Noa laughed and held out her hand. "Jamie! The water. Please?"

"Oh!" Jamie looked at the glass in her hand. "Right. Sorry." She stepped closer to the bath and handed it over. "Sorry."

Noa smiled knowingly as she took the glass. "What were you distracted by?"

"Nothing."

"Sure," Noa said. "Thank you for the water. I was parched."

"Mm-hmm." Jamie moved toward the door. "I'll be right down the hall if you need anything. Music? I can... I can put on music if you want."

"Okay. Sure."

Jamie went into her bedroom and found her phone. She took it back to the bathroom and scrolled through the options. "Any requests?"

"I want to hear what you like."

"Uh-oh. No judgment, then."

Noa laughed. "No promises."

Jamie found a playlist she hoped would prove inoffensive, hit play, and propped the device up so the acoustics of the bathroom would make it sound louder.

"Come find me when you're done."

"Don't run too far."

Jamie smiled and left Noa to her bath. She went into the bedroom and sat down on the edge of her mattress. What was she supposed to do? Go back to work and try to concentrate on measurements and cuts and joints when Noa Laurie was naked in her home? Was she supposed to strip and put on some sexy lingerie so she was ready when Noa got out of the bath? She would feel utterly ridiculous. Besides, there was no guarantee that they would have sex. If she made that assumption and~

Noa was singing. Jamie looked toward the bathroom. She was quiet, barely audible over the music coming from the iPod, but she was definitely singing along. Her voice echoed off the porcelain and tile, like a siren's song caught on the wind. It was a Radiation Canary song, one of their newer ones.

"Empty as a street on Sunday morning," Noa sang, "When the godlies are in church and all of us heathens are sleeping in..."

Jamie smiled and fell back onto the bed. She closed her eyes so she could focus on the rest of the song. At some point her attention slipped. She noticed when the song ended but didn't open her eyes or sit up. She remained where she was and wavered on the line between full sleep and still being awake. Her right hand slipped off her stomach and ended up on the mattress next to her. She didn't bother lifting it back. She just felt so completely comfortable that she didn't want to move a single muscle.

She was finally brought back to consciousness by the sound of water gurgling through the bathtub drain. She opened her eyes and, after a moment to confirm everything she remembered had actually happened, she sat up. She raked her fingers through her hair and smoothed down her shirt. A few minutes passed in which she heard Noa in the bathroom - the sink faucet running, the linen cupboard opening and then softly closing - and then the music stopped. The silence seemed louder than the song that had just been playing.

"Jamie?"

"In here."

Noa appeared in the doorway wearing a black satin robe. The sleeves billowed around her arms before ending just below her elbows. It was cinched tight at her waist but still revealed a wide triangle of her upper chest and a good stretch of leg. She was walking without the use of her cane, but her movements were stiff. Her hair was wet and combed back. Jamie suddenly wished she had a glass of water for herself.

"I found this in the cabinet under the sink," Noa said, plucking at the robe. "I hope it's okay."

"It's... yeah. You look beautiful."

Noa smiled and moved her hand to the doorframe. "Can I come in?"

"Mm-hmm."

Noa stepped into the room. Jamie rubbed her hands on her pants in what she hoped was a subtle move, hoping they would be dry if Noa happened to touch them. Noa stopped in front of where Jamie was sitting and knelt in front of her. She put her hands on Jamie's knees.

"Thank you for being my Lighthouse."

"You're welcome. Thank you for... everything."

Noa stretched forward and Jamie met her halfway for a kiss. Jamie loved the way Noa kissed, loved the feel of her lips. There was a taste to her lips that was probably due to lipstick or something she'd eaten on the plane, but it was intoxicating. After months of having nothing but fantasy to fall back on, she finally knew exactly how Noa kissed. This wasn't a photo taken years ago or a video recorded for someone else, this was new and just for her.

"Jamie," Noa said when she pulled back, "I want to be upfront."

"Please."

"This feels like a first date. I look at you, and I see someone I've never seen before. But at the same time, you're *Jamie*. You're my Jamie, the Lighthouse, the woman I've heard in my dreams for so long. And we're in your house, in your bedroom, and I feel like I've known you for over a year. I look at you and it doesn't feel like the first time I've ever seen you. It feels like a reunion."

"I feel the same way." Jamie brushed her hand over the side of Noa's head, feeling the water in her hair. "You knew my mind. You're still getting to know my body."

Noa let her eyes fall to Jamie's chest. Her voice lowered as well. "In my experience, there's one surefire way to get acquainted with a person's body."

Jamie's heart did a jump-spin. She kept her eyes on Noa's face as she moved her hand to her belt. Noa reached out with both hands to help her.

"Are you sure?" Noa asked. The belt was already undone.

"I'm positive. I want you."

Noa gave a shaky sigh. "I want you, too." Her hands moved faster and she got Jamie's jeans unbuttoned. She started to tug them down.

"Wait..."

"Sorry. I... we can stop..."

Jamie said, "No, we can't, we definitely cannot stop. But... wait..." She twisted and stretched out to grab one of her pillows. She pulled it down and offered it to Noa. "For your knees."

Noa grinned and placed the pillow under her legs. "So considerate, Miss Faris."

"I do what I can for women who are about to have sex with me. I'm a very considerate hostess."

She lifted her hips and Noa pulled down her pants. Jamie kicked them aside, and Noa took the time to also take off Noa's socks to toss them aside. She bent down and kissed the ankle, and Jamie flexed her toes the way Noa had in the bath. Noa smiled and moved her lips in a slow and meandering path, leaving soft kisses along her calf and the inside of her knee. Jamie's reactions grew more pronounced the higher Noa got, until she was trembling with anticipation.

Jamie closed her eyes. She put her hand in Noa's hair and held it so tight that water tricked out over her fingers.

"Noa... please."

"I've been dreaming of what you would taste like," Noa said.

Jamie shuddered and moved her hand to the back of Noa's head. "Please," she said again. This time Noa complied. Jamie rolled her head back and looked at the ceiling. She hadn't been with a woman in so long that she was starting to feel like a fraud for calling herself bisexual. But there was no doubt in her mind now, no question about how she felt. Noa's lips were firm against her, and her tongue was a furtive and flickering presence against every sensitive spot she had. She spread her legs wider and let go of the blanket to begin unbuttoning her blouse, tugging it off with muscles that were reluctant to cooperate with such a mundane task.

"Noa... Noa..." She realized that saying Noa's name could sound like a refusal, and she didn't want any inch of doubt. "Stargirl."

Noa moaned against her and Jamie arched her back. She managed to get her bra off, dropped it, and looked down to see Noa looking up at her. She smiled and pushed the hair off Noa's forehead.

"Hi."

Noa smiled but didn't stop what she was doing. If she had stopped, if she'd let up for even a second, Jamie might have been able to hold out longer than she did. But she'd been waiting for this too long to diminish it, so she didn't fight. She surrendered completely, recalling how every orgasm with Noa seemed like the best she'd ever had. But of course this one was better. She felt this one in her toes, she felt it across her skin, and she released it in a long, low groan.

Noa had moved her head to kiss Jamie's hip. "Look at you," Noa murmured without moving her lips of Jamie's skin. "Just look at you, Lighthouse."

Jamie managed to open her eyes. She looked down at Noa with a denial on her lips, her standard response that she wasn't much to look at, but she couldn't bring herself to say it. Not right then, not when she saw Noa looking up at her with such adoration. So instead she cupped Noa's cheek and brushed her thumb across lips that were shined.

"I know a long time ago you said that you liked how I just treated you like a person," Jamie said, "but I think I have to put you up on a pedestal. Just for right now."

Noa's tongue flicked across the pad of Jamie's thumb. "I think a little worship is to be expected during sex."

"Well, good sex," Jamie said.

"Really fucking fantastic sex." Noa sat up straighter and kissed

Jamie, slipping her tongue into Jamie's mouth as her hands roamed.

Jamie said, "Stand up Stargirl."

Noa did as she was told. Jamie kissed the V of her chest, the skin still soft and damp from the bath. She drew an N with the tip of her tongue and put her hands on Noa's stomach. She flattened them, her fingers curled slightly under the belt of her robe. Noa rested her hands on Jamie's shoulders and gave them an encouraging squeeze. She moved her thumbs in slow circles and Jamie felt the tension and anxiety seep out of her.

Jamie tugged on the belt and it came free. The two halves fell away from each other and exposed a wide lane of Noa's torso. She focused on Noa's stomach, the flat plane of her abdomen and the small dimple of her navel. She kissed Noa's cleavage and dragged her tongue higher, up to her throat, where she opened her mouth and planted a wide-mouthed kiss just above her collarbone. Noa's hands continued to roam across Jamie's shoulders, back, and upper arms. Her skin tingled wherever Noa touched and she hoped she was having the same effect. She leaned back and looked down to see Noa's nipples were erect. She bowed her head and kissed one and, when Noa moaned appreciatively, she took it into her mouth and sucked gently.

"Yes, Jamie," Noa said.

"Come closer." Jamie sat up straighter and curled one arm around Noa's waist, drawing her in. She licked her fingers and reached down, grazing the back of her hand up the inside of Noa's thigh. She started at the knee and moved slowly. Noa linked her fingers on the back of Jamie's neck and planted her feet firmly on the carpet.

"Do you need to lie down?" Jamie asked.

"No. Do it." She kissed Jamie's forehead. "Please."

Jamie rested her cheek against Noa's chest, closed her eyes, and moved her fingers. "If I'm not very good..."

"Shh," Noa whispered. "Just touch me. Please." She hissed through her teeth as Jamie stroked her. First her middle finger, then again with the forefinger added, teasing and exploring. "Jamie..."

"Noa." She kissed the spot of skin that happened to be nearest her lips. Her head moved with the rise and fall of Noa's breathing, and she could hear her heartbeat. The voice that had broken through all the static, the ghost she'd fallen in love with, had magically become a real person. Jamie closed her eyes and eased one finger inside.

"Fuck, Jamie." She sighed. "Fuck, it's been so long..."

Jamie bit her bottom lip. She found Noa's clit with her thumb and teased it as her second finger joined the first.

"Slow?" Jamie asked.

"Fast," Noa gasped. "We can do slow later."

Jamie smiled. She flattened her hand on Noa's back and moved down to her ass, pulling her even closer. She moved her fingers and thumb in response to Noa's breathing and how fast her heart was racing. She lifted her head and focused on Noa's neck. She kissed the spot just beneath her ear and, when Noa growled in response, added her tongue. Noa shuddered and squirmed in Jamie's arms as if she was trying to get away, but then she angled her hips toward Jamie with equal aggressive. She was murmuring, "Yes, yes, yes," until she broke off in a long moan.

Noa pushed on Jamie's shoulder. "Lie down, baby..." Jamie fell back and Noa went with her, lying on top of her. She scooted down until they were properly aligned for a kiss, and Noa pressed her leg between Jamie's thighs. Jamie dragged her fingers over Noa's mound to her stomach, where she circled the navel. Noa looked down and admired Jamie's hands. They were rough, with callouses and little scars standing as evidence of her work. Jamie smiled at the way Noa's body twitched under her touch.

"You never made that sound on the ship," Jamie whispered.

"I can't make myself come the way you can." She nuzzled Jamie's cheek. "What time is it?"

Jamie hadn't looked at the clock. "Around seven. Are you sleepy?"

Noa nodded, her eyes already closed.

"Wait. Don't fall asleep just yet." She slipped out from under Noa and scooted to the edge of the bed. "I bought something a while back in anticipation of today."

Noa opened her eyes at the sound of a drawer being opened. "Baby, I appreciate the thought, but I'm too tired for another round..."

"Not *that*," Jamie said. She held up a long black leash.

It took Noa a few seconds to realize what it was. "You got a tether."

Jamie said, "Of course I did. I just got you here, and I'm not going to risk having you float away. Scoot up by the pillows."

Noa pushed herself toward the headboard, eyes locked on Jamie as she moved naked around the foot of the bed. Jamie knelt on Noa's side of the bed and bent down to attach the tether to the frame. Once it was secured, she sat up and held out her hand.

"Your foot, please."

Noa slid her foot across the mattress. "You know, if you got three more of those..."

Jamie ducked her chin and chuckled adorably. "We'll see how things go." She wrapped the cuff around Noa's ankle and patted down the Velcro. "How's that?"

"It's perfect, Lighthouse."

Jamie visibly shuddered. "Please never stop calling me that."

"C'mere."

Jamie got back into bed, lying on top of Noa, kissing her as she was rolled onto the other side of the bed. Noa snuggled close during the kiss and let her hands travel over Jamie's body. Jamie was tingling all over but tried to focus on Noa's lips. She'd fantasized about this moment, about having Noa in her bed and all the post-coital touching. She tasted herself on Noa's lips and realized she hadn't tasted Noa yet. She made a note to amend that as soon as possible.

But morning would be soon enough.

// POST-MISSION · GROUND CONTROL //

NOA WAS pulled out of sleep by the sound of a dog, Cisco, moving around downstairs. She was lying on her back with the blanket pulled up to her shoulders. Beside her, Jamie was lying on her side facing the wall. She was still naked and clutched the blanket to her chest with one hand, her other curled under the pillow with her face pressed into the bent of her elbow. Noa stared at her, at the wild nest of hair and the stone path of her spine leading down the middle of her back. This was the most candid moment she'd ever gotten of Jamie. With the radio, Jamie could prepare and plan for their conversations. Now she was unguarded in every sense.

Even though they'd fallen asleep very early, they managed to sleep through the entire night. The sun was already up but the sky slowly changed colors through the window. She saw it out of the corner of her eye as she continued staring at Jamie. Her mind was still foggy enough that it might have been five minutes or as many as twenty before Jamie began to stir. She rolled over onto her back, licked her lips, and wiped a hand over her face. She looked at Noa, blinked, and smiled while squinting her eyes.

"Hi."

"Morning," Noa said.

"Morning. I can't see you."

"Oh." Noa lifted her head off the pillow and spotted Jamie's glasses on the nightstand. She reached over her to retrieve them, unfolded the arms, and carefully slipped them on for her. "Better?"

Jamie nodded. "Much." Noa leaned in but Jamie leaned away.

"Mm. No kissing before brushing, please. On the cheek."

Noa adjusted her aim and kissed as close to Jamie's mouth as she dared. "I know this is just a 'first time waking up with someone' anxiety," she said, "but for the record, I couldn't care less about a little morning breath."

Jamie reached up and played with Noa's hair. "I'll file that away for later. I still can't believe you're here. You're really here. You came all this way just for me."

"Of course I did," Noa whispered. "Whoever said it's the journey and not the destination didn't have you waiting on the other side."

Jamie sighed blissfully. "Oh, the hell with it." She moved her hand to the back of Noa's head and pulled her down for a proper good-morning kiss.

Noa repositioned herself to lay on top of Jamie, the tether connecting her left ankle to the bedframe stretching as she moved. Her legs were sore from yesterday's exertion and she was hyper aware of the blankets resting on top of her, but she didn't care. Jamie moved one leg and, when Noa took advantage of the invitation, brought it back up to hook it over her hip. Their kiss deepened, and Noa moved her hands down the front of Jamie's body. Jamie's nipples responded to her touch and Noa bent down to kiss them as her hand moved lower.

"I don't like morning sex," Jamie said against Noa's mouth.

Noa opened her eyes. "I can stop."

"I didn't say that."

"Maybe you don't like morning sex with the wrong person."

Jamie kept her eyes closed. "That. Let's go with that."

Noa pressed her knee into the mattress. The Velcro holding the tether to her ankle ripped and it snapped back to the right side of the bed.

"Oh no," Jamie said. "Don't float away."

"Hold me down," Noa said.

Jamie's thigh tightened on Noa's hip. She put her hands on Noa's back, just above her hips, and pulled her forward. Noa put a hand against the headboard and moved it along the plank until she found a spot narrow enough to wrap her fingers around. She used it to guide herself as she rolled her hips forward as Jamie pressed down to meet her. She focused on Jamie and moved as smoothly as she could. After a few seconds she stopped worrying about elegance and just watched Jamie's face.

"You're gorgeous," she said under her breath.

Jamie was trying to keep her breathing steady but her laughter threw her off. She rolled her head to one side on the pillow. "I love you."

Noa smiled and bowed down to kiss Jamie's neck, making her

writhe underneath her. "Give me your hand," Jamie gasped. Noa reached across Jamie's arm, only to have her pull away. "No. No, your... your *hand...*"

"Oh." Noa put her hand between them. She bit her lip, twisted her wrist, and found Jamie with two of her fingers. Jamie bucked against her with a quiet, "Yes, yes," and Noa watched her come again. When she deflated and sank into the mattress, Noa settled on top of her and watched her face. Jamie put her hand against her cheek, which was bright pink. She wet her lips and made a series of almost inaudible sounds. She finally turned her head and blinked her eyes open to look at Noa.

"How long are you here?"

Noa said, "Well... I kind of just lost my job. So I think my schedule is wide open."

Jamie smiled. Some of Noa's hair had fallen into her face and Jamie reached up to tuck it behind her ear. "Does that mean I have to support you?"

"I can pull my weight. I can find chores to do around the house."

"Like what?"

Noa grinned and slid down Jamie's body.

Jamie sat up straighter, propped up by the pillow. She laughed breathlessly and put a hand on top of Noa's head. "Wait. Wait, it-it's too soon. I don't like to do it again right away."

From under the blankets, Noa said, "You also claimed you didn't like morning sex."

Jamie sighed and surrendered.

The woman made a good argument.

They didn't fall asleep afterward, but they did remain in bed long enough that they were, at the very least, dozing. Noa slipped away from Jamie's side and sat up, planting her feet on the floor. Her back was tight and both thighs felt like they had been replaced by stone copies, but that was actually an improvement from the day before. She placed her hands on the edge of the mattress and took a few deep breaths before she attempted standing.

"Stay."

She looked back at Jamie. Her hair had fallen across her forehead, so Noa reached out and brushed it back. "I'm just going to the bathroom."

"No. No, I mean, you can go to the bathroom, of course. I just meant... stay here. With me. I don't know when you have to be back, or if you made other arrangements since you weren't carrying a bag when you showed up. But I would really like it if you stayed here with me."

"I would love that."

She bent down and kissed Jamie's cheek, out of deference to her 'morning breath' rule.

"Do you need me to find your cane?"

"No, I'm going to try without it. I feel a little less Tin Man today." She shuffled to the door, lifting her feet only as much as necessary. "It's hard to go from doing backflips without a second thought to lunging around a house like Frankenstein."

Jamie propped herself up on her elbows. "Do you need a cheerleader?"

Noa looked back. "Why, do you have a uniform...?"

"I can neither confirm nor deny," Jamie said as she dropped back to the mattress.

"Woman of mystery all of a sudden." She used the doorframe as leverage to limp out into the hallway. "I'll get all your secrets eventually, Jamie Faris. You have my vow."

She was almost to the bathroom when she spotted Cisco on the stairs. He had apparently been alerted that someone was awake by the bedroom door opening, but now he was confronted with this stranger again. He had sunken onto the stairs to look up at her warily. She smiled and, with great difficulty and just a little pain, crouched down so she would seem less threatening to him.

"Hi, Cisco. Hey, pal." She extended her hand slowly, bringing it close to his face so he could get her scent. "If you give me your seal of approval, I'll be sure to sneak you all the best treats. I'm talking food from the table."

"Don't bribe my dog," Jamie shouted from the bedroom.

"You'd get rid of me long before you got rid of him."

Jamie said, "Well. That's true."

Noa leaned closer to Cisco and whispered, "Food from the table. Think about it." She gave his head another rub and headed to the bathroom.

A few minutes later, when Noa slipped back into bed, Jamie wrapped both arms around her and pulled her close. Noa rolled onto her side.

"For the record," Jamie said, "I'd just buy a house for both you and Cisco, and then I would alternate between them."

"I think that could work." She kissed Jamie's hair. "What time do you have to be up?"

"Never."

Noa smiled. That was a plan she could definitely support.

After retrieving Noa's bags from the hotel, they spent the next few days getting to know one another. Their first lengthy excursion from the bedroom was a long walk through Jamie's neighborhood. Cisco quickly figured out that Noa wasn't operating at full capacity and assigned himself as her protector. He was never far from her right hand, keeping his distance so he wouldn't be underfoot but letting her know he was there if she needed him. When they got home, Jamie let Noa feed him a treat for being so good on the walk.

"I didn't know he was a helper animal."

"I didn't either," Jamie said. "I think maybe he just likes you more than he likes me. He's a fickle traitor."

Cisco ignored the criticism.

"How do you feel?" Jamie asked.

Noa rubbed her thigh. "Better. I feel like I ran ten miles instead of walking for half a mile, but it's an improvement."

Jamie said, "Maybe you need more bedrest."

"The doctor said I needed activity to remind my body of how it's supposed to move in a gravity environment. The more I can get up and move around, the..." She trailed off when she saw Jamie's expression and read what she meant. "Oh. Bedrest. Yes, plenty of bedrest. In fact, after all that walking, I think I feel a nap coming on."

They went upstairs, but no doctor would call what followed 'rest.'

On the third day, Jamie woke up to find Noa doing pushups on the floor next to the bed. After breakfast, her hair still wet from the shower, Noa clipped on Cisco's leash and asked if she could take him out for a run. Jamie gave her blessing and watched as they jogged up the driveway. Noa was moving stiffly when she came back, but she was smiling victoriously when she found Jamie in the barn.

"One mile," she said.

"Well done, baby," Jamie said.

Noa wiggled her eyebrows and went inside to take a bath. She came back out forty-five minutes later wearing a pair of jeans and a polo shirt. Jamie was at the lathe and looked up to see Noa watching her. She let the machine wind down and pulled out her ear protection.

"It's strange to just have you... pop up like that."

"Sorry."

"No, I like it. I used to dream about it. Turn around and there you are." She took the piece off the lathe. "Do you want to lend a hand?"

Noa came closer. "Absolutely. What do you need me to do?"

"Just be a second pair of hands."

"I can do that."

They spent the rest of the day working together. Noa was close to useless when it came to the bigger machines, but she could identify tools and brought them to Jamie as needed. She mostly spent the time watching Jamie work. She admired how Jamie could focus entirely on the piece she was currently working on and then bring it together with the rest of the design. It was like magic seeing a piece of furniture being assembled right in front of her.

"You're actually creating something," Noa said as they walked back inside for lunch. "Someone is going to use that chair for the next ten, twenty years. Maybe for the rest of their lives. That's amazing to me. That's so very cool."

Jamie blushed. "Maybe I'll make you something. What do you want?"

"A house."

Jamie laughed. "It'll take me a long time to build a house."

"I can wait."

That night when Jamie came out of the bathroom, there was a wrapped package sitting on her side of the bed. Noa was already sitting with her back against the headboard and her legs folded in front of her. Jamie looked at the package and then looked at Noa. She gestured with her head.

"What is that?"

"Cisco left it there," Noa said without looking up from her phone.

Jamie picked up the present and tore at the wrapping. She peeked inside and laughed when she saw what was inside.

"Well, you did promise."

She pulled out the fluffy rocket ship slippers and put them on before she joined Noa in bed. She thanked Noa with a kiss, which turned into more, which ended up with Jamie wearing nothing but the slippers as she fell asleep on top of Noa.

By that point, Noa had made a full recovery from her time in space. She jogged every morning and did a full workout. Her cane had been propped up against Jamie's bedroom door for so long without being touched that Jamie finally moved it to the hallway closet. It took Noa two full days before she noticed it was missing.

Through it all, they continued getting to know one another. Jamie was afraid they wouldn't have anything to talk about after all their conversations over the radio, but they surprised each other by finding new places to explore. At first Jamie wished she'd brought the cane for herself, but it didn't take long before she was keeping pace with Noa.

At the back of her mind, Jamie thought about Louis' comment that no one had seen her dating anyone. People were certainly seeing her now. Jamie's neighbors were the first to notice, of course. Alf, at the furniture store, saw Noa waiting in the truck when Jamie dropped off some of the items she had been working on.

"Who's the looker?" he asked.

"That's my girlfriend. Noa."

He looked again. "I don't think so."

"What?"

"Hm?"

"You don't think what?"

"You asked if I know her. I don't think so."

Jamie laughed. "Not 'know-her'. Noa. N-O-A."

Alf said, "Huh. Well, she's awful pretty."

"Thanks. I like her."

A few days later, when Jamie was returning some books to the library, Myra smiled at her over the circulation desk. "You haven't been in to use the computer much lately."

"I guess not."

Myra looked like she was trying to hold back an outburst, practically swaying back and forth with the effort of self-restraint. "So... were all these books for you?"

"Yeah. All two of them."

"Well, I just thought... you know... Alf said you had a *girlfriend*, and I thought maybe one of the books was for her. Will she be needing a library card of her own...?"

Jamie just smiled and wished Myra a good day.

A few days later, they went grocery shopping. At that point, Noa had been staying with Jamie for nearly three weeks. There had been no discussion of how long she was going to stay, but they collaborated on the shopping list. When they left for the grocery store, Jamie saw that a hundred dollar bill had been clipped to the list. She pocketed it but didn't bring it up until they were actually roaming the aisles.

"You don't have to pay for my groceries."

Noa shrugged. She was wearing a hoodie over a white T-shirt and jeans. She was also wearing an Astraea baseball cap pulled low over her eyes. "I'm just paying for my share. Plus the groceries I ate over the past few weeks. It probably doesn't even cover all of that."

"Be that as it may," Jamie said, "I appreciate it."

"You're welcome." She picked a can of sauce up off the shelf and examined it. "I know we haven't talked about how long I'm staying."

Jamie rested her arms on the cart handle. "I didn't want to jinx anything by bringing it up. I assume you'll eventually have to go do interviews or go back to your apartment."

"I made sure my apartment was locked up and taken care of for two full years. I don't need to go back early. Besides, that lonely and empty apartment is not exactly appealing after staying at your house."

"Then don't go back."

Noa grinned and put the sauce in Jamie's cart. "Well, I have to go back eventually."

"Says who?"

"Says I don't have anywhere else to live."

Jamie lightly touched Noa's wrist to keep her from walking on. Noa looked at her. "You most certainly do have somewhere to live. I've shared more with you than anyone else. And I only dated Louis for about five months before we were engaged. So if you don't want to go back to your apartment, then don't go back. Stay with me."

Before Noa could answer, someone came around the end of the aisle and almost ran into them. Jamie moved her cart to the side before she realized the new arrival had frozen like a deer in the headlights. Louis had grown a beard since she'd last seen him. It was thin and patchy but it looked well-tended rather than a sign of neglect. He was staring at Jamie, then he shifted his gaze to Noa. Finally he looked down at Jamie's hand resting on Noa's wrist.

Jamie's first instinct was to pull her hand away, but instead she doubled down by shifting her grip so their palms were touching. She linked their fingers and squeezed.

"Hi, Louis."

"Jamie." He stared at Noa.

"This is Noa Laurie."

Louis' eyebrows flickered in confusion. "I... saw you on the news, didn't I?"

"You might have, yes," Noa said.

"You're an astronaut."

"That's right."

He looked at Jamie and then down at his cart. "Wow. Okay."

Jamie was tense, waiting for him to explode or shove his cart against the shelves. Instead he held his head up high and nodded.

"I don't want to get in your way, ladies. I'll let you get back to your shopping."

Jamie blinked in surprise as he maneuvered his cart around theirs and continued down the aisle. "Thank you, Louis."

"Sure."

Jamie and Noa shared a look. Noa raised an eyebrow. Jamie chuckled softly and squeezed.

"Hey. Astronaut lady." Noa looked back. Louis was looking at Jamie. "Don't let her go. You're probably way too smart to need someone like me to tell you something that obvious, but I'm saying it anyway. Whatever happens, just... don't let her go."

"I don't plan to," Noa said.

He nodded. "Good." He smiled at Jamie. "I'll see you around, Jamie."

"It was nice seeing you, Louis."

He turned and pushed his cart around the corner and out of sight. Jamie exhaled and looked at Noa with wide, disbelieving eyes.

"Did that really just happen?"

"I think so." She stepped forward and wrapped Jamie in a tight hug. Jamie buried her face into Noa's shoulder. "Are you okay?"

Jamie nodded. "Yeah. We're blocking the aisle."

Noa held her for another moment before letting her go. Jamie pushed the cart into the next aisle with Noa trailing along beside her.

"He seems like a really nice guy," Noa said. "I'd understand if you were willing to give him a second chance."

Jamie laughed and bumped Noa hard with her hip.

"Keep it up. I'll make you sleep on the floor with Cisco."

// POST-MISSION · LIFTOFF //

NOA CHOSE to do the interview in the breakfast nook where the light was better. She wore her Astraea polo shirt but left her hair down. Jamie thought she looked friendlier and less imposing with her hair down. The screen of her laptop was filled with a live-feed of the noon broadcast from WEKA ("Dayton's news leader!"). For the past five minutes, she had been giving a heavily-edited account of her time aboard the ODIE in honor of the one-year anniversary of her return. She didn't mention Jamie. They eventually got around to revealing the truth to Enver, since it was his mission and he deserved to know what had happened aboard his ship, but it was agreed the general public didn't need to know.

"Will there be another movie, do you think?" the anchorwoman asked.

Noa smiled. "Well, I think you'd have to ask the studios about that. If they want me to consult on the story, I'd be more than willing."

"I would be the first in line to buy a ticket. So what *is* next for you, Colonel Laurie? I assume Enver Crane is knocking down your door to get you back up once the ODIE is spaceworthy again."

"He might be, if he was the type who didn't take no for an answer. He asked me and I told him I wasn't interested. Two near-death experiences are enough. I don't feel like tempting fate a third time."

The anchorwoman laughed. "I suppose a lot of us would feel the same way."

Noa looked down at her hands, folded in her lap. "To answer your question about what's next, I'm still working that out. For now I'm enjoying the private sector. Going to schools, giving talks about pursuing a career in science. And of course, I opened the door for future Mars missions, so now I have to help recruit the astronauts who will be taking that journey."

"You're not the least bit tempted to be on that trip?"

"Not at all." Noa's answer was immediate. "There are far too many qualified individuals vying for a place on those missions. I've had my adventures. I've had more than enough adventures, frankly!" She laughed and looked toward the window. She could see the side of the barn where Jamie was currently hard at work on her latest commission. "Besides, even if I did consider going, I'm enjoying my life on the ground far too much at the moment to go back up."

The anchorwoman said, "Well, you've certainly earned that! We'd like to thank you for joining us today, Colonel Laurie."

"It was my pleasure."

The feed ended, and Noa closed the laptop. She lifted her arms over her head and stretched out her back before standing up. She was barefoot under the table, and Cisco had been laying against her ankles to keep her feet warm. He scrambled up when she moved and she let him lead her to the door. The dog's days were now split between keeping watch over Jamie's workshop and following Noa around when she was actually at home. She tried to keep her traveling limited to a seven days per month, but there were so many schools asking for her to make an appearance. Who knew which speech would be attended by a future Sally Ride or Katherine Johnson? And who knew how long her celebrity would last? She had to take advantage of her ability to inspire while she still could.

Outside she could hear the shrill hum of Jamie's tools. Cisco bounded off the porch and headed toward the barn. Noa stood just outside the back door, hands in her pockets, and tilted her head back. It was daytime so she couldn't see the stars, but the clouds were thick and beautiful. Sometimes she thought she could still feel the ground moving under her feet. There were nights when she still asked Jamie to strap her ankle to the bed after a particularly vivid dream of being back aboard ODIE or the ISS.

In the barn, Jamie saw Cisco from the corner of her eye. She finished the cut she was making and shut off the machine. She was working on a bookshelf for a teenager's bedroom in Pittsboro. It was yet another commission from the website Noa had set up for her. Noa needed the internet, so Jamie finally took the plunge. And when Noa, bored, asked about putting together a website for the business, Jamie agreed. She didn't know how people heard about her or found the site, but the orders started coming in by the end of the first week.

That didn't mean she liked the internet. It was a necessary evil. She was happy to benefit from it, as long as Noa was willing to do all the work.

The dog's arrival meant that Noa's interview was over and it was time for lunch. There was casserole in the fridge, leftovers from their dinner at Adnan's house where Jamie finally told him the whole story about the radio, but Jamie felt like going for a drive. She liked when Noa rolled the window down and let her hand glide through the air currents. It was just one of the many small things she'd discovered that she loved about Noa that couldn't have been seen or properly explained over the radio.

Sometimes it amazed her that she'd fallen in love with just Noa's voice and her mind. Looking back, she would never be satisfied with such a small fraction of the whole. She needed to touch Noa, to watch her wake up, to reach out in the night and feel the warmth of her back next to her in the bed. She could also see how Noa looked at her, the way she smiled when Jamie cuddled close, and how Noa's arms instinctively closed around her when they were lying on the couch to watch a movie. Those moments kept her from doubting how much Noa cared for her, and she didn't know how she'd lived without them for the first year and a half of their relationship.

Once her workspace was cleaned up, Jamie bent down to scratch Cisco's head as he led her out of the barn. Noa was looking at the sky but looked down just as Jamie stepped into the doorway. Noa was still in her jeans and Astraea shirt. Jamie was still wearing her safety goggles, the front of her apron covered in pale yellow shavings. Her hair was still blonde, though it was a bit shaggier now than the day they finally met face-to-face. Noa said it suited her, so she let it grow.

Jamie smiled and took off her goggles. Noa stepped off the porch and walked toward her. Jamie started walking as well. Noa laughed as they closed the distance. They were moving toward each other, just as they had from the day they first spoke.

This time, though, they would meet in the middle.

// END-OF-MISSION //

ALICE KIDD, widower and former dog groomer, didn't hear the doorbell ring, but that was hardly surprising. She kept her hearing aid off in the morning because of the school bus and the children who gathered at the end of her driveway. When she went out to get the mail, she was surprised to find a fruit basket sitting on the top step. She looked up and down the road but didn't see anyone lurking. She looked down at it with a confused tilt of the head. She'd seen on the news about people stealing packages from porches, but *leaving* one...? That had to be new.

She finally picked it up and carried it inside. Maybe one of the women at the church, although she couldn't think of any who had the disposable income for this kind of gift. There was a card visible through the yellow plastic which enshrouded the fruit. She put it down on the kitchen table and used her scissors to carefully open it.

The card was heavy-duty stock. Not expensive, but also not the cheapest option. The message was written in blocky handwriting that she didn't recognize: THANK YOU FOR OPENING THE WINDOW - A FRIEND.

"Well, I never," she muttered. She looked at the kitchen window and confirmed it was closed. She thought for a moment the message could be considered ominous. Old Linda Coyne would have thought it was a warning, that thieves were that very minute lurking in the hedges outside or the fruits had been sprayed with some kind of poison. But Linda was a worrywart who gave herself an ulcer every time she watched the news.

Alice decided there was nothing threatening about the gift. Someone was just being kind. Maybe one of the kids from the youth group or one of the schoolchildren waiting for the bus. Whoever it might have been, she wasn't going to let paranoia get in the way of a kind gesture. Generosity was too uncommon in this world, and she wasn't going to discourage it by responding with fear. She only wished she knew how to repay this 'friend.'

She dug around until she found an apple. She decided to run it under the tap before she took a bite (*"Do you know what they're putting in the tap water?"* Linda would have said, one hand flat against her chest, eyes wide in shock and terror).

As she was taking it to the kitchen, her eye was caught by the china hutch next to the table. She smiled as she always did when she happened to notice the grand old thing. It was brand new but had the feel of something that was a hundred years old. It might even survive that long if she could convince her daughter to take it. She put her hand against the side and stroked the smooth wood. As she admired the craftmanship, she thought of the young woman who had made it for her.

Jamie Faris was a good girl, and kind. When they discussed price, Alice mentioned that she was on a fixed income. She didn't want or expect anything for free, but she asked if there was perhaps an installment plan she could use. Jamie had instead asked if Alice had anything she might be willing to trade. And Alice, to her guilt and shame, had immediately thought of something she'd wanted to be rid of for years. She suggested it and Jamie, poor thing, agreed.

Alice didn't even know if the radio worked. Nelson, her husband, had spent so many years fiddling around with its guts that she would be surprised if he hadn't ended up breaking it. He wanted to boost the signal, wanted to "talk with those scientists down in Antarctica," but to her knowledge he'd never even been able to call Chicago.

Maybe the fruit basket was a sign. She couldn't repay whoever had given it to her, so maybe she could pay it forward and make up some of her debt to Jamie. After all, she'd gotten a hutch and Jamie Faris ended up with some silly shortwave radio.

It was so unfair. Alice would definitely have to find a way to make up for getting the better part of the deal.

"Riley Parra is a strong, badass heroine for those that like their coffee and their cop fiction bitter." - P Industry

No Man's Land isn't the kind of place you go after dark, even if you have a badge. But Detective Riley Parra was born there, and she refuses to surrender it to the drug dealers, killers and criminals who have made it there home. The case of a body stuffed into a drainage pipe leads her to discover that there is far more at stake than she ever imagined.

~ Riley Parra, Season One

"A good novel to while away a few hours in front of the fire." - Kitty Kat Reviews

Three years ago, Sofia Kennedy reported the tragic death of her girlfriend live-on air. Still in the closet even with her closest friends, she was forced to suffer her loss in silence. In the years since she's become isolated and sticks strictly to a routine that prevents her from encountering painful memories of the woman she lost.

Marion Vogt runs a small but well-respected catering service that feeds the elite of Seattle. When Sofia's consumer reporting segment does a story on Marion's company, the two women immediately butt heads. An unintended insult results in a scathing report that nearly shuts down the business. Marion's attempt to defend herself results in a deepening of their conflict until both women are ready to destroy one another.

They quickly find out Seattle can be a very small town when trying to avoid someone. As much as they want to avoid each other, fate keeps forcing Sofia and Marion to cross paths. Before long they realize they'll have to decide if they're going to hold on to bad feelings or risk forgiveness to discover just what they have to offer each other.

~ Breaking Anchor